The Distance Between Us

Books by Bart Yates

LEAVE MYSELF BEHIND

THE BROTHERS BISHOP

THE DISTANCE BETWEEN US

Published by Kensington Publishing Corporation

The Distance Between Us

BART YATES

KENSINGTON BOOKS
http://www.kensingtonbooks.com

KENSINGTON BOOKS are published by

Kensington Publishing Corp.
850 Third Avenue
New York, NY 10022

Library of Congress Control Number: 2008929062
ISBN-13: 978-0-7582-2696-9
ISBN-10: 0-7582-2696-9

First Hardcover Printing: September 2008
10 9 8 7 6 5 4 3 2 1

Printed in the United States of America

For my family.

Acknowledgments

Deepest thanks, yet again, to Gordon Mennenga, for his ruthless editorial eye, good humor and endless patience. Thanks also to Marian Clark for performing honest and gentle triage on the second draft.

For thoughtful feedback and much-needed reassurance on bad days, my thanks to Peder Bartling and Liz Schonhorst.

For answers to random medical questions, my appreciation to Lucas Readinger, Jim Gibson, Abe Assad, Rob Weingeist, and Bill Landis.

For creating the kind of home that feeds the imagination, my thanks to Jim Bynum and John Moriarty.

For legal know-how and generosity of spirit, my gratitude to Ed and Lisa Leff and my brother, Jeff Yates.

For sharing their piano expertise, I am grateful to Peter Cacioppo and Alice Lindsey.

For far too many things to mention, my thanks to Brad Schonhorst, Andrew Knapp, Michael Becker, Libby and Rob Shannon, Jack Manu, Tonja Robins, Rob Burns, Mick Benner and John Perona. A huge thanks also to Sifu Moy Yat Tung (a.k.a. Dr. Robert Squatrito), and my entire kung fu family.

Finally, thanks to my editor at Kensington, John Scognamiglio, for his unflagging support and terrific advice.

"Blessed are those who have no talent!"

—Emerson

"If the only prayer you say in your life is thank you, that would suffice."

—Meister Eckhart

CHAPTER 1

I spend a great deal of time admiring my hands, but that's only because they belong to another woman.

My body turned seventy-one last month and has, of late, begun
to bear a disturbing resemblance to an overripe avocado. If you slit
me down the middle from my neck to my pelvis and peeled off my
bumpy hide, I'm sure you'd find nothing underneath but a gooey,
greenish pulp, riddled with black and brown bruises and completely unusable for anything worthwhile—except maybe as the
base in a suspicious batch of guacamole.

But my hands are only forty or so. My fingers are long and thin
and supple, my palms are soft and smooth, and when I make a fist,
the wrinkles between my knuckles and my wrists vanish, the skin
pulled taut by a layer of fine, strong muscles attached firmly to my
bones.

But as I said, then there's the rest of me.

You bring the garlic and the lime juice, I'll provide the tortilla
chips.

No. Not yet.

I need another drink first. And if you know what's good for you,
you better have one, too.

I open my door and the young man who's come to see about
the attic apartment is standing on the porch, shivering. He's tall

and thin, and he's not wearing a hat or gloves, and all he's got for a coat is a thick blue flannel shirt, three sizes too big for him.

I frown up at him. "It's ten degrees out there, you idiot. Don't you know how to dress in the winter?"

He looks taken aback. "Mrs. Donovan?"

I wince. "Just Hester, please. Are you Alex?"

He nods. "Sorry I'm late. I got lost." His hair is red and curly and wild, spilling over his ears and forehead and down the back of his neck. His chin and cheeks are unevenly dotted with red stubble.

"You need a haircut and a shave," I tell him. "You remind me of an Irish setter I owned as a child. His name was Fergus, and he was run over by a logging truck."

He blinks but doesn't say anything. At least he's not a chatterbox.

I wave him in. "Well, don't just stand there. Come in. And take your shoes off before you make a mess."

He kicks the snow from his soles and steps past me, then bends over to untie his sneakers as I shut the door behind him. He's not wearing socks.

"The stupid streets don't make sense around here," he mutters at the floor. "There are no signs on the corners or anything. What's up with that?"

I point at his bare feet when he straightens. "Aren't you freezing?"

He shrugs. "Not really. I like the cold." His wire-frame glasses have fogged over and he takes them off and wipes them on his shirttail. He squints down at me for a second—his eyes are pale blue—then replaces the glasses on his nose and looks over my shoulder at the fireplace in the living room. He grins. "Sweet. That's an awesome fire." He sniffs. "It even smells great."

"Yes, it does, doesn't it?" I glance at the flames. The fire is so hot it's mostly blue. "I think the wood is a mix of cedar and pine, but there may be a bit of oak as well." I look back at him. "I'm burning my husband's favorite coffee table this afternoon. I believe it was an antique. He swears somebody famous built it, but I can't remember who. Paul Revere, maybe. Or Oprah Winfrey. I always get those two confused, don't you?"

He stares at me.

I retrieve the glass of red wine I set down on the steps a minute ago when I answered the door. "Yes, I know, I probably shouldn't have destroyed it, but I really couldn't be bothered to go out to the woodpile in this cold." I chew on my lip. "Then again, I had to venture out to the carriage house to get the sledgehammer anyway, and I made quite a shambles of the study afterward. What on earth was I thinking? Arthur will be furious with me."

He smiles a little, as if he thinks I'm joking. Poor boy.

I take a sip of wine and study him. He has freckles on his nose, and a small mole on his left temple. I point at the open bottle by my chair in the living room. "Would you care for a glass of merlot? It's not very good, but it helps take the chill off."

He shakes his head. "No thanks. I'm fine."

"Have it your way." I turn around and head for the east staircase. "The apartment is upstairs."

The steps creak under our feet as he follows me. He's silent for a few seconds, but he clears his throat when we get to the first landing.

"Wow. This place is huge." He runs a hand over the mahogany banister and peeks in the doorway of the master bedroom. The late afternoon sun is streaming through the round stained-glass windows on the south wall and lighting the floor and bedspread with patches of red and yellow.

"Wow," he says again. "It's like a church or something in here. The ceilings are so high."

I step beside him and stare in at my room. I don't get much company these days, and I forget how this house appears to strangers.

Bolton, Illinois, is a river town, and though it's now known chiefly as the home of The Carson Conservatory of Music (and, to a lesser degree, Carson's academic sister school, Pritchard University), its original claim to fame was as an industrial port on the Mississippi. In the early 1900s there were dozens of textile mills in Bolton, owned by a few decadently wealthy families who built houses like this one—mansions, really—to live in when they weren't flitting about Europe or picking caviar from their teeth in stuffy salons up and down the East Coast. Then along came the Depression, and most of them were forced to sell their properties for a fraction of what they were worth and move back to New England and New York to lick their wounds—or commit suicide, in a surprising number of cases. Tycoons are apparently quite fragile.

Be that as it may, my husband Arthur's father (who taught philosophy at Pritchard) convinced Pritchard's board to purchase several of the homes as an institutional investment, and he also somehow finagled them into lending him enough money to buy this house—the best of the lot—for himself and his wife.

Knowing Arthur's father as I did, I'm sure it was a shady deal, but I'd be lying if I said I'm not grateful. Our home—*my* home, I mean—is a three-story, elegant old Victorian house with six bedrooms and four full baths, as well as a living room, a study, a music room, and an enormous, tin-paneled kitchen attached to an equally preposterous dining room, with a chandelier the size of a kettledrum chained to the ceiling. In addition, there's a charming, fully furnished attic apartment (from its front windows you can see the Mississippi), a large basement, and a splendid wraparound porch decorated with ornate gingerbread woodwork. The carriage house sits at the top of a circular driveway to the right of the main house, and overlooks a stone garden, complete with a gazebo—and, unfortunately, a hideous, eight-and-a-half foot statue of some obscure Russian saint that Arthur's mother bought at an auction.

I turn away from the bedroom and head up the next flight of stairs and Alex follows me. The third floor has three guest rooms (one of which Arthur used as an office) and a bathroom; Alex eyes the dusty cardboard boxes and scattered paper in the dismantled office with curiosity but I pass by without pausing and ascend the final set of stairs.

I stop in the hallway that connects the various rooms of the attic apartment. I'm panting a little from the climb. "Well, this is it."

He steps past me and looks around, perplexed. "Where's the door?"

"There is no door, I'm afraid."

The only thing separating the attic from the rest of the house is a waist-high banister that runs the length of the hallway. He walks down the hall and peers in at each room—kitchen, living room, bathroom, bedroom—then comes back and stands next to me. The wallpaper behind him is white with small clusters of purple grapes; one of the grape clusters hangs directly above his head, like mistletoe.

He fingers his jeans and stares over the banister at the staircase. "It's nice, but I was hoping there'd be more privacy. I thought there'd be a door."

I sigh. "You needn't worry. No one uses the third floor anymore, so it serves as a buffer between the main house and the apartment. I stay on the first two floors, and as you've noticed, this house is rather large. You'd have all the privacy you need."

He meets my eyes for an instant, then looks away and bites his lip. "I'm sorry. I don't think I can live in a place without a door." He drops his head and curls his long toes in the carpet.

I glare at his scalp and take another sip of wine. "Suit yourself. Give me a moment to rest, and I'll show you out." I wander into the kitchen and sit at the table, dipping my neck to keep from banging my head on the slanted ceiling.

All the rooms up here are a bit misshapen, molded to fit the contour of the roof. The floor in the kitchen is covered with a yellow and gold linoleum, and the cherrywood baseboard running alongside it is dark and polished. Over the stove there's a skylight looking out on the bricks of the house's main chimney, and to the left of the refrigerator is a larger window that opens to the south, thirty or forty feet above the carriage house and the driveway. Each room of the attic has at least two windows, so even though the place is small, there's plenty of light and air, and it doesn't feel claustrophobic at all. I've always loved this apartment. It's a cozy space, warm and clean and quiet, and this boy is a fool for not wanting it.

Alex sticks his head in the doorway and watches me with an anxious expression, as if he thinks I'm preparing to have a stroke.

I point at a picture on the wall, above a small table with an old-fashioned black rotary phone on it. "That's my son Paul. He used to be quite handsome, don't you think?" I swirl the remaining swallow of wine around in my glass. "Now he's got a dreadful beard and a potbelly, and he lumbers about town like a disreputable buffalo. It's ghastly how he's let himself go."

He steps in for a closer look. The photo is a black-and-white shot of Paul standing on the front porch with his arm around one of his first girlfriends. Alex studies it for a minute as I study him. He's very thin and the veins in his hands and feet show through his skin.

He clears his throat. "Your son's still in Bolton? Does he live with you and your husband?"

"Dear God, no. I live alone these days. Arthur and I are separated, and Paul rents a room with an alcoholic clarinetist in one of those seedy little faculty bungalows near the Conservatory. He and his roommate drink single malt scotch and play duets every night until they pass out or throw up, then they get up the next morning and go breathe toxic fumes on their students. It's all very bohemian."

His head bobs up and down to show that he's listening, but he keeps his attention on the photograph. "So he teaches at Carson? What does he play?"

"Paul? He's a cellist. A good one, too, but no one outside of Illinois has ever heard of him because he refuses to leave Bolton, even to tour." I rub my nose to fend off a sneeze. "He has a neurotic aversion to traveling. When he was a little boy we literally had to drag him to the car every time we left town for vacation. I thought he'd outgrow it, but he's just gotten worse."

He taps the picture frame with his knuckle. "How long ago was this taken?"

"Oh, I don't know. Years ago. Paul was in high school, I believe." I play with my lower lip. "I forget the girl's name. Boobsy, maybe, or Blobsy or Barfy or something like that. Her father was one of Arthur's friends, and I thought she was rather adorable. But she only lasted about a week."

I gulp the rest of the wine. "That may be Paul's all-time record. He's had terrible luck with women. They never stick around for long after they've had sex with him." I rest my hand on my chin. "The hair on his back frightens them."

Alex makes a sound that might be a laugh and I look up at the ceiling. It needs fresh paint; the eggshell-white Arthur and I both liked so much is already beginning to flake. Our first and only tenant last year (a philosophy grad student with the unfortunate name of Carmella Croyson) was overly fond of humidity and basically flooded the place with steam all winter long. The paint apparently couldn't stand up to that sort of drenching.

I frown at it and drop my eyes to Alex again. "Where does a child of mine get all that hair, I wonder? Arthur's not exceptionally hirsute, and the men on my side of the family are as bald as potatoes. I must have had an affair with a gorilla before he was born, but you'd think I'd remember something like that, wouldn't you?" I pick lint from the breast of my sweater. "Be a dear and remind me to leave my brandy flask at home the next time I visit the zoo."

He turns around to face me, grinning.

"What?" I demand.

"Nothing."

I raise my eyebrows, irritated, and he shrugs. "You're kind of funny, that's all."

"Oh." I look away. "It's just the wine. It makes my tongue say the oddest things." I wet my finger and run it around the rim of the crystal glass, making it hum an E-flat. "Arthur hates my sense of humor. He didn't always, but he says I've gotten mean in the last few years. I prefer to think of it as being honest."

He doesn't answer, but he leans a shoulder against the wall and puts his hands in his pockets, waiting for me. A light chain necklace hangs loosely in the sparse chest hairs—also red—visible beneath his open collar.

I rub my eyes, suddenly tired. "But honesty is not really Arthur's forte, you see. He tried to tell the truth once, but he claims it gave him diarrhea, so now he avoids it like the plague." I get to my feet, knees popping. "All right, I think I've caught my second wind. Ready to go?"

He nods. "I'm sorry about the apartment. It would be perfect if it had a door."

I purse my lips. "As I said, there's an entire floor between you and the rest of the house. No door can give you more privacy than that. You could run around naked up here with three drunken sorority girls and a German shepherd and no one would ever be the wiser."

He looks away. "It's nothing like that. I just want a door. I don't think I'd feel safe without one."

"Safe from what?"

He pushes his glasses up on his nose and doesn't answer.

I narrow my eyes. "For God's sake, boy, I'm seventy-one years old. Do you think I'm going to murder you in your sleep? I'm altogether harmless."

The sides of his mouth twitch. "Unless you happen to be an antique coffee table?"

That startles a laugh out of me. "Well, yes. Good point. But that was entirely Arthur's fault. He called this afternoon to tell me he'd be over later this week to get the rest of his things, and that set me off a bit. Ordinarily I'm as gentle as a lamb. Ask anyone."

His smile fades. "I'm sorry. I believe you. And I know it's dumb not to jump at a chance to live in a place like this for as little money as you're asking, but I've got to have a door. I don't think I could sleep without one."

I start to argue with him but then shut myself up. Why am I wasting my time trying to convince this stubborn child to live here if he doesn't want to? I'll find someone less fussy; the ad in the paper has only been running for two days, and I've already lined up four other people who want to see the apartment tomorrow.

"Fine." My voice is more curt than I intended. "Shall I show you out, then?"

He looks unhappy. "If you want."

I lead him down the stairs, and neither of us speaks as we pass by the third floor. But when we get to the landing outside my bedroom on the second floor, I step into the room on impulse and wave for him to follow me. "Let's take the other staircase down this time. I might as well show you the rest of the house before you leave."

He hesitates but finally says, "Okay," and trails in behind me.

I flip the light switch on. In the short time since Alex arrived, the sun has already begun to go down, even though it's only a little past four o'clock. I hate how early it gets dark in January; it's so depressing. The fluorescent light leaves awful shadows in the corners of the room and glints coldly from the brass handles on my wardrobe and dresser, and my clean white bedspread looks stark and sterile, like the sheet on a hospital mattress. I hurry through to the other door and sigh with relief when we step on the landing by the west staircase.

"There," I mutter. "That's better."

He stares at me. "Is something wrong?"

"No, not really." I force my shoulders to relax. "Sunsets in the winter should be outlawed, that's all. I seldom go in my bedroom at this time of day because it looks like a morgue in there. I keep expecting to find my own corpse lying faceup on the bed."

I take a deep breath and flick a wrist at the two rooms facing the master bedroom. "Those were Jeremy's and Caitlin's bedrooms once upon a time. My other children."

He glances in the rooms but I don't bother to look with him; I know what's there. Just a bunch of rickety old furniture and empty bookshelves and threadbare carpets. No one ever goes in either room anymore except the woman I hire to clean for me.

He talks with his back to me. "Do they still live in Bolton, too?"

"Caitlin does. She's the head of the English department at Pritchard."

He spins to face me, startled, and laughs. "Oh, my God. Caitlin Donovan is your daughter? I just met her yesterday. I'm taking a creative writing class from her this semester, and I've also got her for English Lit. She seems really nice."

I grunt. "Yes, well, she does have many redeeming qualities. She chews with her mouth closed, for instance, and she never, ever dangles a preposition. It's quite impressive."

He gawks at me. "It sounds like you don't like her."

I snort. "One doesn't *like* Caitlin. One either worships her or flees from her, depending on her mood. You should be careful in her classes, by the way. She had a bad day last semester and ripped the colon out of a graduate student with her bare hands."

I pause. "Don't look at me like that. I'm serious. It was in all the papers."

He laughs again. "How much wine did you say you'd had today?"

I peer in my empty glass and smile at him. "Thank you for reminding me. I believe it's time for a refill."

I lead him down the remaining flight of stairs and stop at the open door by the music room, then I step aside to wait for the predictable reaction.

He stops beside me and gives an obliging gasp. "My God. Look at that piano. It's gorgeous."

"Thank you." I step in the room and caress the black finish of the music rack. My beloved piano is a glorious dinosaur, nearly eleven feet long—two feet longer than an average grand—with ninety-six keys instead of the standard eighty-eight. The body rests on four black tapered legs, each thicker at the top than my torso, and the lid could serve as a wing on a small airplane. "Arthur and I went into serious debt to buy this. It's a one-of-a-kind Bösendorfer. There were only three of this specific model made originally, and the other two were destroyed in fires. There's no other piano like it in the world."

In addition to the exquisite tonal quality of the instrument, the case is what makes it so valuable. Stretching from one end to the other is a hand-painted, enchanting scene of a forest at night under a full moon, with a number of woodland creatures hidden among the trees. The colors are all shades of green and gold and yellow, and the detail is breathtaking. The artist was a man named Jacques Previere, who apparently died from an opium overdose.

Alex stands next to me. "It's gigantic."

"Yes. The movers had a terrible time getting it in the house."

He plunks an "A" on the keyboard. "Do you play?"

I stare at him. "You're joking."

He looks puzzled. "What do you mean?"

"My maiden name is Parker. I'm Hester Parker."

His face stays blank.

I wince. "Dear Lord. You honestly haven't heard of me?"

He shakes his head, embarrassed. "I'm sorry. Should I have?"

I turn toward the door, craving the bottle of wine. He follows me as I speak over my shoulder. "I used to be a concert pianist when I was a young woman. I toured all over Europe and the United

States. Granted, it's been a long time, but I was semi-famous for a while, or so I thought. Not like Rubinstein or Horowitz, of course, but most people have at least heard of me."

He doesn't answer and I enter the living room and retrieve the bottle by the fire. It's half empty. As I refill the glass some of the wine splashes on the frayed Oriental carpet. I stare at the stains and fight back sudden tears. "I was something of a household name, once, believe it or not." I lift my chin and try to smile. "Like Crest, or Alpo. Or Preparation H."

He looks alarmed. "I'm sorry. I didn't mean to upset you."

I wave a hand at him and ease myself down into the leather recliner facing the fire. "It's all right." I swallow a couple of times and sigh. "I've been ridiculously emotional lately. I cried at the grocery store last week because the lettuce was wilted and the bananas were overpriced. The produce manager tried to pacify me with a free box of frozen brussels sprouts, but I was inconsolable." I hold the bottle out toward him. "Are you sure you won't have a drink with me?"

He studies my face for a moment then takes the bottle from my hand. "Where do you keep your wineglasses?"

I point over my shoulder. "In the kitchen, in the cabinet above the sink."

He returns in a moment with a full glass and sits on the edge of the chair facing me. The sun is almost down now and darkness is closing over the house. He rolls the stem of his glass nervously between his fingertips, and the firelight reflects off it, racing back and forth over the spines of the books in the floor-to-ceiling shelves surrounding us.

We stare at each other for a minute in silence until he begins to squirm. "So," he finally blurts. "Do you still play?"

"I fractured my left wrist a number of years ago in an unfortunate tumble on the ice, and it's never really healed properly, not even after surgery. Since then I've been unable to play piano for more than a few minutes at a time, because of a rather debilitating case of carpal tunnel syndrome."

His eyes dart to my wrist and I flex it for him. "Yes, it's still fine for most things. Just not for the kind of beating that Liszt or

Beethoven or Rachmaninoff requires. The last time I tried to play a full concert, by intermission I felt as if someone were digging a corkscrew into my thumb and forearm. It was excruciating, so I had to give up performing in favor of teaching."

I ponder my hands. "There's repertoire available for one-armed pianists, of course, but with a few notable exceptions, it has extremely limited appeal for both soloist and audience. Besides, once you've had two good hands at your disposal . . . well, let's just say it's not much fun playing with only one. It's like trying to run with a single leg."

"I see." His voice is quiet and his face is somber. "Did you make any recordings before your accident?"

"Oh, yes, indeed. Many." I stifle a belch. "Wal-Mart has most of them available on cassette in their bargain bins. They're three dollars and ninety-nine cents each. You better hurry, though, if you want one, because they're selling like hotcakes."

I gaze at the fire and pull at a strand of my hair. "I'm lying, actually. The only place you can find my recordings these days is on eBay, usually after one of my few remaining fans passes away and his heirs auction off his belongings." I sniff. "Then they all run out to the Mall of America, and use the money to buy extremely useful things like Playstations and iPods for their lazy, drooling children. God."

When I look back at him he's grinning again.

I lean forward. "So what brings you to Bolton? I believe you said on the phone that you're transferring to Pritchard this semester?"

He nods and his grin falls away. "Yeah. That's why I need to find a place to live pretty soon. There are no openings in the dorms, and I can only afford to stay at the bed-and-breakfast until classes start next week."

He spins the glass faster in his hands and bars of firelight blur past my eyes.

"Stop that, please. You're going to give me an epileptic seizure."
"Sorry."

"Don't be sorry. Just stop fidgeting." I sink back in my chair and tuck my feet under me. "How old are you?"

"Twenty." He sips at his wine and coughs. "Almost twenty-one. My birthday is in March."

"Oh, dear. I'm giving alcohol to a minor." I raise my glass to him. "Oh, well. Drink up. We'll pretend it's grape juice. I trust this isn't your first time?"

He shakes his head and smiles. "Not even close."

We fall silent again for a moment. A log breaks apart in the fireplace and a small shower of sparks sails up the chimney.

I clear my throat. "So if you're taking my daughter's classes, are you an English major? She only teaches the upper level courses."

"Yeah. Technically I'm a junior, but I'm not sure all my credits are going to transfer."

"Transfer from where?"

He shifts in his chair and looks out the window. "Wow. It's getting really dark outside." He squints at the garden. "Who's that big statue of?"

I stare at the back of his head, wondering why he didn't respond to my question. I suppose I should pursue the matter further, but I can't make myself care enough to try.

"No one knows for sure," I answer. "But it's awful, isn't it?" I take a pistachio from the dish by my elbow and pick the shell apart with my fingernails as I look out the window, too. The statue is barely visible, but I can still make out the stone Bible nestled in the crook of its left arm. "We call him Saint Booger."

He laughs. "Why?"

"No particular reason. Arthur's mother bought it—though only God knows why—without having any idea who it was supposed to be. Some visiting professor once told her he thought it was a Russian saint, but he didn't know the fellow's name, either." I hide a yawn. "So shortly after that, Arthur started calling him Booger, the Patron Saint of Phlegm, and it stuck."

I pop the pistachio in my mouth and chase it down with wine. "It made his mother furious. She'd hoped that having a religious icon in her yard would impress the neighbors, but it was so ugly all people could do was laugh. She was heartbroken."

Alex tilts his head to see better. "He doesn't look so bad from here."

"You should see him up close, in the daytime. He's cross-eyed, and he's missing three fingers on his right hand, and one of his legs is substantially bigger than the other. He also has patches of black mold in his nostrils that resemble armpit hair. It's repulsive."

The grandfather clock in the study behind me chimes once to mark the half-hour: it must be five-thirty. I rest my head on the back of my chair and close my eyes for a moment. "I'd love to get rid of him, but the garbage men refuse to take him. They say he's too heavy and they'd have to hire extra help to get him on their truck."

I open my eyes again and the room takes a few seconds to stop spinning. I reach out a hand and pull the chain on the table lamp to give us more light inside, and the statue disappears, replaced by a mirror image of the living room in the window.

He finally turns away from the outside. "I kind of like him. He looks like he's guarding the house."

I guffaw. "Of course. How appropriate. Saint Booger is my guardian angel. That explains a great deal."

He smiles at me. I offer him the bowl of pistachios and he takes a handful, settling back in his chair to eat them. He puts his wine on the table and starts making a neat pile of shells in his lap, one by one. He focuses on each nut with the intensity of a hungry squirrel, and for a moment he seems to forget I'm in the room with him.

I sip at my wine and watch him, amused by the concentration on his narrow face. There's something very appealing about his expression; it's been a long while since I've seen someone take such conspicuous pleasure in the creature comforts of food and fire. We're both quiet as he eats, but this time the silence doesn't seem to bother him.

After he finishes the pistachios, he collects the shells from his lap and stands up to toss them in the fire. They crack and sizzle as they hit the hot coals. He looks down at me. "Well, I guess I should be going." His voice sounds reluctant.

I stir in my chair. "Or not." The wine is probably interfering with my judgment, but there's something about this boy, something vulnerable and sincere, that makes me not want to let him go. "You can still have the apartment tonight if you want it."

He blinks behind his glasses. "Mrs. Donovan, I really can't."

"Don't call me that, please. It makes me angry, and I'm running out of furniture I can destroy."

He pauses. "Okay. Hester. Anyway, I love your place, and you seem nice and everything, but like I said, I really need to have . . ."

". . . a door," I interrupt. "Yes, I know. You mentioned that several times. It's becoming tiresome, don't you think?"

I get slowly to my feet and stand a foot away from him. He's a good eight or nine inches taller than I am, but I lock eyes with him and he seems to shrink down to my size. "Don't be an idiot, Alex." I've learned to trust my instincts about things like this, and when I speak my voice is certain. "You're moving in."

I don't blink or look away until he nods.

Sometimes you can't reason with people. Sometimes you just have to bully them into doing the right thing.

CHAPTER 2

The boy is coming down the stairs as I'm gathering my things by the door. On his shoulder he's carrying a worn and dirty brown backpack, with a yellow and black patch on the flap that says, *"How would you like it if an animal ate YOU?"* His red hair is uncombed and wet, and he looks half-asleep.

He's been here a week or so, but we've barely spoken since the night he moved in. When he's not in classes at Pritchard, he keeps to himself up in the attic, and even though he's polite when he passes me on his way through the house, he's shown no interest in striking up another conversation.

I nod at him. "Good morning."

"Morning," he grunts. He's dressed in his usual attire: jeans and the blue flannel shirt he uses as a coat. He drops his backpack on the floor and squats to put his shoes on by the old metal milk pail that serves as my umbrella holder. Once again he's not wearing socks.

I finish buttoning my overcoat and peer down at him. "I'm on my way to the Conservatory, and it's right next door to Pritchard. Would you like a ride?"

He fumbles with the laces on his shoes and waits a moment before looking up at me. "Sure, I guess."

I can tell he doesn't know what to think of me. He always watches me warily, as if he thinks I'm getting ready to pop his skull open and scoop out his brain with my fingers if he should dare to drop his guard.

I frown. "You're afraid to get stuck in the car with an old woman driving, aren't you? You probably think I'll weave all over the road and stop to coo at every toddler and starving kitten I see."

He reclaims his backpack and stands again. "I just like walking, that's all."

I study his thin face. "It's quite a hike to Pritchard from here. It must take you nearly an hour. But if you'd rather walk, by all means do so."

He shakes his head. "Nah. I'm running a little late this morning, so I guess a ride would be good."

"I'm a good driver, you know. I haven't had a ticket in nearly twenty years." I search through my red leather purse for my keys. "And the only reason I got that one was because I was listening to the radio at the time. Sergei Pegorav was butchering one of my favorite Schumann pieces—the *Phantasie* in C, do you know it?— and it was such an appalling performance that I got distracted and accidentally ran through a stop light. So as you can see it wasn't really my fault."

I sigh as my fingers find the little mace sprayer that's attached to my key chain. "The policeman who pulled me over disagreed, of course, even when I turned up the radio and pointed out all the horrific ways the piano was being violated by that overrated Russian fop. I told him that instead of wasting my time he should go ticket Pegorav for playing like that, but he was entirely unreasonable and insisted on fining me thirty-five dollars. Can you imagine?"

From his expression I can tell he's trying to decide if I'm serious or not. I am, more or less, but I've been told my face is hard to read.

He follows me out to the carriage house as I pick my way over the two or three inches of fresh snow that fell on the driveway last night. I speak over my shoulder, remembering something.

"Do you mind physical labor, Alex? If you'll agree to keep the porch and the walkways clear this winter, I'll deduct twenty dollars from your rent each time you have to shovel."

His face brightens. "Really? That's pretty pimp."

I scowl at him. "Is that English you're speaking? Do we have a deal or not?"

He grins at me. "Yeah. Deal."

I continue talking as he helps me open the enormous wooden sliding door on the carriage house. "You don't have to shovel the driveway, by the way. I've hired Bernie Lomax to come by with his truck to do that."

My car is a white Toyota Corolla and we get in. It's another bitterly cold morning, but the engine turns over on my first try. I let the car idle for a minute to warm up, and Alex and I sit in silence. He fiddles with the ties on his backpack and stares out the passenger window at the inside of the carriage house. There's not much for him to see except assorted tools hanging here and there, and all my cut firewood stacked high against the rear wall. I flip on the radio and a Brahms violin sonata drifts from the speakers.

"Buckle your seat belt. The roads are always icy this time of year."

He obeys me and I put the car in reverse and step on the acclerator. I give it a little too much gas and we lurch backward faster than I intended, scooting all the way through the open door and into the bright sunshine before I can locate the brake again.

The sudden stop jostles him in his seat a bit and he throws a hand up on the dash. "Jesus!" He turns to gawk at me. "Are you drunk?"

"I beg your pardon?" I glare at him. "I most certainly am not."

He wilts under my gaze. "Sorry," he mutters. "You just startled me a little."

He's so tall his hair brushes against the roof of the car, but in spite of his size, he still looks like a little boy.

I moderate my tone. "I'll attempt to make the rest of the ride smoother for you. You can relax."

We roll down the driveway and out into the street without further mishap, and I put the car in drive. The front wheels take a moment to find traction and the rear of the car slides to the left somewhat before we begin to move forward. From the corner of my eye I see Alex bite his lip and wince.

I ignore that. "So how are your classes going?"

He shrugs. "They're okay." He hesitates. "Your daughter is kind of . . . interesting."

The mention of Caitlin is painful, as always, but I can't help but laugh at his careful choice of words. "I tried to warn you about her, remember?"

"I don't mean it in a bad way. Not really. She's just hard to figure out is all." He's studying me. "She looks like you, though."

I peer at my reflection in the rearview mirror. "Do you think so? Not many people say that."

"Yeah. She's got your eyes, and your cheekbones are the same, too. And you've both got kind of a square jaw." He pauses. "But she's a lot bigger than you are."

I keep my eyes on the road. "She gets her size from Arthur. All our children have towered over me ever since they reached puberty." I blink back tears. "And you're right about her eyes. They come from the Parker side of the family. My father had the same dark green eyes, and so did his father."

We hit another patch of ice by a four-way stop sign and skate a few feet into the intersection before I can regain control of the car. Another vehicle swerves around me, honking, and I exchange black looks with the other driver.

"Shit," Alex mutters. Both of his hands are clutching the dash.

"Oh, for pity's sake. You're behaving like an old woman."

He glowers at me. "That's only because you're driving like one."

I narrow my eyes. "And I suppose you think you could do better?"

He nods. "Yeah, I do. I'm a good driver." He pauses. "Do you want me to take the wheel?"

I face front again and proceed through the intersection, fuming. He fidgets in his seat for the next few blocks and I turn up the radio and stare through the windshield at downtown Bolton until I can decide how best to deal with his rudeness.

My house is on the north side of town, and Carson Conservatory and Pritchard University are on the south side. Bolton is a clean, attractive town, with wide brick streets and dozens of historical buildings and homes lined up along the Mississippi. An imposing courthouse sits in the middle of the village green, next to a pedestrian mall made up of busy bookstores and coffee shops, restaurants, bars, and a plethora of overpriced antique and clothing establishments. There's generally not a lot of money in southern Illinois, but Bolton's association with two thriving academic institutions has kept it more financially sound than many of its neighbors up and down the river.

My silence is bothering Alex. He keeps darting glances at the side of my face and biting his lip.

Good. If I let him stew for a while, he may learn some manners.

He finally clears his throat. "Sorry. I didn't mean to make you mad."

I allow a moment to pass. "You're forgiven." I should just let it go at that, I suppose, but I can't resist a small dig. "Do you talk to your mother that way? If you do, it's a wonder you've lived to be twenty."

He doesn't answer for a few seconds. "I've said a lot worse to her." His voice is subdued.

I wait for more but nothing is forthcoming. I prod him along. "Speaking of your mother, I keep meaning to ask where you grew up. Where's home?"

He turns his head away. "Iowa."

"Oh? Where in Iowa?"

He plays with the button on the glove compartment. "I don't really like to talk about stuff like that." His tone is hostile.

I stare at him, caught off guard. "Why on earth not?"

He meets my gaze. "I just don't. Okay?"

He's being unreasonable, and silly.

"Fine. Shall we discuss the weather, then? How about movies?"

He makes an exasperated gesture with his hands. "I didn't mean that. We can talk about anything you want. Just not my home, or my family." He stares at his shoes on the floor mat and lowers his voice. "Please?"

Without warning, he sounds close to tears, and I reprimand myself for prying. He's right. I have no claim on him, and he's entitled to his privacy, just as much as I am.

I nod. "Forgive me, Alex. I was being discourteous."

I'm expecting him to pout now, but all he does is shrug again. "It's okay. I didn't mean to make such a big deal out of it."

The resentment is gone, replaced by a surprising sweetness.

It seems I've underestimated this boy. It's a rare gift to let go of anger so quickly.

God knows I'm no good at that myself.

We reach the intersection of River Road and Crescent Street, and I pull up to the stoplight and put on my turn signal. Pritchard and Carson are on River Road about a mile and a half from here. Bolton has only eighteen thousand people in it, but when Pritchard University is in session that number goes up to nearly twenty-seven thousand. (Carson Conservatory has as enrollment of less than seven hundred, so if you see a college student around town it's a good bet he attends Pritchard rather than Carson.)

Alex points at the radio. "What's this music?"

I cock my head and listen. The Brahms sonata finished a few moments ago, and has been replaced by an orchestral work I don't immediately recognize. I sift through the possibilites and settle on what seems the most likely.

"Shostakovich, I should think. I don't know this particular piece, but I'm certain it's something of his."

He gapes at me. "You've never heard it before, but you still know who wrote it?"

"The orchestration gives it away. Listen to those cellos, and to the percussion. It's definitely Russian, and mid-twentieth century . . ." I turn up the radio for a few more bars. "Yes. It's Shostakovich. The humor and pathos simply reek of him."

He seems impressed. "How can you do that?"

His admiration is endearing. I smile at him. "Any classical musician worth her salt can do the same thing, child. Every well-known composer has a distinctive style, and I've been trained to recognize it, that's all."

He shakes his head as if he doesn't believe me. "That's really cool. I wish I could do that."

Pritchard's campus looms up on the right, between the road and the river.

"What's your first class?" I ask, slowing.

He sighs. "Creative writing."

"With Caitlin?"

"Yeah. It's in Higdon Hall." He becomes self-conscious. "Sorry. I guess you already know where she teaches."

"Indeed. Higdon Hall has always been closely identified with Caitlin's reign of terror. She used to put the heads of her foes on spikes outside the main doors, but the administration made her stop for fear of declining enrollment."

He laughs. "That's pretty funny."

I pretend to be amused as well, but I don't tell him that it's been years since I've been anywhere near my daughter's domain. Or that my heart is speeding up a great deal at the mere thought of accidentally running into her this morning.

As I pull into the parking lot by the English building, I can see the Mississippi in the distance. Most of the water is frozen on the surface, except for an uneven path down the middle, big enough for tugboats and barges to navigate between the thin black ice reaching out for fifty or sixty yards from each bank toward the center. (This stretch of the Mississippi south of St. Louis is relatively narrow, probably only two or three hundred yards across, and I've been told that towns like Bolton run frequent icebreakers between the locks, keeping the river open for local businesses to ferry items back and forth.) Late at night, from anywhere in Bolton, you can hear the foghorns on the barges as they pass by, wailing in the mist like male banshees, but right now nothing is out there but a small flock of geese or ducks, resting together on the ice by the opposite shore.

I step on the brake by the walkway between Higdon Hall and the cafeteria, and the car slides on the ice again and bangs into the curb before I can do anything about it.

Alex tenses in his seat, then turns to face me. He actually rolls his eyes at me and starts to say something.

I shake my finger at him. "Not a word. Not if you know what's good for you."

He grins at me as he opens his door. "Okay. Whatever." He gets out, then leans his head back in before closing the door. "Thanks for the ride, Hester. See you tonight?"

I nod at him. "Yes. I'll be curled up by the fire with a glass of wine and a book as soon as I finish teaching."

He smiles again. "Word."

I tilt my head. "Excuse me? Is that supposed to mean something?"

His smile broadens. "It just means it sounds good."

I shoo him from the car. "Go to school. I hope my daughter can teach you how to speak properly."

He shuts the door and I watch his back until he disappears into Higdon Hall.

CHAPTER 3

Arthur's car is in the driveway when I get home, blocking access to the carriage house. It's a black Lincoln Continental, with a Carson Conservatory Faculty sticker in the rear window, and the license plate on the back says AMATI (in reference to his cherished and obscenely expensive violin). He's parked right in front of St. Booger, and I have to leave my own car by the curb in the street and walk up to the house. The statue has a slight scowl on its face, and its crossed eyes are staring down at Arthur's car with displeasure, but the severity of poor Booger's expression is undercut by a glob of half-melted snow on his head, in the shape of a beanie.

St. Booger is truly an eyesore. Besides the revolting things I mentioned about him to Alex the other night (the chopped-off fingers, uneven legs, and patches of dead mold sprouting from his nose and ears), one of his cheekbones sticks out more than the other, and there's an unsightly, goiter-like bulge on the left side of his neck. His face is also pocked with dozens of little acne-like craters, probably from standing outside in too many hailstorms. Lord, what an atrocity.

I walk up to the front door and when I step on the porch I can see Arthur's large head and shoulders through the window of my living room. He's wearing a heavy brown sweater, and he's standing with his arms crossed, glaring out at me. I take a deep breath and walk in, knowing exactly how this conversation is likely to go. The love of my life is now my worst enemy, and we haven't had a civil exchange in months.

I take off my coat in the entryway and step into the living room. He's still standing with his back to me.

I sigh. "Why, Arthur! What a pleasant surprise. Have you moved back home, then? You can sleep in the carriage house until we've ironed some things out."

He turns to face me with open anger. His thick gray hair is cut shorter than usual, and his mouth is drawn down at the corners in severe lines, making him look like a toy soldier nutcracker. His skin is blotchy with ire, but he's still a terribly handsome man, with white, even teeth and bushy gray eyebrows the same color as his beard. His eyes are gray, too, and cold, with crow's-feet at the corners.

"Don't you dare start with me, Hester," he rumbles. "Not after what you did to my table."

I sit down in my chair. "I don't understand what you're so upset about, dear. As I mentioned on the phone earlier, it was an unfortunate accident."

"That is unmitigated bullshit." His voice isn't loud, but his words are clipped and fast. "You deliberately destroyed a priceless heirloom out of pure spite and jealousy." He pauses. "No doubt you were drunk at the time, too."

There's a quiet click of the door shutting in the entryway, and I glance over in time to see Alex stepping in. Arthur doesn't hear him, and the boy is out of his line of vision because he's standing behind a partial wall that separates the entry and the living room. I swear silently and keep my eyes on Arthur, hoping Alex will somehow manage to get upstairs without my husband seeing him. Arthur will not take kindly to my having taken on another tenant without his consent. From the brief glimpse I had of Alex's face, I can tell he knows he's stepped into a hornet's nest. He's frozen still in the entryway, next to the umbrella can.

I gaze straight ahead and force a smile. "Why, Arthur, what a terrible thing to say. Haven't you been listening? I already told you that as I was walking through the study, the sledgehammer just slipped out of my hands and fell on your table. I feel sick about it."

Arthur is breathing loudly. "Yes, you mentioned that. But you also failed to explain what you were you doing in the study with a sledgehammer."

"I don't recall." I hug myself. "Don't take this the wrong way, darling, but I rather enjoyed the sound of the hammerhead going through the table top. It made a very satisfying crunch, and splinters went flying every which way."

I can hear the ticking of the grandfather clock in the study. Arthur's voice is almost toneless. "My father gave me that table. Good God, Hester, could you possibly have done anything more childish and selfish?"

His sanctimony is unbearable.

I sit up straight. "Well, yes, Arthur, I believe I could. For instance, I could have had a fifteen-year affair with a sweaty, buxom slut behind my spouse's back. Don't you think that might qualify as being somewhat more 'childish and selfish' than chopping up a piece of furniture?"

He starts to splutter and I cut him off. "Yes, my love, I realize we're speaking of apples and oranges, but I'm just trying to keep things in perspective."

I adjust the sleeve of my dark red sweater. "And by the way, I had the table appraised before I burned it. It was made in the 1970s by a knockoff artist who specialized in cheap imitations of colonial furniture. Your precious heirloom was worth less than a Scooby-Doo TV tray."

"That's a lie." The floor creaks as he steps forward. He's now in a position to see Alex, should he turn his head. Fortunately, he's too fixated on me to notice anything else. He tugs at his full gray beard in frustration. "You know you've done something wrong, and now you're trying to make yourself look better by lying. You've always done that."

He leans down so his face is level with mine, and he puts his palms on the arms of my chair. "You forget how well I know you, Hester." His voice drops. "Do you have any idea how sick I am of you?"

I used to love this man more than my own life, and he loved me just as much. Now all our words to each other hang in the air like nerve gas.

I flinch a little, but I don't look away from him. I refuse to give him the pleasure of winning this dispute.

"Join the club, dear." I clear my throat. "But as long as we're on the subject of telling lies, how's Martha? Would you like to spread her out on our bed this afternoon for old time's sake? I could go out for coffee and give you two kids the run of the place for an hour or so, if you're too self-conscious to do it while I'm here."

He straightens. "There's no talking to you."

He's trying to hide his feelings, but shame is written all over him.

I drum my fingers on my chin and smile. "Or if you prefer, I'll play the piano to help set the mood while the two of you are fornicating. Any requests? How about Stravinksy's *Polka for Circus Elephants?* It might remind Martha of home."

He glowers down at me. "That's not even remotely funny. And for your information, Martha's lost a great deal of weight recently. She looks stunning." He rubs his temples. "Besides, I prefer my women to have a little meat on their bones."

In truth, Martha Predel is a strikingly beautiful woman, and twenty years my junior. But she carries a few extra pounds on her small frame, and I can use this to my advantage. It may be petty, but at this point I'll take whatever weapon comes to hand.

"*A little meat?*" I snort. "The woman is a walking delicatessen."

From the corner of my eye I see Alex put his hand on the doorknob. He's apparently decided to go outside again instead of braving the staircase.

Arthur heaves a sigh. "I've had enough of this. My lawyer told me it was a mistake to come over here until we've come to terms on the house, but I thought that just maybe you'd be capable of being civilized for a few moments while I collected the rest of my . . ."

Alex turns the knob and opens the door just enough to get out, but as he's squeezing through the space he bumps into the metal milk can, and the handle of one of the umbrellas sticking out of it catches on the lip of his pants pocket. The whole can tips over and he makes a wild grab to catch it, but his fingers miss and it crashes on the floor, spitting out a purple and orange umbrella and a silver-tipped walking cane.

Arthur jumps about a foot in the air and spins toward the door. He looks Alex up and down, then swings his head to look at me again. He sees I'm not surprised, and his hands ball into fists.

"Who the hell is that?"

"He lives here, Arthur." I wave Alex in. "Hello, Alex. Don't just stand there. Come in and meet my extremely charming husband. Arthur, this is Alex Pearl. Alex, Arthur Donovan."

Alex walks into the room (after shutting the door and righting the milk can) but when he extends his hand Arthur pretends not to see it. He drops his arm and looks at me for guidance. "I'm sorry, I didn't mean to intrude."

Arthur ignores him. "What do you mean, he lives here? You know damn well you weren't supposed to get another tenant until the divorce is final and we've reached a settlement on the property. Tell him to get out."

I look down at my hands and begin fiddling with my cuticles. "I'll do no such thing. He's already signed the lease."

I'm lying. I haven't had him sign anything.

Arthur gives Alex a black look and the boy takes a step backward. I can't say I blame him. Arthur is overweight and seventy-two years old, but in spite of that he's still quite strong, with thick, round shoulders and a broad chest, and at six-four he's even taller than Alex. However, Arthur wouldn't hurt a fly, physically; he's actually a very gentle man—unlike our son Paul, who would pull the wings off the same fly, with glee.

But that's another story.

Arthur crosses his beefy forearms in front of him. "I don't care what he signed. Get rid of him." He studies Alex with distaste. "I see my wife still has a soft spot for mangy strays. She took in a half-dead cat once that had to be put down for distemper. Have you at least had your shots?"

Alex recoils from the hostility in his tone.

"You're being horribly rude, Arthur." I turn my head to the boy. "Don't pay any attention to him, Alex. He's been suffering from mild hallucinations lately. For instance, he believes, oddly enough, that he still has some say in what happens in this house. Isn't that ridiculous?"

Arthur snatches his coat from the chair behind him. "We'll see how ridiculous I'm being at the pretrial conference." He levels a finger at Alex. "The lease you signed isn't legally valid because this property is under dispute. No matter what Hester tells you, you're going to have to move out immediately. Do I make myself clear?"

Alex drops his head and stares at the floor. He didn't take his shoes off when he came in and there are little clumps of snow melting on the carpet by his feet. Arthur gives me a final look a few seconds later, then sweeps out of the room, smelling like English Leather and pipe smoke.

I stare after him, then look up at Alex again and lower my voice to a stage whisper just as Arthur opens the door. "The doctors think his hallucinations are linked to an overdose of secondhand lard. It's quite sad."

Alex's eyes become huge. I can hear Arthur breathing heavily in the entryway, and I feel a cold draft coming in from outside.

"Go to hell, Hester." His voice is almost civil, but I get ice up my back listening to it.

"You first, dear." I smile brightly. "And do remember to give my love to Martha."

A long silence. "That's very sweet of you, but completely unnecessary. Why give her your love when I can give her this house instead, in just a few weeks?"

My breathing quickens, but all I do is nod. "If that's the case, I'll begin stocking the pantry with Ring Dings and corn chips, so the poor dear won't waste away before you have a chance to get to the grocery store."

The door slams.

For a few seconds Alex and I don't move. We stare at each other in silence as Arthur's car door bangs shut in the driveway, and a moment later we hear his engine rev to life.

Alex lets his breath out with a whoosh. "Jesus."

My lower lip trembles a little. "Quite." I pinch the bridge of my nose. "I'm a bit confused. Arthur left without taking the things he came for." I look up at the boy. "Why do you suppose he did that? I think he's losing his mind."

I get to my feet and jab at the fire with a poker. "I apologize, dear. I had no intention for you to witness that unpleasant little scene."

His forehead is sweating a little. "That's all right. I didn't mean to walk in on you like that." He wipes his hands on his shirt. "Are you okay?"

I set the poker down and adjust my hair. "Why wouldn't I be? That's the most enjoyable conversation Arthur and I have had in ages."

I turn my head, distracted, and scan some of the familiar titles on the bookshelf closest to me: *A History of Western Music* is sandwiched between *Sophie's Choice* and a worn copy of *The Scarlet Letter*. I run my hand over the spines, feeling the dry leather under my fingertips. There's no order of any kind to the books, but there are thousands of them, wall-to-wall and floor-to-ceiling. Everyone in my family is an ardent reader, and I don't believe we've ever thrown out a single book.

When I face Alex again, he's waiting for me. "When do you want me to move out?"

I shake my head with energy. "I don't. Arthur doesn't have a leg to stand on in court, and he knows it." I bend down to straighten the armcover on my chair. "You mustn't mind Arthur, by the way. He behaves like that toward everyone these days."

He looks puzzled. "Then why'd you marry him?"

"I have no idea." I make a face at his expression. "Oh, all right. That's a lie. I adored him, once."

He frowns. "Why?"

I walk past him, toward the kitchen. "I believe I need a drink to answer that. Want one?"

He nods and follows me into the kitchen. I keep talking while fishing through the liquor cabinet next to the pantry. "I met Arthur at a summer music festival in upstate New York in 1958." I dig out a bottle of Black Bush and two crystal highball glasses. "I'd come in third at the Tschaikovsky competition in Moscow that year, and he'd just won some unpronounceable thing in Paris. Anyway, we were both touring a lot in those days, but we'd never met."

I'm standing in front of the window and the sunlight is making a dust curtain in the air between the counter and me. I move over beside the sink and set the glasses down. "We were scheduled to perform the Franck *Sonata in D* together the first night of the festival, so the plan had been to arrive the night before to rehearse it. But Arthur's flight was delayed in Paris and he didn't get there until less than an hour before the performance, so we had no time to even run through it before we had to go out on stage."

I put the bottle on the counter and it catches the light and acts as a prism, projecting a rainbow-colored bar on the floor by my feet until I open the freezer door and block the sunlight with my body. The freezer is stuffed with boxes of Wolfgang Puck's pizzas and Shelton's free-range turkey sausages, and in the door itself is a big bottle of Bombay Gin and another of Beefeater Vodka.

I take out an ice tray and return to the counter. "The way Arthur played the Franck was the most gorgeous thing I've ever heard in my life. Or I should say the way *we* played it, if you'll excuse me for boasting. We were recorded live, incidentally, and . . ."

He interrupts me. "What instrument does he play?"

I drop the ice tray in the sink and round on him. "You're not serious."

He blushes and I stare at him in amazement. "Arthur Donovan is one of the premier violinists in the world. I can understand you not knowing who I am, but how in God's name have you never heard of Arthur? He's been on everything from cereal boxes to *The Tonight Show*."

He shakes his head, clearly embarrassed. I study him for a minute, baffled. "Unbelievable. Someone who's unfamiliar with the great Arthur Donovan. You've lived a charmed life."

I turn back to the sink and retrieve the ice tray. I pry a few cubes out in silence before speaking again. "Anyway, I was telling you about our performance at the festival." The ice lands in the glasses with a few high-pitched clinks. "It was uncanny. I felt like he knew what I was going to do before I did it. We matched each other, nuance for nuance, as if we'd been lovers for years, like Jacqueline du

Pre and old what's-his-name. Half the audience was in tears when we finished, and I felt the same as they did. It was so exquisite it nearly broke my heart."

I glance over my shoulder. "I know how immodest that sounds, but I don't mean it that way. I only mean it was a privilege to be part of that performance."

He shrugs. "That's cool. So that's why you married him? Because of how he played?"

I face him again. "Only partly. He was funny and sweet in those days, too, believe it or not, and he was also very, very beautiful. He had this splendid mane of black hair that came down to his shoulders, and these big gray eyes, and his skin felt like silk. I hopped into bed with him almost the instant we left the stage." I smile. "I could barely walk the next day, and neither could he. Dear God, that was a fun summer."

He grins at me but I barely notice. I fall silent until he prods me along. "Then what?"

I start. "What? Oh. Then the festival ended and I cancelled my fall concert tour to move to Bolton and marry him the following September. End of story."

I look down and pick up the open bottle of whiskey. I pour about three inches into each glass and hand him one of them. "Well, almost the end. Two years after that I broke my wrist and had to quit performing. Then along came Paul, our gifted and spiteful first son, and Jeremy, our sweet, wasted second, and Caitlin, our dear deranged daughter—and before you knew it, forty years passed by, and I never got out of here."

I raise my glass. "Oh, well. Cheers. Here's to callow, stupid young women and the choices they make early in life."

We both take a drink and he winces. "That's pretty strong."

Half of what I gave myself is already gone. "Damn straight." I knock the rest back and pour myself another double shot. "Drink up, Alex."

"I can't. I have a lot of homework to do tonight."

I shake the bottle at him like a policeman's truncheon. "I said drink."

He sighs and takes another sip. "So when did he move out?"

"Less than a year ago. Arthur mourned our relationship for all of two seconds and then shacked up last spring with one of the voice teachers from the Conservatory. Martha Predel is her name. Or Martha soon-to-be *Donovan*, I should say, since they plan to marry as soon as our divorce is final. Martha and Arthur were lovers for years, it turns out, but I never knew about it until recently. I had my suspicions of course, but I was a trusting fool for well over a decade."

I tug on a thin silver chain hanging around my neck. "I hear they threw a lovely dinner party to announce their pending engagement, but for a while there was an ugly rumor floating around town that Martha got hungry before the main entreé could be served, and was forced to eat the caterer to keep up her strength."

He wanders over to the tin-paneled wall and touches the metal with his finger. "You sound kind of bitter."

I bray laughter. He cringes a little as the guffaws echo around the room.

"Me? Bitter?" I come up next to him and lean my shoulder on the wall while watching the side of his face. "Just because I lost the only career I've ever wanted, and no one in my family will speak to me, and the husband I loved more than anybody I've known in my life traded me in after forty-five years of marriage for a wheezing, horse-faced soprano who intends to take my house away from me?"

I swish the whiskey around in my glass. "Don't talk nonsense, boy. These things happen."

I hum a few notes and stare out the window. It's starting to snow, and flakes the size of rose petals are sticking to the roof of the carriage house and slowly covering up the asphalt driveway. I watch them fall for a minute and the pain in my chest eases a bit, in spite of everything. "That's rather pretty, isn't it?"

I take another swallow of my drink. "In retrospect, I don't know which hurt worse. Losing my ability to play piano, or losing my family." I look down at my left wrist and flex it. "I suppose the only difference is the timing. I destroyed my wrist in an instant, you see. Both feet slid out from under me on a patch of ice, and the deed was done. But with Arthur and the children, I was falling for decades, and didn't even know it."

My voice is getting hoarse. "But of course I'm not bitter. Don't be silly. I'm Hester Parker. Hester Parker doesn't succumb to base human emotions like bitterness. Hester Parker is a ray of sunshine, a comforting melody to those in need, a chuckling cherub to all who know and love her. Haven't you noticed?"

He turns to me. My eyes are full of tears, and I reach up to pat his cheek when I see the helpless look on his face. His skin is warm, and dry.

"It's all right, dear. I'm fine. Really." I drop my hand and walk away. "Just don't let me anywhere near a gun."

CHAPTER 4

Alex is outside shoveling the sidewalk when I wake in the morning. I can hear the shovel grating on the concrete as I come down the stairs, and when I look out the front door I see him working. He has his back to me, and all he's wearing, yet again, is sneakers, a pair of jeans and that ratty blue flannel shirt that seems to be the only jacket he owns.

I open the door and in spite of the bright sun a wave of cold air slices through my robe. I yell his name and he jumps and turns around.

I step out on the porch in my slippers. "Come inside this instant and put on some heavier clothes, you idiot!"

He grins at me. "I'm fine. I'm almost done."

"At least wear gloves. You're going to get frostbite, and they'll have to amputate everything on your body except your shaggy little head. You'll spend the rest of your life as a bust on a pedestal."

He shoos me back inside. "Stop worrying, Hester. I'll be right in."

Feebleminded child. I glare at him for a minute but then the wind hits me again and I retreat into the house and slam the door behind me. I make my way to the kitchen to boil water for tea. When the gas is lit on the stove I stare out the window while the kettle pops and hisses.

It must have been quite a storm last night. The porch rail has at least seven inches of new snow piled on top of it. There was a lot of wind, too, it seems; St. Booger is buried in a drift up to his waist.

The front door bangs open and Alex comes in, stomping his feet. His face and hands are almost blue from the cold. "Whew." His glasses are steamed over and he tips his head to look at me over the top of the frames. "That's a lot of snow."

I grunt. "Booger's sporting a new white skirt today. He looks like an aging drag queen."

He laughs and kicks off his shoes. He's not wearing socks again, and his feet are the same color as the rest of his exposed skin. He closes the door behind him and pauses in the entry hall to wipe his glasses on his shirt, then he puts them back on and looks in at me.

I growl at him. "Don't just stand there freezing, you chuckle-head. Come in and get warm. I'm making tea."

He glances at the clock over the sink. "I would, but I need to take a shower and get over to Pritchard. I've got a class with your daughter in less than an hour, and she's kind of strict about being on time."

The kettle starts to whistle behind me and I turn off the stove. "Caitlin's strict about everything. She's in favor of bringing back the pillory for people who don't floss." I stuff a tea ball with some loose-leaf Darjeeling and drop it in a mug. "Don't worry about it. I'll give you a note explaining the only reason you were late was because you were helping me clean out the underwear drawer in her old dresser. I'm sure she'll understand."

He sniggers. "No, thanks. I'd like to live through the day."

"Ah." I fill my mug with hot water and sit at the table. "So I see you've already been exposed to Caitlin's temper."

He shrugs. "Not really. She's just kind of intense, that's all."

I drag the tea ball through the hot water by its chain and listen to it ping against the sides of the mug. "What did she say to you?"

He's standing with one foot on top of the other and leaning his shoulder on the door frame. He won't meet my gaze. "Nothing, really. She was just mad because I was late to class the other day."

"You didn't happen to mention you were renting my attic apartment, did you?"

His eyes touch mine, then dart away. "No, it didn't come up."

I snort. "You're a terrible liar, Alex."

He crosses his arms in front of his chest. "I'm not lying to you."

"Hmm." I drum my fingers on the table and enjoy watching him squirm, but his face starts to darken and I finally decide to let him off the hook. "It's fine, dear. You better hurry or you'll be late for class."

He sighs and runs a hand through his messy red hair. "All she said when I told her I'd moved in was to wish me good luck. But she acted like I'd just stabbed her favorite puppy with an ice pick."

I take out the tea ball and set it down on a cloth napkin. "It's taken her years to perfect that look. She used to trot it out for everyone from paperboys to state senators, but now she seems to reserve it specifically for people who make the mistake of mentioning my name when she's in the room."

He looks unhappy. "I'm sorry. I shouldn't have said anything."

"Don't be silly." I take a sip of tea and wince as it burns my tongue. "I'm rather pleased to find out I can still annoy Caitlin like that, even from a distance. I'd hate to think she's forgotten me entirely."

He dabs at his nose with the cuff of his shirt. "How come she's mad at you?"

"I don't recall."

There's a long silence. He's watching me closely and I start to get irritated. I get up and open the refrigerator, keeping my back to him.

He finally shifts his weight in the doorway and clears his throat. "Well, I guess I better take a shower."

I look over my shoulder. "You might want to think about shaving, too."

He scratches his scraggly chin. "I did just a few days ago. I think it looks cool this way."

I scowl. "Run along and play, dear. Hester's busy."

He grins. "Okay. See you later, then."

I try to maintain the scowl but I can't. His grin gets bigger and he turns around and disappears up the stairs. I can hear him using his long legs to jump over two or three steps at a time.

* * *

Ten minutes after Alex leaves the house, the phone rings. I'm still in the kitchen, washing my breakfast dishes and listening to NPR.

I wipe my hands on a towel and pick up the receiver. "Hello?"

"Mother? Why are you home?"

My breath catches in my throat as I turn down the volume on the radio. "Good morning to you, too, Paul. Why shouldn't I be home? I live here."

"That's not what I mean. Why aren't you teaching today?"

I lean my backside against the counter. "Is that any of your business?"

A pause. "Fine. That's not why I'm calling anyway. I talked to Dad this morning."

The sun pouring in through the window behind me is warm on my shoulders and back. "I see. My condolences."

"Don't be snide. He told me what you did. You're behaving contemptibly."

I watch my long shadow shift on the tin wall in front of me as I straighten. "How nice. Let me get this straight. You've been utterly ignoring me for what, the best part of a year? You've snubbed . . ."

His deep voice, so much like his father's, comes out flat. "I haven't been ignoring you."

"Hush, dear. Don't interrupt." Anger flares in my chest. "You've been a busy little boy this year, haven't you, son? Let's review what you've been up to, shall we?"

"Don't try to make this about me, Mother."

I talk over him. "You've snubbed me time and again on the streets of Bolton and in the halls at the Conservatory. You've bad-mouthed me behind my back in faculty meetings. You had your teaching studio moved to a different floor to get away from me. You've spoken to at least three of my students and managed to convince them to switch to another teacher."

My heart is pounding furiously. "Help me out, here, Paul. Am I forgetting anything? Oh, yes. I almost left out the best part. You also wrote a letter to the dean last semester asking her to consider dismissing me!"

I take a deep breath and fight for control. "There's a lot more I could mention, but let's get to the point."

He snorts. "Already?"

I glare at the phone. "Very funny. The point, my darling boy, is that after all this time, and all of your endearing little shenanigans, it seems you've now decided—on the strength of your father's word, no less—to reconnect this morning for the sole purpose of scolding me. Am I understanding you correctly?"

I listen to the silence on the line and sigh. "How sweet. It warms a mother's heart."

"You've treated me worse than I've treated you," he says quietly. Through the receiver I hear a car horn in the background, then a burst of static from his cell phone. He must be driving somewhere. His voice gets stronger. "And you've treated Dad far worse than that. What's this nonsense about a new tenant?"

I kick at the linoleum floor with the toe of my slipper. "I'm not going to discuss this with you. You've obviously already decided to take your father's side again, no matter what I say."

He coughs his patented two-pack-a-day smoker's cough. "It's a bit hard to take your side when you're always in the wrong. Ever since Jeremy . . ."

I slap the counter with my palm and bite back a scream. "Don't you dare finish that sentence. I don't fancy spending the rest of my life in prison for homicide."

The coldness of his laugh stuns me. "I shouldn't worry about that, Mother." He coughs again. "You already got away with killing one child, remember? I'm sure you can manage it again."

I hurl the receiver at the wall and it explodes into fragments.

The two things my mother said to my brother and me more often than I can count as we were growing up were, "Don't even *think* about going near that with your grubby little fingers," and "Put that down *immediately* before you break it."

Perhaps that's why my oldest memory is of the first time I dared to touch her dearly loved piano.

I was two or three years old at the most, but I remember sitting beside her on the piano bench as she played me a lengthy song. I sat without moving from beginning to end, watching with fascination as her fingers sank into the keys and music flowed from the soundboard and spilled into the living room around us. The piano was an old upright Steinway my mother had been given as a wedding present, and though I must have heard it a thousand times before that day—she practiced every evening for at least an hour—I'm quite sure it was the first time she'd ever allowed me to be so close to it.

When she took her hands off the keyboard, she turned to me and asked, "Wasn't that pretty, sweetheart?"

I didn't know the name of the piece she was playing, of course, but later on I learned it was Ravel's *Pavane pour une Infante defunte*. I remember nodding up at her, then I reached forward before she could stop me and began thunking out the initial ten-note phrase of the melody, just as I'd heard it. Mother grabbed at my wrist, but three pitches had already sounded before she could make contact and suddenly her fingers froze in mid-air and hovered over mine, like a falcon tracking a wild rabbit.

Those seconds are etched in my mind. I remember the feel of the cool, smooth keys under my fingertips, and the lilac smell of my mother's perfume, and the glorious timbre of the notes I was somehow producing, one at a time, just by touching this strange wooden box in front of me. I remember trying not to breathe, because I was sure if I did I'd forget what I was doing, and I'd never be able to make such amazing sounds again.

I think it's significant that before that evening, I have no memory of being alive. I try to conjure up something else, now and then—a caress, a bright color, a sigh—but there's absolutely nothing to latch onto before that lovely, aching melody of Ravel's streamed out of the piano and nudged me into consciousness.

When I finished, I remember Mother gasping, "Dear God in Heaven," but following that I have to rely on her account of what happened. She says she taught me a C major scale and arpeggio, then carried me to my room and tucked me into bed with a kiss before scampering off to share the news of my talent with my father, who was down in his basement workshop attempting to build a lazy Susan for our dining room table.

Knowing my mother as I did, however, I'm rather certain she omitted the part of the story where she first made sure to scrub the keys of her Steinway and remove all traces of my repulsive toddler-grubbiness before heading downstairs.

I've often tried to picture that conversation between my parents. Father was the most unexcitable man who ever lived, and I'm absolutely positive Mother's enthusiasm would have made no impact on him. So I imagine him standing there with a hammer and a few misshapen blocks of wood in front of him, pretending to listen as she prattled on and on. Eventually she would have run out of words, though, and he would have been expected to say something. When nothing was forthcoming, Mother no doubt got exasperated.

"*Harold.*" I can almost hear her. She always said his name as if he were a kindhearted but hopelessly stupid preschooler. "*I've just told you Hester is a musical genius. Are you just going to stand there?*"

Father would have pursed his lips and tried to respond with some kind of appropriate sentiment. "*Well, now. Isn't that nice. Say, do you think I should use white pine for this lazy Susan, or would you prefer something darker?*"

It was usually about this time in their discussions that Mother began pulling at her hair with both hands. It's a wonder she didn't have bald patches all over her scalp. I sometimes suspected (based on one such occasion where I was present and could swear Father winked at me when Mother wasn't looking) that he did this kind of thing on purpose, just to watch her face turn different shades of red.

Be that as it may, from that moment on, when I wasn't in school or eating a meal, I spent nearly every waking hour of my childhood at the piano.

Mother continued to teach me for four years. She was an accomplished pianist in her own right, but by the time I was seven I could play everything she could, so she began driving me to Boston twice a month for my lessons with Joshua Feldstein at The New England Conservatory of Music. At first, Mother always sat in on the lessons, and late at night after we were back in Connecticut and I'd been put to bed, I'd hear her attempting to practice whatever it was Joshua had taught me earlier that day. She kept that up for about a year, but each month she got farther and farther behind, and finally one evening I heard her pounding on the keys in frustration. I listened as Father tried to comfort her, but she wasn't having any: she told him to go away and leave her alone. A few minutes later she slammed the lid down and began to sob. I lay awake in the darkness of my bedroom, torn between childish pride because I knew I'd surpassed my mother, and sorrow because she knew it, too, and was hurt by it.

She stopped attending my lessons, and I never heard her play the piano again. I think she may have practiced when I was out of the house, but she couldn't bring herself to let me hear her after that. I asked her dozens of times to play duets with me, but she always refused, saying, "No, dear, I'd rather just listen to you." She was never mean about it, or resentful, and she often sat in the room while I was practicing, and praised and applauded me on a daily basis. But I always felt bad, because I knew that though she loved me and took considerable pride in my accomplishments, there was nothing she wanted more in the world than to play as I did.

But what could I do? The gift was mine.

I have been asked many times in my life if I wished I'd had a more conventional upbringing. People want to know if I balked at all the practicing, or if I craved more friendship and romance than what I had, or if I ever had any desire to just run out of the house, away from the piano, and flit about in the sunshine like a normal girl.

I tell them I don't remember, but I'm lying.

When I was eleven years old, I won my first national competition playing Beethoven's *Emperor Concerto*. I still have the reel-to-reel recording of that performance; it's one of my best. While my peers were tanning themselves on the beach and guzzling Coca-Cola at the movies, I was making music like few people ever get a chance to make it. While school acquaintances quarreled with their boyfriends and consulted each other about what outfit to wear next

Tuesday, I was casting spells over audiences in every major city in the world, and resurrecting Liszt and Brahms and Tschaikovsky from their respective graves.

I've heard music critics argue that child prodigies are nothing more than highly skilled mimics, with clever fingers and a good ear for aping the subtleties of more mature musicians, but I can tell you that even at eleven I had my own distinct style that had nothing to do with anything I'd heard or been taught. My musical "voice" (and what I had to say with it) has always been my own.

Whatever else I've been called in my life—and the list is endless—no one has ever accused me of being unoriginal. Not even Arthur or my children.

How can I tell you what it was like? What words will serve? For a time, my fingers were full of magic. Sometimes it felt as if I could make a stone dance, or a tree do somersaults, or a river run backwards. I knew the power of walking onstage to bored, polite applause from an audience that had never heard me play, and within the space of an hour, transforming their indifference into a boisterous standing ovation at the end of my performance. On countless occasions, I moved thousands of men and women to tears, and I made them beg for more when I was through, always demanding—and getting—at least three curtain calls before I'd consent to an encore.

God, I loved it all so. And not just because it fed my colossal, pre-adolescent ego. I also loved it (and I'm fully aware how naïve this sounds) because it gave me a chance, night after night, to make something beautiful, and to share it with the world. Laugh if you will, but I felt like a conduit between heaven and earth. And I never once took it for granted, because my mother was always with me, standing offstage with a wistful look on her face.

So here's the simple truth: I would no more exchange those early years of my life for a "regular" childhood than I'd trade a twelve-ounce filet mignon for a can of pickled pig's feet. Arthur accuses me of false modesty for not being more forthright about this, but since there's no way to say something along these lines to people without coming off as even more of a pompous ass than *he* is, I lie to them instead, and tell them I don't remember.

*   *   *

Of all my children, Caitlin has always been, by far, the brightest. In her chosen field—English Literature—she's a respected and widely published scholar, and she's also a surprisingly effective teacher (in spite of a notable lack of patience), as evidenced by her winning Pritchard University's coveted Teacher of the Year Award three times in the last five years. Her critical essays frequently turn up in prominent magazines like *The New York Review of Books* and *Harper's,* and she's considered one of the top experts in the world on both Milton and Donne. She does a great deal of traveling as a guest lecturer to various institutions around the country, where she's wined and dined and treated as royalty, and ever since she assumed the chairmanship of her department seven years ago, the number of English majors at Pritchard has nearly tripled.

She's equally impressive outside her work. Her lifelong hobby of oil painting has always earned her enormous praise, and a few years ago a small but posh contemporary art museum in Chicago even purchased half a dozen of her still lifes to hang in its foyer for a season. Besides that, she can also cook as well as almost any professional chef; her specialty is Italian food, and her dinner parties, though extravagant and far too formal, are the stuff of local legend.

What's not so well known anymore is how good an athlete she is. When she was a young woman she was formidable at both tennis and soccer, and to see her swim was like watching a plump white seal slice through the water. She was preternaturally good at skiing, too, even though she only did it once, on a rare family vacation to Montana.

That particular trip was an ill-conceived notion Arthur dreamed up thirty-some years ago during a long and irritating Christmas break. He'd jammed his fingers at the end of the term and was unable to practice for a few days, and without access to his beloved violin he couldn't tolerate "just sitting around the house." Somehow he got it in his head that a ski trip was the answer to his boredom.

I told him he was out of his mind. "What about Paul? Have you forgotten what he's like whenever he leaves Bolton? We'll have to sedate him to even get him in the car."

"Nonsense. He'll be fine." Arthur always pretended that Paul's strange aversion to travelling wasn't a problem. He was the same about Jeremy's morbid fear of heights, and Caitlin's bizarre daily craving for peanut butter and mustard sandwiches.

My children were, and are, the most neurotic people on the planet.

"Right," I muttered. "We'll get somewhere in the middle of Nebraska and he'll start screaming for us to take him home. We'll have to abandon him at a rest area to get any peace."

He ignored me and I watched him dig our suitcases out of the closet, noticing that his stomach was slightly bigger than when we'd first met.

"Stop that at once, Arthur," I demanded. "You're not thinking clearly. Even if Paul doesn't have a meltdown on the way, you can't hold a ski pole with your fingers like that, and I'm not about to take the chance of destroying my other wrist, too. What do you expect us to do when we get there?"

He shrugged. "I don't know. Read a book. Drink Irish coffee." His eyes flickered. "Take off our clothes by the fire in our room, and have a lengthy discussion while the children frolic on the mountainside."

That kind of suggestion from him used to make my breath quicken and my knees go weak.

Anyway, against my better judgment, we packed the children into our ancient blue Cadillac—Paul began bellowing in the backseat the instant we crossed the Mississippi—and we argued our way across half the country, finally ending up in a sweet little town called Fortune, just north of the Montana border with Wyoming.

Arthur and I spent most of the week in the lodge by the fireplace. I still remember sitting with him on our first day there, nursing a mug of hot cocoa and peppermint schnapps and watching through the large picture window at the front of the building as Paul and Jeremy fell all over each other out on the bunny slope. None of the children had skied before, but after one lesson Caitlin scooted off like a pro, abandoning her ungainly older brothers with a disgusted look on her face. Paul was trying to show Jeremy how to snowplow, but neither of them could get the hang of it and both of them kept tipping over, face first, onto the icy ground. Arthur and I laughed until our sides hurt.

"See?" he said, putting an arm around me on the couch. "Isn't this fun?"

I nodded and smiled. "I had no idea our boys were so good at slapstick. Now all we need is for Caitlin to run over them while they're on the ground, and we'll have enough material for a vaudeville act. Where is she, by the way?"

We scanned the slope and couldn't find her. Arthur frowned and stepped over to the window, but after a moment he turned around again, perplexed.

"I don't see her."

We waited a little longer for her to reappear, but after fifteen minutes had passed I became worried and sent him out to look for her. Just as he got his coat on and headed toward the door, though, Caitlin came winging into sight from under the trees near the bottom of the most challenging adult slope. She must have gotten on the T-bar and ridden it up the mountain all by herself. I called out to Arthur and I rose to my feet to watch her finish her descent.

She had on a purple and white stocking cap with a long tail, and her coat was brown with a furry collar. She flew out of the woods with her knees bent and her upper body crouched low over her skis, and the tail of her cap twitched around on her back like a spastic snake. She passed several slower skiers who were headed toward the clearly marked shute that would eventually disgorge them into a fenced-in corral at the bottom of the slope, where they could either get back on the lift for another ride up the mountain or remove their skis and return to the lodge. Caitlin weaved around the others in line with astonishing competence, and I murmured to myself in appreciation of her newly acquired skill.

She safely reached the upper lip of the shute, but then with no warning she broke away at full speed from the line of skiers, and without so much as a glance at them or at the signs pointing the direction she should go to end her run, she dodged under a flimsy wire barrier and shot across the flat, icy ground directly in front of the lodge. She dug her poles into the wet snow by a sign that read

"NO SKIING ALLOWED THIS SIDE OF FENCE," and aimed herself like an arrow at where I stood watching from inside.

My heart leapt into my throat when I realized she was going much too fast to be able to stop before hitting the building. She obviously didn't understand the peril she was in, because even though her lips were partly open and her eyes were squinting with concentration, there was not even a hint of fear in her face.

I put my hand to my mouth, and a woman next to me gasped and held up her arms toward the window as if that might stop the inevitable collision. I was dimly aware of Arthur calling out Caitlin's name in panic from somewhere behind me, yet I couldn't do anything but stand in mute horror and watch as my daughter raced toward a terrible smashup with the rough log walls and thick glass that separated us. She had to be going at least thirty miles an hour, and I was sure the impact would kill her.

I found my voice again and cried out just as Caitlin veered away from the lodge with a showy turn to her right, spraying an avalanche of snow at the window that pelted against the panes like a handful of gravel and blotted out my ability to see her. An instant later the spotty white curtain slid off the glass all at once, streaking it with water, and there was Caitlin standing before me, leaning on her ski poles in a studied, casual pose. She met my eyes and gave me a huge, impudent grin.

I swore and shook my fist at her and ran outside, screaming. I ordered her out of her ski boots and marched her back inside and up to our room past a crowd of amused strangers. Arthur and I then took turns yelling at her for nearly an hour, and afterwards she was confined to the lodge for the rest of the vacation, where she had to endure the torture of watching Paul and Jeremy cavort about on the bunny slope without her.

It felt like the right thing to do because of how she had frightened us, but in hindsight I think we were dead wrong to punish her like that. All I allowed her to see was my anger, and she deserved better.

I should also have told her how proud I was. Granted, it was a stupid stunt that almost got her maimed or worse, but she was magnificent on those skis, and I wish I had reacted differently. Children sometimes take idiotic risks, but they ought to be forgiven anyway, to honor the sheer audacity required to attempt such things. I wish now I had rewarded her in some way for her courage, or at least applauded her briefly before confining her to her quarters.

My God, she was fearless that day. She was strong, and fast, and as graceful as a hawk plummeting out of the sky, and I'll never forget it, especially because she's since lost most of those qualities, and I miss seeing them in her.

But I digress.

Getting back to what I was saying before: my daughter has multiple skills—teaching, writing, painting, cooking, athletics. She's terrifyingly smart, and she used to be brave, and if she's not exactly kind, she's at least capable of mercy on occasion.

But none of that has ever mattered to her.

What Caitlin has always wanted more than anything else is to be a musician. Her heart and soul are stuffed with an almost indecent love of music—especially the meaty, sprawling piano concertos from the Romantic period—and ever since she was a small child, she's dreamed of one day being able to play Tschaikovsky and Brahms and Chopin. When she's not teaching, she's glued to classical music stations on the radio, and she's a walking library of obscure musicological facts about every composer from Binchois to Stravinsky.

Unfortunately, she's also the only person in our family with no musical aptitude whatsoever.

I suppose I shouldn't say *no* musical aptitude; she slogged her way through some semi-difficult repertoire on her flute in high school, and she also managed to play, eventually, one or two medium-level sonatas on the piano that were nearly recognizable as Beethoven and Schubert by the time she performed them. But when your parents are Arthur Donovan and Hester Parker, and your brothers are Paul and Jeremy Donovan, if you aren't a virtuoso, too, you stick out like a gangrenous thumb.

And she's never forgiven Arthur and me for that. She wanted our talent, and to this very day she seems to believe we somehow de-liberately deprived her of it when we conceived her, for no reason but to spite her. Jeremy and Paul, in contrast, have never been the targets of her jealousy; I daresay when you detest your parents as much as she does, you have no rage to spare for something as trivial as sibling rivalry.

CHAPTER 5

"No, no, no, Miranda." I lean down and push her right hand out of the way to make room for mine on the keyboard. "You're making it sound like elevator music, for God's sake. Do it like this."

I pound out the opening measures to the Scherzo of Prokofiev's *Second Piano Concerto*, exaggerating the accents and the dynamics to make sure she hears what I want her to do. "Understand? Put some muscle into it."

She nods her empty blond head and plays the phrase exactly the same as she did before I corrected her. I bang my fist down on the lid of the piano and she almost falls off the bench.

"Are you listening to me?" I demand. "Sloppy performers like you are the reason nobody younger than fifty listens to classical music anymore. They think it's all boneless, insipid tripe that no one with a pulse can possibly respond to. Dear God, girl, are you breathing? Listen to what you're playing. Can't you hear the fire in it?"

Her eyes, rimmed with dark blue mascara, well up, and her bright red lips quiver.

Oh, for pity's sake. I hate it when they cry.

I sigh. I'm in a foul mood and I'm taking it out on this poor child. She's actually not a bad player, but I don't have the patience at this given moment to deal with Miranda Moore's fragile self-esteem.

I grunt and pat her on the shoulder. "There, there. Buck up, dear." I force my voice to soften. "If you're going to make it in this business you need to grow thicker skin."

Her voice shakes. "I'm sorry, Ms. Parker, but it's just . . ." She leans over and grabs a tissue from the box on my desk and blows her nose.

I wait for her to get hold of herself. "Yes? It's just what?"

She shrugs her shoulders and fresh tears roll down her cheeks. "Last week you told me I was playing too loudly, so I worked really hard on being more musical and more subtle, and now you want me to play louder again. I don't know what you want."

My temper re-ignites. "What I want is for you to pay attention to what I'm saying."

She quails. "I'm trying . . ."

"No, you're not. You're just going through the motions. A lobotomized chimpanzee could play with more feeling."

Her shoulders begin to tremble and I pause to rub my temples and collect my thoughts.

I should have stayed home this afternoon. It was idiotic to come to work. The argument with Paul on the phone earlier this morning was reason enough to cancel lessons for the rest of the day, even if I hadn't also had a dreadful meeting with my lawyer afterwards.

The fight with Paul was par for the course, but my conversation with Phillip Hogan was a disaster. The gist of what he had to say today was (in direct contradiction to what he predicted a month ago, when he agreed to represent me) that I am now likely to lose my house to Arthur. He told me Arthur has a much larger chance of winning the house in the settlement than he had originally believed.

And he also told me—more or less—that I should just give up.

I suddenly can't seem to govern my chin, and Miranda is gawking at me. I look away and struggle with my emotions.

Maybe I shouldn't be teaching any longer. My students would all be better off and so would I. Maybe all I'm good for these days is terrorizing hapless young musicians like this little girl, and instead of doing that I should just retire and sit in peace by my fireplace. At least there I can't do any more harm. At least there I'll be warm and safe.

A shudder runs through me.

My fireplace.

God. What am I thinking? I won't even have a fireplace when Arthur is done with me. He won't be happy until he's tossed my naked body out in the snow for the wolves to feed on.

How did it come to this? How did I ever end up here? Have I been such a bad person that I've somehow earned this?

I don't think I have the courage to answer those questions.

The last few years come crashing into my mind. All the lies I've told, all my cruelty, all my selfishness. Everything I've done to my husband, everything I've done to my children, everything I've done to myself. The list is enormous, even if you subtract all the times I was sorely provoked. Is that why this is happening now? Is this what I get for living as I have?

And beyond all that, far beyond, there's Jeremy.

No. I will not think of that right now. I will not. There are limits to how much blame I'm willing to take on.

Maybe Paul was right to try to get me fired. Maybe I should just accept the inevitable and step down with dignity. Maybe Arthur and Martha deserve the house more than I do. Maybe . . .

A fugitive spasm of anger tightens the muscles in my chest.

Like hell they do.

Whatever I am, whatever I have done, Arthur is, and has done, too.

With an effort I lift my head and look in Miranda's eyes. I speak as clearly as I can. "Look, child. I'm a crabby old woman and I can be difficult at times, but I can also make you a better pianist than you've ever dreamed of being, if you'll just bear with me."

I nudge her shoulder. "Move over."

She slides to the left on the bench and I sit beside her. I put both hands on the piano and start to play the Prokofiev again. My left wrist immediately begins to ache, but I ignore it and plunge my fingers into the keys.

"Be adaptable is all I'm saying," I murmur as I play. "Be soft when you're supposed to be soft, be loud when you're supposed to be loud. Think. Use your brain. Use your ears. The phrasing will tell you what to do if you just listen."

She sniffs. "But it says *mezzo forte* there, not *fortissimo.*"

"So what?" I snap. "Dynamics are relative. So is everything else, for that matter. Hush now and I'll show you."

I can't help myself. I know how much this will hurt but right at this moment, I don't care. I'll dope myself out later on Motrin and brandy.

I dig in and the music explodes around us; my fury couples with Prokofiev's genius, and the notes fly through the air like shrapnel. I close my eyes and breathe, and I let myself play for nearly a minute, in spite of the horrific pain in my wrist. Miranda disappears from my mind, and so does Paul, then Arthur, then Caitlin—all vanishing one by one, shoved out of the spotlight by wild, pungent chords and unpredictable, frenzied runs.

After that I move on to the worries about my house and my future. I may have no control over anything else, but I can control this particular piano long enough to vanquish *those* feeble anxieties. When they're gone, I jettison the awareness of my damaged old body, and then I go deeper, tossing out memory after hateful memory, hunting them down and destroying them like rabid animals. I use whatever hurts as kindling, burning it all up inside of me, feeding it a stick at a time into the raging inferno in the center of my chest that used to be my heart.

It builds and builds and builds until finally there's nothing left but Jeremy.

Jeremy is always the last to go.

Most days I give up long before he departs, but today not even he can survive the noisy apocalypse I'm making. In my mind, he stands in front of me and begs for my attention, but I just play louder and louder, and he eventually has no recourse but to cover his ears and step into the blaze, too. Before my eyes he turns into flame, then ash, and still I keep playing.

There's nothing in the world but this wall of sound and fire I've created. While it's still standing, nothing can touch me. Nero may have fiddled while Rome burned, but Nero was a rank amateur compared to me. Rome be damned.

If I had the stamina I'd burn the whole bloody, stinking world to a cinder.

I know that Jeremy and all the rest will reappear, phoenix-like, the instant I stop, so I refuse to quit until my left hand goes numb, and it's all I can do to not scream. The pain is overwhelming, but it's preferable to what's waiting for me when it's gone.

Burn, damn you, burn.

I can't take it any longer.

The music ends abruptly and I open my eyes. I have to bite my lips to keep from whimpering.

My studio is just as I left it a moment ago. The two Steinway grands are still sitting side by side, beneath the picture window looking out over Carson Conservatory's small but tasteful campus, bleak and gray in the late afternoon light of winter. The yellow carnations I brought with me today are also still here, fragrant and bright in a tall vase on the top shelf of the bookcase by my desk.

It's all so familiar. On the surface, nothing has changed.

My life is just as much a disaster as it was before I sat down to play, my prospects for a decent tomorrow are just as grim. I'm still losing my house, I'm still at war with my family, I'm still tired and old and angry. All of this is true, and yet somehow there is a difference now, however slight.

I feel like me again.

It's not much, but I guess it will have to do.

I let my hands fall from the piano into my lap. Miranda is watching me with her mouth half-open; her eyes are enormous.

She swallows several times and finally clears her throat.

"I didn't know Prokofiev could sound like that," she whispers. "I didn't know anything could sound like that." She seems dazed. "That was the most amazing thing I've ever heard."

I thank her as gently as I'm able. "So now do you understand what it is I'm after? Do you hear what I'm talking about?"

She shakes her head. "I hear what you want, but there's no way I'll ever be able to play like that." Her voice is diffident.

I stand up, cradling my left wrist. "Of course you will," I say. "All it takes is patience and practice."

I watch her go, her face full of wonder. She's practically floating with inspiration.

She doesn't yet know a lie when she hears one.

She's right, I fear. She'll never play as I play. Oh, she has enough talent that she may eventually be able to execute the notes as well, and she has enough discipline to build herself a decent career as a musician. Ten years from now she may even be something of a name in the world; she has ample poise and grace when she's performing, and a rare physical beauty audiences will likely respond to. I predict she'll be well reviewed, and many younger musicians will no doubt flock to her for lessons and guidance.

But Miranda Moore will never have what it takes to play like me.

It's not a question of talent or ambition; it's a question of character. She doesn't have the passion; she doesn't have the endurance; she doesn't have the self-honesty necessary for fusing her heart and mind to her fingers. And most damning of all, she doesn't have the guts to live the kind of life that would teach her these things.

I can't fault her for that, I suppose. Most people are just like her.

I lift my head and fill my lungs with air, then I let it all out again a second later with a heavy sigh.

For better or worse, there's only one Hester Parker.

Prior to our children being born—and before I shattered my wrist—Arthur and I were frequently asked to perform together. The best concert we gave was in 1966, in Boston's Symphony Hall, and I can still recall the entire program. We played the *Violin Sonata* by Darius Milhaud, and Ernst Bloch's *Baal Shem,* and the third *Violin Sonata* by Brahms, and Rachmaninoff's *Romance and Danse hongroise.* The audience nearly rioted at the end of all that, and after they finally let us off the stage (four encores later), we escaped to the city's North End for a midnight dinner at a quiet Italian restaurant, near Old North Church.

Being a classical music celebrity is an odd thing, because your fame is so limited. One moment you can be standing in front of a packed concert hall, receiving a ridiculous amount of adulation from what seems to be the entire population of the planet, and the next you're out dining in public, unnoticed by anyone.

I remember Arthur bringing up this strange phenomenon that night, over an exquisite bottle of chianti and two vast platefuls of spaghetti and meatballs. I looked up from my meal to find him surveying our surroundings with an expression of utter satisfaction.

"What is it, dear?" I asked. "Is the wine kicking in?"

Arthur wasn't much of a drinker in those days, and could become positively giddy after one or two swallows of anything containing alcohol. His boyishness at those times was one of the things I found the most charming about him. But then again, we were newly married, and very much in love, and almost everything he did delighted me.

"Yes, as a matter of fact," he beamed. "But I was also just thinking how nice it is to be an anonymous deity."

I smiled. Off-kilter statements such as this were daily fare from him. "Pardon me?"

"Think about it. A mere . . ." He glanced at his watch. ". . . hour and a half ago, we were being treated like the Beatles, and now we're just a couple of nobodies. There's not a soul in this place who's ever heard of us." He picked up his fork and poked at a meatball, giggling. "Of course, our audience is somewhat different, isn't it? Most of our fans have blue hair, for one thing."

I waited for him to go on. When he was in a chatty mood, which was most of the time, I mostly just listened to him talk.

"What I mean," he continued, "is that I love this. It's the best of both worlds, really. We get to be treated like emperors half the time, and regular human beings the other half. Who else can say that?"

I wrapped a piece of spaghetti around the tines of my fork. "Radio talk show hosts? Politicians?"

"Radio personalities don't count. They're just disembodied voices. It's easier for them to be anonymous." He played with the melted wax drippings on the candle in the middle of the table. "And politicians are *never* anonymous. They have power, and people with power are always being stalked, and never really get away from the public eye."

His face wrinkled with concentration. "That's the secret. Most celebrities have power, but we have no power at all. We just have talent, and there's a real difference between the two." He seemed pleased with this analysis. "Power comes from words, and we only deal with emotion. And since our art doesn't rely on words, we have no power to effect political change in the world." He nodded, as if agreeing with himself. "And that's the reason we have no name recognition outside of our art, of course."

I dabbed a piece of garlic bread into a bowl of olive oil. "I see." I leaned forward to tease him. "What was your name again, by the way? You look familiar, but I can't place you."

His smile grew, and he put his foot on my chair, between my legs. He'd somehow gotten his shoe off, and I could feel his toes work their way under my skirt.

I flushed. "We're in public, darling," I admonished. "If you wish to remain *anonymous* at this establishment, you might want to exercise a bit of care."

He licked his lips, aroused. "The tablecloth goes all the way to the floor. No one can see what I'm doing."

He was so handsome back then. So tall, and strong, and sensuous. I loved watching his fingers toy with his plate and his utensils, I loved watching his gray eyes as they studied my face.

I was having considerable difficulty focusing. "So you think we have no power, but pop musicians do?"

He shrugged. "Of course they do. They use words. Their music is *about* something. If they want to make a political statement with their songs, they can." He fed more wax from the base of the candle into the flame at the top. "And I know what you're going to say. *'What about arias, and lieder?'*"

I raised my eyebrows. "As a matter of fact, that was exactly what I was going to say."

He waved his fork at me, and the waiter came over because he thought he was being summoned. Arthur apologized and the waiter withdrew to a corner, with a knowing expression on his face. He was no doubt aware of our under-the-table mischief, tablecloth or no.

Arthur waved his fork again, less dramatically. "Think about it. Arias and lieder are more often than not about ridiculous things, like flea-bitten cats sitting in the window, or lost scarves. And when they're serious, they're always too specific to an individual character's problems to have a political agenda, or a broader social message."

His foot was pressing softly against my undergarments as he said this, and I opened my legs a little wider for him as I pretended to be absorbed in my spaghetti.

I cleared my throat. My voice was husky. "I'm afraid I can't agree with you on that point. Your logic has gaps in it."

His toes found their way past the elastic band around my thigh. "Perhaps." He spoke in a whisper. "But I've found a much more interesting gap."

We didn't finish our meal that night. We left money on the table and exited the restaurant long before the bill arrived, and barely made it back to our car before losing all of our clothes, and our sense of decorum, too. We were young, and attractive, and insatiable, and this was the way most of our meals ended, as I remember it.

And Arthur was right, incidentally.

We may have been powerless in the real world, but we were also gods.

I hear them on the lawn, at two-twenty in the morning. I rise from my bed and make my way to the window, and peek out the curtains to see who in the world is making such a ruckus at this hour.

There's enough light from the street to make out two figures in my driveway, sprawled on the snowy ground in front of St. Booger's pedestal, like supplicants at the feet of the Pope. One of them is howling at the moon, apparently, and the other is cackling like a madman. Even through the heavy leaded glass of my window I can hear them carrying on.

The howling one is Alex, but I have no idea who the other boy is. Good Lord. They appear to be drunk as skunks, and the neighbors are likely to call the police any second. I draw my fist back to bang on the glass, but all at once they get to their feet and the noise stops as they appear to confer about something or other.

I should be angry at their thoughtlessness, I suppose, but as long as they've stopped making a public nuisance of themselves there's no real harm done. Besides, they didn't wake me. I haven't had a good night's sleep since Arthur moved out, and before Alex and his friend showed up tonight all I was doing was staring at the ceiling. To be honest I'm almost grateful for their buffoonery; the thoughts I was having made for poor company.

I used to love this bedroom. Arthur actually carried me into it on our wedding night (his parents were still living at the time but had relocated to an assisted living facility in St. Louis two years earlier), and for decades it was my favorite place on earth. It has high, graceful ceilings, a bench seat by the windows, and a working fireplace in the corner. The original wood floor is polished and smooth and welcoming, and I adore it, but in the winter Arthur and I always covered it with an enormous Oriental rug, which at the moment is warm and luxurious under my bare feet. The bed is king-sized and soft, and crowded with inviting pillows and quilts and afghans, and we often spent entire weekends up here, nestled in the sheets, making love and sleeping, only leaving the room to forage for food, or to use the toilet.

But now it's just a big empty room, with a big empty bed in the middle of it, and I hate it.

Outside, Alex steps up within a foot of St. Booger and raises his head to look the statue in the face as his hands do something near his waist. The other boy comes over and stands next to him, and it takes me a moment to realize what they're doing.

They're urinating on poor old Booger.

I sigh and return to my bed. St. Booger's dignity is the least of my concerns at the moment, and I'll speak to Alex tomorrow morning when he's sobered up again.

I have excellent hearing and my bedroom door is open, so when they trip into the entryway downstairs I still hear them, even though they're attempting to be quiet.

"Shh." Alex's whisper drifts up the steps. "Hester's asleep."

"Who's Hester?"

This voice is deeper and louder than Alex's, and he's slurring his words.

"My landlady," Alex answers. "Remember? Professor Donovan's mom."

"Oh, *fuck!*"

I stifle a laugh in my bed. It seems that Caitlin's students are still terrified of her.

"I forgot all about that," he continues. "If she's half as bad as Donovan, she'll probably shoot us or call the cops or something."

"Nah, it's okay." Alex's voice gets harder to hear; he's apparently stepped into either the kitchen or the living room for some reason. "She's not like that."

The voices fall silent for a minute, then I hear Alex yelp from the kitchen. "What the hell?"

"What happened?" His friend must still be standing in the entryway.

"*Shh, Eric!* Keep your voice down," Alex hisses. There's a pause. "I just stepped on something sharp."

I almost start laughing again.

The phone. I never did clean up the mess I made when I broke the phone after speaking to Paul. There are chunks of plastic all over the floor, and the ruined receiver is dangling from the wall on its cord like a lynched man.

"You okay?" Eric asks.

"Yeah. I'm not bleeding or anything. It just hurt like hell."

Alex has now returned to the entryway, and a moment later I hear their footsteps as they near the landing by my bedroom.

"What'd you get?" Eric whispers.

"Whiskey, I think. I couldn't really see 'cause it was so dark in there."

I sit up in bed. They're stealing my alcohol?

"She doesn't care if you drink her booze?"

"I doubt it. She's pretty cool."

There's affection in his tone, and it catches me by surprise and makes me hesitate, long enough for them to move off the landing on their way up to the next floor.

"Besides," Alex's voice is nearing the edge of my hearing. "As much as she drinks, I doubt she'll even notice a bottle missing."

I blink in the darkness, and I lie down again, filled with an abrupt sadness. I'll deal with him in the morning.

CHAPTER 6

"Morning."

I'm fooling with the teakettle on the stove when I hear the soft voice behind me, and I jump a little and spin around to face the intruder with a hand on my throat.

Alex is standing in the kitchen doorway, wearing nothing but a pair of jeans. He's rail-thin and pale, with freckles on his shoulders, and a V-shaped patch of light red hair in the middle of his chest.

I glare at him. "Good God, boy, are you trying to give me a heart attack?" I take a jagged breath. "I should make you wear a cowbell around your neck so I'll be able to hear you coming."

He grins at me and leans on the door frame. "Sorry. I didn't mean to frighten you."

"I suppose I'll forgive you this time." I turn back to the stove. "I'm making tea. Would you like some?"

"No, thanks. I've got somebody waiting for me upstairs."

I decide to play dumb. "An overnight guest? How scandalous." I hesitate as a new thought strikes me. It's really none of my business, but I can't help being curious. I test him. "Well, *she's* welcome to join us, too."

He flushes a little and begins to stammer, shaking his head. "It's a he. He's a he, I mean. His name's Eric."

He really couldn't be any more transparent, and my heart goes out to him.

I raise my eyebrows. "Oh, my. The plot thickens."

His blush spreads. "No, it's not like that. We're just friends."

"I see."

I tilt my head to the side and study his face. He and Eric may indeed be "just friends," but there's more going on here than that. A crush, maybe?

Lord. I wouldn't be his age again for anything in the world.

He's squirming under my scrutiny and I finally turn away to get my favorite mug from the cupboard. It's dark red, with white, hand-painted snowflakes on it. Caitlin created it for me years ago, in her high school ceramics class.

I face him again. "So will your friend want some tea, then, do you think?"

He's fiddling with his silver neck chain, and his expression relaxes. "No, I don't think so. But I was wondering if you had any aspirin I could borrow? We had kind of a rough night."

I drop a tea bag in the mug and pour hot water over it, then seat myself at the table. "I assumed as much." I indicate the liquor cabinet with my thumb. "How did you enjoy my brandy, by the way?"

The cabinet door is standing open, just as I found it this morning.

His white skin gets even whiter, and he hangs his head to avoid my gaze.

"I'm sorry, Hester," he says quietly. "We were really drunk and the bars were closed and I was going to put the bottle back before I went to bed but then I passed out and forgot all about it. I know I shouldn't have taken your brandy but we didn't even drink much of it, and I'll buy you a new bottle and I promise I won't ever . . ."

I shift in my chair and he runs out of words. The room is deathly silent.

A patch of warm sun coming through the window paints a stripe across his naked stomach, but the floor must be cold under his feet. He flexes his toes and waits for me to say something. A faint chiming floats down the hall behind him as the grandfather clock in the study goes off. It rings eleven times in the stillness before stopping again. He crosses his arms over his chest and raises his eyes.

I play with the string on my tea bag, swirling it around in my mug. I dunk the bag a few more times then let go of it.

"Relax, dear. You're not in trouble." I remain stern. "At least not too much. You and your friend pilfering my brandy is the least of my worries."

He heaves a sigh of relief and starts to say something else but I cut him off by shaking a long finger at him.

"Mind you, the next time I won't be so lenient." I turn my attention back to my tea. I'm tired and on edge this morning, neither of which is his fault. "I'm going to need every drop of alcohol I've got to keep me sedated over the next few weeks, so don't push your luck. Understood?"

He clears his throat. "Okay." It's clear he feels bad, but doesn't know what to do about it. "Are you all right?"

I rally a little, straightening in my chair. "Right as rain, dear. Don't worry about Hester." I wave a hand. "There's some Motrin in that drawer by the sink. Help yourself. I buy the stuff by the truck-load."

The drawer is crammed full of letters and rubber bands and other assorted junk, but he finds the Motrin right away and dumps a handful of pills in his palm. He's watching me from the corner of his eye, as if he's trying to determine my mood. I ignore him, but once the drawer is closed again he doesn't leave.

"What happened to the phone that was in here?" he asks. "It was in a million pieces when I got home last night."

My eyes drift to the vacant phone jack on the wall. "Nothing, really. I was just redecorating yesterday and didn't get around to tidying things up again until this morning." I look back at my tea. "Telephones simply do not belong in kitchens."

He waits for more but I remain quiet, so after a minute he thanks me for the Motrin and starts to head back upstairs. Before he gets to the door I call his name and he turns to face me.

I look him up and down and give him a slight smile. "That's a rather nice outfit you're wearing, incidentally. Wherever did you get it?"

He blushes instantly, and I toss my head and laugh, delighted.

I've always been an unrepentant coquette (Arthur once told me in a jealous snit that I'd flirt with a pimply iguana, if no other male was available) but at this stage in my life I certainly don't mean anything by it, and most especially not with this child. But Alex doesn't know that, and my manner seems to have thrown him for quite a loop. Nor can I resist poking at him a little more; I think he deserves a large dose of embarrassment for his behavior last night.

I adopt my best sultry attitude, caressing my throat with the tip of a finger and dropping my voice to a husky murmur. "Oh, come now. Surely you don't think that I no longer pay attention when there's such an attractive, available young man in the room?"

His eyes go wide with dismay, and he begins to stutter. I watch him wriggle about for as long as I can bear it, then I trot out his own words from the staircase last night. "Or did you think that *with as much as I drink, I simply wouldn't notice?*"

He stops blathering, and his face goes still.

Whatever else this boy is, he isn't stupid.

"Oh, shit. You heard us talking last night, didn't you?"

I nod. "Yes, indeed."

He gets a rueful look on his face and sighs. "And now you're just fucking with me to get even, right?"

"Very good." I reward him with a smile. "My ears still work just fine, by the way, in spite of my raging, epic alcoholism." I pause. "Not to mention my uncontrollable penchant for seducing virile, eligible college men such as yourself."

He shuffles from foot to foot for a moment, speechless. My mirth gets the better of me then, and I begin to laugh in earnest. I expect him to either sulk or protest, but once again it appears I've underestimated him; he has the good grace to know when he's been beaten, and he even manages a weak, mortified chuckle before he flees the room.

I think I might grow fond of this boy, given enough time.

Living with three brilliant children was not easy, even in their pre-teen years. If they had been bright and docile it would have been one thing, but they were as volatile as they were intelligent, and even when they were very young they could not be easily cowed, and ordinary things such as bath times and bedtimes often turned into substantive, presidential-type debates, or drawn-out battle campaigns with multitiered strategies, endless flanking maneuvers, and shifting alliances.

Paul, as the oldest, believed himself to be their leader, but in truth, Caitlin was always the real power behind the sibling throne—which I'm eternally grateful for, because if Paul *had* been in charge, he would have quickly turned the house into a Gothic, indoor version of *Lord of the Flies* before he reached puberty. Jeremy played the role of counselor to the queen, recognizing that his younger sister had a far subtler and more devious mind than Paul, and was more likely to come up with effective ways to subvert any and all rules Arthur and I attempted to enforce.

For instance, one Saturday afternoon I made the familiar weekly demand that they all clean their rooms. Normal children might have thrown tantrums, stalled, or whined to have avoided a chore like this, but such tactics were far too unrefined for the Donovan brood. In fact, at first I was foolish enough to believe that for once they were actually going to do as I asked without a struggle. I made the request on the front porch, and they rose without a word, as one, to do my bidding.

Or so I thought.

When I went to check on their progress, Caitlin's room looked as if it had been ransacked by the KGB. The floor was cluttered knee-deep with everything that had been on her shelves and in her closet, and she was nowhere to be found. Paul and Jeremy's rooms, however, were neat as pins, but the boys, too, were absent, and the house was silent. I went hunting for them, and given that all three were under ten years old at the time, I began to panic when a thorough search of the premises turned up nothing. I went to the kitchen and started making phone calls, attempting to track them down.

No one knew of their whereabouts. Arthur was out of town, none of the neighbors had seen them, and likewise none of their friends. I fretted by the phone for nearly half an hour, wondering if I should alert the police, but then I thought I heard a noise upstairs, coming from either Jeremy's or Caitlin's bedroom. I made a mad dash for the steps and came to a halt on the landing outside their open doors.

Caitlin's room was now perfectly clean and orderly, and Jeremy's was a disaster.

And my children were still nowhere to be found.

Thus began a game of cat and mouse that lasted for nearly two hours before I finally snared one of the "mice." It was Paul I first trapped; I hid in Arthur's study and caught him climbing out of an empty clothes hamper in one of the guest rooms across the hall when he thought I was elsewhere in the house.

To this day, I still have no idea how the three of them evaded capture for so long, or accomplished this feat of alternating de-struction and restoration. I ran all over the house, I waited in dark corners and I stood guard on stairwells, but they somehow worked their devilry, again and again. If Paul hadn't become impatient, there's no telling how much longer they could have kept it up, but once I had him in custody I coerced him into betraying the others, and soon I had all three at work under close supervision, undoing their most recent damage.

I was so torn between amusement and rage that I couldn't speak coherently for the rest of the day, but I eventually found out it had all been Caitlin's idea, and she had been planning this for some time.

When I asked her why she had decided on this course of action, all she said was, "Because I like making you crazy, Mom."

It was outright rebellion, but with an ingenious twist, and it was calculated to push every button in my parental body.

Incidentally, Caitlin was five years old, Paul was nine, and Jeremy was seven.

Thank God they stopped cooperating when they got older.

I'm leaning out the door, retrieving my mail from the box on the porch when Alex walks Eric downstairs to let him out. I'm not in-clined to be meeting a stranger at the moment and it puts me in a bit of snit to do so, because I'm still wearing my robe and slippers even though it's almost noon, and my hair is a fright. I step back in-side and frown at them as they reach the bottom of the stairs.

My eyes do a slow sweep of Eric. He's a handsome child, as tall as Alex but more muscular, with light blue eyes and stately cheekbones. Unfortunately, the effect is altogether spoiled by a silly stocking cap, which has a single orange antenna on it rising up from the crown of his head like a wildflower.

"That cap is utterly ridiculous," I growl, dropping my gaze to thumb through a small pile of envelopes and magazines in my hands.

He grins at me, unabashed. "Hi. I'm Eric Weber, Alex's friend." He holds out his hand. "My mom hates this cap, too. That's why I bought it."

I warm to his friendliness in spite of myself. "Good for you. I'm sure your poor mother appreciates the aggravation." I take his fingers in my own and smile up at him. "I'm Hester Parker. Alex's senile slumlord."

He nods for a second, then his smile falls away and he blinks. "Wait a minute. Hester *Parker?*" He stares into my face and tightens his grip on my hand. "Oh, my God. I don't believe it." He looks dumbfounded. "Jesus Christ. You're really her."

"You've heard of me?" My ego doesn't get stroked very often these days, and I'm more pleased than I should be by his undisguised awe. "I'm shocked."

He laughs and shakes his head. "Of course I've heard of you. My mom and dad have every record you ever made. I grew up listening to you." He releases me and cuffs the back of Alex's head. "Dude, I thought you said your landlady's last name was Donovan. Why didn't you tell me you were living with Hester Parker?"

Alex glances at me, startled, and I raise my eyebrows at him. He flushes and looks back at Eric. "I didn't think you'd know who she was," he mutters, rubbing his head.

I smooth the front of my robe. "I mentioned to Alex that I used to be a concert pianist of some reputation, but it appears he didn't believe me."

"Yes, I did," he protests. "I even went to the library and listened to one of your recordings the other day. I meant to tell you how much I liked it but I forgot."

That surprises me even more than Eric knowing who I am. I didn't think Alex had any curiosity about me at all.

Eric suddenly slaps his forehead. "I'm so stupid. You're Professor Donovan's mom, right?"

I should have seen this coming. It always does.

I nod stiffly. "I'm afraid so."

He chews on his lip. "Wow. Then that means her dad must be . . . holy shit." He looks thunderstruck.

And here we are again.

"I couldn't have said it any better myself." Frost creeps into my voice. "Caitlin's father is indeed the magnificent Arthur Donovan." I inspect my fingernails before continuing. "Although I'm personally convinced that Caitlin was implanted in my womb by a hostile alien. One of these years I'm going to insist on a DNA test to prove it."

Eric laughs, unfazed by the bitterness in my tone. "Yeah, that's a good idea." He shakes his head again. "What a trip. My writing teacher's parents are Hester Parker and Arthur Donovan. I can't believe I've never made that connection before. I knew you guys lived in Bolton, but . . ."

He rattles on and on, but the mention of Arthur and Caitlin has stolen most of the pleasure out of his flattery. He eventually seems to notice I'm not saying anything else and slowly trails off under my quiet inspection.

He looks at the floor, uncomfortable. "Well, anyway, my folks will freak out when I tell them," he finishes lamely.

There's an awkward silence, and he squats to put on his shoes in a hurry. I look down at the top of his head, feeling an unexpected sense of remorse for quashing his enthusiasm. I should apologize for my manners, but I don't know what to say; it seems lately that every conversation I have ends on a sour note.

Except with my new tenant, for some reason.

I glance over at Alex as this occurs to me, and I catch him watching me with a thoughtful expression.

I force a smile. "Do you see those unusual cloth garments your friend has on his feet, dear?" I ask. "Those are called 'socks,' and you wear them inside your shoes. Perhaps Eric will be kind enough to show you how to put some on, if you ask nicely."

He smiles back at me. He's all dressed now, except for his feet. "I would, but I don't own any."

I sigh in mock exasperation, glad to be speaking about some-thing besides my family. "Oh yes, I forgot. You were a homeless, naked orphan when I found you on my porch."

Eric laughs and stands up, at ease again. "That sounds about right." He jabs Alex in the ribs. "I'll take you to the Salvation Army later, if you want. Mrs. Parker's right, buddy. Your wardrobe could really use an update."

Alex scowls at him. "Is that where you got that classy Bugs Bunny shirt you're wearing under your coat?"

He grins. "Ha. You're even funnier than you look." He holds out his fist for Alex to hit with his own, which seems to be their genera-tion's equivalent of a firm handshake. "So I'll see you on campus this afternoon?"

Alex nods.

"Cool." He gives Alex a quick hug, startling him.

I watch Alex's face over Eric's shoulder as he hugs him back; he closes his eyes and breathes deeply, as if he's inhaling the other boy's scent.

Eric releases Alex and turns to face me. "It was awesome meet-ing you, Mrs. Parker. This is probably rude to ask, but if I bring over some of my mom and dad's old record albums, do you think I could get you to sign them?"

"Of course, child. I'd be delighted." I pause. "But only after you return my brandy."

He blushes and begins to stammer, but then he realizes I'm teas-ing him and he laughs and says good-bye. Alex and I stand side by side and watch him walk across the porch and down the driveway past St. Booger.

"He's quite attractive," I murmur. "And sweet, too, I should think."

He doesn't answer. Whatever he's feeling about Eric, he's not about to reveal it.

After a minute I clear my throat again. "Which recording of mine did you listen to?"

He tilts his head to look down at me. "Bach's *French Suites*. It was great. I mean, you were great. I've never heard anything like that before."

"Ah." I lean my head on the screen door. My breath fogs up the windowpane. "I made that recording the same year I married Arthur. He always claimed it was my best, but at that point in our relationship I could have played 'Chopsticks' with my knees and he would have thought it was divinely inspired."

A car swings into the driveway and shoots up toward the house. It's a red Volvo. I sag away from the glass as the car screeches to a halt next to the carriage house.

"How lovely," I say. "It seems we have a surprise visitor."

"Who is it?" he asks.

I don't look at him. My eyes are fixed on the large, hairy man climbing out of the Volvo.

I take a deep breath. "I'm afraid you'd better make yourself scarce, dear. This is likely to be exceptionally unpleasant."

He touches my shoulder. I try to mask my agitation, but my body gives it away by trembling.

"Who is it?" he repeats.

I purse my lips. "Who else?" I mutter. "The prodigal son, of course. My darling boy, Paul."

CHAPTER 7

When did my son and I become enemies?

Paul is even heavier than he was the last time I saw him, and as he walks toward the house I can see him panting for air. His brown beard is wild and thick, and it's speckled with small white dots that have recently sprouted all over it like mildew on a basement wall. Even before he reaches the porch I can see the fury in his face; his forehead is red and furrowed, and his eyes are narrow, puffy slits.

Dear God, how I've grown to detest this man.

It wasn't always this way between us. Truly. Once upon a time, we even *liked* each other. I have a snapshot somewhere of the two of us in the music room, sitting side by side on the piano bench, when he was only twenty years old, and in the picture we're looking at each other with open affection. His arm is touching mine, and his cello is resting on the floor beside the piano, next to a music stand and a chair.

Paul had a lovely smile when he was younger. His brown, liquid eyes were alert and intelligent, his face was delicate, and his body, though never athletic, was trim and elegant. He was the best looking of my children, and in many ways my favorite—partly because he was the oldest (and arguably the most musically talented), but mostly because he had a pointed sense of humor very similar to mine.

I don't remember why we were sitting at the piano together; I don't even remember if it was Arthur or Caitlin or Jeremy who took the photo. But what I do remember is that our being close like that wasn't a rare thing in those days. We had many such moments, probably even hundreds, and the camera just happened to catch us in the middle of one.

But that was a very long time ago.

He slips a little on a patch of ice in the driveway and then clumps up the steps and glares at me through the window of the screen door. I lock eyes with him and make no move to invite him in.

Alex hasn't left my side yet. I know I should order him upstairs to the safety of his apartment, but I don't have the heart to face Paul alone. Not that I expect Alex to be of much use in handling Paul, but I very much want someone nearby right now who doesn't hate me.

Paul seizes the handle of the screen door and flings it wide. Cold air pours around me into the house.

"Hello, sweetheart." I make my voice pleasant. "How kind of you to come see me."

"Let me in, Mother. We need to talk." He sounds more like Arthur with each passing day, down to the threatening growl and the petulant, clipped syllables his father trots out whenever he feels he's not being shown proper deference. "It's freezing out here."

His head swings to Alex and he falls silent for a moment as he studies him. "So this is your new tenant, I suppose? How convenient. He's one of the main things we need to discuss." He continues scrutinizing the boy for some time with an odd expression on his face.

I make no move to allow him in the house. "I'm really not in the mood for company today, Paul. Why don't you run along home, and come back again in the spring?"

He leans one beefy paw on the door frame and towers over me. "I don't have time for this. Are you going to allow me in, or not?"

I pick some sleep residue out of the corner of my eye with a pinky finger. "That depends. Can you keep a civil tongue in your head?"

He pauses. "You have the gall to speak to me about civility?"

I motion for Alex to stand back and I begin shutting the main door. "Wrong answer."

Paul rears back in disbelief. "For God's sake, Mother." His breathing quickens. "Don't you dare close this . . ."

The rest of his sentence is lost and Alex and I stare at each other in the entryway. He looks uneasy. There's a second of silence, then Paul begins beating on the door and cursing.

"Goddammit, Mother!" His words are somewhat muffled through the wood, but still easy to make out. "I will not be treated like this! Open this fucking door this moment!"

"He knows full well it's unlocked, and he could barge right in if he wanted to," I tell Alex. "But of course, being Paul, he'd rather make a scene on the porch for the entire neighborhood to see."

BAM BAM BAM! "Mother!" BAM BAM! "Goddammit!" BAM BAM BAM! "Let me in, right now! You're behaving like a four-year-old!"

BAM BAM BAM BAM BAM!

The noise abruptly stops.

Alex crosses his arms over his chest and clears his throat nervously. "Is he going to leave now?" he asks.

"Wait," I whisper.

A minute passes. Suddenly a soft knock sounds on the curtained panel window to the left of the door. I raise the curtain and Paul's forehead is pressed against the glass. He says something I can't hear.

I raise my voice to carry. "What, dear?" I cup my hand to my ear. "Say that again, will you?"

He grimaces but stays silent.

Alex shuffles his feet. "I think he said, 'Please, Mother,'" he mumbles.

"Really?" I pull the door open and beam at Paul. "I'm so proud of you, dear. You've learned some manners! Who's been tutoring you? Annie Sullivan? Goodness, first Helen Keller, now you."

He eyes me with distaste. "Very amusing. Are you done playing games now?"

"Don't be ridiculous, Paul." I let the smile fall from my face. "I'm having far too much fun to stop, aren't you?"

He doesn't answer. For an instant there's a flash of something in his eyes that I haven't seen in a long time—a deep, aching sadness I remember noticing quite often when he was a child. Pain flares momentarily in my chest in response, but I push it away.

"Well, don't just stand there." I step back and wave him in. "Welcome home, son."

On the night he turned sixteen, Paul wandered into the kitchen, long after Jeremy and Caitlin had gone to bed. Arthur was out of town on tour, and Paul, who'd spent the bulk of the evening practicing in the music room with the new—and ludicrously expensive—Hill and Sons cello bow we'd bought him for his birthday, took a break around midnight and came to find me as I was finally getting around to cleaning up the supper things in the sink.

"Want help?"

"Of course."

I washed and he dried, and we had the radio on as we worked. It was semi-dark in the kitchen, with the only light in the room coming from the shaded bulb over the window above the sink. The station we were listening to was playing a Boccherini symphony, and Paul snorted after a few minutes and growled, "Is this stupid piece *ever* going to end?"

I rewarded him with an approving smile. His intolerance for dull music was beginning to rival mine.

"Soon." I rinsed suds from a plate and handed it to him. "But first there will be a fatuous deceptive cadence, followed by an insipid coda, and then—assuming the orchestra is still alive, of course—there will be a flourish in the violins, announcing the arrival of the last three utterly predictable chords: tonic-six, dominant, tonic."

I rubbed my chin on my shoulder. "It just occurred to me that Boccherini has almost certainly been reincarnated as Barry Manilow. Someone in authority should be notified, don't you think?"

He grinned. "So why are we still listening to this?"

"Good question. The sad truth is I was too lazy to change the station, but please do so at once."

"Nah." His smile widened. "I want to hear you rip apart the next piece they play, too." He handed the plate back. "You missed a spot."

I grunted. "The imbeciles who run classical music stations could be giving air time to Brahms or Stravinsky, and instead they choose *Luigi Boccherini*. It's enough to make you want to open your wrists in the bathtub."

He shook his head in mock disapproval. "You're a snob, Mom."

"Of course I am. The only people worth knowing are snobs, dear." I pause to look down my nose at him. "Incidentally, if you're not a full-fledged snob by the time you're an adult, I intend to disown you."

He laughed. "I wouldn't worry. With you and Dad as my role models, what are the chances I'll be anything else?"

I chuckled. "Good point."

We worked for a while in companionable silence, then I remembered something and glanced over my shoulder at the table. "I see you received a letter from the admissions office at Yale today."

Paul was due to graduate high school a year early, and colleges and universities around the country were already beginning to court him.

He shrugged. "Yeah, but I don't want to go there. It's too far away."

We had been arguing for months about what schools he should apply to for his undergraduate degree. He wanted to stay in Bolton and take lessons at Carson with the same cello teacher he'd had for the last four years (Martin Duvitsky, a talented pedagogue—and, alas, a second-rate performer), but Arthur and I both believed his career would best be served by placing him with a well-known teacher in a larger city. I didn't want another disagreement that night, but his stubbornness about staying in Bolton at all costs was starting to annoy me.

I pretended to return my attention to my hands in the soapy water. "Yale is close to where I grew up, you know. You might actually like New England if you gave it half a chance."

He wasn't fooled by my attempt at nonchalance. An edge worked its way into his voice. "I said I don't want to, Mom, okay?"

I darted a look at his handsome face. "Don't pout, Paul. I was just making a suggestion."

"I'm not pouting, I'm pissed off. There's a difference." He tipped his chin down in the same way I do when I'm irritated. "And I'm only pissed off because it's a shitty suggestion. What's wrong with me wanting to stay here in Bolton and go to the Conservatory? Are you that anxious to get rid of me?"

"Right at this moment, you mean?"

"Ha ha. Very funny."

I put a damp hand on his wrist. "If I thought Carson Conservatory was the best place for you to go to college, I'd tie you to the radiator to keep you from leaving, even if you wanted to go someplace else. But it isn't the best place for you, so . . ."

He made a face. "That's fucked up. What about what *I* want? It's my life."

"Your vocabulary is getting much too colorful for my taste." I let go of him. "It's your father's fault. He's been swearing around you children ever since you were born."

He rolled his eyes. "Whatever."

I put the last pile of silverware in the dish drainer and pulled the plug in the sink, then I took the towel from him when he was through with it and dried my hands.

"I'm sorry to sound like a cliché, son, but it's my responsibility to make decisions for you until you're old enough to make them for yourself."

"I'm not five, Mom, I'm sixteen." He leaned against the counter. "As of today. Remember? I'm not a little kid anymore."

I studied him. He was taller than me by a good six inches, and all the baby fat had long since left his face. His eyes were passionate and bright, like Arthur's, and his shoulders and chest were filling out daily, so fast I could almost see it happening. The peach fuzz on his face was also getting noticeably darker.

He was right. He wasn't a child anymore. But he was wrong, too, because when it came to making crucial decisions about his future, he was still very much an infant.

I walked over to the liquor cabinet and pulled out a bottle of Bushmills Irish Whiskey and two glasses. He eyed me with distrust as I poured us each a double shot and gestured for him to sit across from me at the kitchen table. He hesitated for a moment before acquiescing.

"Your father would kill me if he knew I was doing this with you." I pushed a glass in front of him.

He stared at me. "You're not serious. You want me to drink this?"

His voice, too, was now a young man's, and it still startled me sometimes to hear how deep and husky it had gotten. Just a few short months ago people used to mistake him for me on the phone.

I smiled. "We're having a drink together to celebrate your birthday. You're old enough that a shot or two of whiskey won't kill you." I looked into his eyes. "Don't tell me you've never gotten drunk with your friends before."

He shook his head. "I haven't. I tried a beer at Tony's one time but I didn't like it." He blushed a little. "I poured it out when I went to the bathroom."

He saw I didn't believe him and got exasperated with me. "Honest to God, Mom. I'm telling the truth. Besides that crappy white wine you let me taste last Christmas I've never had anything else to drink."

I blinked. "I see. Good for you." I cleared my throat. "Well. This isn't beer or wine. In truth, you probably won't like it, either, but it's far more efficient." I raised my glass to him. "Cheers, my love. And happy birthday."

He didn't lift his glass. "Why are we doing this? What are you up to?"

I shrugged. "No reason, really. I just want to acknowledge that you're getting older, as you said."

He ran his tongue over his teeth the way he always does when he's thinking. "So is this your way of saying that you'll stop bugging me about where I want to go to school?"

"Absolutely not. It just means you're getting older. Now shut up and drink your whiskey like a good boy."

He looked away and sighed. "Figures."

I kept my arm in the air. "My shoulder is getting rather tired, dear."

After a long moment he finally raised his glass, too, and clinked it against mine.

"Whatever," he mumbled. "I guess I'll take what I can get."

"Some joker's been urinating on St. Booger." Paul steps through the door and storms past me. He makes a beeline for the living room, impaling Alex with a glare on the way.

I close the door and lean against it. "Stray dogs have always treated poor old Booger abominably." I raise my eyebrows at Alex and he flushes. "I believe they see him as a fire hydrant with legs."

Paul reaches the fireplace and turns so his back is to the blaze. "If that's the case, then there's a mutt running around the neighborhood who knows the alphabet." He takes off his black ulster overcoat and tosses it over the arm of one of the chairs. "The letters 'c' through 'f' are scribbled in piss in the snow covering Booger's feet."

Alex kicks at the rug and mouths the word "sorry" at me.

I push off from the door and gesture for him to follow me into the living room. He trails along behind me, and when I sit in my chair he stands at my side like an overly attentive waiter. Paul eyes him with ill-humor, and Alex studies the floor.

"So." I break the silence with a cold syllable. "What did you want to speak with me about, Paul?"

He crosses his arms and rests them on his substantial paunch. He gives Alex yet another black look, then drops his gaze to my face. "We need to discuss this in private, Mother, don't you think?"

Alex makes a small noise and turns to leave.

I catch his wrist, and I'm amazed at how warm his skin is. He must have an oven for a heart. My own fingers are freezing.

"Stay put, dear." I look into his pale, expressive face. "Please."

His eyes dart to Paul and then back to me. He's terribly uncomfortable, but after a minute he favors me with a feeble attempt at a smile, then nods.

I release him and turn back to Paul. "Alex is fine right where he is, son. He lives here, unlike someone else I could name."

"Oh, for God's sake," Paul snaps. "Stop being so goddamn childish. I've come to see you about a personal family matter, and this . . .

this barefoot street urchin you've taken in has absolutely no business hearing any of it."

I sigh. "I don't think you're going to say anything Alex hasn't already heard from your unconscionably rude father." I pull at my ear. "For instance, you're going to tell me that this house doesn't *legally* belong to me, right?" I stress the word "legally" in an imitation of Paul's pompous tone. "And I had *absolutely* no right to rent the attic apartment to Alex, and therefore I'm a *horrible* person."

I bestow a pleasant smile on him. "How am I doing?"

He bares his tobacco-stained teeth. "You're a mind reader. But you left some things out, too."

"I can't imagine what."

"Oh, no?" He leans forward and the floor creaks. "For starters, how about the wanton destruction of Dad's table?"

"Good God." I yawn. "Not that again."

"That table was worth a fortune, not to mention the sentimental value it had for Dad."

I roll my eyes. "As I said to Arthur, it was an accident. How many times must I apologize for that?"

"A few thousand, I should imagine," he says dryly. "But never mind. In retrospect, that's the least of your transgressions."

"Oh? And what else have I done?"

He sucks on his front teeth. "You started a ridiculous rumor about me at the Conservatory."

I cross my legs and drum my fingers on my kneecap. "I did no such thing."

"Yes, you did. And you owe me an apology for it."

"Now who's being childish?"

He picks something invisible from the sleeve of his bulky sweater. "You told the dean the reason I was late to one of my students' lessons this semester was because I was hungover."

"Oh, dear." I sigh again. "Well, you *were* hungover, son. I saw you that morning, remember? Your breath smelled like the punchbowl at a frat party." I settle back in my chair. "Or possibly the toilet bowl. Take your pick."

Alex stirs, and when I glance up at him he's covering his mouth in a fake cough, trying not to laugh.

Paul shakes a warning finger at him. "You shut up." He faces me again after a moment. "Control your pet poodle, Mother, or I'll toss him out on the street."

The threat is real. I know my son, and I know what he's capable of. I clear my throat. "You'll do no such thing, Paul. And by the way, I didn't speak to the dean of my own volition. She came to me."

He snorts. "You don't play the innocent very well, Mother. You couldn't wait to tell her, could you? You probably scampered down the hall to her office immediately after speaking to me."

"I'm getting bored with this, darling. The only reason I knew you'd been drinking was because you've always been indifferent to proper oral hygiene, and that's hardly my fault. If you'd bothered to brush your teeth before coming to work, I might never have known." I straighten the striped arm covering on my chair. "Now do you have anything else to call me on the carpet for, or may I go take a nap?"

His breathing gets louder. "How about the juvenile things you've been saying at the Conservatory about Dad and Martha?"

"What things, dear? Why would I waste my time talking about those two overfed lovebirds?"

He tugs at his tangled beard. "I heard two of your students laughing uproariously in the hallway last week." His voice goes flat. "One of them said you'd told her that Martha had gone in for emergency liposuction, but the doctor slipped during surgery and accidentally removed Dad's penis instead."

Alex makes a choking sound.

Paul's head snaps up and his face turns a frightening shade of red. "So you think this is funny, punk?" He lurches forward and Alex backs away from him in a panic.

I throw up a warning hand. "Paul!"

He ignores me and keeps moving toward Alex.

I slam my fist down on the coffee table beside my chair and both of them jump. Alex uses the opportunity to slip behind me, and Paul's eyes flick back and forth between us.

"How predictable," I murmur into the charged stillness.

Paul focuses on me and some of the color leaves his puffy cheeks and forehead. "What are you talking about?" he grates.

"You've always been a coward, my love. Even as a child, you only dared to bully the people who posed no threat to you."

He rears back, stung, which is what I intended. I want his rage directed where it belongs.

I look over my shoulder at Alex. "I apologize for my son, dear. You'd better go upstairs before he loses control and proves himself to be a barbarian."

I expect him to bolt for the stairs, but he surprises me by hesitating. "Are you sure?" he whispers.

"Get out of here," Paul rasps. "Right now."

Alex doesn't budge. He doesn't even look at Paul.

Well, well. It seems as if my sweet young tenant has more of a spine than I gave him credit for.

"I'll be fine, Alex," I murmur. "Jabba the Hutt will be leaving shortly."

"Charming, Mother," Paul spits.

Alex waits another moment, then nods. "Okay. But give a yell if you need me."

Paul sniggers, but Alex ignores him. I turn to face Paul again and Alex exits the room. A second later I hear him running lightly up the stairs to his apartment.

Paul sneers and steps back to the fire. "How nice. You've made a friend. Too bad he'll be moving out so soon."

I refuse to let him rile me further. "I think it's time for you to go home, Paul. I have nothing else to say to you."

His face freezes. "That's strange, because I have so much more to say to you."

"I'm afraid it will have to wait." The flames in the fireplace behind him are beginning to die. "There's a limit to how many ugly confrontations I'll have with a family member in this room, this month. By the way, is Caitlin planning an assault, too? If she is, tell her to call ahead, would you? I'm booked solid until next August."

He shrugs, impatient. "As you well know, I have no idea what Caitlin's doing. We never speak." He pauses, and his voice changes ever so slightly. "But if I had to guess, I'd say she's probably out looking for a leper to chastise."

When he was younger, a running joke between us was Caitlin's legendary impatience with other people's problems.

I nod, unable to stop myself from participating. "Indeed. The last time I saw her, she'd just finished browbeating a quadriplegic about the evils of a sedentary lifestyle."

He nearly smiles, and for the briefest instance, our eyes meet without animosity. I can't even remember the last time that happened. But as soon as he realizes we're not being hateful to each other any longer, his face ices over.

He bends to snatch up his coat from the other chair. "Fine, I'll go," he rumbles. "But before I do, I'm giving you fair warning that you'd better get that kid out of here." He shakes his head. "Jesus. I'm surprised you haven't already got him wearing Jeremy's old clothes."

I blink. "I beg your pardon?"

He glowers. "Oh, come on. Don't pretend you don't know what I'm talking about."

In truth, I don't have any idea what he means. Is he comparing Alex to Jeremy? The two of them are nothing alike.

"Hush, now. You're giving me a headache." I point over my shoulder. "Do show yourself out, will you, dear?" I lift my head. "And don't bother coming back anytime soon."

We gaze at each other with mutual belligerence for a minute, then he barrels out of the room without saying another word. The door slams behind him a few seconds later, and I close my eyes until I hear his car roar out of the driveway.

I get to the landing on the third floor, and after catching my breath I call up to the attic apartment. "Alex? It's safe to come out of hiding."

I hear a chair scrape on the floor in his kitchen, then a few seconds later he appears at the top of the stairs, looking a bit flustered. "Are you all right?"

I shrug. "More or less. May I come up?"

He glances over his shoulder. "Uh, yeah. Just give me a second to straighten up, okay?"

I frown. "There's no need for that. Not unless you've been making blood sacrifices to Satan on my clean linoleum, or something along those lines."

I start up the stairs and panic flares across his face. "Wait, Hester. Please? It's a mess up here and I don't want you to see it like this."

I'm halfway up the steps by now and I catch a distinctive whiff of something I haven't smelled in a long time. I stop still and put my hands on my hips. "Oh, my. Are you smoking marijuana, Alex?"

His cheeks and forehead turn crimson to match his hair. He begins to stutter. "No, I'm . . . it's not, I mean, it is, but it's just something I . . . oh, shit." He looks like he wants to cry, and he hangs his head.

I continue climbing the stairs. When I get to the top I stand in front of him and wait for him to look up. After he finally meets my eyes, I reach up and pat him on the shoulder. "It's hardly the first time I've encountered pot, dear." I pause. "Or that it's been smoked in this house, for that matter. I've been a musician my entire life, remember?"

He blinks behind his glasses. "You're not mad?"

I shrug. "That depends. Are you willing to share?"

His face goes blank. "Holy shit, Hester. You smoke weed?"

"Well, no, not really. It's been at least thirty years since the last time." I shrug. "But then again, no one's offered me any since then, either." I gesture for him to lead the way. "Shall we?"

He laughs. "Sweet. Come on in."

He spins around on his bare heels and I follow him into the kitchen. I'm surprised at how clean things are; there are dishes drying in the rack next to the sink, and the white- and gold-flecked counter is sparkling in the sunlight coming through the windows. Aside from a plastic sandwich bag and a cheap red ashtray on the table (and a pungent wisp of smoke still hanging in the air like a shredded phantom), the entire room is spotless.

"I'm impressed." I sit kitty-corner to him at the table. The window next to me is open an inch, but the cold air blowing through it is more than offset by the warmth in the rest of the room. "You're a much better housekeeper than I thought you'd be."

He takes a pinch of marijuana from the plastic bag before looking up. "Yeah, I like to keep it neat. I get depressed when things are messy."

He builds a small green mound in the ashtray, then he takes a brass pipe about the size of a cigarette and mashes the end of it into his pile, tamping the pot in tightly. He examines his handiwork with a critical eye, then offers me the pipe, along with a lighter he digs out of his front pants pocket.

I stare at the things on my palm. "I'm afraid you're going to have to talk me through this. I don't remember what I'm supposed to do."

He grins again. "It's easy. You just put it in your mouth, then you light up and hold the smoke in as long as you can." He leans forward as I put the pipe between my lips and flick the lighter. "Yep, just like that. Don't take too big a drag, though, since you're not used to it. This stuff is great, but it's pretty harsh."

I fill my lungs and immediately wish I hadn't. I only manage to keep the smoke in for a few seconds, then my throat ignites and I begin to cough in spasms.

Alex's face fills with concern when I can't seem to stop. "Are you okay?"

I can't answer because I'm too busy hacking.

"Oh, God!" Alex hops to his feet and hovers over me. "Should I call an ambulance?"

I shake my head, still coughing, and wave my hand at the sink. "No, I'm fine," I gasp. "Just get me some water, please."

He flies to the counter and fumbles a glass out of the cabinet, almost dropping it before he manages to get it under the tap. He hurries over to me and I trade him his pipe and lighter for the water. He remains standing as I take a few sips, and he doesn't step back until he's convinced I'm not going to die. I slowly straighten in my seat and he drops into his chair with a relieved sigh.

A few more coughs shake my body. "God," I croak, wiping my face with my wrist. "Those horrid fundamentalists are absolutely right. That stuff *should* be illegal."

He checks out the end of the pipe. "Jesus." He shakes his head. "No wonder you had a fit like that. You cashed it all out in one toke." He begins to laugh. "That's awesome, Hester. You're gonna be so fucking stoned in a minute, you won't believe it. This shit is hardcore."

I settle back in my chair with a growl. "Good, because otherwise

I just reenacted the Marlboro Man's last few moments on earth for nothing."

He refills the pipe for himself and lights it. The green grass stuffed in its tip becomes a glowing red ember as he inhales, then fades away to ash soon after he removes his thumb from the lighter. His shoulders twitch as he suppresses a cough, but other than that he seems unaffected.

My scalp is starting to itch, and my eyelids are trying to come together. I giggle. "Oops. I believe something out of the ordinary is happening."

He aims his chin at the ceiling and releases a plume of smoke from his lips. He looks like a steam whistle on a train engine. I giggle again.

He laughs. "You're already getting wasted, aren't you?"

I draw myself up. "Nonsense. I'm only pretending."

He snorts. "Uh huh." He extends the pipe toward me again but I shake my head and he sets it back in the ashtray. He rubs his neck. "So is your son always like that?"

It takes me a moment to realize he's expecting an answer. "Like what, dear?"

He shrugs. "You know. Pissed off. And kind of, I don't know, kind of . . . well, mean, I guess."

"Oh, that. Yes, I'm afraid so. But what Paul lacks in charm, he more than makes up for in malice and aggression." I tug at my lip. "Do you still have my brandy? I'd very much like a glass."

He flushes and hops up again. "Sorry. I stuck it in the cabinet after breakfast this morning, just to get it out of the way, then I forgot about it again. I was going to bring it back to you later." He pulls the bottle out from under the sink.

"That's fine," I murmur. "I'm glad it's still up here. We should make it a point to squirrel away at least one container of liquor in every room in the house." I smile at him. "Did you know that when you're embarrassed your face turns the same shade as your hair?"

My ears feel heavy. My head tips first toward my left shoulder, then back toward my right. I watch Alex dig out two more glasses from his stash above the counter, but it seems to take him forever to return to the table.

He sits down again and fills the glasses. The brandy comes out of the bottle in slow motion, like runny gold ketchup.

"So how come he's like that?" Alex asks.

"Who?"

"You know. Paul." He pushes my drink toward me. "Why's he such a prick?"

I raise my glass and stare through the liquor at him. "Well, between us, I blame his parents. Especially his unstable mother." I down the brandy in a single gulp, and instant heat spreads from my throat to my belly. "The wicked old witch should be burned at the stake."

I expect him to smile, but he doesn't. He sips his drink and studies me.

I point at the bottle. "May I have another shot, dear?" I look out the window, down at St. Booger. From this angle, the snow on the statue's head looks like a white football helmet. "Paul wasn't always like this," I say. "Twenty years ago he really wasn't all that different from you."

There's a long pause. The metal legs on his chair creak as he shifts his weight. "How do you mean?"

I keep my back towards him. "He was gentle, and thoughtful. Just like you. And ever so much kinder than he is now."

I lean toward the window and expel a "hah" of hot air to steam it up. I write my name in the resulting fog, and my finger makes soft squeaking noises on the moist glass.

Alex stirs behind me, and when he speaks, his voice is strangely subdued. "Do you still love him?"

I freeze for a moment, and the silence in the air between us vibrates like a piano string.

"No." I bite my lip. "Isn't that awful?" I turn away from the window and find that my drink has been refilled. "God knows Paul needs the love, but he'll have to find it elsewhere, I'm afraid. I'm fresh out."

The marijuana is making me sluggish. My hand swims through the air and latches with effort onto my brandy. "Oh, well. Down the hatch."

He drains his glass, too. "That's kind of sad, isn't it?"

"I suppose." I make a face. "But how in the world am I still supposed to care for that man?"

His pale blue eyes are troubled behind his spectacles. "But you're his mom."

"True enough. Yet the older he gets the less that means to me."

His expression bothers me, and I roll my eyes. "Oh, stop looking at me like that. It's perfectly natural to despise your children. Animals devour their young all the time, and no one makes a fuss about *that*, do they?"

He shakes his head. "You're being weird. Maybe you shouldn't smoke pot anymore."

I smile at him. "On the contrary. I'm feeling extraordinarily clear-headed. Perhaps I should become a dealer so I can buy my marijuana in bulk." I glance over his shoulder at the far wall and Paul's high school picture is staring back at me. I feel my smile evaporate.

I settle my gaze on Alex. "I'm sorry to break this to you, darling, but the unconditional love that's supposed to exist in families is a childish fantasy. A mother's affection can be revoked at the drop of a hat. And the people in the world who need love the most—like my vile, turgid son, Paul—are the ones who will never get it, because they no longer deserve it."

He doesn't answer me, and he seems upset. I almost ask him what's bothering him, but before I can he excuses himself to use the bathroom.

He's far too sensitive for his own good.

CHAPTER 8

In the eyes of the world, Hester Parker should have, long ago, been "put out to pasture."

Just ask anybody.

She is a relic from a forgotten era, a dotard, and a cracked antique in society's attic. She is a poster child for every sorry old has-been who clings like a leech to bygone glory, refusing to retire with dignity and make room for the next generation.

I even heard through the grapevine last year that I'd died.

The dean's secretary, Marla Sorenson, scurried up to me in the hallway at school one morning with the news; she told me her phone had been ringing off the hook. It seems somebody, somewhere, had seen an obituary for a retired composer/pianist from Illinois named Hester *Parkinson*, and was confused by the similarity between our names and ages. Several of my colleagues on the East Coast swallowed the report without question; many called Arthur to offer their condolences, and the piano faculty at Juilliard went so far as to send a lovely bouquet of flowers in care of Carson Conservatory, for use during my memorial service.

On one level it was all very amusing and touching, but on another it illustrated—with grisly clarity—just how far from the limelight I've fallen.

When Vladimir Horowitz died, he was eulogized by every major newspaper and magazine in the country. Radio stations from Los Angeles to New York rebroadcast his most popular recitals, ad in-

finitum, and every time you flipped on the public television chan-
nel there was Vladimir again, hamming it up at his final performance in Carnegie Hall.

By way of contrast, no one of stature in the vulturous press even
bothered to inquire about the possibility of poor old Hester
Parker's demise. It's not that they didn't hear about it, mind you—
but no reporter outside of Bolton could be enticed to follow up on
a story that simply wasn't considered newsworthy.

The first of my colleagues who phoned Arthur to console him
told me later that all Arthur said to debunk the rumor was, "Hester
dead? Don't be ridiculous. The only way to kill Hester is to cut off
her head and stuff her mouth full of garlic."

She thought Arthur was joking, hence the reason she chose to
share that little tidbit with me.

"Oh, yes," I agreed. "Arthur is very witty."

But I digress.

My anonymous status notwithstanding, I still manage to pack in
a crowd whenever I'm required to give a master class in the concert
hall at Carson, and today is no exception. The national media may
never again pay any attention to me, but locally, at least, I am yet
considered to have a smidgeon of entertainment value (not unlike
the bearded lady in a traveling freak show). And while there is precious little comfort in such limited notoriety, at this juncture I'll
take what I can get.

Though to be honest, it's a mystery why anybody would want to
see me teach one of these things, has-been or not.

There are musicians who never feel alive unless a student is present. For them, nothing measures up to the thrill of helping a raw
talent evolve into something resembling a mature artist. Such people live for the moment of revelation in a protégé's eyes, that instant of connection when they say a magic word, and the student's
brain opens wide to receive it. Mentors such as these may be fine
players in their own right—although they are rarely first-rate—but
their passion is not about playing. All they truly care about is passing on the "sacred flame." More often than not, they are zealots
and/or tyrants, and they are gifted amateur psychologists, and once
in an aeon they may even be saints. But they are not performers.

They are teachers.

And while there are numerous examples of musicians who have been equally terrific at teaching *and* performing (Leonard Bernstein and Isaac Stern, to name two), if you got them in private, they would tell you their hearts belonged, mostly, to one discipline or the other. Both fields of study require commitment and enormous patience; both call for talent and sacrifice and heartache. But no honest musician is as invested in one facet of the art as much as the other—unless he or she is schizophrenic.

You are either a teacher, or you are a performer.

And I am a performer.

Which is why I'm always flabbergasted when the unwashed multitudes flock to these once-a-semester classes, as they have this afternoon. Especially since I am no longer able to do much playing myself, which implies that the audience, in defiance of all logic, must be coming primarily to observe my questionable prowess as a teacher.

Granted, the spectator sport aspect of a master class also has something to do with the heavy attendance. I've long believed most people show up for these things for the same reason the Romans packed the Colosseum whenever the lions were lunching on Christians. They're hoping the open lesson format of the class will turn into an emotional bloodbath—say, for instance, an ugly clash of egos between a young virtuoso and the more experienced musician leading the session, or, even better, a painful public dismemberment of said virtuoso if he finds he is unable to do what is asked of him.

It's most unsavory, and thus irresistible.

As I walk onstage to begin the session, a hush spreads through the auditorium. Since this is not a concert per se, the houselights have not been dimmed and I can clearly see who's here. I scan the crowd for familiar faces and am shocked to find my daughter Caitlin staring back at me from the back of the room, sitting off in a corner by herself. She's wearing a bright green dress and her best glower, and when my eyes lock with hers, she sniffs and looks away.

Dear God. What on earth is *she* doing here?

I haven't seen her since. . . .

I rip my attention away from her. My heart is beating rapidly but I keep my face expressionless and continue my sweep of the audience. A moment later I get another unpleasant jolt when I find Arthur planted—a portly, angry weed—in a row of Conservatory faculty members. He's a head taller (and half a foot wider) than anyone near him, but I pretend not to notice him. He frowns and says something to Ben Hessling, the viola teacher, and both of them smirk.

So. Arthur has turned Ben against me, too. That stings, but I'm not surprised. Ben doesn't have a single opinion that somebody with more of a backbone hasn't spoon-fed to him.

I square my shoulders and turn away from them. It's time to begin the class. Arthur and Caitlin be damned. I have a job to do, and I will not let their presence rattle me. I suppose I should count my blessings that Paul isn't here as well.

I take a deep breath to calm my nerves. I can smell the fresh wax on the floor at my feet, mixing with the scent of mildew coming from the heavy, red cloth curtains tied back at the corners of the stage. Dust and stale human sweat hangs in the air, only slightly diluted by the odor of old leather and wool pouring from the seats behind me. The familiar stench is a comfort; I've been on a thousand stages in a thousand concert halls, and they all smell the same.

The recital hall at Carson seats five hundred (three hundred in the orchestra section, and a hundred each in the mezzanine and top balcony). The upper levels are closed today, forcing an intimacy between the watchers and the watched. The stage itself is large and rounded, with a polished wooden floor, and a Baldwin grand piano has been rolled out to the center, its lid raised high for full volume. Four alcoves surround the stage, each sheltering a white marble bust of one of the "biggies"—Bach, Mozart, Beethoven, and Brahms— perched on stout, black Roman pillars, like demigods.

I'm scheduled to work with three pianists today. One of them is a student from Carson, and another is a young lady from Northwestern University who drove down from Evanston. Both are proficient players, but the star of the day is already seated at the piano, waiting for me. He's a special guest from Russia, in town this week as part of an exchange program our development director set up with her counterpart at the Moscow Conservatory.

I walk up to him and he rises from the bench to shake my hand, introducing himself in a thick Slavic accent as Viktor Katavasov.

"It is a great honor to meet you, Ms. Parker," he tells me, gripping my fingers. He's a handsome, black-haired boy in his late teens, with long arms and legs, and a huge nose, rubbed raw and red from an apparent head cold. He lowers his voice so the audience can't hear him. "Thank you so much for agreeing to teach me today. I'm very nervous to play for you."

His English is good, even with the accent.

I nod at him and whisper back. "There's no need to be nervous. I'm largely tone-deaf, and heavily medicated."

His smile brightens. "Ah, yes. Dr. Pavlovskaya warned me about your sense of humor."

His teacher in Moscow is Olga Pavlovskaya, an old friend and professional rival from my touring and competition days.

I smile back at him. "That's too bad. It's more fun when people think I'm serious." I press his hand warmly. "You can relax, dear. Olga has been singing your praises for months in her e-mails, and she never exaggerates. How is she doing, by the way?"

He beams. "She is very well, thank you. She told me to give you all her love, and she misses you terribly."

I feel a sudden constriction in my throat and have to fight back tears. I give his hand another squeeze and look away. I'm being a mawkish old fool, but my daughter and husband have me feeling singularly vulnerable right now, and any affection at all, even from the other side of the world, is almost more than I can bear.

I take hold of myself again and gesture for Viktor to sit, then I face the audience.

"Good afternoon." I'm relieved to hear my voice come out strong and controlled. "My, this is quite a throng. Should I be flattered, or was there nothing but reruns of *Cops* on television?"

Chuckles. I let my glance pass over Arthur and he rolls his eyes. He used to chide me for what he called "working the crowd." He once told me I was a pianist, not a comedienne, and that I cheapened myself with what he considered "feeble attempts at stand-up routines."

I told him jealousy was not an attractive quality in a man.

"As you're no doubt aware," I continue, "this brave soul sitting at the piano behind me is visiting from Russia." I turn to acknowledge Victor and he sniffles and wipes his nose on the sleeve of his thick gray sweater. Olga's students have always had zero stage presence, so I decide to let this breach of performance etiquette slide. "I understand Viktor will be playing a Chopin *Polonaise* for us." I tilt my head at him. "Is that right, dear?"

He shakes his head. "No, I'm sorry, Ms. Parker, but Dr. Pavlovskaya suggested that I perform instead one of the *Nocturnes.*"

I close my eyes for an instant. Oh, no. Please.

This can't be happening. Olga, you treacherous old fool. What have you done?

I glare at him. "Let me guess. *Number 1 in C minor?*"

He blinks. "How did you know?"

There's no escape from this now. I have no choice but to make the best of it.

I wave a hand. "No matter. That will be fine, Viktor. You may proceed whenever you're ready."

He cracks his knuckles and takes a deep breath, and I move gingerly to the chair provided for me next to the piano bench, where I can see his hands. I sit and try to seem unaffected, but after a pause my gaze returns against my will to Arthur, then to Caitlin.

They're the only ones here who know what this is going to do to me.

God. I can't bear it. Arthur is actually waiting for me to look at him, and there's open compassion on his face. I don't dare show any reaction, and a moment later he turns away. Caitlin is staring at her lap.

Viktor's long fingers sink into the keyboard and I jerk a little in my chair as the wistful, elegiac first notes crawl out of the open lid of the piano and limp across the stage. I close my eyes again and nearly moan aloud.

My only hope is that he'll mangle it. Because otherwise I'm likely to come apart at the seams.

It's not really Olga's fault. It's mine. We had a discussion a few years back about the repertoire we each favored in lessons, and I lied to her about why I no longer teach this *Nocturne* to my students. All she knows is that it used to be my signature encore piece in the old days, and that I had grown tired of it. She no doubt thought it would be a good, harmless prank for Viktor to spring it on me this way.

Well, that's what I get for lying.

I open my eyes again and brace myself for what's coming.

Unfortunately, the boy plays very well. His phrasing is limpid and thoughtful, and as the music gains in power and speed he displays an admirable restraint, avoiding the sentimental excess that so often mars the performances of young pianists. His hands are big and strong, but he isn't afraid to use them lightly; he's saving his energy for the finale. There's an intensity to his expression that reminds me of Olga, an almost frightening loss of self in his concentration. It also reminds me of me, I suppose.

The melody begins its slow, relentless buildup, and I can't block it out any longer.

This was Jeremy's favorite piece.

Jeremy.

My sweet, stupid son.

When he was a child, he would come into the music room at home while I was practicing, and he would lie on the floor and listen patiently to whatever I was working on. My injury didn't allow me to play for any length of time without causing enormous discomfort, so I'd eventually take a break and peer over the piano at him.

"Jeremy." I'd make a face. "Not again, surely. Not today. My wrist hurts too much."

He'd beg. "Please? Just once more, okay?"

I must have played it for him a hundred times over the course of his adolescence. The piece is only six minutes long, but it covers the emotional gamut, and as he grew older, I'd look up when I was done, and he would always have tears in his eyes.

I asked him once why he liked it so much if it made him sad, and he shrugged.

"I don't know." He ran a hand through his unruly blond hair. "It's not just sadness, though. It's everything. Everything all at once." He grinned at me. "And you already know that, otherwise you wouldn't play it the way you do."

He couldn't have been more than fourteen when he said those words.

Jeremy played the French horn. He started off on piano, as did all my children, but when he was seven years old we took him to a concert at the Conservatory. The orchestra was performing Beethoven's Seventh, and he sat through the entire symphony without moving, his gaze glued to the horns and his face slack with wonder. All the way home in the car he whistled the theme to the finale, waving his arms around in the backseat like a mad conductor and annoying Paul with a barrage of rude remarks about the cello (Paul's instrument). I don't recall most of his comments, but when he made the proclamation that "the horn is the voice of God, but the cello is a farting walrus with strings attached to its head," Paul seemed to believe he'd gone too far.

"Shut the fuck up, you little pisshead!" He reached around Caitlin and wrenched Jeremy's arm with brutal intensity. "I'm going to fucking kill you!"

Paul never did develop much patience for his younger brother when they were children. They were only three years apart, and Jeremy's mouth was merciless. He knew better than anyone else how to make Paul dissolve into a screaming lunatic, and the beatings he took because of it never seemed to discourage him from giving his tongue free rein.

I remember walking in the house one day after work and stumbling into a war zone. The table and chairs in the kitchen were overturned, and Paul had Jeremy cornered by the refrigerator and was ruthlessly punching him in the stomach, again and again, because Jeremy had been making fun of a slight lisp Paul had at the time. Both of them were bawling and Jeremy could barely talk, but every time he was struck, he'd croak, "Thtop it, Paul, pleath thtop it."

"I can't help thpeaking like that!" Paul wailed. "I hate you, I hate you!"

I separated them but just as Paul was beginning to calm down again, Jeremy whispered from behind the safety of my back, "Thankth, Mom. He wath hurting me."

Paul went berserk. He seized a steak knife from the silverware drawer and began chasing Jeremy through the house. I caught him before he could commit fratricide, but he nearly stabbed me in the leg as I wrestled him to the ground. Jeremy locked himself in a nearby bathroom and began to sing loudly, over and over, "Thith ith the dawning of the age of Aquariuth, the age of Aquariuth . . ."

That was a rather long day.

And yet most of the time they were quite close. They played music together frequently and watched television every night, and when they were older I would often find them sitting side by side on the front porch in the evening, listening to the radio and talking. Occasionally I'd hear them laughing like fools over something incomprehensible, a private joke made up of endless shared memories and intimately understood facial expressions, bewildering catchphrases, and crude sound effects.

In other words, everything that makes up the muddled and reason-defying language of brothers.

They weren't just siblings, you see. They were also friends.

That's why Paul is still so angry with me. He has few friends, and Jeremy was one of the only people in the world he actually loved, and so he blames me for everything that happened. It's as if he thinks I could have changed the outcome, could have somehow prevented Jeremy from doing what he did.

It's what my entire family believes.

Which is so grossly unfair, I want to scream. They have no idea what they're talking about. None. I was the only one there with Jeremy at the end. The only one. I know what happened, and I know what I did was right. But they have never listened to my side of the story.

I yank my attention back to the present, trying to concentrate on Viktor's few foibles as a player. I'm supposed to spend at least forty-five minutes of the class on him, and if I can just endure the initial run-through, I may be able to immerse myself in the nuts and bolts of his interpretation for the rest of the time, and avoid more of this senseless wallowing in the past.

Who am I kidding?

I'm not wallowing. I'm drowning.

Dear God, this hurts. The music feels as if it's eating a hole in my flesh, one caustic note at a time. How can it possibly still hurt this much?

I'm not going to make it. I'm going to have to walk offstage any second now. Viktor's almost arrived at the climax in the *Nocturne*, the place where all hell breaks loose, and I won't survive it, not this time. It's far too laden with memory, too rich with grief and longing and despair. If I were playing, I might be able to harness the notes and discharge some of the pain that way, letting it sluice out of me like sewage water from a pipe. But having to sit here and simply listen is torture.

His phrasing is exquisite. He connects one idea to the next in a seamless line, like a master storyteller, and his rests almost throb with tension. My only complaint so far is with his left hand; it has a slight tendency to overpower his right. It's a minor problem, but I fixate on it with gratitude. Any flaw at all is a welcome distraction.

God damn him. If he'd only miss a note now and then, it would make this so much easier.

I turn my head away from the audience as my eyes fill with tears.

God damn Chopin, too, while we're at it. And God damn Olga and our development director, and God damn Arthur and Caitlin, and God damn everyone in this room who expects me to hear this hateful piece right now without falling apart. All I want to do is go home, and sit with Alex again in the kitchen attic as we did yesterday, and lose myself in alcohol and undemanding conversation.

I blink to clear my vision and begin to rise slowly from my chair to leave the stage, but Viktor suddenly leans forward and sinks the weight of his forearms into the keyboard, and the music erupts into the air around me. I fall back in my seat and drop my head on my chest in defeat.

No qualified teacher would take Jeremy as a student until he was older, but the instant he turned ten we couldn't put him off any longer. Arthur and I would have preferred for him to take up a string instrument or continue with the piano, but after Sandra Means at the Conservatory agreed to teach him, Jeremy insisted we buy him a horn, and he began to practice with the single-minded devotion of an idiot savant. By the time he was twelve he could play almost anything in the repertoire. Orchestral excerpts from Mahler and Richard Strauss were standard fare, and he blared them out his bedroom window every day after school. It's a wonder the neighbors never complained, because you could hear him from five blocks away.

When he was fifteen, he won a young artist's competition with the Chicago Symphony, and almost every music school in the country that was worth a damn started trying to recruit him. Paul was already at Carson by then, but Jeremy—who was always far less afraid of the world than his brother—decided he wanted to go to Philadelphia to study at the Curtis Institute, and he somehow managed to convince Arthur and me that he didn't need to finish high school first.

"What are you guys so worried about?" he demanded when we dared to argue with him. "Curtis doesn't require a high school diploma." He paced in a circle around the kitchen table. "And after I've been to a school like Curtis, no one will give a shit that I once dropped out of high school."

Arthur looked at me and shrugged. "He has a point, Hester."

I scowled back at him. "Yes, darling, he does. Unfortunately, it's on top of his malformed little head." I grunted. "And you have one, too, if you're thinking this is a good idea."

Jeremy's eyes, gray and brilliant like his father's, scanned my face for signs of weakening. He knew he'd won Arthur over (as usual) and had only me to contend with.

"Come on, Mom," he nudged. "You know I'm right."

"No, Jeremy, I don't know that at all." I rose to my feet to go get a drink. "I'd like for you to have something of a normal childhood, son." I raised my eyebrows at Arthur. "Neither your father nor I ever did, and I think we owe you that opportunity."

Arthur frowned. "Oh, for God's sake. What are you implying?"

"I'm not implying anything, dear." I made my way to the liquor cabinet and dragged out a full bottle of Glenlivet. "I'm simply trying to prevent our middle child from becoming a psychotherapist's wet dream a decade from now."

He waved his hand. "You're being absurd. I'd say we turned out rather well, in spite of our unorthodox upbringings."

"That's debatable." I held out the bottle of scotch for his inspection and he nodded his head. I took two glasses from the cabinet to pour us both a shot. "You, for instance, have an alarming number of personality disorders."

"Name one," he growled.

"Fine, I will," I said, amused by his defensiveness. "You're unable to go to sleep at night until you've plumped your pillow exactly eleven times."

He stiffened. "That's a harmless habit I've had since childhood. It doesn't affect my sleep one way or the other."

I laughed. "Yes, dear. Whatever you say."

He ignored that. "Regardless, you know full well neither of us would have survived a so-called 'normal' childhood. The boredom alone would have killed us."

I plunked the glasses down on the table before turning back to Jeremy. "All I'm saying is that something may happen in the next two years of high school that you might wish you hadn't missed out on later in life."

"Like what?" he demanded. "Another fascinating discussion about blackheads in health class? Another rousing shirts-versus-skins basketball game in gym?" He rolled his eyes. "Jesus, Mom. Don't be obtuse."

He won that argument, of course. He always won, no matter what. He always got what he wanted, in the end.

And with that thought, the image I've fought so hard to keep out of my mind comes back full force.

His face. His clean, smooth face turned up to the winter sky. His lovely gray eyes, empty and unblinking.

And so much blood in the snow. So very much blood.

I wrap my arms around my ribs and stifle a sob.

My face is still turned away from the audience, but by now everyone in the hall must know something is wrong. I can feel their eyes fixed on me. And there's no time to recover before I have to speak again. Viktor is almost through with the piece, and when he's done,

I'll be expected to rise to my feet and launch into a scintillating dis-section of his performance.

And I can't. I simply can't do it.

My son. My beautiful boy.

Oh, God. How am I going to live with the shame of this break-down? I'm disintegrating in front of a roomful of people, and no one except Arthur and Caitlin has any idea why.

Viktor's right hand spins out the last few melancholy notes, and then he sounds the final three chords, expertly milking the silence between them. There's a long moment of profound stillness after the final one, and he doesn't move a muscle. In spite of what I'm feeling, I can't help but admire his artistry. He has the audience in the palm of his hand.

The applause starts, but before it can get going full tilt, he sneezes, then lifts the waist of his sweater to his face and loudly blows his nose on it. His thin, hairy stomach is exposed to the room. When he drops the gray sweater again, there are two wet patches near the hem in front, with a thin ribbon of yellowish mucus running be-tween them like a tightrope. Viktor looks down at the mess he's made, then he looks back up at me and shrugs apologetically.

The applause turns to raucous laughter.

Oh, praise the Lord.

As a rule, I do not believe in a "Higher Power." As a child, I was raised in a semi-devout Methodist household, but by the time I was a teenager, God was no more real to me than Mr. Ed, the talking horse, and I have seen nothing in the nearly sixty years since to change my mind.

But today I may be forced to make an exception to that rule. Be-cause nothing less than divine intervention could have been the cause of such a glorious and abrupt change of mood in my psyche and in the concert hall.

I feel as if Viktor had tossed a bucket of filthy ice water on me. I'm so appalled by his gross display that my grief has been trans-formed on the spot into stunned indignation. I've never seen such an act of blasphemy on the stage, and every ounce of sadness in me is gone, replaced, as if by magic, by an almost overwhelming desire to slap this ridiculous child senseless for desecrating such a magnificent performance in this manner.

And yet nothing short of this kind of egregious behavior could have pulled me out of the well I had fallen into.

So I say again, praise God. Today I am a believer.

Praise God for not giving Olga Pavlovskaya the ability to teach proper stage conduct, and praise God for the farcical timing of Viktor's sneeze, and praise God, most of all, for the much-maligned, incurable common cold. It's all I can do to refrain from rushing forward and kissing this hapless youngster on his chapped Slavic lips.

A moment before, all eyes in the hall had been riveted on me, attempting to discover the source of my odd histrionics during the Chopin piece, but now there is loud chatter and scattered guffaws, and a palpable feeling of expectation as the audience awaits my reaction.

I fear they know my reputation too well.

I once flung a musical score at a student's head during a master class, simply because he made the mistake of scratching his armpit during a cadenza. I daresay that story is common knowledge to most of the people in this room, and what the Russian boy has just done is a far worse crime than that—and so, no doubt the audience is now gleefully anticipating Viktor's impending evisceration.

And if it were any other day than this, I'd be happy to oblige them.

I turn and glance at Arthur. My eyes must be red-rimmed, but hopefully the crowd will now believe the cause of this is rage.

I clear my throat and lift my voice to carry, but I keep my tone mild. "Arthur, dear, do you happen to have a clean handkerchief on you? Viktor's sweater isn't very absorbent, and it appears to be chafing his nose somewhat."

The room ignites with fresh, surprised laughter, and Viktor flushes. Caitlin, of course, only scowls at me.

But Arthur meets my gaze fully, and in his expression is something I never thought to see again: understanding. He knows exactly what's been going on in my mind, and he's trying without success to fight back a smile of affection.

He's a fool for trying.

No matter what he feels about me anymore, it's simply not in him to resist the appeal of an absurd situation like this, and he should know better. I let my eyes linger on him for a few seconds, and he doesn't look away, and for that small space of time it's as if we never separated. All our years together are in that gaze, and he finally reaches wordlessly into his pocket—conscious, as ever, of being the center of attention—and he pulls out a handkerchief. It's white and spotless, and he waves it in the air above his head, like a flag of surrender.

And I can almost remember why I loved him so.

CHAPTER 9

The reception following the master class is in the lobby outside the concert hall, and the very first thing I see as I enter the room is Martha Predel, helping herself to the cookies and punch.

Martha Predel. My husband's mistress.

Good God. The nerve of that woman. The unmitigated gall.

She didn't attend the master class, of course (she can't bear to see me receiving attention on the stage), but I should have known I'd find her here afterwards, waiting to provoke me. She lives for any such chance she can find to appear in public with Arthur at her side—especially when she knows I'll be in the room as well, and won't be able to avoid the two of them.

She's wearing a loose, white and pink, full-length dress that manages to hide the less appealing aspects of her figure and brings out her striking red hair, and she's beaming a toothy, besotted smile at Arthur, standing next to her. I see the moment when she becomes aware of me across the room; she takes hold of Arthur's arm in a proprietary manner and pretends not to notice me.

This reception is supposed to be in *my* honor, and she's beside *my* husband, acting for all the world as if she has every right to be here.

I will not tolerate such brazen disrespect. Certainly not from Martha Moonface Predel.

For fifteen years Martha acted like my bosom friend. For fifteen years she greeted me gaily in the hall here at the Conservatory, made congenial small talk, and peppered me with flattery. For fifteen years, she played the part of a deferential colleague, begging for advice and assistance on numerous projects, and showering me with gratitude whenever I would attempt to help her.

And for fifteen years that harlot made a fool of me.

I will never know how many times she and Arthur crept off for "nooners" in his studio, or weekend getaways when he was touring. I will never know how often they slept together in my bed when I was out of town at seminars or judging competitions. I will never know how often they laughed about poor deluded Hester, or how frequently they patted themselves on the back for their enormous success at pulling the wool over my eyes.

In point of fact, if you had asked me during that decade and a half what I thought of Martha, I would have told you she was a simple, mildly-talented musician, with a good heart and inoffensive manners. She was conscientious, and pleasant, and she could be counted on for a supportive smile or a soft word on bleak days. More often than not, I might even have told you that I *liked* her.

Well, the joke's on Hester. And it's quite a knee-slapper, isn't it? Martha Predel took my husband, she took my life, and she took my happiness. She took my right to walk down the hall without receiving stealthy, pitying glances from my peers and my students, and she took my peace of mind, and she took a great deal of my self-respect.

In other words, she took everything I had that was worth having. And she accomplished this mighty feat of larceny in sly, bite-sized increments, so I never even noticed it happening. Like a malicious blue jay, she floated into my territory while my back was turned, and ate all the precious eggs in my nest, one by one.

And now, or so I'm told, she also intends to take my house.

A killing rage swells inside me.

The smell of brewed coffee is in the air, and people are bunching together in groups of two or three to make small talk and gossip. I paste a benign expression on my face and begin sauntering toward the refreshment table, pausing here and there to acknowledge the compliments and greetings from colleagues who speak to me on my way, but I keep Martha in my line of sight the entire time, and I gradually close the gap between us.

I will make that woman pay for having the audacity to show up at *my* reception.

"Hello, Mother."

The cold, familiar voice behind me stops my feet before I can reach the table, and my heart lurches in my chest as I gather the strength to turn around and face my daughter.

We haven't spoken in a year. And before that, not since Jeremy's funeral.

I greet her as pleasantly as I can. "Why, hello, Caitlin. I thought I saw you in the audience today. It's sweet of you to come."

The lobby is a large, bright room with a wide set of stairs in the middle, and windows reaching from floor to ceiling all around us. Caitlin is standing with her back to the staircase, wearing a dress the same shade of green—the color of a sickly fern frond—as her eyes.

My eyes, as Alex noted in the car a few days ago.

She squints at me, frowning at the afternoon sunlight coming through the windows. There's a long, awkward pause as we study each other.

"So how have you been?" she finally asks.

I don't know what to say to her. There's far too much pain and anger here for both of us, and speaking to each other is likely to do nothing but cause more damage. I'm sure she still believes I'm to blame for Jeremy's death, and God knows I haven't yet found it in my heart to forgive her for not telling me about Arthur's affair—the knowledge of which both she and Paul were privy to long before I was.

But what else can I do but answer her? "Well enough. And you?"

She sniffs. "Fine." She indicates my husband's mistress with a tilt of her head. "You shouldn't let Martha get to you, you know."

Caitlin is much larger than I am. I'm five-foot-four and weigh no more than a hundred pounds dripping wet, while Caitlin is five-eight and much stockier. She's not fat, mind you, but she has wide shoulders and hips, and somewhat bulky thighs and shins. She's certainly not unattractive, but neither has she ever been what you could describe as beautiful. (When I was younger, I was something of "a looker," but Caitlin inherited more of her father's physical characteristics, which unfortunately suit a man better than a woman.) Still, her shoulder-length black hair is thick and shiny and very soft, and her skin is clear, and her hands are long-fingered and elegant, with small knuckles and short unpainted nails. She also has a restless energy about her that is quite compelling and no doubt serves her well in the classroom.

I glance over my shoulder. "You're imagining things, darling. I'm simply on my way to the refreshment table for a glass of punch. I didn't even know Martha was here."

I catch Martha watching Caitlin and me. I narrow my eyes at her and turn back to Caitlin again. "I should at least give my regards to the old girl, don't you think?"

"Actually, no. I don't." She adjusts her dress because it's bunching up over her wide shoulders. She notices me watching her and she pauses, blushing.

Paul and Jeremy used to tease her for those shoulders; they called her "Princess Quasimodo" and "Lawrence of Arabia's pet camel," and they would favor her daily with witty remarks such as, "Don't you have to go ring the cathedral bells now?" or "Could you drain your hump for me, Caitlin? I'm thirsty."

She bore it all with a kind of stoic calm, though, because she was always smart enough to know, even as a very young girl, that if she responded in anger to anything her brothers said, the only result would be an escalation of the verbal abuse. Instead, she got even by embarrassing them in public as often as possible, with clever guerrilla tactics—such as running up to them in crowded rooms to demand that they stop wearing her makeup and panties without asking, or delivering such *bon mots* as, "So Paul, how's that new plastic sheet on your bed working out for you?"

Paul and Jeremy never stood a chance against her, really.

In truth, they were a little afraid of her, because they didn't know just how far she'd go to humiliate them. Oh, they could be cruel at times, and they were always insensitive—yet underneath all the scathing gibes they aimed at her was a furtive, grudging compassion, an inborn reluctance to go for their little sister's jugular. Caitlin, alas, never had any such qualms, and they were wise not to test her limits.

I shouldn't admit this, but I've always admired her for that.

She greets an acquaintance walking by, then resumes her homily about Martha. "You're just jealous, Mother. She's not worth your time."

I don't know how she's able to determine what's going on in my head, but it bothers me that I'm so easy for her to read.

"Jealous? Of Martha?" I pick a white hair from the front of my black skirt. "Don't be absurd."

She rolls her eyes. "Uh huh."

"Believe what you want. I'm no more jealous of Martha Predel than I am of the Pillsbury Doughboy."

She sighs. "I thought you might have grown up by now, but I see that honesty is still too much of a leap for you."

No one in the universe can provoke me faster than Caitlin. No one.

The spiteful words are out of my mouth before I can stop them. "Speaking of growing up, I have to say I'm surprised to see you here today, dear. I know how difficult it is for you to watch others play the piano the way you always wished you could."

She pales and takes an involuntary step backward. "Lovely, Mother," she whispers. "Very kind."

I can barely hear her for all the chatter in the room, but the hurt on her face is plain. I close my eyes for an instant, hating myself. Whatever we've done to each other, she deserves better from me than this.

I start to apologize, but she cuts me off.

"It doesn't matter." She turns to go. "I really didn't expect anything else from you."

She begins to walk past me, and I put my hand on her arm to stop her. She halts for me, but she pulls away from my grip.

"Caitlin." I drop my voice so no one else can hear me. "Why *are* you here? It's been forever since I've seen you."

She hesitates and won't meet my gaze. Standing this close I can smell her perfume; it's subtle and pleasant, with a faint suggestion of lilies.

"I don't know." She shrugs. "I'd heard the Russian boy was going to be here and decided to come. That's all."

Oscar Schneider, the skeletal oboe teacher, appears out of the crowd and starts to angle toward us, but neither Caitlin nor I spare him more than a slight nod and he takes the hint and moves away again. Dear old Oscar. He's one of the few faculty members here at Carson with a functional brain in his head.

"No." I peer into her eyes. "I mean, why are you at this reception, and why are you speaking to me again?"

She grunts. "This is hardly a *rapprochement,* if that's what you're implying. I still want nothing to do with you."

"I suspected as much." I clear my throat. "Which brings us back to my question. Why are you here, then?"

For an instant, her lower lip trembles and she sighs. "Idle curiosity, I suppose."

I can't believe what I'm seeing. If I didn't know better, I'd swear she's fighting tears.

Caitlin never cries. Ever.

I start to reach for her again and she recoils.

"Don't touch me." She steps back and gets control of herself again. She crosses her arms over her chest and frowns at me. "And drop the solicitous act, too, while you're at it. It's making me sick to my stomach."

I study her for a moment. "Now who's being dishonest?"

She sees the smile I can't prevent and her face hardens. "Oh, please, Mother. Do you think I've forgotten who and what you are? Or what you did?" Her voice is brittle. "Do you really think I could ever forget?"

I was an imbecile to let down my guard with her. A complete imbecile.

I'm close to tears again as I shake my head. "Of course not. I imagine it's far too rewarding to continue scapegoating me for something you know nothing about."

I turn away before she can say anything else and resume my journey toward the reception table.

Nothing ever changes between us. Nothing.

When I discovered I was pregnant with a daughter, I was thrilled. I adored my boys, but I had always wanted a little girl, too. I was sure we'd be instant best friends the moment she emerged from my womb, and I foresaw endless, intimate talks with her about music and art, and literature and drama, and boys and men. I fantasized about how she'd look and behave as a graceful, spirited teenager, and later, as a young, lighthearted adult. I couldn't wait to share my life with her, and to teach her what she needed to know to survive and flourish as a woman, and to watch her grow into maturity and wisdom, as I knew she eventually would.

Needless to say, things didn't turn out exactly the way I'd envisioned.

From the moment she was born, we never truly connected. She always preferred her father's company, forever running to him if she was injured or upset, and keeping her distance from me even when Arthur wasn't there. Nor did she warm to me any further as she grew older. Our conversations, though polite, were often awkward, and whenever one of us would attempt to be affectionate with the other, it usually felt strained. The boys and I were allies from the start, kindred spirits, but I've never known how to speak to Caitlin, nor has she known how to approach me without setting my teeth on edge.

Yet there was love between us, once. There really was. It was a crippled, tenuous sort of love, but it existed, especially when she was a little girl. In moments of weakness, she would occasionally let me hold her, and I would stroke her hair and feel her small heart beating against mine, and for the duration of that embrace I would feel the barriers between us crumble and fall, like the walls of a sand castle, and I would hum softly to her until she fell asleep. And now and then she would take my hand in the yard or on the street, and she'd walk at my side for a bit, and she'd look up and ask me questions about this or that.

And when she said the word "Mother" back then, it didn't even come out sounding like a curse.

I swallow past the lump in my throat and force myself to forget about Caitlin. I have bigger fish to fry, and I'm going to go fry them, right now.

Arthur and Martha are still standing where they were when I began my quarrel with my daughter, but they've since started speaking to Bonnie Norton, the dean of Carson Conservatory's music faculty. Bonnie is a harpsichordist and a musicologist, and she is also, of course, my boss—which is no doubt why Arthur and Martha have her cornered at this moment. They're obviously counting on Bonnie's presence to deter me from dealing with them in the manner they deserve.

Idiots.

Bonnie has her back to me, beside the table, and Arthur and Martha are facing her, doing their best not to acknowledge my approach. I step into the space between Bonnie and Arthur and exchange greetings with them.

Martha pretends to be surprised at my appearance. "Why, hello, Hester. I'm sorry I missed your class today. I understand it was quite entertaining." She gives me a smug smile and leans her head on Arthur's shoulder.

It's all I can do to keep from plucking her eyes out. This is outrageous. The woman has no shame. Arthur at least has the grace to look uncomfortable.

I return her smile. "Hello, Martha. I see you've found the cookies." I glance at the full tray on the table. "I assume you'll be needing a doggie bag?"

She lowers the plate she was using as a trough and glares. She has magnificent blue eyes, and what they used to call a Roman nose, pronounced and angular and lovely. Thank God she wrestles with her weight; it's the only sure way I know to get under her skin.

Arthur drops his meaty arm over her shoulders and shakes his head at me in disbelief. "For God's sake, Hester," he growls. "Don't start. Not here, not now."

It's as if the moment of rapport in the concert hall a few minutes ago never happened.

Bonnie eyes the rest of us and makes a graceless attempt at redirecting the conversation. "Hester. That was a tremendous class. Really."

With her nervous mannerisms and emaciated body, Bonnie always reminds me of a Chihuahua. She takes my arm and tries to lead me apart from the others. "I especially appreciated your insights into the Chopin. I was just saying a moment ago that no one knows the Romantics like you do."

I rip my eyes away from Arthur's protective embrace of Martha and turn to Bonnie. "That's very generous of you, dear. Yes, I'm quite fond of Chopin." I give a conspiratorial chuckle and plant my feet in the ground, refusing to be herded. "Even though he was a bit of a scoundrel, really. For instance, did you know that while he was in a supposedly monogamous relationship with George Sand, he was also having an affair with a brainless, unbathed, stubby little village girl?"

Martha blanches and Arthur looks as if he's having a grand mal seizure. He grinds his teeth together and tugs at his gray beard with his free hand. "I'm warning you, Hester."

"Warning me about what, darling? I thought you'd rather enjoy hearing about another musically famous lecher with deplorable taste in mistresses."

Bonnie's grip on my arm tightens. "Please, Hester. Stop this."

Silence is forming around our small group as other people in the vicinity become aware of the altercation.

I wince, and lie. "That's my bad arm, Bonnie."

She flinches and lets go, but then narrows her eyes at me. "It isn't either. You broke your left wrist, not your right."

"Oh, yes, silly me. What I meant was, mind your own business, Bonnie. This has nothing to do with you."

She tightens her jaw. "Anything that happens in this building between faculty members is my business, Hester. Watch yourself."

"Excuse me?" I can't believe my ears. This yapping little bureaucrat actually thinks she can rein me in. I draw myself up to put her in her place, too, but all of a sudden Caitlin reappears on my other side and interrupts for no apparent reason.

She gives a cold nod to Arthur. "Hi, Dad." She examines him

with hostility. "You look ridiculous with that beard. How have you been?"

It's heartening to see she now despises Arthur as much as she despises me. That's a relatively new development; up until this last year she always reserved the lion's share of her wrath for me, and basically ignored Arthur. But much can change in a year.

His nod is equally chilly. "I'm well." He waits a moment before deciding to simulate polite behavior. "And you?"

"Fine." Caitlin shrugs. "Ever since I disowned both you and Mother, my life has been quite good. But thanks for asking. Really." She sniffs. "I so much appreciate your pathetic mimicking of fatherly concern."

The hurt on Arthur's face is unfeigned. He's not used to the change in their relationship, and whatever psychic armor he's constructed thus far to ward off her attacks is woefully inadequate. Caitlin may not be a virtuoso on the piano or the violin, but she has a genius for hatred.

"That's unnecessary," he says. "I don't deserve that from you, do I?"

The cruelty in her smile surprises even me. "Are you really going to attempt to take the high moral ground here, Dad? I wouldn't bother, if I were you."

He bristles and starts to say something else but she turns to Martha before he can get the words out.

Her voice, oddly, becomes almost civil. "Hello, Martha. You look wonderful today." She pauses. "Have you lost weight?"

If I didn't know better, I could swear she was being sincere.

Martha, surprised, puffs up at the compliment. "Thank you, Caitlin." She gives me a pointed glance before going on. "Yes, I've found a terrific diet and it's doing wonders."

I nod with enthusiasm. "It certainly is!"

She gapes at me.

"Honestly, Martha, I'm being serious." I play with one of my earrings. In truth, she's gorgeous, and it makes me furious. "I really do believe you've lost at least a chin or two since I last saw you. Congratulations."

Bonnie seizes my arm again and pinches me. "That is absolutely *enough.*"

Martha purses her lips. "You have no right to speak to me like that."

My control begins to slide. "And you have no right to speak to me at all, Martha. Lying whores should be seen and not heard."

Tears of fury spring into her eyes and she begins to sputter. Arthur is so irate he's trembling. He looks at me for a long time with complete scorn, all the while fussing with his beard, then he turns his head back to Martha and squeezes her shoulders again.

"Don't pay attention to Hester, sweetheart," he murmurs loud enough for us all to hear. "She's just bitter because she lost her looks so many years ago." His hand drifts up to stroke her hair.

"Arthur!" Bonnie barks. "Not another word."

"Don't, Dad," Caitlin whispers.

Arthur ignores them both. "And not only that, she also knows I never loved her the way I love you." He kisses her cheek twice. "Ever." He fixes me with his arctic gray eyes, unblinking. "So pity poor old Hester, but don't let her get to you, okay?"

In some dim corner of my mind, I'm aware that the rest of the room has now fallen silent, except for a few nervous coughs somewhere behind me. Someone tosses something into the garbage; I can hear the creaking of the hinged metal lid on the top of the trash can as it swings back and forth. Out of the corner of my eye I see Viktor, watching me with concern. He's standing a few feet away with his arms folded over his soiled sweater. He looks like a lost little boy. Miranda Moore is here as well, in a cluster with several of my other students.

I feel dead inside. It's queer how dead I feel. "That's true enough, I suppose." I grope for words. "And far be it from me to argue with you about the quality of your so-called 'love.'"

I take a deep breath, recovering, and reach around Bonnie to retrieve a plastic cup full of pink fruit punch from the end of the refreshment table. "But then again . . ."

They're all watching me. Arthur, Martha, Bonnie, Caitlin, and the entire lobby full of people. Arthur's mouth is pressed into a thin, angry line, Martha has a triumphant gleam in her eye, Bonnie seems torn between sympathy and indignation. Caitlin, though, just looks resigned, as if she knows what's coming. She catches my eye, and a sad smile flickers across her face.

My smart girl. She's always been my smart girl.

". . . but then again," I repeat, "how could I possibly compare to Martha? It's not a fair contest." I cough before continuing. "After all, I'm just a human being, Arthur. If I'd known about your perverse fetish for flabby, bucktoothed Jersey cows, I never would have married you in the first place."

The stillness in the room is almost unbearable. Arthur releases Martha in a convulsive motion and takes a heavy, threatening step toward me, but then he seems to remember where he is and grinds to a halt again.

The dead feeling is gone, ousted by a sudden, cleansing wrath.

I raise my glass and salute him. "Well, kudos for your defiance of those bothersome bestiality laws, dear." I salute Martha as well. "To your health, Martha. Or, as you'd say it in your charming native tongue: MOO."

There's a gasp or two behind me, and what I could swear is several people trying very hard not to laugh.

Oh, my. Martha is so agitated her adorable Roman nose is quivering. And Arthur is clearly beside himself, too; he's almost panting with fury.

Without warning, Martha snaps. She cocks her arm back and with a loud hiss she flings her plate of cookies at me. I duck to get out of the way, but it turns out to be unnecessary; her aim is terrible. Aside from a half-eaten Oreo hitting Bonnie with some force in the stomach, all the rest of the goodies fall short and land harmlessly on the red carpet at our feet. The paper plate itself careens off Caitlin's thigh and glides under the table.

We all stare at Martha in amazement.

"How dare you!" she screams. Her whole body is shaking. "You vicious, horrid old *cunt*!"

I calmly inspect my drink. "Why are you so upset, sweetheart? Is my bovine pronunciation incorrect? Let me try again. Moo. Is that better?" I draw out the vowels for her. "Moooo? Moooo!"

She screams again and lunges forward. Arthur catches her arm as I toss my fruit punch in her face, ice and all. Her eyes go wide and she stands frozen in horror as the punch cascades down the front of her pretty dress.

Bonnie and Caitlin have disappeared somewhere when I wasn't looking. The cowards.

"Oh, dear," I cluck. "That's likely to leave a stain."

Arthur's words are quiet. "You'll pay for this, Hester. I swear to God, you'll pay for this." He grunts profanities in a steady stream as he moves to comfort Martha. He steps on a green-frosted sugar cookie on the way, crumbling it into dust.

The entire room seems to be holding its breath to see what will happen next. The show isn't over, not by a long shot. Martha is a serious drama queen, and we're all expecting a marvelous tantrum. Divas are so predictable.

Bless her. She doesn't let us down.

She turns into a madwoman. She throws herself at me again and again, but Arthur has both arms wrapped around her and won't let her go, and she howls and spits like a cat in a bathtub.

I applaud. "Bravissima, Martha! What a lovely aria. You've never been in better voice."

She covers her face and wails and bleats. "Make her staaaahhhhhp, Arthur, make her staaaaahhhpp! Pleeaaasse! Aaarrthuuuuurrrr . . ."

This is the happiest I've been in months.

I wait for her to quiet down again so I can say something else. Maybe I can actually cause her to have a stroke.

From out of the blue, Bonnie and Caitlin, working in tandem, seize me from both sides and escort me, protesting, to the lobby entrance. Caitlin is wearing her coat and Bonnie is carrying mine, along with my purse.

"What are you two simpletons doing?" I demand. "Have you lost your minds?"

Neither answers. I get one last glimpse of Arthur's splotchy, enraged face, then Bonnie pushes me through the door and out into the cold. I struggle to get away from them, but they don't let go of me until we're standing several feet away from the entrance. I continue to berate them even when we finally come to a stop on the concrete steps of the fine arts building. Caitlin ignores my tirade and moves to the side, breathing hard.

Bonnie stuffs my coat in my arms and tells me to shut up. Her voice is ragged and tired.

I bridle. "There's no need to be rude, Bonnie."

She hugs herself for warmth and searches my face.

I'm in no mood to be scrutinized by a dull-witted harpsichordist. "Is there a problem?" I demand. "I really don't appreciate being manhandled, by the way. I'm tempted to file a complaint."

She shifts her weight and grimaces. "I may have to fire you for this, Hester. "

I stare at her for a long time. "I'm tenured. You can't fire me for something this trivial." My breath turns to mist in the air and I put my coat on automatically, shivering.

"Don't be so sure about that." She hands me my purse when my hands are free. "Your tenure may indeed be an obstacle to your removal, but I promise that if I decide to get rid of you, you'll be gone, one way or another." She kicks at a piece of ice on the top step and rubs her temples. "In any case, don't bother to come back to work again until I call you."

With an abrupt nod to Caitlin, she turns away and disappears into the building again, leaving my daughter and me together outside. While the door remains open I can hear the ongoing pandemonium in the lobby. Martha is still bellowing at the top of her lungs and no one seems to know what to do with her. The door shuts again, showing me my reflection in the steamy glass.

The exhilaration I was feeling a moment ago is altogether gone, banished by shock and a sudden, horrible weariness. Arthur's apoplectic expression as I was being ushered out of the reception flashes through my mind; I don't think I've ever seen such hatred on a human face.

Surely that's not the reaction I wanted. Was it?

Surely not.

I examine myself as if I were a stranger, and my throat closes up. Dear Lord, I'm tired. From my shiny black shoes to my thin white hair, I look terribly old. Old and feeble.

I very much want to go home now.

I button my coat in silence before glancing at Caitlin's image in the door.

She frowns at me. "You've looked better, Mother."

I sigh. Good old Caitlin. I can always count on her when I'm feeling down.

"Yes, I'm well aware of that, thank you, dear." I pat my hair and open my purse to get my gloves and car keys.

She doesn't answer, and when I look up again her face in the glass is expressionless. Her eyes probe mine in the crude mirror, no doubt looking for a weakness to exploit.

Damn her.

I may be down, but I'm not so far down as that.

I force a smile and turn around again. "But a little wear and tear is to be expected, don't you think?" I have to fight to control the tremor in my hands as I tug on my gloves. "After all, these formal receptions take a great deal out of me. They're so dreadfully *boring*."

There's a long silence, but eventually the corners of her mouth turn up, just as I knew they would.

"God, Hester." She shakes her head. "You really haven't changed a bit, have you?"

She spins on her heels then and leaves me alone on the steps, wondering if I only imagined the faint note of tenderness in her voice as she spoke my name.

CHAPTER 10

"I don't want to do this, Mother."

Caitlin was standing by the piano, clutching her flute in front of her stocky chest as if it were a talisman against evil. Her thirteen-year-old face was twisted in misery as she glared at each of us, sitting together in a knot a few feet away from her. Arthur and I were sharing a piano bench in the middle of the room, and the boys were sprawled on the floor in front of us, leaning against each other and giggling like old drinking buddies at their favorite bar.

Caitlin was preparing for an audition with the St. Louis Youth Symphony the next day, and Arthur and I had thought it would be wise for her to play her orchestral excerpts and scales for an "audience" prior to the audition itself, to help her get over her pre-performance jitters. She had agreed with our plan at first, but now that she was on the spot in our music room, she was digging in her heels.

"I know you don't want to, dear, but it's for your own good," I told her. "And there's nothing to be embarrassed about. We're your family."

Arthur nodded. "Besides that, we've all been through this sort of thing more times than you can count, and you couldn't ask for a more sympathetic set of ears."

She rolled her eyes.

"That's right," Paul chimed in. "Just play, Caitlin. Jeremy and I promise not to make fun of you."

I reached down and ran my fingers through his clean brown hair. Arthur and I had spoken to both boys about being kind to their sister when it came to her musical endeavors, because we all knew how sensitive she was about her modest skills on the flute and the piano.

"Yeah," Jeremy said. "We'll just smirk behind our hands. You won't even notice we're doing it."

I jabbed him in the kidney with my toe. "Ignore him, Caitlin. There will be no smirking."

She held her flute tighter. "I said I don't want to."

Arthur's well of patience, never very deep, was quickly drying up. "For God's sake, child. Just be a good girl and trust that your mother and I know what we're doing, okay? It will only take ten minutes, and you'll feel much better about your audition when you're done."

I didn't know why she was being so obtuse, but thus far I wasn't taking her behavior too seriously. It was a superb spring afternoon outside, and the sun coming through the windows was lighting up the forest painting on the sides of my piano. Every time I looked at this imaginary forest, I saw something new. This morning I'd found what appeared to be the tail of a black squirrel, hidden in the crook of a tree.

I tried to jolly Caitlin along, so we could be done with this and enjoy the rest of the day. "The sooner you get through this, darling, the sooner you can go back to reading in your room and pretending none of us exist. Why don't you just start with a few major scales? You're quite competent at those."

"No," she said, adamant. "This dumb audition was your idea anyway, and you never even asked me if I wanted to be in the stupid symphony in the first place. You're just worried I'll play badly tomorrow and embarrass all of you in front of the whole world."

I blinked. "That's an absurd thing to say. Of course we want you to do well, but the only way you could possibly embarrass us is by doing what you're doing right now."

She stared at the floor. "No."

Jeremy spoke up. " If you're nervous, just picture Mom and Dad in their underwear. You'll be so traumatized you won't have to worry about anything else." He shuddered. "Oh, shit. Forget I said that, okay?"

The corners of her mouth quirked up, in spite of herself.

Paul laughed. "Yeah, that's good. Think about Dad in a pair of tighty-whities." He cackled. "And wearing one of Mom's bras, too, while you're at it." He glanced over his shoulder at Arthur. "You're starting to get man-boobs, by the way, Dad. I've been meaning to tell you that a bra might be a really good idea."

Arthur leaned over and gave Paul a shove, causing him to lose his balance and topple into Jeremy. Jeremy fell over, too, and both boys ended up flat on the floor, chortling.

Arthur glowered down at them. "I don't have 'man-boobs,' as you call them. I've simply been doing push-ups lately, if you must know, and my pectoral muscles have been getting larger as a result."

The boys laughed harder. Arthur's physical vanity was an easy target, and the children dearly loved to wind him up. I had to bite my cheeks to keep from laughing, too. The only push-up Arthur ever did was when he lifted himself from our mattress each morning on his way to the shower. He loathed exercise of any kind, and his sedentary lifestyle was beginning to catch up to him.

Jeremy rolled out from under his brother, fighting for oxygen. "Oh, I see. Those are your pectorals, then. Thank God. I thought they were silicone implants."

Paul howled and held his stomach. "Yeah, same here. I'm really relieved to know you're such an athlete, Dad. I was worried you might have been playing around with hormone therapy instead, so you and Mom could have a lesbian relationship."

Jeremy buried his face in Paul's side, choking with mirth.

"All right, all right," Arthur growled. "That's enough." He spoke with wounded dignity, but it was mostly an act. He knew quite well that both of them adored him, and he loved watching our sons have fun together, even when their silliness was at his expense. "Let's settle down. This nonsense isn't helping your sister to focus."

He returned his attention to our daughter, who was watching her siblings writhe about on the floor with an odd, bruised expression. Their closeness was something she was seldom part of, and her anger now seemed to be tinged with sadness, too.

When the boys were younger, they invented an asinine game called "Donkey Butt," which required four things—a Nerf ball, a basketball hoop, a piano, and the ability to make oneself belch. The rules of the game were as follows: Player One would shoot a basket, belch, and play a note on the piano. Player Two would follow suit, but play two notes—the first being the note Player One had played, the other of his own choosing. Player One would add a third note on his next turn, and so on, until a player at last bungled the notes in the sequence and lost the game. The real "catch" was that neither player was allowed to look at the keyboard as his opponent added a note. This posed no real obstacle in the first rounds (both boys were blessed with perfect pitch), but their impromptu "melodies" could sometimes exceed twenty notes, and were all over the keyboard, so eventually it became quite difficult, even for them.

And for Caitlin, it was impossible.

Her memory was more than equal to the task, but her musical "ear" was not. Nor did she have any inclination to grossness, or horseplay, which were both at the heart of everything her brothers did together. I don't believe Paul and Jeremy ever intended to exclude her from their relationship, but games such as these were exclusive by nature. In short, there was very little overlap between their world and hers, and though I knew she often felt like a third wheel around them, I could see no way—aside from asking the boys to give up the things they enjoyed doing together whenever she was around—to make her feel more welcome.

"I don't need to focus," she now blurted. "What I need is to be left alone. I'll be fine at the audition tomorrow, okay?"

Arthur ignored her. "Start with something really easy, sweetheart," he coaxed. "How about a 'C' scale?"

She stomped on the rug. "Why are you guys making me do this? What's the big deal?"

I put a hand on Arthur's arm. "We're only doing this for your sake, Caitlin. It would be good for you to earn a spot in the Youth Symphony."

She snorted. "You mean it might make me feel like less of a failure."

There wasn't much I could say to that. She was right, and we both knew it.

Arthur and I wanted so badly for her to succeed at something musical, because we saw, daily, how it hurt her to be so overshadowed by the rest of us. In any other family but ours, she would have been the golden child, due to her exceptional talents in many other fields. But with us, she could only see herself as the runt of the litter.

"You are not a failure." Arthur put his elbows on his knees and stared into her eyes. "And you can do this audition, if you'll just try."

Jeremy and Paul had finally sobered and were sitting upright again. Jeremy was watching Caitlin closely.

He cleared his throat before speaking to Arthur and me. "Don't make her do it if she doesn't want to, okay?" His voice became gentle. "It's just a stupid audition, Caitlin. It doesn't matter at all."

There were sudden tears on her face. "That's easy for you to say." She waved her flute at the rest of us. "It's easy for *all* of you to say. There's not one of you who's ever been anything less than Wolfgang *Fucking* Mozart." She brushed away her tears with impatience. "It's not fair. I'm sick of being the house retard."

Paul, too, was looking at her with concern. Unfortunately, tact was not one of his strong points, even when he was attempting to be kind.

"You're not a retard," he said. "You're just . . . I don't know. You're just musically challenged."

Caitlin flinched and Jeremy tried to shush him.

"Don't be an ass, man," he muttered. "That makes her sound like she should be in special ed courses or something."

Paul took umbrage at this. "That's not what I meant, and you know it." He turned back to Caitlin. "I just meant that music isn't your thing. We all know you're smarter than shit at everything else." He looked away. "Hell, you're smarter than all of us put together."

This was the first time I'd ever heard either of the boys acknowledge Caitlin's superior intelligence. The balance of power among the three of them was a tricky thing, and it was only her exposed vulnerability that allowed him to make this concession.

But it didn't help.

"So what?" she snapped. "Do you think that matters with this family?" She gazed with grief into the music on the stand in front of her. "I could win a Nobel Prize, and Mom and Dad wouldn't even notice. They'd just say, 'Caitlin, who?'"

Arthur and I were both stunned by this announcement. But while he just sat there in bewilderment, I was on my feet in an instant, enraged.

"That is the single most idiotic thing I've ever heard," I fired off. "Why in God's name would you say such a thing?"

"Don't, Mom," Jeremy implored. "She's just upset."

"Oh, hush, Jeremy." I turned back to Caitlin. "Do you really think your father and I give a damn that you're not exactly Jean-Pierre Rampal when it comes to the flute?"

She lifted her eyes from her stand and peered into my face. Her cheeks and forehead were flushed, and her nose was running. "Yes," she whispered. "I think you give a damn about that, Mother. You'll never admit it, of course, but that's the truth. The only thing that matters to either of you is music, and if you say otherwise, you're lying."

I fell into a troubled silence in the face of her conviction. She wasn't completely wrong, and I didn't know how to answer her.

Arthur and I loved Caitlin dearly, and were proud of her, in our fashion, for her mind, and her spirit, and her many, many gifts. But music was the heart and soul of our existence, and she was our only child who couldn't speak the language that we—and the boys—so effortlessly understood. And with that being the case—as Caitlin and I both knew it was—what could I say to her that wouldn't be a lie?

There are moments in my life that have stood out as particularly awful. This was one of them.

She spun away from whatever she saw in my expression, then, and she ran from the room. We all sat there, quietly, feeling sick, as we heard her feet on the stairs, and the door to her bedroom slamming shut. Arthur got up without a word and went to talk to her, but suffice it to say, she didn't end up playing for us that day.

And the next day her audition was a disaster. She played as badly as she could, as if to further illustrate her point.

On the drive home from St. Louis afterwards, I thought about my own mother. I thought about what my talent had done to her, and now to my daughter, as well. I hated that Caitlin was suffering, and, believe me, I would have given her a kidney, or a lung, to make her happy. Without a moment's hesitation, I would have reached into my own body and ripped out all my organs for her to use as spare parts.

But I also remember thinking, with shame, that even if there were a way to pull my talent out of me in the same manner, and hand it over to Caitlin, I probably would not be willing to do so.

Because my gift meant more to me than she did.

That's a horrible thing for a mother to say, but it's the truth. And it's just as true today as it was then.

I can assure you I am not proud of this. But nothing in my life has ever mattered more to me than my musical ability. Not my parents, not my children, not even Arthur. It is the only thing I own that no one else can touch, nor sully, and it is mine forever.

I hear music in each and every one of my dreams. I always have; even as a little girl this was the case. It was only when I was older that I realized most people don't have the same experience. And the thoughts that flit through my head when I'm awake often come with a melody of some kind as well, like a libretto for an opera. I do this automatically, and I couldn't stop if I tried. Nor do I want to. I require notes more than food, polyrhythms more than air.

And it's the same for Arthur. Our passion for music, and our ability to play it, is the strongest bond we have.

Caitlin was the apple of Arthur's eye. He doted on her because she was our youngest child, and our only daughter. Every time he came home from a tour, he brought her a gift—candy sometimes, or a sweater, or a book she'd been wanting—and he'd more often than not forget to pick up anything for the boys. Even when she was a teenager he would still sing her to sleep sometimes, when she'd let him, and she was the only person he'd allow in his study when he was in there reading. She shared his love of books, and silence, and the two of them would curl up together on his big chair for hours on cold winter afternoons, turning pages and not speaking.

But even so, Caitlin knew all too well where she truly stood with him. How could she not? Music always came first for Arthur, just as it did for me.

And I'm only beginning to understand the cost of this, for each of us.

CHAPTER 11

It's after four in the morning when Alex comes home, but I've been sitting here in the kitchen since two-fifteen, drinking chamomile tea (with brandy, of course), hoping desperately that it might put me to sleep. The fiasco at the reception earlier today—yesterday, now, I suppose—has been playing itself over and over in my mind, like an evil little melody. Especially the last part, when Arthur's face filled with disgust and loathing.

Disgust and loathing for me, as he bent over Martha.

To console her. And protect her.

From me.

Dear God. I may never sleep again.

The small lamp over the sink is the only light in the room I'm using, and there are shadows everywhere, beneath the table and the chairs, at the base of the cabinets and walls and appliances, and lurking around everything on the counters—the bread box, the microwave, the toaster, the spice rack. I'm living in a house of shadows, and they appall me. But I'm too tired to get up and turn on the lights, too tired to do anything but nurse my drink in the darkness.

When Alex opens the door I jump in my chair, frightened by the noise. He steps in and shuts the door behind him, then stands in the entryway, peering in at me. He's lost in the shadows, too; I can scarcely see his face from across the room.

"Hester?" he asks. "What are you still doing up?"

There's something wrong with his voice.

"Nothing, child. Nothing at all." I beckon him to come closer.

He keeps his distance. "The door wasn't locked. You should always lock your door at night."

His words are muffled and hesitant.

"I left it open for you." I gesture at him again. "Alex? What's wrong? Come in here and let me see you."

"I have my key," he murmurs. "It's not safe for you to keep the door unlocked, Hester. You're a little old woman, alone in a big house, full of antiques and stuff. Somebody could break in, and hurt you or something." He steps closer, into the circle of light by the sink. "It's not safe," he repeats.

His left eye is black and blue, and one side of his jaw is swollen. He's shivering violently, and there's a visible patch of dried blood at the corner of his mouth.

I shoot to my feet. "For God's sake, boy. What happened to you?"

"I'm fine," he whispers. "Don't make a big deal, okay? It was just a scuffle."

He's also intoxicated; the sour smell of beer fills the room.

"I beg your pardon? A scuffle?" I step over to him and put my hand up to examine his injuries. He shies away at first, but then allows me to put my fingers on his chin. I turn his head toward the light and wince. "You look as if you've been worked over by an angry mob, and you're asking me to not make a 'big deal' out of it." I release him in frustration. "So what should I make a fuss about, then? A public stoning?"

He just shrugs. "I'm okay, Hester. Really."

I look closer at him; there's a crust of ice on his flannel shirt and his jeans. I touch his collar and find it damp.

"Your clothes are wet, too! How did that happen?"

He gives me a twisted grin. "I fell into a ditch walking home, and broke through the ice. The water was a couple of feet deep underneath." He tries to pretend this is all a joke. "Oops."

"I see." I glare at him. "I assume this stupidity happened during your brawl?"

"After. I guess I wasn't paying much attention where I was going."

I push him toward the stairs. "Get out of those clothes immedi-ately, and go take a hot bath. You'll catch your death running around like that in this weather."

He nods and says okay, but then he just stares at me for a while. I give him another nudge and tell him to hurry, and he nods several more times before saying okay again and turning away.

Something in the set of his shoulders as he shuffles across the room twists at my heart. I don't know what happened to him tonight, but I'm certain it goes far deeper than a 'scuffle' and a mishap in a ditch.

"Alex?"

He stops but doesn't turn, as if he knows what I'm going to ask and doesn't want to face me. "Yeah?"

"Who hit you?"

He draws a slow breath, and lets it out again before answering. "Eric." His voice cracks. "It was Eric."

Eric. The likable, attractive boy who spent the night with him re-cently. The boy I believe I referred to at the time as "sweet."

Oh, dear. I think I can make an educated guess about what hap-pened between them tonight.

I bite my lip and soften my tone as much as I'm able. "Go get cleaned up, and warm, and then come back down if you feel like it. I'll make you a hot toddy, and we can talk."

He finally looks over his shoulder at me. "Okay." He studies me for a moment. "Are you sad about something, Hester? You look sad."

I pull back, surprised. I was so fixated on him I'd almost forgot-ten why I was sitting in my kitchen at four in the morning, drinking brandy.

Arthur and Martha. Caitlin, and Paul, and Jeremy.

My job, my house.

My life.

Despair wells up and I frown, not wanting to discuss any of this with him at the moment, for fear of coming undone. "What does that have to do with anything?"

He doesn't answer, and I look away, my lower lip quivering. I want him to take the hint and go away, now, like a normal human being would, but he doesn't budge. He simply stands there, waiting for me.

Irritating child.

As if he knows that I'm as bad off as he is. As if he's actually concerned about me, in spite of his own obvious problems. As if I matter to him.

He's still waiting.

I blink away tears, moved by his stubbornness.

The despair eases a bit, and I take a deep breath and look up at him again. "Yes, dear. I'm afraid I am a bit low this morning." I gaze into his damaged face for a long time. "But then again, I'm not the only one, am I?"

His blue eyes fill.

I shoo him upstairs. "Go get warm, son, right now. Then come back down here, if you can stay awake that long." I hug myself and sigh. "I believe it's time we had a long talk, don't you?"

By the time Alex returns to the kitchen, I've managed to rouse myself enough to turn on the overhead light and assemble the ingredients for his hot toddy. It's too bright in here now, but at least the worst of the shadows have been herded into hiding beneath the refrigerator and the liquor cabinet.

I'm standing at the counter slicing a lemon when he steps into the room after his shower. He's dressed in a white T-shirt and dark blue sweatpants, and of course he's barefoot. He looks a bit less fragile now, although his bruised eye is still ghastly and the skin on his jaw is scraped raw.

He winces at the light. "Wow. That's really bright."

"Yes, it is," I agree. "If you'd like, we can go into the living room after I'm done brewing this potion."

He shrugs. "That's okay. This is fine."

I turn to pour hot tea from the pot into two mugs. He comes over to see what I'm doing and raises his eyebrows.

"There's tea in a hot toddy?" He leans over and gives the steam rising from the mugs a suspicious sniff. "What else goes in it?"

I add the other ingredients as I list them aloud: "A few drops of honey . . . two shots of brandy, like this . . . and a slice of lemon.

There. Perfect." I pause, considering, and reach for the bottle of Courvoisier again. "Did I say two shots of brandy? I meant three."

He manages a tired grin. His long red hair is wet, but for once it's combed. "You're just making this up as you go along, aren't you?"

I smile back at him and wave him toward a seat at the table. "I'm told that some primitives don't put tea in their hot toddies, but I prefer not to associate with people of that ilk." I bring him his mug and set it in front of him. "Let this cool a mite before you drink it."

I settle across from him with my own mug, and we sit in silence for a while. I decide to not speak first; if he wants to talk about what happened to him earlier tonight, he will.

He sips at his drink and stares at the table. The grin he dredged up a moment ago is gone again, replaced by a bone-deep misery that declares itself in the slackness of his chin and the corners of his mouth. The seconds tick by and the house is so quiet it feels as if it's holding its breath, waiting to hear what he has to say. The furnace is temporarily off and the air in the room is cool and light, and I can feel a draught pass through my hair, like a ghostly finger.

He clears his throat and raises his eyes to my face. "Did you ever do anything horrible, Hester?" His hands tremble a little as they cup the mug in front of him. "I mean, like something so bad you can't even believe you did it?"

In an instant, Jeremy is in my mind, standing on the roof in the cold.

I close my eyes, then force myself to open them again. "Of course I have, child." I lick my dry lips. "But so has almost everybody, I'd imagine." I pause. "Why do you ask?"

He begins to shake. The quiver starts in his shoulders and works its way down his entire back as his eyes spill tears on his cheeks. "I did something bad tonight, Hester. Really, really bad." He releases his mug and puts his face in his hands. When he speaks again I can barely understand him. "It's not the first time, either."

I gaze at the crown of his head. With his hair wet like this I can see a line of his scalp, pale and vulnerable under the dark red mass. He seems disinclined to continue, so I try to ease his way.

"You did something with Eric you regret?" I ask.

He nods. "Yeah." He swallows several times and fights to control his breathing. "We got wasted in his dorm room, and he passed out on his bed. And then . . ." he drops his hands and stares into my face, ". . . and then I started to do stuff to him while he was blacked out."

His eyes are red and bleak, and his normally attractive face is knotted with anguish. "I unzipped his pants and started, you know, started to . . ." The rest of his sentence is utterly lost, mangled by sobs.

I sigh. "And I take it he woke up?"

Another nod. "Yeah." He wipes his runny nose on his short sleeve. "He opened his eyes all of a sudden and completely lost it when he saw what I was doing. Like he went fucking nuts, and started beating the shit out of me." He dissolves in another spate of tears. "All I wanted was to be close to him. That's all. I didn't mean anything bad."

I reach across the table and squeeze his thin wrist. "I know, dear."

And I do know. I really do.

He's looking at me skeptically, as if he's expecting censure rather than consolation. On some level he probably even wants to be punished, as a way to atone for his perceived "sin."

But I can't help him with that.

I've done so many things in my life I'm not proud of, and would take back in an heartbeat if I could. Drunken indiscretions not so different than his (including a botched attempt to seduce another pianist at his own engagement party when I was seventeen), and harsh words and deeds aimed at family and friends and colleagues, and harmful, ugly actions reserved for total strangers and the world in general.

Witness my behavior at yesterday's reception, for example.

So if he's seeking condemnation tonight for being young, lustful and foolish, he's come to the wrong place.

I lean forward and search his eyes. "As such things are measured, Alex, what you did this evening doesn't sound so terrible."

He shakes his head violently and pulls away from my grip. "You don't understand," he blurts. "Didn't you hear what I said? This wasn't the first time! I did it the other night, too, only he didn't wake up then because I didn't go as far."

I twine my hands around my mug for warmth. "Even so, I think you're being a bit hard on yourself, don't you?"

"Am I?" He laughs, and it's a dreadful sound. "What if I told you that I did the exact same thing last semester with another guy, in my hometown, too? And that time it got so bad the guy woke up my whole family screaming for help, because I was bigger than he was and he couldn't make me stop by himself?"

I flinch a little without meaning to, and he sees it and closes his eyes. When he opens them and speaks again, his voice is dripping with self-laceration.

"His name was Wei-shan. He was a Chinese exchange student at Buckland." He sees the question on my face and halts to give me an impatient explanation. "Buckland's the college in my hometown. My mom works there."

Ah. So that's where he attended school before transferring to Pritchard this term. I know next to nothing of Buckland, other than it being a small liberal arts college somewhere in Iowa.

"Anyway, Wes—that's what everybody called Wei-shan—came to stay with me and my family at Thanksgiving, because the dorms were closed," he continues. "He had to share my bed since it's a small house, and we were drunk and stoned and one thing led to another, and I thought he was into it, too, but he wasn't and then things got so fucked up I can't even begin to describe it."

But he does.

He tells me about the Chinese boy bucking beneath him and bellowing in panic as Alex attempted to cover his mouth and calm him down. He tells me how he, Alex, realized at the last moment that Wei-shan wasn't just "wrestling" with him as he'd first thought, and he was trying to defuse the situation when his parents and his two younger sisters barged into the bedroom and saw both boys naked on the bed, with Alex pinning the smaller, struggling, and nearly incoherent Wei-shan beneath him. He tells me how his parents—conservative Lutherans—gave him no opportunity to explain what was happening, and instead threw him out into the night with nothing but a backpack full of clothes and toiletries. And he tells me of arranging a transfer to Pritchard over Christmas vacation, and how he somehow managed to cobble together enough loans and grants and scholarships to cover his tuition and living expenses, after his parents withdrew all financial support.

I listen to him until the flood of words becomes a trickle and finally dries up, and then I watch him drink his hot toddy and wait for me to say something.

I clear my throat at last. "I see." I sip my drink. "So you've had no contact with your family since Thanksgiving?"

He blinks, apparently anticipating a different response. "None. They told me they never want to see me again." He searches my face for some sign as to what I'm thinking. "So I guess you must think I'm a piece of shit?"

I shake my head. "Not at all. I don't believe for a moment you intended harm to either of those boys, or that you would have continued to try to force yourself upon them once it became clear to you what their wishes were."

His eyes are a wasteland. "You weren't there, Hester. You didn't see what I was like." He stares at the wall. "I may have stopped tonight if Eric had asked me nicely instead of punching me in the face, but I'm not sure at all about that. And even though I *was* going to let go of Wei-shan when I finally figured out he wasn't playing, I sure as hell didn't let myself see how upset he was getting until he was a complete basket case."

His head swings back around and he pierces me with his gaze. "I'm a fucking asshole, Hester. A sick fucking asshole." Once again, his face crumbles, like a sand castle. "I don't think I can live with myself after this."

The desolation in his voice is the twin of what I've been feeling for years. I can't help but wonder if mine is as obvious.

"Yes, you can." I take several calming breaths. "You can live with anything, if you have to."

And without intending it, I begin to tell him about Jeremy.

CHAPTER 12

When Jeremy finished his undergraduate degree at Curtis he was only twenty years old, but by then he'd already been a member of the Philadelphia Orchestra for two years, and had won four young artist concerto competitions around the country. He was also a featured soloist with the Boston Symphony at Tanglewood in the summer between his junior and senior years, and had released an album of chamber music, in collaboration with some of the top names in the business. *The New York Times* had referred to him as "a magnificent, prodigiously gifted musician," and the *Los Angeles Times* dubbed him "the finest young classical artist to emerge in the United States, bar none, in the last decade." Elijah Jenkins (that crotchety old tosspot at the *New Yorker*) even went so far as to joke, "Scoff if you must, but it seems plain to me that wunderkind Jeremy Donovan has made a bargain with Satan. Granted, his sterling musical pedigree accounts for much of his vaunted prowess on the French horn, but not even a child of Arthur Donovan and Hester Parker can do such impossible things without supernatural assistance."

I mention all this not only as a gloating mother, but also by way of explanation for why Carson Conservatory was so eager to offer him a faculty position immediately following his graduation, in spite of his age and lack of an advanced degree. Arthur and I didn't even have to pull any strings for him; the instant Jeremy received his diploma he was contacted, without our knowledge, by Bonnie

Norton, who somehow wooed him back to Carson, even though he was receiving teaching offers from all over the world. (Nor was teaching his only option; he could easily have walked into any of half a dozen major symphony positions available at the time, in cities as diverse and appealing as San Francisco or London.) I know for a fact he was offered a tenure track position at no less than three major universities.

But he chose to return home instead.

Until the moment he called to tell us the news, I had been certain Jeremy would be our one child to leave the nest forever, and nothing could have astonished me more than to hear he was taking the job at Carson, and would be home by the end of the week.

I stared at the phone receiver for a moment, dumbfounded.

"Why in God's name would you do such a thing?" I barked. "Did you injure your head?"

"I'm fine, Mother." He laughed. "Believe it or not, I thought you'd be happy to have me home again."

"That's not the point, and you know it." I put my hand over the mouthpiece to talk to Arthur, who had just walked into the room. "Jeremy says Bonnie offered him a job, and the glue-sniffing idiot is actually going to take it. Can you believe the stupidity?"

Arthur crowed. "That's fantastic!" He tried to seize the phone, and failing that, contented himself with bellowing so Jeremy could hear him. "Hurry home, son!"

"Oh, hush, Arthur." I spoke to Jeremy again. "Pay no attention to the dimwit in the background. All I'm saying is you should take a while and spread your wings. Go do something exciting before you settle down."

"Like what?" Jeremy giggled. "Join the Hare Krishnas? Become a ninja?"

He loved getting my goat.

"Don't be difficult." I paused. "I only want what's best for you, son. You have the opportunity right now to build a wonderful life. There's nothing for you in Bolton that can possibly equal what you'll get elsewhere."

He grunted. "Nothing except a great job at one of the top music schools in the country. Nothing except my home and my entire family, including my wonderfully supportive mother. Nothing except easy access to Chicago and St. Louis and anywhere else on the planet I want to go, by plane." He hesitated. "Come on, Hester. Why all the resistance? What's going on?"

All my children called me by my first name when they were irritated with me. It was as if they were too ashamed at those moments to claim me as their mother.

"I just want you to stop and think a little bit." I played with the phone cord. "I was forced to abandon my solo career when I was only slightly older than you are now, and I can't tell you how much I missed it when it was gone." I turned my back on Arthur, so he couldn't see my face. "I'm afraid if you move home this soon after college, you'll become like Paul, and settle for less than you should."

Paul, too, had been hired at Carson a year before, after earning his master's degree, and had since made it clear he had no intention of leaving for the rest of his life. (In his case, Arthur and I *had* pulled strings to get him the job; unlike his younger brother, Paul had no claim to fame aside from having "Donovan" as a last name. Not that he didn't deserve the position, mind you—he was, and is, one of the finest cellists in America—but without our assistance, Carson would have overlooked him for somebody with a more established reputation.) I had, of course, argued with him, too, about staying in Bolton, but given his deep-seated phobia regarding the outside world—and his likely inability to survive elsewhere—my resistance was only halfhearted.

But Jeremy had no such handicap.

Jeremy snorted. "Don't be dumb. I love Paul, but I've never been like him. Why should I start now?"

"I'm just saying that teaching may end up sapping the energy you need to sustain your soloist aspirations."

"Oh, for God's sake." I could hear him grinding his teeth. "The only thing that ever saps my energy is talking to you." He took a deep breath. "Dad tours six months a year, every year, and teaching at Carson hasn't slowed him down at all. Why should it be any different for me?"

I didn't answer and after a moment amusement crept back into his voice. "And by the way, I'm beginning to understand why Dad enjoys leaving home so much."

I glared at the phone. "That's very droll, Jeremy. When your music career collapses perhaps you can earn a living as a court jester. I can hardly wait to see you in your pointy slippers and your codpiece." I sighed. "Fine. Move back to Bolton, then. See if I care when the entire world forgets who you are."

He was unfazed, of course. "There's my optimistic girl," he said brightly. "Always so gracious in defeat." His tone mellowed. "I'll be fine, Mother. I promise."

When he was sweet, I had no defense against him.

"You better be," I whispered. "You don't get a second chance at life."

"Are you sure?" He laughed again, breaking the mood. "I forgot to mention I've become a Jehovah's Witness, and I get to come back and live happily ever after, no matter what. It's a hell of a deal, don't you think?" There was a predictable beat of silence. "Incidentally, do you have room for a few dozen boxes of pamphlets in your basement?"

I hung up on him, fuming.

He called back within seconds. "Lighten up, would you? I'll be home in a few days, and I'll let you lecture me for as long as you want. Think how much fun you'll have." There was another pause. "Oh, yeah. I also forgot to tell you earlier how much I love you."

He hung up before I could answer, and I listened to the dial tone for a long time afterwards.

So for a while all the Donovans were living in the same house again. (When Jeremy returned to Bolton, Caitlin was beginning college at Northwestern, but she still came home "to visit" virtually every weekend.) And no, it wasn't all picnics and parties and happy gatherings at the holidays, but for the first year or so it was peaceful enough, even pleasant. We had many common interests, and there was always good music-making to be had, and company when you wanted it, and more often than not some kind of stimulating argument going on.

Paul stayed in the attic apartment, and Jeremy and Caitlin slept in their rooms on the second floor, across the hall from Arthur and me. That kind of proximity between five prima donnas may seem like a recipe for open warfare, but Arthur was touring a great deal that year, and as Jeremy began receiving invitations to perform elsewhere, he, too (as promised), was soon spending much of his time on the road. In addition to that, Caitlin was in Chicago five days a week, and Paul and I were both in demand at Carson, so with all these comings and goings, it was a crapshoot who would be home on any given night, and privacy, when needed, was usually not hard to come by—especially in a house the size of ours.

The brawls that did break out were mostly between the children, although Arthur and I seldom managed to stay out of the fray when a heated "discussion" was going on. Nine times out of ten, Paul was the instigator of the feud, but Caitlin, too, could never resist being part of a good bloodbath; the two of them thrived on confrontation, especially when the other was involved.

And then there was Jeremy.

Since his return to Bolton, Jeremy had, surprisingly, taken on the role of peacekeeper in the family, but now and then he'd wake in a wretched mood and pick a fight with Paul or Caitlin, for no other purpose than to rile them up. The mean streak he'd evinced as a child almost never surfaced as an adult—thankfully—but when it did, the tension level in the house ratcheted up several notches.

I remember a battle royal, particularly, that Jeremy caused in this fashion, and it happened to be on one of those rare occasions when all five of us were home. Caitlin and I were in the kitchen on a Saturday morning having a quiet breakfast, and both of us looked up when Jeremy appeared in the doorway, with rumpled hair and a black frown.

"Good morning," I said. "Would you like some tea?"

He shook his head and wandered over to the refrigerator to hunt for his breakfast. He was barefoot and bare chested, and had on a pair of jeans. He was awfully thin; his ribs stuck out and he looked as if a lapdog could knock him down. When he walked by the table I smelled cigarette smoke oozing from his pores.

Both he and Paul smoked far more than was good for them. I

didn't allow them to smoke in the house, so when they were home they went outside dozens of times a day, no matter what the weather, to stand beside St. Booger and get their fix.

Caitlin smelled the smoke, too; her nose wrinkled up. "What's your new cologne called? *Eau de Ashtray?*"

This kind of jab from Caitlin was by no means unusual; ordinarily Jeremy wouldn't have thought a thing of it.

He glared over the open refrigerator door at her. "I'm impressed you can smell anything over that rotting tuna fish perfume you seem to favor."

Paul was not above this kind of crude rejoinder, but for Jeremy it was quite harsh.

"Jeremy!" I chided. "That's beneath you."

"Don't bother, Mother. He's just looking for attention." Caitlin narrowed her eyes at him. "I'm so glad to see that you aren't intimidated by women to the point where you feel the need to lash out at them in the most childish manner possible."

He snorted and poked his head back in the refrigerator. "Oh, don't be so sensitive, Caitlin." He pulled out a package of English muffins, a stick of butter and a pitcher of orange juice and closed the door with his foot. "I was just attempting to remind you of the concept of proper feminine hygiene. Mother apparently neglected that part of your training."

On cue, Paul wandered into the room in a bathrobe, bleary-eyed. "Part of what training?"

"Never you mind." I pointed a finger at Jeremy. "Stop this prepubescent behavior immediately. What's gotten into you?"

"Nothing." He put down the orange juice and the butter on the table and then stole my knife to slice his English muffin in half. He looked around. "Where's the toaster?"

I took back my knife and handed him a clean one from the pile on the table before pointing toward the counter. "There, next to the microwave."

"Why'd you move it?" he grumbled. "It's been by the stove forever."

Paul plopped down in the chair at the opposite end of the table from me. "I meant to congratulate you for that, Mother. Relocating the toaster was truly a bold move." He reached for a bagel. "I had no idea you were such a rebel."

Caitlin was drumming her fingers on the tablecloth; a sure sign that she was planning a retaliatory strike against Jeremy.

I attempted to divert her before she could speak. "Caitlin, dear, what was that book you were telling me about last week? The mathematical one with Bach in it?"

She raised a dark eyebrow at me. "*Gödel, Escher, Bach*, and stop pretending you don't remember." She stared over her shoulder at Jeremy, who had moved over to the toaster and was standing with his back to us. "Speaking of genital hygiene, Jeremy . . ."

"Excuse me?" Arthur shuffled into the kitchen, dressed in casual slacks and a sweatshirt. "I'm rather certain I don't want to hear the end of that sentence, sweetheart."

Jeremy turned around. "I do. Go ahead, little sis. Let me have it."

She ran her tongue around on her teeth under her lip, a habit I'd been trying to break her of for years because it made her look like a thoughtful monkey. "Well, I was just going to say that while cleaning *any* part of yourself would be a distinct improvement, I understand why you've especially avoided using soap and water on your groin." She peered into her teacup. "After all, the scars from when Sarah neutered you must be difficult reminders of your pre-eunuch existence."

Sarah Weinstein had been Jeremy's only serious girlfriend since he moved back home. She severed their relationship after a few months, however, and for weeks afterwards Jeremy had been heartbroken, moping around the house and bursting into tears every time her name was mentioned. He still wasn't entirely over her.

His thin, handsome face purpled and his voice dropped. "I can't believe you just said that."

I could. Caitlin always said whatever was guaranteed to hurt the most. Always.

"Oh, don't be so sensitive, Jeremy," she mimicked with precision.

Paul hid a smile behind his hand.

"That's enough," Arthur said flatly. "I've had a very long week, and I don't want to listen to this bickering while I'm having breakfast."

His "long week" of touring had ended—in a rather animalistic fashion, I blush to add—the previous night in our bed.

"Yes, indeed," I murmured. "Your father is exhausted. It's a wonder the poor old dear made it down the stairs this morning without assistance."

He tried to suppress a boyish grin without success. "Behave yourself, Hester. The last thing we need right now is another child in the room."

But Jeremy was only getting warmed up.

He crossed his arms over his chest. "As long as we're on the subject of ex-lovers, shall we talk about Sebastian?"

"Don't you dare, Jeremy," Caitlin warned, flushing. "Don't you *fucking* dare."

We all stared at her, caught off guard by her ferocity.

"Go ahead, Jeremy," Paul interjected, leaning forward, "I think I'd like to hear this."

"Shut up, Paul," Arthur grunted. He sat across from Caitlin and put his elbows on the table. He cleared his throat after a moment and assumed a casual attitude. "Who's this Sebastian, darling?"

I tapped my chin with my index finger. "Yes, I believe I'd like to know that, too. Do tell."

Caitlin's love life—or lack thereof—was a total mystery to her father and me. She had always been notoriously tightlipped about the subject of men and romance (so much so that in private Arthur and I had often speculated about her sexuality), and while it was possible she had been in and out of love on numerous occasions, we had been given no reason to believe this was the case, especially considering she was barely eighteen.

She fidgeted with her napkin. "Nobody. Just an acquaintance."

Jeremy nodded. "Hmm. I see. An acquaintance." His English muffin popped up and he half-turned to deal with it. "So do you allow all of your acquaintances to ride you bareback like a circus pony?"

There was a stunned silence, then Paul burst out laughing. "Way to go, Caitlin. You finally got laid!"

She rose to her feet, furious, flipped her long black hair off her forehead and locked eyes with Jeremy. "You are the lowest of the low. I will never forgive you for this."

Jeremy gave her a sweet smile and turned to Paul. "You'd think losing her virginity would have made her more affable, wouldn't you?"

Paul chortled. "Maybe Sebastian didn't know what he was doing. I'm not surprised, though. With a name like that it had to have been his first time, too."

"Shut up, Paul," Arthur and I said at the same time, without heat, then we stared at each other, at a loss for words.

Neither of us were prudes, nor were we naïve enough to be shaken overmuch by this type of disclosure. Mind you, I wasn't thrilled to hear that my daughter was now sexually active, but what surprised me far more than Caitlin's loss of virginity was that Jeremy knew about it before I did.

Arthur glanced over at Jeremy and then back to our daughter, still on her feet and rigid with indignation. "Is this true, sweetheart?" He was apparently thinking along the same lines as I. "And if it is, why did you tell Jeremy?"

Jeremy winked at Caitlin in a conspiratorial fashion, not at all fazed by her rage. "Shall I relate the story, or do you want to? It's a good one."

"Goddamn you," she whispered. "I will never trust you again."

His smile faltered, but I believe I was the only one who saw that, because he recovered in the blink of an eye. He sauntered over to the table and slid into the chair beside Paul, acting for all the world as if this was nothing more than a pleasant family conversation over breakfast.

"Let's set the stage first, shall we?" He buttered his English muffin slices while talking. "It was a dark and stormy night . . ."

"Shut the fuck up!" Caitlin snarled.

Arthur frowned at her. "I understand you're upset, honey, but there's no need to use obscene language."

I laughed. "Oh, that's rich, dear. Where do you think she learned to speak like that? During her long stint in the merchant marines?"

He stuck out his jaw. "Don't start with me, Hester."

Jeremy cleared his throat. "You guys are interrupting my story."

Caitlin balled her hands into fists and pressed her knuckles into the table top. "There is no *story,* you sadistic piece of shit."

Paul reached over to Jeremy's plate and claimed half of the English muffin. "Don't be so modest, Caitlin. Let's hear all the gory details. For instance, was there leather involved? Or maybe some handcuffs?"

Jeremy giggled. "None that I saw."

Paul gaped at him. "Good God, you actually witnessed our little sister's deflowering and didn't take pictures?" He bit off a large chunk of muffin and spoke with his mouth full. "I am so disappointed in you."

"He didn't see a *thing.* Not a *goddamn thing.*" Caitlin slapped the table in frustration and all the dinnerware jumped. "I swear to God, Jeremy, I'll make you regret this for the rest of your life."

I snatched up my mug but not before most of the tea in it had sloshed over the rim and made a mess. "Calm yourself, Caitlin." I dabbed at the spilled liquid with my napkin. "You're overreacting."

She glared at me. "I can't believe you just said that, Mother! Jeremy is humiliating me in front of all of you and you're just sitting there, letting him!"

I sighed. "I only meant that if you're worried about your father and I punishing you for something like this, you have nothing to fear. It's fine, as long as you're being careful."

Tears filled her eyes and she shook her head violently. "For God's sake, Hester. Do you think I'm worried about a *spanking*? I'm asking you to shut him up because what he's talking about is nobody else's business! I'm an adult and I have a right to my privacy, even in this stupid, dysfunctional family."

I nodded. "You're right, of course. Jeremy . . ."

"Our family is not dysfunctional," Arthur objected. "A little high-strung perhaps, but not dysfunctional."

We all stared at him in silence.

"Why are you all looking at me like that?" he demanded, flush-ing. "I'm just tired of hearing my children run this family down. It's not healthy."

There was another long pause, broken at last by an exaggerated cough from Jeremy.

"As I was saying," he continued, "I showed up at Caitlin's dorm room one evening last semester while I was in Chicago, thinking I'd surprise her by taking her out for a late night snack or something, but when she answered the door I got quite a shock."

Caitlin began to hop up and down. "Goddamn you! *Shut your fucking mouth!*"

Paul took the rest of Jeremy's English muffin since Jeremy wasn't eating. "You certainly seem to have fucking on the brain, Caitlin."

"Shut up, Paul!" she howled.

Jeremy made a clucking sound with his tongue. "She only opened the door a crack, but I was still able to see that all she was wearing was a sheet, wrapped around her shoulders."

Caitlin stalked away from the table, headed for the stairway. "I'm done with this conversation. You can all go to hell."

He raised his voice, stopping her in her tracks before she could reach the door. "And when I looked over her head, what do you think I saw sprawled out naked on her bed?"

He nursed the quiet with the intensity of a seasoned actor. Caitlin was directly behind him now, staring at the floor. Jeremy kept his back to her deliberately, and made eye contact with the rest of us, studying each of our faces in turn. He came to me last, and I shook my head at him and mouthed the words, "Please stop this."

He ignored me and resumed his narrative. "It was a rather beau-tiful young man, obviously asleep, face up." He raised his eyebrows. "Granted, I couldn't see much of him because there was only about a two-inch strip of light coming from the hallway, but I could still make out a muscled thigh, and a hairless, sculpted torso, and a chin so flat and chiseled you could use it for a doorstop."

He turned his head slightly, to speak over his shoulder. "How old is Sebastian, by the way? Are you sure he's legal? He looked about sixteen."

She didn't answer.

Jeremy grinned. "No matter, I suppose. Anyway, when Caitlin saw it was me, she tried to slam the door in my face—that was quite rude, darling, by the way—but when she realized I had seen her dozing boy toy, she stepped into the hallway and lectured me about the *dire* need for secrecy and the *earth-shattering* consequences that would result for everybody involved, should I reveal what I had seen to anyone."

He shrugged. "Oops, now I've done it." He staged a yawn. "Could you pass the salt, Mother?"

Caitlin spoke without turning around. "You made a promise to me that night to keep what you saw between us. A promise." She spun to face us. "But now that the secret's out and you're all having a good laugh, maybe you should also know that Sebastian happens to be my best friend's husband, and I feel like shit about sleeping with him." She sobbed. "Pretty funny stuff, huh?"

Arthur and I flinched and Paul emitted a low whistle.

Jeremy wheeled in his chair. "What?" His voice was thin. "You didn't tell me that. All you said was a lot of melodramatic stuff about your right to privacy." He foundered for words. "It sounded lame, and I thought you were just being eighteen. I'm sorry, okay? If you'd told me this then, I wouldn't have said anything."

I studied the red birthmark on his back, on his left shoulder blade, in the shape of a half-moon, and tried to think of something appropriate to say under the circumstances. Nothing came to me. Arthur muttered something about "poor judgment all around," but Caitlin didn't hear him.

"Oh, you're sorry, are you?" She gave Jeremy a brittle, phony smile. "Fine. That makes it all better, then. No hard feelings. We'll just pretend like this never happened."

"If I could take it back, I would, but I can't." He turned back to the table, chewing on his cheeks. "What else can I say?"

His apology, far from calming her down, incensed her further. Her voice became strident. "How about something along the lines of *'I'm a complete piece of shit, Caitlin, and it's no wonder Sarah dumped me, because I'm pathetic and scrawny and worthless?'*"

His expression froze. "Tell me something, Caitlin." He picked up a fork and poked the tips of his fingers with the tines. "How soon after I left you that night were you guys humping again? Fifteen minutes? An hour? Have you and his wife ever had a threesome?"

Tears spilled from her eyes and ran down her face. "You goddamn bastard."

"Stop, Jeremy," Paul muttered, surprising all of us. "That's enough."

Arthur gazed at me in helpless supplication from across the table, giving me his patented "For God's sake, do something" look. I made a face at him and put my spoon down next to my cereal bowl, intending to go to Caitlin and hug her.

I never got the chance.

Caitlin leapt at Jeremy and landed on his back, and he crumpled under her assault and flew forward into the table, knocking it over. Everything on it went flying as Jeremy's chair tipped over, too, and the next thing I knew Caitlin was sitting on top of him on the floor in a puddle of milk and tea and orange juice, slapping his face and shoulders with all her strength.

He didn't fight back. He just allowed her to hit him, over and over, until Arthur and Paul finally lurched into motion and dragged her off.

Caitlin didn't attempt to break away once they had her on her feet, and the three of them stood in shocked silence, looking down at Jeremy. I think Caitlin was as amazed as the rest of us at what had just occurred. I was still in my chair, immobilized, with an upside-down bowl of Rice Krispies in my lap.

Jeremy slowly sat up. His eyes were bright with disregarded tears. Caitlin had been hitting him hard enough to leave livid handprints all over his skin.

He cleared his throat and ran his fingers through his matted hair. "Well. I don't know about the rest of you, but I really think we should do these family breakfasts more often." He stared at the mess around him and sighed. "Is this what they mean by quality time?"

That was not a stellar day for the Donovan family.

But this sort of chaos wasn't the norm in our household. It really wasn't. We had many, many times together when nothing was broken, and no sordid secrets were revealed, and no one hated anybody else. And in retrospect, the good times far outweighed the bad.

Honestly, they did.

It's just that the bad times stick in the memory more, for some reason. And I believe they also point the way to understanding what happened, finally, to Jeremy. Good moments in one's life are just that—good moments. They go nowhere, they just *are*. But bad moments have a clear destination. You may not know where they're headed at the time, but later, when the story is fully told, they're as easy to follow as footprints in the snow.

Anyway, as angry as Caitlin was that morning, she eventually forgave Jeremy, because most of the time he was as good as gold, and when Jeremy was killed no one took it worse than she did, not even Paul.

Oh, dear. There I go again.

I'm lying, of course.

One person took it far, far worse.

And that's as it should be, really. After all, when you're the party most directly responsible for another's death, you should be the one who suffers the most, don't you agree?

CHAPTER 13

"I'm driving." Alex reaches for my car keys when I remove them from my purse in the entryway.

"You most certainly are not," I snap, holding them away from him.

We're on our way to the grocery store. It's mid-afternoon on a Monday and ordinarily I'd be teaching and he'd be in class, but Bonnie Norton still hasn't called to give me permission to return to work, and Alex is playing hooky from Pritchard, for fear of running into Eric.

He puts his hands on his hips. "Hester. There's freezing rain all over the roads today. It'll be really slick out."

"I'm fully aware of the condition of the roads," I sniff. "Which is why I'm the one who should be driving. I have far more experience behind the wheel."

"Maybe," he mutters, "but you still drive like shit."

I bristle and he rushes to head off the explosion. "I'm just saying I'm a really good winter driver. You can pretend I'm your chauffeur and order me around and stuff, like in that old chick flick my mom used to watch all the time. *Driving Miss Doofus*, or something like that."

I shake my fist at him. "I have no need of a chauffeur! I'm an excellent driver, no matter the weather." As fond as I'm becoming of him, I will not allow him to treat me in this fashion. "And if I were you, I'd begin groveling immediately, unless you intend to to walk to the grocery store."

He rolls his eyes. "Oh, for God's sake. I'm just trying to help."

"That may be, but I require no assistance from a chauvinistic young man who is getting much too big for his britches. Do I make myself clear?"

I'm more on edge than I should be. Tomorrow is the pretrial conference with Arthur and our lawyers, and worrying about it is making me irritable.

He grimaces. "Okay, fine, whatever. You drive. But I'm going to wear a motorcycle helmet and ride in the back seat."

As infuriating as his attitude is, I must say I'm pleased to see him put up a bit of a fight. When he finally went to bed after our heart-to-heart, pre-dawn discussion this morning at the kitchen table, he trailed up the stairs to his apartment like a zombie. Yet here he is a mere nine and a half hours laters, bruised and rumpled—and highly annoying—but at least functional.

I wave him outside. "Be a dear and go open the carriage house door for me," I grate. "Then stand perfectly still in the middle of the driveway, so I can run over you."

He steps out on the porch and shivers as the cold wind hits him. "You might want to hold off on that," he grunts as I follow after him. "What if you get stuck in a snow bank and need a push or something?"

He glances over his shoulder and flashes an insolent grin at me.

I grit my teeth. "Just hurry up and get in the car."

"Peanut butter and soy sauce?" I eye his corner of the grocery cart. "Is that all you're purchasing?"

He shrugs. "I'm getting bread, too, and some toilet paper."

"I see. You've got all the major food groups covered, then." I frown up at him. "No wonder you're so thin. You're living on a star-vation diet."

Bolton's sole grocery store is a Hy-Vee, and it's clean and pleas-ant, but quite small. If I were more interested in cooking, as is my daughter, I'd be forced to venture up to St. Louis on a regular basis to acquire more exotic fare, but since most of what I eat is either frozen or canned, this little market suits my needs.

Alex yawns. "I've got rice and beans at home, and milk, and some fruit and lettuce. I eat fine." He picks up a jar of pickles, then puts it back on the shelves. "Besides, I'm kind of on a tight budget."

His parents should be boiled alive for cutting him off as they have. It's a miracle he's managed to put together enough financial aid to keep a roof over his head, let alone food in his non-existent belly.

He makes a face as we pass the meat counter. "Beef," he reads aloud. "Poultry. Pork." He rolls his eyes. "I guess it wouldn't sell as well if they were honest and said what it really is, right? Butchered Cow. Plucked Bird. Slaughtered Pig."

Other than this bit of vegetarian snobbery, he's been almost totally silent since our mild spat at the house regarding my driving. I don't believe he's upset with me (although he did make an obnoxious show of covering both eyes with his hands when I brushed up against the highway median near an intersection on our way here), but his mood feels heavy again, as if his trouble with Eric is consuming him. I try to distract him.

"So have there been any new developments in your creative writing class since we last spoke of it?" I pretend to be absorbed in my shopping list. "Has my daughter disemboweled anybody recently?"

Before he can answer, Karla Greenbauer, my accountant's secretary, rolls by with a cart full of red meat and M&M's, and stops to greet me. I merely nod at her and keep walking to avoid a conversation. Once we're safely away, Alex glances down at me with an inquiring expression.

I reach for some horseradish. "That woman will talk your head off. I once said hello to her and she latched onto my ear like a deer tick." The horseradish joins the honey mustard and the capons in a corner by my purse, and we turn the corner to enter the bread aisle. "So tell me about Caitlin's class."

Alex rubs at his eyes with the back of his wrist. "There's not much to tell. Especially considering that I skipped this morning."

"Oh, yes." I stand on my toes to retrieve a box of croutons from the top shelf. "I forgot. I imagine you'll be caned for that."

"Nah." He pauses by the bread rack and tugs off a loaf of Roman Meal. "She'll just lecture me in front of the class next time, and threaten to give my scholarship to somebody else." The corner of his mouth twitches, and his tone abruptly changes as he does a startling imitation of Caitlin. *"Don't think for a moment you're exempt from playing by the rules, young man, no matter whom you're unfortunate enough to have for a landlord. Do we understand one another?"*

His impression is perfect, down to my daughter's icy, imperious glare and her flawless, haughty diction.

I stop still and laugh, even though it doesn't escape my notice that Caitlin must have said something much along these lines for him to ape her so well now. "That's quite impressive, dear. You're a gifted mimic. For a moment there I was afraid I'd given birth to you."

He flushes a bit, smiling. "When I imitated her for Eric he about split a gut laughing." He starts to say something else, stops, then decides to keep on talking. "He doesn't like her very much at all," he confides. "He thinks she's a total whack-job."

His smile is gone as fast as it appeared. "I'm really sorry. I shouldn't have told you that."

"Not to worry." I pat his arm. "Truer words were never spoken."

Poor Caitlin. It saddens me to hear her students are so aware of her shortcomings. You'd think a brilliant woman like her might be better able to conceal the less savory aspects of her personality, but a duck could sooner type the Magna Carta than Caitlin could repress her chronic hostility.

I've never agreed with the theory that one's faults make one endearing to others. People are drawn to strength and repulsed by weakness; vulnerability is only attractive when it's something cute and inoffensive, like having a soft spot for teddy bears, or an uncontrollable midnight craving for chocolate macaroons.

But Caitlin is all too much her mother's daughter, and she inherited the worst aspects of my temper, and then some. And a bad temper is neither cute nor inoffensive, and it's harder to hide than a clubfoot.

"Hester?"

Alex is watching me, looking chagrined. He probably thinks he's the cause of my sudden mood shift.

I pat him again. "I'm fine, dear. My mind just wandered off." I commence walking again, pushing the cart in front of me. "I'm done in this aisle, I believe. Let's head on to the tea section, shall we?"

We turn the corner and nearly collide with another cart coming the other way. I look up to apologize to whomever is driving it, and my breath catches in my throat.

It's Caitlin herself, looming up next to a Campbell's soup display, as if I had conjured her out of thin air simply by thinking about her.

I'm too flustered to greet her at first, and she stares at the two of us for a long time before speaking. "Hello, Hester," she says at last. She sets a can of New England clam chowder in the kiddie seat of her cart and narrows her eyes at Alex. "Hello, Alex."

She's wearing a knee-length, coal-black coat and a bright wool scarf the same color as Alex's crimson hair.

Alex mutters hi and fiddles with a price tag on a shelf.

Her cart only has a few items in it; I see milk and eggs and some wheat germ, all lined up on one side of the basket like children at a playground fence.

"Why, hello there, Caitlin." I force a smile. "How good to see you again so soon after our last encounter."

She runs a hand through her thick black hair. "I feel blessed." Her tone is corrosive. "I would have thought you'd be at home, sharpening your claws for the pretrial conference tomorrow."

I have no idea how she knows about *that*, considering she doesn't speak to either Arthur or Paul.

"I haven't seen you here in years, dear. Don't you usually shop in the big city?"

She doesn't bother to answer me; she's too busy studying the boy. "You missed class today, Alex. I assumed you were sick."

He shakes his head. "Nah, I'm sorry, I just overslept." He glances over at me. "I forgot something. I'll be back in a minute, okay?"

His discomfort is so obvious I can't help but be amused. I nod at him and he touches me on the arm before beating a hasty retreat around the corner, leaving Caitlin and me staring after him.

I sigh. "I think he's in mortal terror of you, dear. Whatever do you do to your students?"

She scowls. "I expect them to show up. I expect them to work." She adjusts her scarf with impatience. "I awarded Alex a sizable scholarship to allow him to transfer here this semester, but I fear that was a mistake. He's lazy and irresponsible, and he seems to be making a series of poor choices." Her eyes flit to my forearm, where the boy rested his fingers a moment ago. "Especially when it comes to selecting his friends."

I search her face in surprise. Am I reading her correctly?

"Dear God." I raise my eyebrows. "You're jealous of him."

She blinks. "Don't be absurd."

I laugh. "That's it, isn't it? That's why you've been giving him such a hard time in class. You're actually jealous of our friendship." I laugh again. "That's rather sweet, darling. I'm flattered."

Her hands tighten on the handle of her grocery cart, and her cheeks redden. "If you think for a moment I care one way or another about the sick little *Harold and Maude* relationship you've got going on with Alex Pearl, you're delusional," she grates. "Perhaps you should consider a move into the Alzheimer's wing of an assisted living facility, after Dad finally takes the house away from you."

It's odd, but for once my own temper doesn't flare in response to hers. I simply watch her carefully, as my amusement at her resentment of Alex deepens.

"Surely you're not really suggesting Alex and I are having an affair?" I throw back my head and almost shriek with delight. "Oh, my. You should mention that to him when he gets back, dear. He'll turn green and begin to projectile vomit at the very notion."

The more I think about it, the funnier it gets, especially because my daughter is mortified by my response. My laughter echoes down the aisle, and a gentleman I don't recognize at the other end by the coffee cans looks over at us and smiles.

Caitlin winces. "All *right*, Hester," she snaps. "Stop making a fool of yourself. It's not that funny." She pushes her cart closer to me, and lowers her voice. "I wasn't saying I thought the two of you were having an affair. I was only making the point that your relationship is inappropriate."

The earnestness in her tone is a warning. I've rattled her cage, and now she wants revenge.

I slowly regain control of my breathing. "Oh? And why is that?"

She leans in to whisper. "Because any idiot can see he's a very troubled young man, who needs stable people in his life, not more insanity. And the only reason you've taken him in as a tenant—and apparently adopted him as well—is for absolutely selfish purposes. You just want to create another Jeremy for yourself."

My spine stiffens. "That's ridiculous."

I flash back to my recent conversation with Paul. The two of them *must* be talking to each other again, then. Just as they did when they discovered Arthur's infidelity, and decided to keep it a secret from me.

"Is it? I don't think so." Her eyes bore into mine. "You should be careful, Hester. He's not even your own flesh and blood, and you're using him to make yourself feel better." She snorts. "And to make Dad as angry as humanly possible, too, of course. That goes without saying."

"Alex has nothing to do with either Jeremy or your father," I hiss.

It's her turn to laugh. "Of course not. And fairy dust can make you fly."

Alex reappears from around the corner before I can respond, and she steps back and resumes her normal voice as he draws closer.

"But as I said, what you do is of no concern to me." She makes sure he's within earshot before continuing. "Go ahead and keep hanging candy canes and gingerbread cookies on your walls, and entice whomever you wish into your oven."

She steps past me with a self-satisfied air, knowing she's knocked me off center. "Don't miss any more of my classes, Alex," she admonishes over her shoulder before leaving the aisle. "I don't believe you can afford to lose your scholarship, can you?"

She exits in a flash of black and red, like an enormous crow with a piece of my large intestine wrapped around its neck.

Alex comes up to the cart, nonplussed. He looks after Caitlin, then back at me. "What was *that* all about?" he asks.

I gather myself together again. "What was what about, dear?"

"That stuff about candy canes and ovens."

"It's nothing. My daughter was just being her usual cheerful self."

He nods and stares after her again. "I'm sorry I left you alone with her, but she creeps me out. She's just way too intense." He peers down at me, worried. "Do you think that maybe she heard us talking about her?"

I consider this for a moment. "No. If she'd heard us discussing her before we accidentally stumbled upon her foxhole, the two of us would now be nothing but hamburger for the Hy-Vee butcher." I resume pushing the cart, determined to thrust aside her accusations. "She keeps a chain saw in her purse for such things, by the way, and a hockey mask. Did you know that?"

He laughs. It's a sweet laugh, young and warm and full of life. It seems for the moment he's forgotten to be depressed.

"You crack me up, Hester," he tells me. "You say the funniest damn things about your own family."

"I'm not joking. The authorities will one day find a collection of vital organs and severed limbs in her freezer. Mark my words."

He laughs again, and I continue to banter with him as well as I'm able, for his sake as well as mine.

When we finish our shopping, I may even let him drive us home. He needs the experience, and I'm not feeling particularly well. Tomorrow's meeting must be weighing on me more than I want to admit.

I don't care what Caitlin says. I am not using this boy for anything.

CHAPTER 14

"You're going to love this," Jeremy said, lifting a flashlight from the seat between us and placing it in his lap. He unrolled his window and the freezing winter air filled the car. "Trust me."

Caitlin leaned forward from the back seat, which she was sharing with Paul. "What are you up to, Jeremy? Why did you drag us all down here?"

It was a good question. It was nearly midnight, and Paul and Caitlin and I had been at home a few minutes beforehand, getting ready for bed, when Jeremy had charged in the front door, reeking of coffee and cigarettes, and demanded we all come with him for a "quick outing." He said he had something "phenomenal" to show us, and it couldn't possibly wait. We balked at first, of course, but eventually gave in, knowing full well it was no use arguing with him when he was in one of his manic moods. If we had refused to go he would have kept at us all night, so after a vain show of resistance we dressed and followed him out to the car, badgering him with questions, which he declined to answer.

"You'll see," he kept repeating, chuckling to himself like a deranged chicken, as he drove us through the darkened streets of Bolton, down to a dilapidated dock on the outskirts of town, on the east bank of the Mississippi River. He parked the car as close to the water as he could get, with the hood pointed toward the river, then shut off the engine and the headlights.

"You'll see," he said again, in response to Caitlin's question. "Just be patient for a little while longer."

There was a barge coming toward us, following the narrow, jagged path of open black water the icebreakers had carved for it down the middle of the river. An enormous spotlight was mounted on the boat's cabin, and the light swept across the mostly frozen surface of the Mississippi, bouncing from bank to bank. Its foghorn blared every minute or so, long and low and sad. It was an abysmally dark night out, with the moon and stars obscured by the clouds, and the only sources of light in all that blackness were the spotlight on the barge and the dim glow coming from downtown Bolton itself, a mile or two behind us.

I peered at Jeremy seated next to me in the car, and even though we'd been at the dock for some time and my eyes had adjusted to the darkness, I could still barely make out the pale white blob of his face as he rested his chin on the steering wheel. The foghorn sounded again, and he shifted in his seat to look at me.

"I believe it's looking for its mommy," he said. He seemed oblivious to the arctic blast coming through his open window.

Paul's head appeared next to Caitlin's between us. "What did you just say?"

Jeremy tipped his chin at the river. "The barge. Its mommy must have left it alone at the mall or some such thing, and now it can't find her."

Paul sighed in disgust. "You're a moron, Jeremy. Honest to God. Can we go home now? I'm freezing my ass off."

"Me, too," Caitlin complained. "Can we hurry this along? I mean, whatever it is we're doing?"

Jeremy had just turned sixteen a month prior to this, so Caitlin was fourteen and Paul nineteen. I was sleepy and grumpy that night, and all three of them were irritating me more than usual.

"Far be it from me to join the lynch mob, dear," I growled at Jeremy, "but for once I'm in agreement with your impatient siblings. Perhaps we should wait to do whatever you have in mind until your father is back from England. I would hate for him to miss out on all the extravagant fun we're having."

He ignored me. "I'm serious about the barge, you guys." He giggled. "For your information, I happen to be a barge expert."

Paul huffed in exasperation and his breath tickled my ear. "Can I smoke, Mom? If I have to sit in this goddamn freezing car at midnight with my lunatic brother holding us hostage, then I should at least get to smoke."

I turned my head and gave him a loving peck on the cheek. "Of course you can, darling. So long as you're at least twenty feet from the car, and standing downwind."

"Amen," Caitlin said. "Make it thirty feet."

Paul jabbed her in the ribs and she jabbed him back.

"Quit it," she commanded. "I can't believe you let them smoke at all, Mother. Especially Jeremy. He's still a minor."

Arthur and I had forbidden the boys to smoke in our presence, or in the house, or in our vehicles. But we had also decided, after countless heated arguments and fruitless lectures, that it was a doomed effort to try to enforce any further discipline than that on them.

"It's hardly as if I've given them my blessing, Caitlin," I snapped. "If the knuckleheads want to kill themselves when I'm not around, there's not much I can do about it."

Jeremy proceeded with his patter, as if none of us had spoken. "As an example, this barge is only about six months old. The short feathers on the tips of its wings will fall out as it gets older." He held the flashlight out the open window with his left arm and rested it on the side mirror, but he didn't turn it on yet. "Another fascinating characteristic of barges is how they'll disguise themselves as sticks or exotic grasses to blend in with the scenery. In the wild some have even been observed . . ." he abruptly cut off, and his voice dropped to a whisper as the barge passed directly in front of us. "Here we go."

The flashlight flared to life in his hand and he pointed it straight at the cabin of the barge, presumably aiming it at the person who was steering the thing. The light hit the windows of the cabin and bounced from them, and Jeremy began to cackle.

The spotlight on the barge stopped dead and hovered in one spot for a few seconds, as if stunned by such blatant insolence, then it began to swing toward us in a slow arc, gathering speed as it hunted us down. It skittered over the last few feet of river in front of us and leapt over the bank, plowing through the dry reeds and gravel like a dog chasing a rabbit.

"What the hell?" Paul blurted behind me.

"Uh oh!" Jeremy wailed. "Here it comes!"

The light hit us full force and I fell back in my seat and threw up my arms to shield my eyes.

"Jesus Christ!" Caitlin screamed, as we were all dazzled and blinded in a circle of paralyzing white fire. The snow on the ground around the car flared up, too, reflecting the light tenfold.

Jeremy jerked the flashlight out of the window and buried his face in my shoulder. "Yeehaw!" he howled. "It's pretty bright, isn't it, Mom?"

"You fool!" I snapped. "Get us out of here immediately, before we all have to learn to read Braille!"

Caitlin slapped at the back of his head in indignation. "Jeremy! You knew this was going to happen, didn't you?"

"Yep!" He dodged her blows. "Isn't it wonderful?"

The barge pilot continued punishing us for a good half minute before he finally tired of the game and set us free. The light drifted off in mindless silence to seek the river again, nosing its way over drifts of snow and a small log sticking up out of the ice.

Jeremy sat up again, moving slowly. His breath was coming in hitches. "Goddamn, I'm seeing spots," he gasped.

"Me, too." Paul's voice had a rare hint of hilarity in it. He'd collapsed back into his seat and was rubbing at his eyes. "Shit. You dick. I may never see again."

"Yeah, I know." Jeremy flicked off the flashlight in his lap to let our pupils adjust to the darkness again. "Sorry about that. But I didn't want to spoil the surprise by warning you." He patted my wrist. "I've done that about a dozen times now."

Caitlin was calming down. "I see." There was a trace of unwonted humor in her voice as well. "Any particular reason, or are you just out of your mind?"

He rolled up his window before answering, and in the pause I could somehow feel his good spirits vanish, as abruptly as if a switch had been thrown. The mood in the car altered in that instant as well; Paul and Caitlin were just as attuned to him as I was. Jeremy turned away from the rest of us and rested his forehead against the cold glass of the driver's door.

"It's like being an astronaut on the moon or something," he said in the stillness. "Know what I mean?"

All the levity had fled from his voice, replaced by something somber and frightening we'd all heard there before, a kind of hopeless yearning that seemed to have no source and no boundaries. He fiddled with the key chain in the ignition but didn't turn on the engine. "It's as if I'm out walking around on craters and hills in the dark, and all of a sudden the sun comes over the horizon, and, bam! It's instant obliteration." He paused again and his words faded to a whisper. "I love it."

Even as a baby he had been prone to bizarre changes in disposition like this, and I had grown accustomed to them to the degree that they no longer shocked me as much as they perhaps should have. They still disturbed me, of course, but I knew from long experience that he would rally soon enough, if I just left him alone.

Caitlin reached out a hand and put it in his hair. Gestures of affection like this from her were a rarity, but Jeremy somehow brought them out in her.

"What is it, Jeremy? What's wrong?" she asked him.

He shook his head to dislodge her fingers. "Nothing." He started the car. "I just wanted you guys to see this tonight, that's all."

"Great," Paul muttered. "That's just great." The inexplicable longing in his brother's voice always upset him whenever it surfaced, but being Paul, of course, he would never admit it. "Can we go home now?"

CHAPTER 15

About two years after Jeremy began teaching at Carson, Paul decided to move across town into one of the faculty bungalows on the grounds of the Conservatory. (These so-called bungalows—Jeremy referred to them as "bungholes," irritating Paul to no end—are little more than a row of flimsy shacks the Conservatory put up next to the river around World War I, to provide low-income housing for some of its grossly underpaid faculty. Nowadays the salaries at Carson are more than adequate to buy a decent home in Bolton, of course, but many of the younger teachers still seem to find the shacks inexplicably charming.) Paul tried to convince Jeremy to move in with him, but Jeremy declined the invitation, preferring the attic apartment Paul was vacating. A few months later Caitlin began her master's degree in Ann Arbor, and with her removal to Michigan and Paul's conspicuous absence from our daily home life, Jeremy took on his role of "only child" with gusto.

He'd sit next to me by the fire in the evenings when Arthur was on the road, and peer up from his newspaper now and then with a quizzical expression.

"What is it, dear?" I'd ask.

He'd pull at his ear. "Well, it's nothing really. I was just wondering why you didn't smother Paul and Caitlin at birth." He wouldn't wait for an answer to questions such as these; he only asked them to amuse me. "I'm serious. I would have enjoyed my childhood so much more without having to share you and Dad with those two leeches."

"Liar," I'd murmur. "You adore Paul and Caitlin, and you know it."

"Once upon a time, maybe." He'd pour himself another shot of whatever we were drinking for a nightcap. "But Paul's turning into something of an ogre, and Caitlin is fast becoming a first-class shrew. You may not see it yet, but I do." He'd hold his glass up for a toast. "Well, here's to how they were before the body snatchers got to them."

I thought he was joking. I didn't know he had the gift of prophecy.

Quite often the two of us played music in the evenings until my wrist couldn't take it anymore, wading through all the literature for horn and piano. We read everything from Saint-Saens to Mozart to Maxwell Davies, and even though I could only handle about five minutes at a time (with frequent stops for self-medication) we played the hell out of whatever caught our fancy until, at last, I'd be forced to cry uncle. I shouldn't have done it, of course, because the pain was intense, and afterwards I'd always have to ice my hand like an injured athlete to reduce the swelling. But I could never resist the temptation; it brought me too much pleasure.

When Arthur was home the three of us would occasionally even tackle a little of the Brahms trio (one of my personal favorites, but far too demanding for me to endure more than a few pages in one sitting), and it's a pity there are no recordings of those impromptu performances, because both Arthur and Jeremy were transcendent. There were only a handful of musicians in the world who could match either of them, and rather than competing for "alpha-musician" status as you might have expected a normal father and a son to do, they feasted on each other's abilities with true joy, using the opportunity to explore all the extreme possibilities of their instruments. Arthur was slightly more refined, of course, and could never refrain from showing off what his additional years had taught him, but Jeremy had an intensity that Arthur could not rival.

And to Arthur's credit, he didn't try. He let Jeremy take the lead when it came to passion, and he contented himself with being witty and restrained, and the combination of Jeremy's youthful fire and Arthur's polished maturity was heartbreaking to hear. They were equals, and both knew it—even though admitting such a thing was beyond either of them.

Nor was I too shabby, myself.

I may have had a ruined wrist, but I was still more than able to hold my own, even in such rarefied company. When my left hand wouldn't allow me to do what was required, I'd find a way to compensate by using right-hand techniques I've never seen another pianist do, or even attempt to do. And when that failed, I'd come up with methods to manipulate the music itself, employing artistic license with a vengeance to solve various problems imposed by my physical limitations. My disability gave me a new understanding of my own talent, and I tapped into a reservoir of resources I hadn't known was at my disposal. I learned to shade every note with an entire palette of bewitching colors; I taught myself to fill each silence with texture and meaning.

One time I looked up in irritation when Arthur and Jeremy both missed an entrance at the end of a piano solo, only to find them gaping at me. When I asked what the problem was, neither answered at first.

"Why are you just sitting there?" I demanded. "Have you forgotten how to count?"

Arthur finally shook his head and cleared his throat. "That was exceptional, Hester. Truly." His voice was full of wonder. "You'd never know you were injured."

Jeremy nodded. "Yeah. Jesus, Mom. What's gotten into you? That was fucking outrageous."

I believe I actually blushed. It felt so wonderful to be admired again for my playing, especially by those two. It gave me no illusions about regaining my performance career, of course; I was permanently maimed, and we all knew it. No matter how I tried to gut it out, I simply could not make it through an entire movement without stopping, and therefore I was useless on the stage.

But I could still make my husband and my son look at me as if I'd just turned water into wine.

Anyway, that type of "family" activity, though splendid, was rare, because Jeremy tended to make himself scarce when Arthur was around. It's not that the two of them didn't get along; it's more that Jeremy was slowly beginning to distance himself from everybody but me.

When I say "slowly," I mean "glacially," by the way. The only reason I noticed anything wrong at all was because I saw him every day, week after week, season after season, whenever he wasn't touring. At first I attributed his darkening moods to the usual causes for such behavior—the weather, or a touch of the flu, or an argument with a co-worker. But as time passed by, I began to suspect something else was going on besides his native inclination to occasional crankiness and depression.

How do you know when somebody's spirit is dissolving? When does it become apparent that the will to live is utterly gone?

I was with my mother when she died, and with her, the transition was obvious. She had severe cancer, she refused chemotherapy, and she chose to spend her last few days at home. I sat beside her bed and watched the light flee from her eyes all at once; she'd had enough pain, and that was it—she was gone, regardless of how much longer her body lived.

But with Jeremy, it wasn't like that. He didn't have cancer, he wasn't sick. He had more good days than bad, he was often cheerful, he never seemed so far down that he couldn't spring back from whatever was troubling him. To me, there was always light in his eyes.

A false light, it turned out. No more trustworthy than a reflection on the water.

So the years passed. He fell in love with several girls (red-haired, imbecilic Gina lasted the longest, but feckless, desperate Shelley was the most promising), yet none of these relationships panned out. As he grew older he began to tour less, preferring to stay home, but his playing didn't suffer as a result; if anything, he continued to grow in mastery, and he started to develop a formidable reputation as a teacher as well. He never had any inclination to move out of the attic apartment, he spent more and more time alone, and he quarreled frequently with everybody, including me.

He laughed, he cried. He dreamed, he drank, he copulated, he made music. He smoked his cigarettes, and he taught his students, and sometimes he sat on the porch for hours, silent and still as St. Booger, staring at the street. He loved and was loved in return, he read thousands of books (he was particularly fond of science fiction and fantasy), he listened to the radio every evening before bed, and he read the sports section of the newspaper every morning during baseball season, tracking—with fanatical devotion—the progress of the Chicago Cubs, even though he never once went to see them play. He complained about the weather, he loathed politics and television, and he toyed with the idea of attending church every once in a while, even though he didn't really believe in God and found the whole concept of organized religion incomprehensible.

In other words, he lived a somewhat normal life.

But through it all he was still Jeremy. Funny, manic Jeremy Donovan, brilliant and gifted, acerbic and impatient, sweet and generous. For more than a dozen years after he returned from Curtis, there was only the everyday fact of him in the house, the solid, living and breathing human being who was my middle child and became my closest friend.

And until the last few months of his life, it never crossed my mind he could ever be any different, or that a time might come when he would ask me to kill him.

I began to find him up on the roof every so often, usually after work, but sometimes in the mornings, too, before the neighborhood woke up. If it had been anyone else, this might not have seemed so odd—the view from our roof was spectacular, and there was a small, flat area on the east side of the house, overlooking the driveway, that was accessible from the kitchen window of the attic apartment. It could be quite pleasant to sit up there with the town of Bolton spread out before you, and watch the boat traffic on the Mississippi River in the distance.

But heights had always horrified Jeremy. When he was a child, he would never go near the windows in the attic apartment, let alone venture on the roof. As bad as Paul was about traveling, Jeremy was far worse about heights; whenever he'd go up a flight of stairs in our house he'd clutch at the banister for dear life and keep his eyes fixed on his feet until he reached the landing. (Paul and

Caitlin tormented him for this, of course, and would often follow him up the stairs, begging him to turn around and look down at them. He'd ignore them until they'd try to unbalance him by slapping at his heels, then he'd bellow for me to come intervene.) For some reason, his phobia of heights didn't extend to airplanes; as long as he had an aisle seat in the plane, he said flying never bothered him. And in the attic he survived by keeping the window curtains closed all the time, and hanging sheets from ceiling to floor in his hallway, so he couldn't see the staircase as he went from room to room.

Dear Lord, he was odd.

Be that as it may, the first time he did his roof walk, I saw him when I stepped out to the driveway to get in my car for an early morning meeting at Carson. As I put my hand on the handle of the car door, I heard my name called from far above me, and I spun around on the asphalt next to St. Booger and gawked up at Jeremy. He was standing on the flat area of the roof, the toes of his shoes sticking over the edge of the shingles.

"Jeremy!" I screamed. "What in the name of God are you doing up there? Come down this instant!"

His laugh reverberated off the walls of the carriage house behind me. "Okay! I'll be right there!"

I ran back inside and made it up the stairs in about ten seconds flat (I was considerably younger then; nowadays it feels as if it takes me the better part of an afternoon to reach the attic from the ground floor), then I barreled through Jeremy's kitchen and poked my head out the open window. The sun was in my face so I had to shield my eyes to see him. He was still perched on the edge of the roof like a massive, brooding dove, staring down at the driveway.

I didn't say anything at first because I didn't want to startle him, but he knew I was there anyway.

"Morning, Mother," he said over his shoulder. It was the middle of May and there was a light, cool breeze blowing. His voice was calm and pleasant, but he wouldn't turn to meet my eyes. "It's lovely up here, isn't it?"

"Jeremy." I felt myself trembling; I knew for certain this was no idle game he was playing. "What on earth is wrong?"

His thin shoulders shrugged under a clean white T-shirt. "Nothing. I'm just getting some fresh air." He giggled like a little boy. "And how are you today?"

I cleared my throat. "Not very damn well, thank you. You're frightening me."

"I'm sorry." He held his arms away from his sides like a diver. "Wanna bet I could do a triple-gainer before I hit the ground?"

In spite of the circumstances my temper flared. "I believe a belly-flop is more your style. Now come inside before somebody calls the police."

He snorted. "Yeah, you're right." He dropped his arms. "A fancy dive is beyond my athletic ability. I bet Caitlin could do it, though." He sighed. "How about a cannonball, then? If I jumped far enough I might even end up with St. Booger's head up my butt." He finally turned around and met my gaze. "I don't know about you, but I'm thinking my ass would be a distinct improvement over that face of his. Don't you agree?"

The sun lit up his hair, and he smiled at me.

Something in his expression made my stomach twist. I smiled back at him as well as I was able. "Don't flatter yourself, dear. You'd make a terrible lawn ornament." I held out my hand to him. "Please come back inside."

He chuckled and tried to pretend he was joking. "You worry too much, Hester. I'm merely attempting to conquer my fear of heights."

His heels were still perilously close to the edge, and it seemed as if he were almost leaning backwards.

"I'm certain there are better ways to deal with your fear than this." I struggled to go along with his casual act. "Hypnosis, for example? Or perhaps some extensive shock therapy, followed by a full frontal lobotomy."

A touch of genuine amusement crept back into his voice. "That's inappropriate humor, Mother, even for you. Your roofside manner leaves a lot to be desired." His body relaxed, ever so slightly.

"Jeremy." I leaned forward a little more, putting my shoulders through the window, but when he tensed I halted. "Please tell me why you're out here."

He shrugged again and studied his grass-stained sneakers. "Nothing in particular. Just doing some thinking."

"Thinking about what?"

"Lots of stuff. Nothing too important, really."

"You're on the roof at . . ." I glanced at my watch. ". . . six-thirty in the morning, thinking about nothing?"

He pulled at the front of his shirt, twisting the fabric in his fingers. "Well, not nothing, exactly. I was mainly thinking about the nature of musical talent."

"I see." I glared up at him. "And exactly how much have you had to drink?"

"Nothing." He hesitated. "Not for several hours, at least. And actually, I've been thinking about talent in general. It doesn't have to be musical, it could be anything."

I leaned on the windowsill and waited as patiently as I could, knowing he'd continue at his own pace, and interrupting again would only aggravate him.

He looked back up at me. "But musical talent is what I have, so that's what I was thinking about specifically." All of a sudden he squatted down and my heart almost stopped. His rump was hanging off the roof, but he seemed insensible to the danger. His eyes were now on the same level as mine, and he stared into my pupils, unblinking. "Do you think talent like our family has is a good thing?"

"Of course it's a good thing. What else could it be?"

"A lot of things, actually. Some much less savory than others." He cocked his head. "You mean you've never really thought about this before?"

"Thought about what?" I demanded. "And please stop doing that with your head. You look as if you're begging for a Milk-Bone biscuit."

He ignored that. "So you honestly haven't thought about what our talent may have done to us?"

I forced the exasperation out of my voice. "I don't have the first idea of what you're talking about, Jeremy. Can you explain it to me?"

He nodded. "Okay. I'll try." He wiped his nose on his shirtsleeve.

"Let's start with you, shall we?" He paused for an instant and then words began pouring out of him, as if he were reciting a prepared speech. "You're Hester Parker, one of the leading concert pianists of the twentieth century, and it's safe to say that very, very few people, living or dead, can measure up to you for pure musical aptitude."

He held up a hand to forestall me from saying anything. "I'm not kissing your butt, Mother, I'm just trying to make a point. Yes, you could argue with me about this or that person, but we're talking about maybe a couple hundred pianists over the last few centuries who were, or are, at your level, so the bottom line is you've got a shitload of talent. Right? So okay, that being said, here's the thing." He mimed playing a piano in the air. "For all the talent you've got in your scrappy little body, can you say you're happy?"

He didn't wait for an answer, he just plunged on.

"Now let's take a tour of history. Who's probably the biggest musical genius of all time? Mozart or Beethoven, right? Whichever, take your pick, they're both on the shortlist, okay? Now look at their lives. Pathetic, disastrous, and lonely. Right?" He was getting more and more agitated. "Then there's Schubert, Schumann, and Brahms: ditto for all of them. And Wagner was a pervert, Stravinsky was an irascible old bastard, Mahler had a death wish, and oh yeah, Tchaikovksy! God, don't even get me started on that sad old poof. I could go on and on and on, but let's . . ."

A bee whizzed by his head and he took a violent swing at it with his fist and almost tumbled off the roof. I gasped in horror as he braced himself and settled back into position. His face blanched a little, but he didn't move away from the edge.

I decided to engage him in this ridiculous conversation, because it was the only way I could think of to get him back inside. "Why are you getting so worked up over this, son? As far as I'm concerned, a little personal angst is a small price to pay for the *Ring* cycle, or *Don Giovanni.*"

For the life of me I couldn't fathom what had gotten into him; his eyes were filling with tears. "You're wrong, Mom. You're as wrong as can be. It's a huge price, and you're paying it, and so am I, and Dad, and Paul, and even Caitlin, in her own field."

I blinked. "What do you mean?"

He shook his head. "You're so blind, Hester. You really don't see it. How can somebody so smart be so stupid?"

Despite my best intentions, anger crept into my voice again. "Given your location at the moment, that should be my line, I believe."

He flinched at my tone and I bit my lip. Wonderful. My son was on the roof, in immediate jeopardy, and I was goading him. Brilliant.

I forced myself to be calm. "You're not making any sense, darling. What's this price you think we're all paying? To my mind, I haven't paid a thing I wouldn't pay ten times over for what I've been given."

He just stared at me as if I were babbling in Swahili. Then he began to hum a few bars of something it took me a moment to recognize.

"*Tosca?*" I asked.

He nodded. "Very good. The third act. It's the part where she leaps to her death, remember?"

I fell silent again, confused and terrified.

He continued humming for a minute but when he realized that I hadn't said anything else, he finally let the tune trail off and sighed. "Don't worry, Mom. I'm just pushing your buttons. I'm fine."

There was such desolation in his voice, such longing.

I held out my hand to him again in desperation and tried a new tack. "You didn't let me answer your earlier question."

"What question?" he whispered.

"You asked me a few moments ago if I was happy. Yes, I am. I'm very happy."

"Liar." He blotted at his tears with his palms and grimaced. "You are not."

I raised my voice. "Yes, I am."

"No, you're not." He let his hands drop, and one fell on the roof with a thump, like a dead bird. "You drink yourself to sleep every night, you always have music playing in the background because you can't stand hearing your own thoughts, you won't admit to yourself that Dad's likely having an affair, and you never get through a single day without wishing you had your wrist back the way it was before your accident."

He said all this flatly, in a drone, never once taking his red, puffy eyes from my face.

I stared at him in shock. I had suspected Arthur of infidelity for the last few months, but I had said nothing to anybody about it, nor had any of the children mentioned anything prior to this. Hearing Jeremy say it so bluntly caught me by surprise, and I felt a dull ache begin behind my breastbone as I struggled to find the words to refute him.

I opened and closed my mouth several times before I could summon an argument.

"I'm trying to sort out which of those statements is the most absurd." I ran my fingers over the sill and worried at the head of a nail sticking up from the wood. "First of all, you're making it sound as if my drinking is a problem, which it isn't. Secondly, I listen to music because I like listening to music, and my thoughts are hardly erased just because my ears are otherwise engaged." I paused to gauge his reaction, but he showed no outward sign of what he was thinking. "As far as my wrist goes, of course I want it back the way it was, but I've learned to live with that. And that accusation about your father is . . ." I bit my lip. ". . . well, it's simply preposterous."

He rested his chin on his knees and picked up where he left off, as if I hadn't said anything at all. "But really, these are only surface disturbances, aren't they, Mother? Your unhappiness is directly rooted in your talent. The more talented you are, the more unhappy you are." He straightened his back and fiddled with the hem on the leg of his jeans. "It sucks, but that's just the way it works."

I grimaced. "That's the dumbest thing I've ever heard in my life. Do you honestly believe that Joe and Jane Normal are happier as a general rule than those of us with an appreciable gift?"

He nodded again. "Yes. That's exactly what I'm saying."

I tugged at my ear. "Not only is that elitist, it's also patently false. There are millions of people in the world who would give up virtually everything they own to be recognized as outstanding in a chosen field."

"Yes, and if they were given that opportunity, it would destroy them as surely as it's destroyed us."

My frustration was building. "Speak for yourself, please. I, for one, am hardly *destroyed,* as you put it." My lower back was beginning to ache from leaning forward all this time. "And if you think that pain and self-doubt and neurosis are the birthright of the artistically gifted, I suggest you spend a day sitting at Willie's Diner downtown."

Willie's was a blue-collar restaurant in Bolton, frequented daily by an assortment of eccentric townspeople—including my personal favorites: Sylvia Simpson, the jaundiced, dishonest pet store owner who never wore anything but yellow blouses and green pants, and Dylan Crowell, her fawning, incoherent assistant, who stank of cat urine and birdcages.

Jeremy sniffed. "That's not what I'm saying, Mother. Of course human suffering is universal." He closed his eyes for a moment and moved his lips, as if praying. "But my point is that talent exacerbates the situation a hundredfold. Do you think for a moment I'd be up here on the roof, thinking about stepping off, if I weren't a prodigy?" He opened his eyes again. "My gift is what makes me dissatisfied with everything else in the world."

I didn't want to upset him further, but he was sounding more petulant than distressed at this point, so some of my fear had abated. And to tell the truth, I was irritated because he was being unbelievably pigheaded.

"Look at me, Jeremy."

His eyes were wandering around the sky, but now they fluttered back to my face.

"You're behaving like a spoiled brat," I scolded. "Poor little Jeremy Donovan. Oh, the *humanity.* You're telling me you can't handle the pressure of being special, so you're going to end it all?" I frowned. "I think a better plan might be a spanking and a nap, don't you?"

He flushed a little, stung. "You're not listening to what I'm saying."

"No, I'm not," I agreed. "Self-pity bores me, and every time I hear yet another 'sensitive artist' bellyaching about how difficult his life is, I want to cut my own ears off like Van Gogh, so as not to have to listen to it anymore. Now come inside and stop spouting nonsense."

I said this last in my most commanding voice, and to my surprise, he did what I asked.

But that was only the first time.

He was out there the next week, too, and then again a month later, and each time he had a different, equally silly complaint. The second time he was upset because a student had been "disrespectful" during a lesson, the third time was after he felt he had performed below his usual level at a concert the previous night. He never did this when Arthur or anybody else was at home, and he could be counted on to time his breakdowns to coincide with my comings and goings, so I would be sure to find him on my way in or out of the house.

And I always managed to talk him down, usually with a mixture of threats, praise and ridicule. He would argue with me for a while, then he would finally become sullen and stop acting the fool. After he was back inside the house, he would recover completely, becoming cheerful and relaxed, and our lives would return to normal.

For a time.

But whenever he experienced one of these lapses, he begged me not to tell Arthur or anybody else about it. He'd swear to never do it again, and he'd insist he was fine and didn't need professional assistance.

And God help me, I believed him.

Or, more accurately, I *chose* to believe him, because it was easier than doing what I should have done. A number of times I went so far as to call a therapist to set up an appointment for him, but somehow Jeremy always managed to jolly me out of forcing him to go, convincing me I was "blowing things out of proportion," and all he needed was "time and patience to work things through."

He'd put his thin, warm arms around me when he said these things, and he spoke with remorse and sincerity, and I fell for it every time. I agreed to keep these episodes between us, just as he asked, so Paul and Caitlin were oblivious to the situation, and if Arthur suspected something was amiss, he was too preoccupied at that point with his own double life to pester us with any questions.

I could use this opportunity to assign more of the blame to Arthur for what happened later, but that would be unfair. To be unconditionally honest, I was rather flattered that Jeremy was willing to share this troubled part of himself with me and nobody else, and even though the nature of this secret of ours was disquieting, the closeness that grew between us was addictive. (It was the same kind of pleasure I had experienced once as a little girl, after rescuing a small dog that had fallen off a stone ledge in the garden with a leash around its neck. The poor creature was choking to death when I released her from her collar, and for the rest of the day, she was glued to my heels everywhere I went, like a pagan worshipper at the feet of a god.) The adoration in Jeremy's eyes as he expressed his gratitude for my help in regaining his sanity was a potent, lovely drug, and it lulled me to sleep with a placid smile on my face, just as he had intended it to.

And then one winter day things went a little differently up on the roof.

CHAPTER 16

My hands are still shaking as I step into the house and hang my coat on the rack. I believe they were also doing that on the steering wheel all the way home from the courthouse, but I don't remember the drive; the streets and houses of Bolton were no more real to me than a backdrop in a theater, the people on the sidewalks nothing but stick figures.

All I could see was Arthur's implacable face at the pretrial conference. All I could hear was Arthur's voice. Arthur's terrible, wounded old voice, telling me he was going to take my home away from me in court next month.

Our home.

There was no mercy left in him this morning. No mercy, and no kindness, and no decency.

I want a drink, very badly.

But not yet. There's something else I need to do first. Right now.

I kick off my shoes and hurry through the living room in my stockings, and I'm nearly running by the time I reach the other side. My heart is pounding as I pass through the doorway into the music room, but I barely break stride until I'm standing next to my piano.

It's still here, of course, just as always. Waiting for me to return to it, like a dozing, patient old beast in its den.

Arthur offered to sell the house to me today, but for an outrageous price he knew I could not afford. Not unless I sell my piano, first, which he knows I will never do. He only made the offer to antagonize me.

Damn him.

God damn him.

I catch my breath and rest my hand on the piano's massive lid, pressing my palm into the smooth, black, varnished wood. My heart gradually slows, and after a minute I lift the lid and secure it on its short peg, then I sit on the bench and let my head loll from side to side, doing my best to loosen the kinks in my neck and shoulders. There's warmth all across my back from the radiator behind me, and the humidifier in the corner is keeping the air moist and comfortable. I close my eyes for a moment, and clasp my hands in my lap, and settle myself into the peace and quiet.

Priests pray, and Buddhist monks meditate. Dancers launch themselves into the air, and artists paint—or sculpt, or draw—and writers put pen to paper, or stare at a blank computer screen for hours on end. We all do what we have to do, to get by, and to make sense of the world. Those of us with a "calling" of any sort surrender ourselves to a rigid, daily discipline, and we steep ourselves in technique and shared lore, and we do what we can to serve whatever it is we think we're serving, be it a deity or an art. We do this, at first, because we think it will bring us joy (or comfort, or recognition), but in the end we find we're doing it only because we know of no other way to live, and we feel we have no other choice left to us.

And so I play piano. This is my prayer, my meditation. My dance, my canvas, my poem. I sink my fingers into the keyboard just as innumerable pianists before me have done, and I seek clarity and absolution in strict, intricate counterpoint, escape and redemption in melody and chordal structure. I will fail, of course, just as I do every time I play, but that's beside the point, I think. The soul of music, to a true musician, is the fabled face of God: it's not really meant to be seen, full-on, by the naked human eye. But I've had glimpses of that ancient, lyrical soul, again and again, and each glimpse has earned me a profound moment of grace, a transcendent instant outside of time—and an absolute, if temporary, relief from my burdens. So I persist, vainly, in trying to remove all the veils, until nothing is left but blinding, eternal glory.

Did I say earlier that I don't believe in God?

Well, I lied. I do believe.

But the God I bow down before does not answer prayers. It does not sit on a throne, it does not traffic in locusts and plague, and it does not care a whit about you, or me, or your Aunt Juanita, or your cat. It cares only for the earsplitting peal of the trumpet, the hum of the low "E" string on the bass, and the shocking thud you feel deep in your gut when someone strikes a bass drum behind you. Wind instruments, and voices and strings and brass, and perhaps occasional birdsong are its angels; concert halls and recording studios are its churches and its synagogues.

Music is my God, of course. A god with no country, a god with no bible, and a god with no conscience. And I have given my life to it.

And what does that make me?

Nothing, really. Nothing at all.

I am nothing but a very angry, lonely old pagan worshipper, with uncommonly gifted fingers, a crippled wrist, and a broken heart.

Unbidden, the famous second movement from Beethoven's *Pathétique Sonata* fills the room. I let it come out unchecked, let it pour through me like clean water from a faucet. It saturates the house, then the yard, then the neighborhood; it drowns downtown Bolton, and southern Illinois, and the entire Midwest. It floods city after city, and continent after continent, and sends every would-be Noah scurrying for his ark and galoshes before I finish. But as soon as the last notes sound, the tap is turned off. The water reverses its flow, the sun reemerges, the earth dries itself again in a single second.

Just as if the magnificent, grief-obliterating flood I created with my own two hands—and the skill and training of a lifetime—had never happened.

My wrist is a nightmare of fire. I let my head fall forward on my chest, and all my anguish and loss returns with the physical pain, and the silence.

"Jesus, Hester."

I jerk in surprise on the bench. Alex is standing in the doorway, watching me. I have no idea how long he's been there.

I somehow muster a response. "Alex. I didn't realize you were home."

"Where else would I be?" He gives me a lopsided grin. "No one else wants me around." He takes a tentative step into the room, and his face becomes solemn. "What was that song you just played?"

I close the keyboard lid and sigh. "Something of Beethoven's. An Adagio."

He puts his hands in his pants pockets. "It was . . ." He stops, searching for words. "That was gorgeous, Hester." He shakes his head. "Really. It was unbelievable."

I rise to my feet and try to hide the shooting pain in my forearm. "Thank you for saying that, dear. It is a lovely piece, isn't it?"

He nods, but then steps closer and examines my face. "You hurt your wrist again, didn't you?" He searches my eyes. "Oh. Your meeting went bad, too."

I blink at him. "Dear God. Am I that easy to read?"

"Sort of." He falls into step beside me as I move toward the kitchen. "And now you want a cocktail, right?"

I grimace. "No. I want at least a *dozen* cocktails, Nostradamus."

As we walk through the living room, the fear of losing my home assails me again. My lawyer tried to comfort me today by telling me I could always buy another house if I lost this one in court, but he doesn't have any idea what that would do to me.

I've lived here my entire adult life, raised my family here, slept and breathed and dreamed and cried here. And I intend to die here as well, when the time comes. I know every square inch of this place; every hallway and every corner triggers a memory that otherwise would be irretrievable. The music we've made here as a family, and the love we shared together, is part of the walls and the floors.

I mean that literally. If you cut into the wood of this house with a knife, I would bleed in sympathy, like a stigmatic. How could it be otherwise?

This is where I first learned what the word *love* really meant. This is where Arthur and I began our life together, and watched our squalling infants lurch and stumble their way into maturity, one after the other. This is where Paul sat beside me on the porch after my mother died, and cried with me, and stroked my hair as if I were a little girl. This is where Caitlin asked to paint my portrait for her art class, and actually danced around me in surprised pleasure, like a sprite, when I said yes. This is where Jeremy stood on the kitchen table for my fiftieth birthday and sang "God Save the Queen" at the top of his lungs while Arthur squirted him from across the room with the dish sprayer.

This is where Paul and Jeremy, indignant and stuttering, attempted to explain to me why a pet turtle they'd stolen from a neighbor's house was entitled to political asylum. This is where I found Caitlin asleep on the living room floor with her head resting on a chessboard, and Arthur snoozing next to her with an open thesaurus on his belly. This is where the boys dressed as sumo wrestlers for Halloween, and then as Starsky and Hutch, and once (most notably) as Luciano Pavarotti and Mirella Freni.

This is where I cooked everything from sloppy Joes to ratatouille to beef bourguignon for my ravenous and finicky children. This is where on any given day of the year I could walk in the front door and be greeted by the living, breathing melodies of Vivaldi, or Haydn, or Mendelssohn, or Copland, expertly played on a cello, or a French horn, or a violin. And this is where Arthur removed all my clothes by the fireplace in our bedroom one unforgettable New Year's Eve, when we had the place to ourselves. He refused to hurry, and his fingers traced, for many hours, the flickering shadows cast by the fire over my bare skin.

And I will not give it up. Not to Arthur, not to anybody. Arthur gets a new wife, and a new chance at life after our divorce. I will be damned if he gets this house, too. It belongs to me.

This is my home. I don't know who I am without it.

CHAPTER 17

So Jeremy was waiting for me when I returned home from work one cold February afternoon, a little before sunset. As I pulled into the driveway I saw him on the edge of the roof again, not wearing a coat, and hugging himself for warmth.

"Oh, for pity's sake," I muttered to myself in the car. "Bless his pointed little head."

I pulled up in front of St. Booger, turned off the engine and stepped out into the inch or two of fresh snow on the driveway.

"Welcome home, Hester!" Jeremy called down.

I glared up at him without answering. Before I could get into the house, our next-door neighbor (doddering old Edith Schumaker, who has since died of lung cancer) opened her front door and hailed me, hobbling out on her porch with a cigarette dangling from her mouth.

"He's been up there quite a while, Hester," she said in what she intended to be a whisper, but came out as a shout. She was nearly as deaf as Beethoven. "I was getting ready to call you at work, but then I saw your car pulling into the driveway."

"Thank you, Edith." I raised my voice and spoke with exaggerated mouth movement, so she could read my lips. "He's just getting a breath of fresh air. It's nothing to be concerned about."

She shook her head. "Damn fool's going to get himself killed doing that sort of thing. It's probably icy up there."

She was loud enough for Jeremy to hear her.

"Hi, Edith!" he bellowed. "Come on up and we'll go dancing! And by the way, you look sexy as hell!"

Edith waved her cigarette at him and blew a plume of smoke into the air. "You be careful up there, young man!"

"No worries!" he responded. "Trust me! I'm like a mountain goat." He paused for a moment, then began to bleat at the top of his lungs.

Edith shot me a worried look and I felt myself flush with embarrassment.

"He's fine," I reassured her. "You go on back inside now, before you catch your death of cold."

"BAAAA!" Jeremy bawled. "BAAAA!"

I bid Edith an abrupt goodbye and made my exit, sensing something unusual in Jeremy's mood, a brittle edge to his voice I hadn't heard there before. I rushed by St. Booger and almost fell in the driveway en route to the porch.

"Oops! Easy does it, Hester!" Jeremy scolded. "You've only got one good wrist left!"

"Shut up, you idiot!" I barked back at him.

"BAAAA!" he replied.

The house was cold and dark as I made my way up the stairs. Jeremy usually had the fire going by the time I came home, and the thermostat turned up where I liked it, but that afternoon he'd neglected to make the place more comfortable. God only knew how long he'd been up there. I passed by Arthur's and my bedroom on the first landing at a pretty good clip, and sailed by Arthur's office on the third floor, but when I finally reached the attic apartment, I was seriously winded.

I ground to a halt in the attic hallway to catch my breath. When I saw what awaited me there, my hand went to my throat.

Jeremy's apartment, normally neat as a pin, was in ruins. The rugs had been ripped to shreds and flung throughout the place as if by a mad bird, the wallpaper in the hall itself had been clawed from the walls and was balled up by the kitchen door, along with the sheets he used as a screen to block his view of the staircase. I glanced in the living room, and all of his albums (he had hundreds of them) were shattered on the floor, mixed in with buckets of black soil from all the plants he'd upended. And in the kitchen he'd been hurling dishes into the open refrigerator, apparently, because there was a tremendous pile of broken pottery inside it, spilling out in an avalanche at its base.

He must have been tearing the place apart for hours.

I picked my way gingerly through the wreckage in the kitchen, to the open window by the table.

Jeremy was prepared for my arrival; he was facing me and smiling when I poked my head out into the cold air.

"Hello, Mother." He sounded utterly rational. "It's good to see you."

This semblance of sanity alarmed me far more than anything else could have. His demeanor was jovial, his speech polite and measured. But underneath all the surface lucidity was a fever of some kind, and I could feel the heat in his gaze.

"Jeremy." I took a slow, ragged breath, and then another, waiting for my heart to slow. "What is it this time, dear? What's wrong?"

"Wrong?" he cocked his eyebrow. "Whatever do you mean?"

I threw up my hands. "Oh, my mistake, then. You've just been rearranging your apartment, is that it?"

"Oh, that." He chuckled. "I had a bit of tantrum earlier, that's all. But I'm all better now."

It was bitterly cold up here; even given that the attic apartment was always hot, the warmth from the house behind me couldn't compete with the freezing wind pouring in through the open window. Jeremy was dressed in black slacks, a pair of brown slippers, and a white button-down shirt with long sleeves, and his face and hands were shivering and blue from the cold. The temperature was plummeting as the sun sank lower in the sky.

"Jeremy. You must come inside." I leaned forward to plead with him. "Please. We'll talk about whatever is bothering you once you're warm again."

"You worry too much, Hester." This had become his standard line whenever I found him up here. "It's not good for your blood pressure, you know."

"My blood pressure will be just fine when you stop being a fool," I snapped. "You're going to get frostbite."

He bent forward and put his hands on his knees to peer into my eyes. "It's no good, Mother. I can't bear it any longer."

The forced jollity was gone from his tone, replaced by something distant and lonely. My heart twisted in response.

"Bear what?" I whispered.

"This." He made a circling gesture with his hands, indicating who knows what. "All of it. I mean, what's the point?"

He cleared his throat and fought to control his trembling lips. "Day in and day out, it's the same thing. For all of us." He played with a button on his shirt. "Do you see what I mean? We get up, we go to work, we make music or whatnot, we interact with other people. Then we come home, watch the news, read a book, stare at the television, whatever—then we go to bed, either alone or with someone else, and we dream, and the next day it starts all over again."

He shrugged, thinking. "And that's it, really. That's all there is. I mean, sure, we do other things, too. We sweat, we shower. We eat and shit. We fall in and out of love. We swear at the mailman for dropping our magazines in the snow, and we hug the kids for doing their chores, and we argue about where we should eat for lunch on Fridays. We whack off or hump our brains out when we're horny, we drink booze when we're edgy, and some of us even pray before we fall asleep at night, even though most of us know for a fact it doesn't do a damn bit of good."

I opened my mouth to speak, but he wasn't finished.

"Just hear me out, okay, Hester?" He waited for my nod. "It's not bad, but it's not good, either. There's joy sometimes, but it's always, always unclean, muddied up by pain and waste and grief. And today I woke up, and realized that I've had thirty-three years of that sort of thing, and I don't want to play anymore, that's all." He sniffed. "It's a stupid game, with no rules and no referee. And no matter what I do, it's going to end the same way, so why bother playing at all?"

My tongue felt numb in my mouth. "Tell me what happened today, son."

He shrugged. "Nothing, really. Shanda Cartwright threw a little hissy fit this morning in rehearsal that pissed me off royally, but it wasn't a big deal by itself."

Shanda was the flute instructor at Carson, and she had the brains of a toadstool.

"You let Shanda put you in this kind of a snit?"

He shook his head. "Not at all. I couldn't care less about her. But while she was going off about this and that petty irritation, it suddenly occurred to me she was just a symptom of something much, much worse."

The sun was almost to the horizon, now; it looked as if it were caught in the upper branches of an oak tree across the street. It was orange and red and stunning, and I watched it for a moment, distracted and moved—in spite of where we were—by how beautiful it was.

My nose was running and I swiped at it with a hanky I had in my coat. "What was she a symptom of, dear?" I had to keep him talking, it was the only thing that ever calmed him down.

"Futility. Stupidity." He searched for more words. "Blind, unthinking existence, I suppose." He straightened. "Take your pick, but it wasn't pretty."

"Oh, God," I sighed, relieved to be back on familiar ground. "In other words, you're complaining about having too much talent and brains again?" I slapped the windowsill for emphasis. "When in God's name are you going to grow up?"

Every other time we'd done this routine, this strategy had brought him back to himself. I would simply shame him into seeing how childish he was being, and the crisis would be averted, yet again. I had no reason to believe this time would be any different.

But this day, he didn't get angry, or defensive. He didn't flinch, or stiffen, or show any outward sign of resentment or embarrassment. He just smiled at me.

Did I mention he had dimples on his cheeks when he smiled? They were small and tight, like two little staples, one on each side of his mouth.

"Oh, Hester," he said. "My problem isn't a lack of maturity. It really isn't." He paused. "It's cowardice."

I shivered. "I don't understand."

"It's simple, really." He took a small step backward, closer to the edge. He was only about a foot away from it now. "I want out, but I don't have the balls to do it myself." He locked eyes with me. "So will you help me, Mother?"

My blood was ice. My skin was the same temperature as the wind, my face was as blank and immobile as St. Booger's.

"I will not." I forced the words out past frozen lips. "Come inside this instant, and stop talking nonsense."

There was compassion in his expression. He was examining my features closely, as if he hadn't seen me in a very long time. "I want you to know this has nothing to do with you. Or anybody else, for that matter. It's just life I'm tired of. That's all." He cocked his head at me. "Can you please help me out?"

I put my foot up on the chair next to the window in the kitchen and began to climb out on the roof. He took another step backward, but I didn't stop. I had been overtaken by a sense of urgency, and I knew I had to get to him right away.

He was only inches from the edge when I cleared the window and had both of my knees on the roof.

He smiled again. "That's my girl," he said. "I knew I could count on you."

I rose to my feet, knees popping. The wind blew my hair around like a fan, and I blinked away tears from the coldness of it. "I want you to come inside with me, son," I whispered.

He sighed. "No can do." He put his hands in his pants pockets. "All I need is a little nudge, okay?"

I was about five feet away, and I took a step toward him to close the gap.

He watched my slow progress, unconcerned. "Do you remember the Chopin piece I always asked you to play for me when I was a kid?" he asked, for no reason I could think of.

His voice was wistful, and warm, and I hesitated.

"Of course I do," I answered. "How could I forget? You made me play it for you nearly every day."

He nodded. "Yeah. I did, didn't I?" All of a sudden, he was crying. His shoulders were shaking and his breath was coming in hitches. "Well, that's the way I thought life was supposed to be. Like in the music, I mean. Full of longing and pain, too, of course, but in the end, more about glory than anything else." He fought to control his voice. "Not the other way around. Do you see, Hester? Tell me you see that."

I could barely understand him through his sobs.

I took another step forward, and held my arms out to him. "Come inside, Jeremy. Come back where it's safe."

He didn't seem to notice me getting closer. He just wept, and let his head fall forward on his chest.

"Oh, Mother," he said. "You always made it seem so beautiful."

I was weeping, too. I wanted nothing more than to hold him next to me, and he was almost in reach. I opened my arms to gather him in, and I took the final step.

And so did he.

CHAPTER 18

"Alex? Are you awake yet?"

I hear light footsteps in the hall above my head and he leans over the banister, dressed in nothing but a pair of dark green boxer shorts. "Yeah. Sort of."

I smile up at him from the landing by Arthur's old studio. "Did someone steal your clothes, child?"

In spite of the anxiety he must be feeling about the day ahead of him, he manages to grin back at me. He seems even more vulnerable than usual in his bare skin.

"Nah," he answers. "In fact, I was thinking of starting a nudist colony up here." He yawns and smooths his tangled red hair with his fingers. "Can I put an ad in the newspaper?"

He's begun teasing me a great deal lately.

"I'd rather you didn't. Anybody who answers such an advertisement in this town is likely to be somewhat alarming." I yawn, too; I've only been up for a few minutes. "You're still planning on going to school today, aren't you?"

He hasn't attended his classes at Pritchard for well over a week, ever since his fight with Eric. He's terrified of seeing him again.

Near-panic crosses his features, but he controls it with an effort. "Yeah. I'm gonna take a shower in a minute and then head out."

We had another long talk last night, and I believe I finally convinced him of the necessity of returning to his normal routine, in spite of his skittishness. But it was a hard sell. He wasn't just worried about facing Eric; he was also concerned Eric may have blabbed to other people, and the news would be "all over campus."

"*It's exactly what happened at Buckland last semester, with Wei-shan,*" he said. "*Everybody started looking at me like I was a rapist or something, after Thanksgiving.*" He stared at his hands on the kitchen table. "*What if that shit happens here, too?*"

I tried to calm him. "I'm sure you're just imagining what people were thinking of you." I managed to sound far more certain than I felt. "Besides, Eric isn't Wei-shan, and a university like Pritchard is far less prone to rumor-mongering than a tiny school like Buckland. You're worrying over nothing."

He blinked back tears. "It wasn't my imagination, Hester. Everybody knew." He stared over at the stove. "But then again, I guess it wasn't Wei-shan who said something back home, so maybe you're right. Maybe Eric won't tell, either."

That surprised me. "What do you mean, it wasn't Wei-shan who said something?"

"It was my mom." He shrugged. "At least I'm pretty sure it was. I suppose it could have been one of my sisters, instead, but I don't think so."

I gaped at him, indignant. "Surely you're mistaken. Surely your own mother wouldn't have broadcasted something like that about you?"

He tried to smile. "Families sure get fucked up fast, don't they?" He ran a finger through the water ring his glass had left on the table. "Did I tell you I spent Christmas in a Motel 8 outside of Chicago? I tried to go to a cousin's house, first, and my grandma's, too, but Mom had called around and warned all the relatives to not let me stay with them." The smile faltered. "It wasn't so bad, though. I watched It's a Wonderful Life *on the tube, and got majorly stoned."*

When he saw the look in my eyes, he leaned forward as if it were me who needed consolation. "It's okay, Hester. Seriously. I'm over it." He hesitated. "But I don't want to put myself through something like that again if I don't have to. Know what I mean? Especially not so soon after last time."

My heart went out to him, but I couldn't stay silent. "I'm afraid you're going to have to, my dear. And it needs to be sooner rather than later. I wish you could hide here with me forever, but you can't. You've already got a great deal of catching up to do in your classes, and each day you stay away from school is just making things worse for you. Surely you see that?"

He'd looked as if I were force-feeding him a dead rat, but he eventually nodded, and agreed to return to Pritchard.

What I didn't tell him is he'll likely be so far behind in Caitlin's courses already—she piles on a stupefying amount of homework, each and every class period—that I fear she may indeed carry out her threat to revoke his scholarship.

Which would leave him with no other choice than to drop out of school immediately.

"Good for you," I say now, pushing aside my worries for his future. I study him. "You're not intending to smoke marijuana before you go, are you?"

He blinks. "Yeah, I am, as a matter of fact. Want some?"

I cringe. "Good God, no."

He grimaces at my expression. "You're getting ready to tell me I'm an idiot, aren't you?"

That tickles me, for some reason. "It would seem I no longer need to." I cock my head at him. "Alex, dear. Think for a moment, please. You'll need all your wits about you today, don't you agree?"

He doesn't like being mothered, and I can tell he's annoyed at me for saying this. But in the end he sighs and nods his head.

"Okay, okay," he mumbles. "I won't smoke."

I reward him with another smile. "Don't mumble, please."

He sighs again, and repeats—in a louder, more exasperated voice—his pledge not to smoke.

I nod, satisfied. "Good. Hurry up and shower, then come down and have a quick breakfast with me. I'm warming up some frozen cinnamon rolls from the bakery."

He cranes his neck toward his living room, presumably looking at the clock on the wall in there. "I don't have time for breakfast, Hester. Not if I'm going to walk."

I start down the stairs. "You have time. I'll drive you."

* * *

He steps into the kitchen a few minutes later with wet hair and clean clothes. As he pulls out his chair, I set a plate with a cinnamon roll the size of a grapefruit on the table in front of him, next to a glass of orange juice and a steaming mug of hot tea. The roll is fresh from the oven, and the smell of cinnamon and sugar is filling the room. Ordinarily he'd wolf down a treat like this, but today he just stares at his plate as if he's contemplating throwing up on it.

"That's huge," he grunts. "I can't eat it." He sinks heavily in his chair.

I sit across from him and butter my own roll, which is quite a bit smaller. "Have a bite or two, then," I tell him. "The rest will keep."

He's miserable. His lower lip is trembling, and he's pale and withdrawn. I observe him from the corner of my eye, knowing there's not much I can do for him at the moment, no matter how much I'd like to help. Guilt and worry and fear are circling around him like large, hungry buzzards, and nothing I can say will change the truth of that. I know these predatory birds all too well, and they are impervious to reason, deaf to supplication, and fully armored against all conventional weapons.

But you have to try to beat them back, anyway.

"It will be all right, Alex." My voice is quiet. "You'll get through this day."

He raises his head and stares into my eyes. "Are you sure about that?" He looks away and bites his lip. "I keep going over and over in my mind what I can say to Eric to get him to forgive me, but everything I think of sounds stupid."

He pushes back from the table and gets up, unable to sit still.

I glance at my watch. "Where are you going?" I ask. "We have plenty of time before we need to leave."

He steps over to the entryway and comes back to the table a moment later, carrying his shoes. "I'm just gonna finished getting dressed." He sits in the chair again and tries to fit his right foot into a sneaker, but his hands are trembling so badly he can't seem to do it. He gives up and lets the shoe drop to the floor, and he sits there with his bare foot on the chair and his chin on his knee.

He looks up at me again in despair. "Do you know how pathetic

I am?" He's on the verge of tears. "I was just thinking that maybe if I wore socks, Eric would like me again."

I smile at him, as gently as I can. "Yes, I'm sure you're right, dear. Socks are the solution to all your problems."

There's a long pause, and his throat works as he swallows.

"I don't know what to do, Hester," he chokes out. "What am I supposed to do?"

"I don't really know." I try to find words to comfort him, even though I know there are none. "You put on your shoes. You have a bite to eat, and you go on with your day. It's all any of us can do, really." I take a sip of tea. "And if I were you, I wouldn't say a word to Eric. He's . . . well, right now he's poisonous to you."

He lowers his head. "That's not his fault."

My silverware pings against my plate as I cut into my roll. "I know it's not. But that doesn't make him any less . . . toxic for you at the moment." I take a bite and swallow. "Sometimes you can't fix things, Alex. No matter how much it hurts, you just have to let them be, and do nothing but sit around with an ache in your chest, and an ocean of acid in your stomach."

That ache, and that acid, are as familiar to me as the keys on my piano. I'd do anything to spare him from having to experience them, but I can't.

He shakes his head. "But if I don't do something, I'm going to die," he whispers.

He isn't being intentionally theatrical. He's young, and he's suffering, and he can't see his way past the feelings he's having right at this moment. And probably the worst thing I can do is to tell him the truth: that he will indeed survive this, and go on, and then one or two years from now, he'll do something else that will cause him at least as much pain, which he will also survive. And then (assuming he maintains a firm grip on his lovely, restless old soul, which I think he will) there will be a next time, and a next, and a next, for the remainder of his life.

Because desire is a nearly unbreakable habit, as is the impulse to act on it. The only thing that sometimes changes—and this is only if you're very fortunate—is the object of your desire. You can call it karma, I suppose, or recurring bad luck, if you prefer a less fate-oriented explanation. But the truth of being human is that what we *want* defines us, and dictates all our actions, and leads us into temptation. Again, and again, and again, world without end.

But as I said, he probably doesn't need to hear that indigestible piece of news right at this moment.

I nod. "I know it feels that way. Believe me, I really do. But I'm hoping you'll be smarter than me, and not waste your time as I have, attempting to win back someone who doesn't want to be around you anymore."

His eyes well up, and I bite my lip.

"Forgive me, son," I murmur. "I'm sorry to put it so bluntly, but there it is. Pining after somebody you can't have only leads to anger, and anger leads to serious consequences down the road." I try to smile. "And believe me, you're much better off doing nothing—and feeling the way you feel now—than acting out and making things ten times worse."

Alex is openly crying, now.

So much for my little pep talk.

I close my eyes briefly, and struggle, yet again, with my own grief, which is flaring up in response to his. But when I open them once more, I'm surprised to find him looking straight at me.

"Thank you," he says roughly.

He knows I'm hurting, too, of course. I'm sure he's just being polite to a fatuous old woman, to spare my feelings and make me feel good. But I appreciate the effort.

I clear my throat. "For what?"

He doesn't answer. But as I search his haggard features more closely, it seems to me that something else is there, now, besides panic and despair. It takes me a moment to recognize this new thing, and when I do, it becomes difficult to swallow the bite of roll in my mouth.

I may be wrong, but I could swear that what I'm seeing on his face is love.

It changes nothing, and it helps neither of us with our separate dilemmas. But as I feel an answering affection rising up in me, I realize that at least he's not alone any longer.

And neither am I.

"What is it, dear?" I ask him. "Why are you looking at me like that?"

He shrugs, and gives me the faintest hint of a smile. "I don't know." He swipes at his eyes with the back of his hand. "You're just making more sense today than you usually do, is all," he says gruffly. "I guess it's kind of freaking me out."

He's trying to pull himself together, trying to move on to something other than sorrow. And I believe he's doing this as much for me as for himself.

My eyes are full now, too, but I do my best to play along with him. "I see," I say after a minute, sniffling. "Well, be a good boy and eat your cinnamon roll. The ant poison I put in the frosting shouldn't go to waste."

His grin widens, becoming more real. I watch him slowly draw his shoulders up, attempting to be brave. He picks up his knife and reaches for the butter, but his fingers are still shaking a little.

I was the only member of my family to see Jeremy's body in the driveway. Deaf old Edith next door called the police when she noticed me standing out there by him, and by the time Arthur and the children arrived home, most of the emergency personnel had already come and gone, including a man from Leeman's Funeral Home, whose job it was to cart my son away in the mortuary vehicle.

What was left of my son.

He'd landed on his tailbone on the asphalt, and the back of his skull hit immediately afterwards, with enough force to split it open and fling a three-foot trail of blood and brains across the snow and ice in the driveway. His face survived more or less intact, though, and his lovely gray eyes were still open, as if he were waiting to see the first stars appear, following the sunset.

I did not kneel next to him. I did not hold his body, nor feel the warmth leave it.

I simply stood there, staring down at him for an eternity. I didn't move, or make a scene, or rend my garments. I did not weep, nor did I begin to keen. In fact, I'm fairly certain I made no noise at all.

Until I felt Edith's arms around me.

I remember convulsing with grief as she held me. I remember hearing the sirens approaching, and I remember thinking the sound I issued in response was nearly an octave lower than that of the sirens, but it was just as loud and jarring to my ears. I believe I kept making that racket for a long time, as more and more policemen and paramedics showed up, but everyone was very kind to me, and no one made me stop until I ran out of steam, and at last fell silent. My throat felt as if I would never speak again, but somehow my voice continued to work, and that's when the questions started.

Half an hour later I was back inside, watching through the living room window as an investigator and the county medical examiner conferred in the driveway, standing next to St. Booger. Several fire trucks were parked nearby, providing illumination with their powerful spotlights. Our entire yard was bathed in so much light it might as well have been high noon out there. I could see more of our neighbors in the street by then, watching the proceedings, but the police kept them away from the house.

The investigator was Carlos Bernal, who had been in the same class with Caitlin in high school, and had also been in our home several times as a teenager. He was the one who asked me about what had happened on the roof, and he listened without any expression on his face when I told him that Jeremy slipped and fell while watching the sunset with me.

He knew I was being dishonest, of course. He'd spoken to Edith before he spoke to me, and even though she hadn't actually seen Jeremy fall, she'd seen how erratically he was behaving beforehand, and Carlos was more than capable of putting two and two together.

But he didn't demand the truth from me. He knew me, and he knew my family, and he simply stood there watching me for a long time before finally asking another question.

"Mrs. Donovan," he said. His eyes were sad and compassionate. "Are you sure this is what you want me to tell the medical examiner?" He hesitated. "He'll believe what I tell him, I think, because the . . ." He searched for words. ". . . the physical evidence here is consistent with that of an accidental death. But are you sure your memory isn't playing tricks on you?"

I took a long, shuddering breath. "Surely you don't suspect me of foul play, Carlos?"

He shook his head, firmly. "No. I don't." He put his hand on my shoulder. "But I just want you to be absolutely positive this is the story you want people to hear about how Jeremy died."

When he was in high school, he had been a quiet, bright boy, who for a time had chased after my daughter with no success. He was still a quiet, bright boy, and I suddenly recalled Caitlin telling me the news that he had married a woman from Oklahoma, who was pregnant with his child. He was going to be a father soon.

I stared at the floor and nodded. "I'm sure."

I watched his feet shuffle from side to side for a while. "Okay," he said at last, squeezing my shoulder. A moment later he left me in peace, and went outside to lie for me.

For the life of me, I don't know why he chose to handle the situation that way. Maybe he thought it might ease my suffering to allow me to conceal Jeremy's suicide, or maybe he decided that, in the end, there was nothing to be gained by reporting it any differently. Either way, Jeremy was dead. Dear Edith, too, maintained her silence about what she suspected, so the articles that came out in the papers the next day had headlines like "Virtuoso Musician Plummets to His Death in Tragic Accident." There were a few mumbled rumors of suicide, of course, but to my knowledge no one took them seriously.

I don't know much. I don't know if I did the right thing, and I don't know if the truth of Jeremy's death would have served a higher purpose, had it been reported. But one thing I *do* know is this:

If there's a heaven, there's a VIP suite in it reserved solely for people like Carlos Bernal and Edith Schumaker. For what it's worth, they both have my fervent gratitude, until the end of time.

Anyway, as I was saying, my family was not on hand to witness the grotesque events in our driveway. This was ten years or so before cell phones were in every pocket and purse, and although the police had begun calling everywhere I could think to tell them to try, it took over an hour before Arthur finally showed up. Paul and Caitlin arrived half an hour after their father, but within seconds of each other.

Arthur had been at a recording studio in St. Louis that morning, and should have returned much earlier in the day. (I now suspect he was with Martha Predel at the moment Jeremy jumped, but I have no proof of this.) It was fully dark outside when he at last pulled into the driveway, but the light from the porch allowed me to see him step from his car, toting his violin. Almost everyone else had left by then, but Carlos and a uniformed officer were still standing by the house, tying up loose ends. I ran for the door, desperate to reach Arthur and tell him what had occurred before he heard the news from them.

Edith was in the living room with me; she had refused to go home and leave me by myself. She called out behind me as I tore the front door open. Arthur was next to the officers by then, but they hadn't yet had time to explain what they were doing there.

He saw it in my face before I said a word. My feet stopped moving after I was out on the porch, and I watched him glance anxiously over Carlos's shoulder at me. At first there was relief in his expression, and I realized he'd feared something had happened to me. He almost smiled, then, but all at once his cheeks went slack as he studied me more closely, and he shook his head, twice. His legs gave out on him, and he fell on the ground, clutching his violin case to his thick chest.

I kneeled next to him, as I wasn't able to do for Jeremy. I held his body, the way I should have held our son's, and the two of us sat there in the snow, sobbing under the cold glare of the porch light. The two policemen and Edith hovered over us, wanting to help, but there was nothing they could do except wait nearby, and watch us grieve for our boy.

By the time our remaining children came home, Arthur and I were alone in the house, waiting for them. Unfortunately, both Paul and Caitlin had already been alerted, by strangers, to the news about their brother. Paul had been at his cottage, taking a nap all afternoon, with the phone unplugged, but the police had finally tired of trying to call him, and had instead sent an officer to knock on his door. And Caitlin, who had recently moved back to Bolton to teach at Pritchard, had been unearthed in a basement room at the university library, where she often sequestered herself to "get away from interruptions."

Paul pulled into the driveway mere seconds ahead of Caitlin, and Arthur and I went outside to meet them. The moon was up by then, and there was light enough to see by. The four of us were moving in slow motion, it seemed, and it took a lifetime to reach each other next to the carriage house.

And so we came together at last, in stunned, nightmarish silence, to face the reality of Jeremy's death. Our eyes met, and we embraced, and we tried to speak, and we cried. When that ran its course, we did nothing at all except stand there, witless and drained. I found myself becoming a cliché, against my will, because I couldn't conceive of an original way to mourn. Every gesture I made seemed preordained, every word I uttered felt scripted. When I had awakened in the morning there were still five of us, but that evening there were only four, and the simple math of this equation made no sense to me. Arthur and Paul and Caitlin were just as lost as I was; none of us knew what to do, or how to behave. It's a wonder we eventually remembered to come in out of the cold and the darkness.

Sometimes this sort of thing brings a family closer together, or so I'm told.

But sometimes it tears it apart.

It didn't take very long for the Donovan clan to come undone. I don't know why this was so, but it seems to me the groundwork for our dissolution must have already been laid, years ago, unbeknownst to me, because otherwise there would have been no reason for things to have gone as sour as they did. Regardless, once we began to speak, all our karmic chickens—an entire flock of them—came home to roost.

We sat by the fire in the living room for a few minutes, and I told the children what I had already told Arthur—namely about all the times I had found Jeremy on the roof, and what had passed between us, especially this afternoon. But while Arthur had taken in this information quietly, with only a whispered "You mustn't blame yourself, Hester," as his reaction, Paul and Caitlin were floored, and instantly furious.

And more unforgiving than I'd ever dreamed possible.

Paul was drinking scotch, and his first response was to stand up and fling his glass into the flames. The glass shattered and the fire ignited the alcohol with a tremendous "whoosh" of heat and light; it was a miracle nothing close to the fireplace was burned before the flames subsided again. I didn't have a chance to object to his behavior, though, because he was yelling at me before I could recover from the shock.

"You were up there how many times?" he howled. "You *knew* he was suicidal, and you never said anything about it?"

"Sit down, Paul," Arthur demanded. "Control yourself."

"Fuck you, Dad," Paul shot back. "Did you know about this, too?"

Caitlin was more contained, but just as livid. "Why would Jeremy do such a thing, Mother?" She kept her seat, but her back was rigid and her voice cut like a scythe. "Why in the name of God did you go out on the roof? He as much as told you he was going to jump if you did just that."

I tried to answer her, but Paul cut me off. "Yes, Mother. Do tell us what was going through your mind." His ruddy face was streaked with tears. "Jeremy's been depressed his whole goddamn life, but he's never acted on it until you decided to play a game of tag with him." He stumbled over to the fireplace and rested his forehead on the mantel shelf. "Oh, Jesus," he sobbed. "What have you done?"

Arthur tried to defend me. He really did. "That's enough, from both of you." He was so overcome with grief that he could barely make himself understood, but he tried. "Your mother is not to blame for this."

Caitlin leaned forward and glared at him. "Then who is, Dad? Who else knew how bad things had gotten? Did you? Did Paul and I?" There were tears on her cheeks as well. "Of course we didn't. Jeremy didn't say a word to anybody else except Hester." She turned her glare on me. "And you did what you've always done with him and Paul, didn't you? You coddled him, and you decided you knew best how to deal with his condition."

She dropped her gaze and stared blindly at the floor. "Hester always knows best, especially when it comes to her darling wunderkind boys."

The bitterness in her tone was appalling.

"His condition?" My voice was a small, dead thing. The combined weight of their assault and my own guilt and pain was destroying me. "Which condition are you referring to?"

"His goddamn depression, of course," Paul snapped, spinning around again. "Don't be stupid." He turned his rage on his sister. "And what the fuck are you talking about, Caitlin? Hester's never coddled me a day in my life. She was too busy wiping Jeremy's ass every time he farted, or babying you because you couldn't . . ." He made a face and looked away. "Fuck it," he mumbled. "Never mind."

Caitlin blinked. "Because I couldn't what, Paul?"

He didn't answer her.

Arthur made another attempt to calm them down. "We need to stop this, right now. None of us is thinking clearly, and this is the absolute worst time possible to turn on each other. Jeremy didn't kill himself because Hester spoiled him, or any such nonsense." We were sitting close to each other, and he reached for my hand to hold it. "And criticizing your mother serves no purpose at all. We weren't up there, and we can't possibly know what made him do what he did."

Caitlin shook her head, hard enough to dislodge a tear from her chin. "That's the whole point, Dad. We weren't up there. But Hester was up there at least half a dozen times with him before today. She's *known* there's been a problem for months, and she's never told us anything." She studied my face. "You enjoyed having him all to yourself, didn't you? You loved that feeling of being needed so much that you weren't about to share any part of it with the rest of us."

And with that cruel, all-too-accurate statement, she fell to pieces, just like that. She buried her face in her hands and wept as if the entire world were ending. I don't know if it was because she saw what her words were doing to me, or if she simply could no longer beat back the full horror of Jeremy's death. She'd wept in the driveway before, but that display was nothing to this flood now pouring from her.

And to my undying shame, I didn't go to her. The ugliness she had shown preceding this breakdown had devastated me, and all I could do was watch her from a distance, with wounded pride, and despair, and a burning self-hatred.

Arthur, too, did nothing. I don't know what kept him in his chair. Loyalty to me, perhaps, or some kind of psychic paralysis. Either way, he didn't move, and the two of us, in frightening stillness, watched our daughter implode in front of us. It was our single greatest failing as parents, I believe, and maybe the only opportunity we would ever have to draw what was left of our family together again, in a way that would allow for some kind of healing.

But we chose not to. We didn't know any better.

Which left Paul in charge of caring for her.

"For God's sake, Caitlin," he growled down at her bowed head. "Get a grip."

He meant it kindly enough. Honestly, he did. There was even love in his voice, if you knew how to listen for it. But if you weren't listening closely, all you would have heard was his impatience, and his exasperation.

Caitlin's head snapped up. Her face was distorted and red, and her eyes were wild with anguish and rage. She looked at her brother for a moment, and then at Arthur, and then at me. It seemed as if she were searching for something she had lost, and was frantic to recover.

But whatever she was looking for, she couldn't find it in our faces.

She picked up her purse, and she rose from her chair.

"Where are you going?" Paul asked, as she walked toward the door.

"Somewhere else," she replied, putting on her winter coat. "Anyplace that's not here."

I didn't stop her. I didn't tell her that this was her home, and that she belonged here, especially after a day like this. She may have been waiting for me to say something to that effect, but my tongue refused to make the effort. Arthur's hand tightened on mine, but he, too, said not a word.

And so she left.

Her departure was the last straw for Paul, as well. He began to rant at both of us, but the worst of his vilification was directed at me. He went on and on, but the gist of it was that I "killed Jeremy," and "drove away Caitlin," and I was "responsible for everything that's wrong with this family." He was incoherent with grief and frustration, and more than once I saw madness in his eyes.

You'll forgive me if I don't wish to recount all of that particular speech.

Suffice it to say, it didn't end well. Paul, too, collapsed in despair, and disappeared into the night after Caitlin, leaving Arthur and me alone in our huge, cold, empty house.

And leaving us as well—for all intents and purposes—with three dead children, instead of one.

CHAPTER 19

Bonnie Norton is being ridiculous. And devious, too.

After dropping Alex off at Pritchard this morning, I returned home and called Bonnie at the Conservatory, but Marla—her secretary—told me Bonnie had instructed her to say, should I call, that "the dean is considering your situation carefully, and will be in touch with you as soon as she reaches a decision." When I inquired about what was being done with my students, she informed me, cryptically, that they were being "taken care of," and would not elaborate.

Which means, of course, that Bonnie has shuffled them off to other teachers, at least temporarily. And the fact that not even one of my pupils has contacted me to ask what's going on (not even pretty little Miranda Moore, who adores me) tells me Bonnie has likely warned all of them away in an attempt to further isolate me from the Conservatory community.

Either that, or my students themselves are too disgusted by my behavior at last week's master class reception to wish to speak with me.

The doorbell rings, interrupting my dark thoughts. I glance up from my chair in the living room and peer out at the porch through the window, to see who it is.

Dear God. It's Paul, again.

I get to my feet with an effort. I'm exhausted and sad this morning—it's not even noon yet—and I'm in no condition to deal with another of his fits of pique. I check the mirror on the wall in the entryway before opening the door; I don't want him to see me looking too disheveled. I'm pleased to see my hair is combed, and my blouse and slacks—both dark green—are presentable. My light blue slippers don't go with the ensemble, but there's no time to change footwear, so they'll have to do.

I take a deep breath and open the door, to find Paul waiting in ambush on the other side. He's already holding the screen door open, and leaning in, so he can begin badgering me without delay.

"Hello, Hester," he growls. The day is bitterly cold again, and he's glaring down at me from behind his bisonesque beard.

"Paul." I cross my arms and refuse to shiver in the frigid air. "Why have you come back?"

"Let me in, and I'll tell you," he says. His heavy, strong hand slips on the handle of the screen door and he almost falls at my feet.

Lord. He's thoroughly, absolutely besotted. His breath stinks of alcohol and cigarettes, and his eyes are unfocused and fairly secreting hostility. I glance around him and see his red Volvo next to St. Booger in the driveway; its bumper is mere inches away from the statue's pedestal, which means Paul missed the turn in the driveway by several feet, and even jumped his vehicle over the brick lip of Booger's stone garden before managing to apply the brakes.

"I think not," I say firmly. "You're drunk, and I have no intention of speaking to you while you're in this condition."

He pulls himself to his full height. "Don't you dare fucking judge me for being a little shitfaced. If you're not already drunk yourself, you will be soon, and we both know it."

He's not slurring his words at all, but he's speaking with exaggerated precision.

I begin to close the door. "Goodbye, Paul. You might wish to use your cell phone to call a taxi to take you home."

He steps in closer and puts an arm out to prevent the door from shutting. "We're going to talk now," he states. "Right now."

He's looming over me, and his face is flushed, and his voice is low and mean. What in heaven's name has gotten into him? I'm used to him being unreasonable, but there's something else going on here I haven't seen from him before, and I have no clue what may have set him off. But I believe he may be drunk enough to hurt me.

For the first time in my life, I find myself physically afraid of one of my own children.

I step forward and glare up into his eyes. I will not let him see my fright. "Leave this house immediately, son, or I will call the police and have you arrested."

He snorts and pretends to be unconcerned, but he abruptly drops his hand from the door. "I want you to throw that fucking kid out, Hester," he blurts. "I'm done fucking around. He's got no business being in Jeremy's apartment. No fucking business at all." He shakes a finger in my face. "And then you need to get out, too, and let Dad have his own goddamn house back."

Jeremy's apartment? What on earth?

I slap his hand out of the way. "Have you been swilling absinthe, or something similarly brain-damaging? If you'll recall, we had another tenant in the apartment last year, and you didn't care one way or another about that. What are you so upset about?"

The reddened skin on his face tightens. "Caitlin said you're treating this little shit like some kind of fucking foster kid. Like little fucking Jeremy Junior." Spittle flies from his lips; he hasn't sworn this much since he was in junior high.

So I was right. Caitlin and he are speaking again, and they seem to be united in jealousy about my relationship with Alex. That in itself is a bit of a shocker, but Paul's having worked himself up into this much of a rage over it makes no sense at all. What caused this sudden burst of saber rattling?

I study him, trying to see past the current drunken stupor into his convoluted psyche. Why would he be jealous now of my relationship with Alex—a virtual stranger to him? Does he truly believe I'm attempting to supplant Jeremy? And how can I talk to him about any of this when his bloodstream is so polluted with alcohol?

I can't, of course. And I won't.

"We're done talking, Paul. Go home, get sober, and get some sleep. If you still want to talk when you're lucid, then you know where to find me."

He leans down and begins to scream in my face. "Fuck you, Hester! We're gonna talk now, and you're gonna get rid of that skinny piece of crap tenant upstairs, and you're gonna stop being such a bitch to Dad!"

His breath is foul and hot, and his teeth and tongue are about two inches from my nose. I reach up and slap him, hard, across the face. He tries to grab my hand but misses and loses his balance, staggering backward.

I grasp the handle of the screen door and yell at him. "I'm calling the police this instant! You can either leave now on your own, or you can leave in handcuffs in a few minutes!"

He regains his footing and stands there in front of me, swaying. His eyes are thin slits and his forehead is mottled and veiny. For a moment, I think he's preparing to charge me, but then he spins around and stomps over to his car, leaving a trail of uneven footsteps behind him in the snow. He pops the driver's door open on the Volvo and nearly falls into the front seat.

"Fuck you, Hester!" he bellows. "Fuck you, fuck you, *fuck you*!"

The sun is shining on the snow, and it's a bright day. He's too far away for me to be sure, but I could swear there are tears on his face and in his beard, glistening in the sunlight. It could be sweat, I suppose, but his face is contorted, too.

Just as it was on the day he learned of Jeremy's death.

My heart twists to look at him as he slams the door and starts the engine. He pops the car into reverse and it surges back down the driveway, miraculously staying off the lawn and shooting out into the middle of the street without hitting anything.

And the second he comes to a stop and shifts into first gear, Alex appears on the sidewalk at the end of the block.

I fly off the porch and onto the driveway in my slippers, with my heart in my throat. Alex is walking fast with his head down and hasn't yet seen Paul, but Paul is peering intently out the windshield at the approaching boy. He takes his foot off the brake and the car glides forward, its tires crunching over the snow and ice on the pavement as it nears Alex. I reach the sidewalk at the same moment Alex draws even with Paul's car, but I'm still half a block away from the two of them.

What in God's name is Alex doing home this early? He was supposed to be in class until late afternoon.

Paul rolls down the window and sticks his beefy, hairy head out
the window. "Hey, shithead! Get over here!"

Alex looks up, startled. He sees Paul before he sees me, and his
face darkens with fear.

My heart is beating wildly and I nearly take a spill on the sidewalk, but I somehow find the breath to call out. "Alex! Ignore him,
and run this way."

I may have been able to prevent my son from attacking me, but I
have no illusions about what he's likely to do to Alex if I can't keep
them apart.

Alex turns at the sound of my voice and sees me running toward
him. He glances over at Paul again, then picks up his pace and
moves to meet me. Good boy.

"Hey, I'm talking to you, punk!" Paul rages. "Get your ass over
here!"

Alex grinds to a halt on the sidewalk. I'm only ten feet away from
him now and I can see his face harden as he turns to face Paul.

*Oh, Lord. Please don't do this, child. You have no idea what
you're doing.*

I reach his side just as he raises his voice to carry across the
street. "What do you want, Paul?"

My chest is heaving from the run and from anxiety, but I take
Alex's arm in a firm grip and tug at him.

Paul is bellowing again. "It's *Mister* Donovan, and I want you to
get your ass over here, so we can have a conversation without the
whole fucking neighborhood hearing it."

Alex looks down at me. His eyes are remarkably calm as he studies me, and his face fills with concern. "Hester," he whispers. "Where's
your coat? Why are you outside in your slippers?"

"I'm trying to save your life, you idiot," I gasp. "Paul's dead
drunk right now, and very, very dangerous. Don't you dare go near
him."

He swings his attention back to Paul, and gazes at him for a long
time. Paul is simply sitting there, leaning out the window, waiting.
Alex takes a deep breath and then reaches down to pat my hand.

"I'll be right back. I promise." He extricates himself from my clutching fingers. "I'll be careful." He steps away from me, picking his way through the knee-deep snow on top of the lawn between the sidewalk and the curb, and when he reaches the street he approaches the car with caution.

The snow is too deep for me to get through it without breaking my neck, especially in these slippers. I'll freeze to death soon if I don't get back inside, but I fling my arms around myself and do a dance of frustration on the sidewalk.

"Come back here immediately, you little jackass!" I hiss at his back.

He ignores me and stops a few feet away from Paul's door. Even from that distance he must be able to smell the booze on my son.

Paul has one arm hanging out the window of the car, and he's glaring at Alex, and all of a sudden it occurs to me how much Paul and Caitlin look like each other, and their father, too. Paul's eyes are brown and Caitlin's are green, but they both have the same belligerent glower Arthur has when he's angry, the same brooding intensity.

Paul takes a drag on his cigarette and blows the smoke in Alex's direction. "I just tried to visit my darling mother, but she wouldn't let me in the door." He's pretending not to see me. "The bitch even threatened to call the police if I didn't leave."

The wind takes the smoke away before it reaches Alex, and I watch it vanish, along with the steam from his breath. He's standing at an angle to the Volvo, just out of Paul's reach, and I can see his face as he appraises my son. His expression is flat and unreadable.

He shrugs. "Good for her." His face may be composed, but his voice is high with tension. "What do you want to talk to me about?"

Paul's forehead and cheeks get redder and he leans out the door a little more. "I want you to move out of my dad's house. And I mean right now. Today."

"Alex," I cry out. "Come back over here. Please?"

He doesn't answer, or turn to look at me. He's entirely focused on Paul. "It's not your dad's house," he says quietly. "It's Hester's."

I wince. Is the little fool *trying* to get himself killed?

Paul sits bolt upright, and almost bangs his head on the roof of the car.

"Shut your fucking hole, asswipe! And stay the fuck out of my family's business, or I'll fucking kill you. Do you understand?"

His hand is hovering by the handle of the door, ready to open it. Alex's eyes dart to me and up to the house, as if considering his options. He could probably outrun Paul with no problem by himself, but if he has to tow me along with him his speed advantage is nil.

"You pathetic little piece of shit," my son continues. "Who the fuck do you think you are? I'm doing you a favor by telling you to move out." He pauses for another puff and raises his eyebrows. "Surely you realize you're living with the biggest goddamn cunt in the universe?"

I don't even bother to pay attention to this crude statement; Paul is unhinged at the moment, and doesn't even know what he's saying.

But Alex's reaction is somewhat different.

Without a moment's hesitation he steps forward and punches Paul in the face as hard as he can. Paul reels back, blood spurting from his nose, and Alex starts kicking the side of his car like a madman.

"Shut the hell up about Hester!" he yells. "What kind of a dickhead talks like that about his own mom?"

"Stop it, Alex," I scream. "Please, please, stop it!"

Paul recovers and flings the door open so hard it makes a loud popping noise right before it swings back at him in force as he's trying to get out. It slams into his legs and he screams in rage, and then he slides past it and falls down on the icy street. Alex gives the Volvo one more solid kick, right in the headlight, and glass goes flying with a high, sharp crack.

Paul is up on his knees by then. "You little fucker!"

"Run, Alex," I wail. "Run!"

Alex hops back a few feet, to get distance from Paul. I look both directions in a panic to see if there's anyone nearby I can ask for help, but the street is empty.

Alex shakes out his hand; I wouldn't be surprised if he broke a knuckle or two when he struck Paul. "You shouldn't talk about your mom like that," he says coldly. "She deserves better from you."

Paul is on his feet, and he's panting for air so badly it looks as if he might collapse. But he's huge, and he's out of his mind with rage, and I know there's no way Alex can handle him in a fight, even though Paul is drunk and middle-aged, and in horrible shape.

"She deserves nothing from me except my contempt." Paul almost sounds calm as he starts lumbering toward Alex. "I'm going to tear your fucking head off, kid. And then I'm going to have you arrested for assault, and what you just did to my car."

Alex is watching him warily. "No, *Paul*, I don't think you are," he tells him. He should be smarter than to goad my son like this, but his pride won't let him stop. "Because Hester and I are going back home in a second, and we'll call the cops. And then they'll put your fat ass in jail for public intox." He wipes his nose on his sleeve. "How does a night in jail sound to you?"

Paul blinks and stops moving forward. "The cops will believe me, not you. I'm the one who's fucking bleeding."

He *is* bleeding. His brown and white beard has patches of red in it, and the front of his coat is getting drops on it, too.

Alex shrugs. "They'll also believe you're fucking wasted, dude. You smell like a scratch and sniff ad for Dewar's."

Paul may be completely drunk, but he's not stupid. He pauses for a moment, then he starts swearing in a low stream. He kicks at the street several times before finally getting back in his car, and he slams the door once he's behind the wheel.

He gives Alex a frightening smile through his open window. "I'll see you again, then," he says. "Very, very soon."

Alex nods and rolls his eyes, pretending to be unconcerned. "I'm terrified. Music teachers scare the shit out of me."

In truth, he should be wetting his pants. Paul is insane at the moment, and he wants to hurt Alex more than anything else in the world. He may even be crazy enough to try to kill the boy in spite of the consequences.

Without warning, he pops the car in gear, cranks the wheel in Alex's direction and stomps on the accelerator. Alex barely makes it to the side of the road before Paul slams into the curb at his heels; the Volvo bucks and stalls out as Alex scrambles to my side and hustles me behind the safety of a large tree a few feet away. The snow on the grass slows us down, but I'm glad it's there because it's also keeping Paul from getting any traction. He turns the engine over and revs it a few times, and for an instant I think he's going to just keep on coming, no matter what.

But at last he backs off into the street. The front left tire of the Volvo wobbles a bit. Paul sticks his head out the window, and waggles a finger at Alex. He's not even looking at me.

"See you around, Alex. That's a promise."

My heart is in my throat as Alex and I watch him drive away. The car weaves from side to side down the road, like a snake. We look at each other in frozen silence for what seems like forever, until the wind becomes unbearable and herds us back home.

I can't stop trembling. Between the cold and the fear of the last few minutes, my limbs are quivering as if with palsy, and the warmth of the house isn't helping at all. Alex is standing next to me at the kitchen window, and he looks frazzled and half-mad.

I'm sure I appear much the same to him.

Without even thinking about it, I begin assembling the ingredients for Irish coffee. It's only ten past noon, but I desperately need something to calm my nerves and get my blood moving again. Alex watches as I grind the coffee beans, then he moves over to the door and kicks his shoes off. He pads back into the kitchen on bare feet and holds out his left hand for me to see. The middle knuckle is swollen and red.

"I hit him really hard," he says. "I think I broke his nose."

His pale blue eyes are enormous, and he seems to be in a state of shock.

"I wouldn't be surprised." I clear my throat, not at all sure of how to proceed with this bizarre conversation. Part of me is furious with him, but my voice remains gentle. "And do you believe this was a wise course of action?"

He nods. "Yeah. He called you a name." His tone is matter-of-fact, but there's an edge of hysteria in it, too.

"You're lucky to be alive." I breathe once, then again. "Striking him was absolutely the worst thing you could have done, child."

A lecture will do no good at this point, I know, but I don't know what else to do. The coffeemaker begins to percolate.

He makes a face. "He was way too drunk to catch me. But I think . . ." He trails off for a moment, then he bites his lip and continues. "I think he'll be back before too long." He meets my gaze. "Am I right?"

I don't answer him. He's still holding his hand out, looking at it, so I take it by the wrist and inspect it. "Can you bend your fingers?"

He flexes them for me, making a fist and wincing. "Sort of."

"It needs ice." I order him to sit at the table, and I get some ice cubes from the freezer and wrap them in a dish towel. "Put this on your hand for a few minutes."

He obeys me, and I finish making the Irish coffee, grateful for the distraction. He watches me without comment as I wander around the kitchen, and I pour him a mug, too, and sit across from him in silence. We're both too rattled to talk. I'm sure there are other things I should be doing, but I can't seem to think what they might be.

The sun is flooding through the window over the sink, reflecting off the tin panels on the walls, and the patch of sky I can see from where I'm sitting is a deep, vibrant blue. I can just make out the top of St. Booger's head; it appears as if the birds have been using it for target practice, because even from this distance I can detect several thin black streaks decorating his snow-covered scalp.

There stand I, I muse, and smile in spite of myself.

I gather my thoughts as best as I'm able and lean forward. "So why on earth did you get so angry with him?"

Alex waves a hand and blushes. "It doesn't really matter."

"Surely it's not just because he called me a name?" I hesitate. "He's always been partial to the word 'cunt,' by the way. Sometimes he even uses it affectionately."

His eyes flicker with anger. "What kind of a person says something like that to his own mom?"

I reach across the table and pat his forearm. "Sticks and stones, dear." I smooth the fabric on the sleeve of his flannel shirt. "And thank you for being upset on my behalf, but you shouldn't have let him get to you. He was quite drunk." I grip his arm for a moment. "But now that you've angered him, I fear what he may do to you if he indeed gets it in his head to come back."

He sighs. "I know. I hope he forgets all about it, but I don't think that's going to happen. He was bleeding a lot, and I think he's going to hunt me down the first chance he gets." He slumps forward and rests his head on the table. A lock of his red hair brushes against my fingers. "God, what a day."

I squeeze his arm again and decide to put Paul out of my mind for the time being, as best as I can. If he returns, I'll find a way to deal with him then.

"Did you see Eric today?" I ask.

"Yeah," he grunts into the tabletop. "He even tried to stop your whacko daughter from castrating me in public."

I wince. "You had a run-in with Caitlin, too?" I release him. "And Eric intervened?"

The top of his head bobs on the table. "Yeah. She was pretending to be pissed because I skipped classes this week, but it was really because I live with you. So I basically told her she was full of shit, and she kicked me out of her room. But before I walked out Eric spoke up and told her he thought she was being unfair." He turns his face so that his freckled cheek presses against his sleeve. He looks worn out. "She was still yelling at him when I left."

He closes his eyes. "Then I waited outside to thank Eric after class, but when he saw me, he told me he only said something to her because she was being such a bitch, and not to think we're still friends because we're not." His voice roughens. "That's why I came home early."

"Oh, dear." I take a big swallow of my Irish coffee. It's really too hot to drink, yet, but I quickly take another, not caring if I scald my mouth. "And here I was, feeling sorry for myself simply because my oldest child threatened me on the porch this morning, and then attempted to run over both of us."

He lifts his head and gawks at me. "He threatened you?"

I pinch the bridge of my nose. "Well, no, not in so many words.

He just blustered a great deal, and wouldn't leave until I mentioned the police."

I push his mug closer to him and tell him to drink, and he complies. A trace of whipped cream ends up on his upper lip.

He licks at it. "So he was already pissed when he saw me."

"I'm afraid so. I apologize for the poor timing."

The phone on the wall rings and we both jump in our chairs. Alex stares at it.

"You got a new phone in here." He removes the makeshift ice pack from his injured hand. "When did you do that?"

"I took the one from Arthur's office this morning."

It rings again, and I make no move to answer it.

He manages a grin. "I thought you said you got rid of the one that was in here because phones don't belong in kitchens."

I grin back. "I lied, of course. I was embarrassed for destroying it during a tantrum."

Ring. Ring. Ring.

The answering machine in the library finally picks up; my recorded voice floats across the entryway and into the kitchen, greeting the caller in polite, no-nonsense tones.

Another woman's voice begins speaking after the beep.

"Hi, Hester." It's Marla Sorenson, the dean's secretary. I'd recognize her voice anywhere; she wheezes a great deal. "It's Marla. Listen, I just got a call from Walter at campus security, saying the police arrested Paul for being drunk and disorderly." Wheeze. "Apparently he got in a fight with Evan a few minutes ago, and Evan called the cops on him. Walter says Evan has some bruises, and is threatening to press charges, but he's also pretty drunk, so it may all blow over." Another wheeze. "Sorry to be the one to tell you, but I thought you should know what was happening."

She hangs up without saying good-bye.

I suppose I should be grateful for the update, but Marla only called because she enjoys being the bearer of bad tidings. Nothing makes her happier than to ruin someone else's day.

"Who's Evan?" Alex asks in the stillness.

I pour more whiskey into my coffee mug. "Evan McCartney.

Paul's roommate. The clarinet teacher at Carson." For some reason, an image of Paul as a young man, sitting at my piano, laughing, pops into my mind just then. I shake my head to clear it. "This is a bit of good news for us, I believe."

"Huh? Why?" Alex cocks his head; he didn't used to do that. It takes me a moment to realize where he picked that habit up.

Dear God. He's imitating me. I don't know if I should be flattered or horrified.

I hold out the bottle to him. "Because if Paul's in jail, he can't come after you. Or me, either, for that matter. At least until he sobers up and bails himself out, that is."

He takes the whiskey and pours more in his mug, too. "Maybe we should call the cops, too, and file a complaint. That way he'll be seriously screwed, and they may keep him for a few days."

I almost agree, then remember something. "We better not. You could get in trouble for striking him." I chew on my lip. "Unless we said it was self-defense?"

He perks up for a moment as he considers this, but then his face sags again and he sighs. "I don't think that will work."

"Why not?"

"Because I also kicked the shit out of his car."

I cock my head, too, before I can catch myself. "Did that do much damage, do you think?"

"Yeah, some. I kicked it about five or six times. And I broke his headlight, too, remember?" He unbuttons his flannel shirt and shrugs out of it; he's wearing a ragged black T-shirt with a quarter-sized hole in the collar.

"Oh, yes. I'd forgotten. Why in God's name did you do that, by the way? Wasn't punching him enough?"

He flushes and takes another drink. "I kind of lost control," he mumbles into his mug.

"Yes, you most certainly did." I'm torn between affection and irritation. "But I'm sure the judge will be very understanding when you're hauled into court for assault."

He hangs his head. "I know. It was stupid. But I just couldn't help it. He was being such a prick."

I massage my temples and wonder if I should call my lawyer to alert him to this latest potential legal snafu. I'm beginning to get a terrible headache. "Is there anything else of Paul's you feel compelled to break at the moment, besides his nose and his headlight?" I demand peevishly. "His arms and legs, maybe? His dinnerware?"

He looks so woeful that despite everything I almost laugh.

I cease my interrogation. "Oh, Alex." I take a shaky breath. "What on earth is the matter with the two of us?"

His mouth twitches. "I don't know."

We finish our drinks and switch to straight whiskey, and we bat around our alternatives: lawyer vs. no lawyer, police vs. no police, how to protect ourselves vs. trying to make peace with Paul. We get nowhere, because every choice either has a significant downside, or is really no choice at all.

The phone rings again.

"What now?" I mutter.

Once more, I let the answering machine intercept the call. Alex and I are both less tense this time as we wait to see who's on the other end of the phone; at least the alcohol is having the desired effect.

It's Oscar Schneider, the oboe instructor at Carson.

"Hello, Hester, it's Oscar." His voice is dry and polite, and uncharacteristically nervous. "Could you give me a call when you get a chance? I was wondering if you'd like to have dinner with me this coming weekend." There's a pause. "I'd really enjoy that."

He gabbles on for a moment, says thank you and hangs up.

Alex and I stare at each other, and I feel myself blushing.

"Damn." He giggles. "That dude wants to hook up with you, Hester." He throws back his head and laughs at my discomfiture. "Who is he, anyway? You've never mentioned him before."

I make a face. "Oscar's an old friend, and I'm sure he's only interested in a platonic relationship."

In truth, I'm baffled by this development; Oscar has never once expressed any desire to see me outside of work. Of course, I was never available before this year, and he's too much of a gentleman to have approached me until it was clear to him that Arthur was permanently out of the picture.

"Uh huh." Alex reaches for the bottle, which is draining rather quickly. "Do you like him, though? Is he hot?"

I fake a growl. "He's nearly my age, so 'hot' is hardly the word I would use to describe him." I give him my best wilting glare. "And we have far more serious matters to attend to than Oscar Schneider's possible sex appeal, don't you think?"

He's not intimidated by me at all anymore. His smile doesn't alter in the slightest. "I think it's cool, and you should go out with him."

I snag the bottle back from him, not trusting him to fill our glasses at this point.

"Yes, well, thank you for your input. But I seldom pay attention to dating advice from bare-knuckled brawlers."

He laughs harder, and I can't help but smile. It's lovely to see him enjoying himself for once, even if it's at my expense.

I refill our glasses, and the phone rings, yet again.

I sigh, annoyed. "I wish people would allow us to drink in peace, don't you?" I blink at my watch. "After all, it's nearly one in the afternoon, and they can't really expect us to be sober at such an ungodly hour."

Alex nods. "Maybe it's your boyfriend Oscar again, hoping to catch you in person. Do you want me to answer and make him jealous?"

The machine picks up before I can retort, and Alex mimics the greeting of my recorded voice, matching it word for word: *"Hello, this is Hester Parker's residence, please leave a message if you would like me to return your call."*

"Very impressive." I sniff. "Apparently there's parrot blood in your family's gene pool."

The caller begins to speak and I stiffen. "Hello, Hester, it's Bonnie Norton. Call me back as soon as you get this." She sounds abrupt and cold. "You need to make an appointment to see me."

She rings off without any further explanation.

The laughter is gone from Alex's face; he knows about the free-for-all with Martha following the master class, of course, and Bonnie's tone just now did not bode well for my future at Carson Conservatory.

"Your boss?" he asks, subdued.

"Yes. The dean." I feign disinterest. "I fear my days as a piano teacher may be numbered."

"I thought you said you had tenure. How can they get rid of you?" He's indignant. "You're famous, Hester. There's no way they'll fire you."

I snort. "My tenure—and my reputation—may indeed protect me from the consequences of flinging a drink on Martha at a public reception, but I'm not counting on it. In the end, they may not be enough to save my job."

"Why not?"

"Because Bonnie Norton is a mule of a woman, and if she's decided she wants me gone, it's likely she'll find a way to do it." I stare at the tawny gold liquid in my glass, admiring its reflective qualities as the sunlight hits it. "Even if she failed to dismiss me, she could make my professional life a daily torment, and I'd eventually be forced to resign of my own free will. I know how she works. I've seen her do this sort of thing before, and she always gets what she wants, sooner or later."

He doesn't know what to say to that, but he gazes at me with compassion, and I have to quell an impulse to cry. The last person to look at me like that was Jeremy. The similarity between the two of them finally hits home, and it's all I can do to not run around the table and plead with this sweet young man to take me in his arms and comfort me, the way my son might have if he were still alive.

Jeremy had a gift for expressing love. He's the only one of my children I can say that about. As a little boy a day never passed without him climbing into my lap at least a dozen times in the course of an afternoon, or resting his head on my shoulder in the car, or crawling up beside me on the couch while I was napping. Even when he was in junior high and high school, he was perfectly at ease with embracing Arthur or me in public, right in front of his friends, who wouldn't be caught dead doing the same thing with their parents. He was especially adept at knowing when I was down, and could be counted on to show up at my side, like magic, whenever I needed a reminder that I wasn't alone, or forgotten, and never would be.

He didn't lose this capacity, either, as he got older. I remember one time, specifically, shortly after he began teaching at the conservatory, when he came to find me in my studio. I had just received news that a former student of mine, Sarah Lawson, had won the Van Cliburn International Piano Competition, and had been invited to do a series of prestigious recordings as a result. Though I was honestly thrilled for Sarah—and had strutted about like an obnoxious peacock in front of all my colleagues—I was feeling more than a bit sad, too. Her success was an unexpectedly difficult reminder of what I had once been as a pianist, and would never be again. But I said nothing to anybody about this, and I believe nobody in the world knew what I was feeling. Nor did I have any intention of telling a soul.

But Jeremy knew anyway.

He showed up at my studio that day, and walked in, unannounced. I was sitting at my desk, pawing through a score, and I looked up and greeted him, as cheerfully as I always did. He said nothing in reply; he only stared across the room at me for a moment, then walked over to stand behind my chair. I tilted my head back and started to ask what was the matter, but before I could speak he leaned down and put his arms around me, very gently. His cheek pressed into mine, and he held me, and he never said a word. But in his silence was understanding, and compassion, and grief for what I had lost. And there was love, too, of course.

I surrendered, then, and let myself cry. There was never any point in dissembling with Jeremy. He always knew what was in my heart, and always would.

It seems Paul and Caitlin may have been partly right, after all, about why I took Alex in.

Oh, Jesus. I miss Jeremy so very much.

I pull myself together. The last thing Alex needs right now is to have a weepy old woman on his hands.

"Oh, well." I drain my glass in a single gulp. "There's no sense in worrying about Bonnie at this particular moment." A silly notion occurs to me. "Do you know how to play the piano?"

"What?" He looks confused. "Where did *that* question come from?"

"Just answer me, boy. Do you play the piano, or not?"

He yawns, long and loud, before replying. He has silver fillings in several of his lower molars. "Not really, no." He plays with the hole in his collar. "I had a few lessons when I was a kid, but I don't remember much about it."

I slap the table lightly and prepare to stand. "Well, come on, then. There's no time like the present."

He laughs when he realizes I'm serious. "You're crazy. I'm way too drunk to play the piano."

"That's certainly never stopped me." I pick up the bottle and my empty glass and rise to my feet. "Are you coming? I've had a brainstorm. Once I'm unemployed, I intend to open a new music salon in town. I'll be considered the Nadia Boulanger of Bolton, Illinois."

"Who's Nadia Boulanger?"

I roll my eyes. "Your education has been appalling. Let's just hope you have enough talent to offset that deficiency."

He indicates his damaged fist. "What about this? I've got a gimp hand, Hester."

"That makes two of us, dear. Come along."

We almost make it to the music room before the phone rings for the umpteenth time. We stand in the living room and listen to the message, and halfway through it I thrust the things I'm carrying into Alex's hands and run as fast as I can to pick up the receiver before the caller hangs up.

Chapter 20

"**H**urry, Alex!" I call across the living room, hoping my quavering voice will carry through the door of the small bathroom off the study. "We have to leave right this moment!"

I'm in a panic. The last phone call was from a nurse at the emergency room; she told me that Arthur has apparently had a massive heart attack, and is now in surgery.

"Alex!" I cry again.

"I'm coming!" he yells back. "Just a sec!"

I'd leave him, but I'm too much of a wreck to drive myself, and Alex offered to act as my chauffeur. But he insisted he needed to relieve himself first, and he's been in the bathroom for *days*. I have my coat and shoes on, and somehow I'm holding my purse, but when any of that happened is beyond my comprehension.

The doorbell rings behind me, and I spin around to answer it. I have no idea who this could be, and I don't care.

"I'll be outside!" I holler. "I'm pulling out of the driveway in fifteen seconds!"

"Dammit, Hester!" he bellows. "I'll be right there! Don't go anyplace without me, okay?"

I fling the front door open and find Alex's friend, Eric, gawking in at me through the glass on the screen door. I step out on the porch to confront him.

"We don't have time for you right now, Eric." My voice is far colder than the wind; I make no effort to warm it. "There's been an emergency, and we're leaving."

Alex is suddenly beside me. "Eric?" He's got his flannel shirt on at least, but he's still barefoot and standing on one leg, struggling to pull on a sneaker. "What are you doing here?" He sounds thunderstruck, as if this tall boy on our porch with the idiotic orange antenna sprouting from his head is the living Christ.

I dig through my purse in a frenzy, searching for my car keys. "We don't have time for this, Alex. We need to go immediately." I can't find the keys and I explode. "Goddammit! Where are my *fucking* car keys?"

I don't believe I've ever said that word in my entire life.

Alex puts a firm hand on my shoulder. "I've got them, Hester. You gave them to me already, remember?"

"What's wrong?" Eric asks in a small voice.

"Arthur's had a heart attack." Alex has managed to get both shoes on, at last, but neither is tied, and the tongue on one of them is mangled up in the laces.

Eric blinks. "Arthur Donovan? Her husband?"

"*Yes,* Arthur Donovan, my husband!" I snap, stepping around him. "We're leaving now, Alex."

I walk toward the carriage house as fast I'm able, then glance back after a few steps to see if Alex is following. He's still standing beside Eric with a vulnerable, addled look on his face, but when he meets my eyes his confusion vanishes.

"I've really gotta go," he says to Eric. "Sorry, man. Can you come back later?"

"Sure." Eric frowns and takes a closer look at him. "Hey, you're drunk as shit, dude. You can barely stand up straight. You really shouldn't be driving like that."

"I'm okay." Alex sees me nearly prancing with impatience and finally moves in my direction.

He trips on something invisible on the sidewalk and falls down facefirst in a snowbank.

"Shit," he says, rolling over and looking up at the sky.

"For God's sake!" I scream. "Would you please stop mucking around?"

Eric helps him to his feet and takes the keys from him. "I'll drive. Neither of you guys should be behind the wheel of a car right now."

Alex is brushing himself off in what seems like slow motion. A broad, astonished grin nearly splits his cheeks apart. "Are you sure? Don't you have other stuff to do?"

I stomp on the sidewalk. "*Somebody* drive! I don't care who!"

"It's fine," Eric says, leading Alex toward me by the elbow. "It's cool."

Caitlin and Martha are in the waiting room at the hospital when we arrive. They're seated side by side, facing the door, and when they see me enter they vie with one another to see who can give me the more spiteful frown. I walk over to them with Alex and Eric at my heels.

Caitlin rises to her feet. She doesn't bother with a greeting. "Dad's in surgery right now." She hesitates. "He's already been in there for over an hour, but we were told that it doesn't look good, and he might be in there for the better part of the day."

Her voice is even more curt than usual; no doubt she believes Arthur's heart condition is somehow my fault.

"Hello, dear." I'm calmer now than I was at the house, and as I was filling out the necessary paperwork at the front desk after my arrival, I promised myself I was going to remain in control—and civil—for the duration of this ordeal. "Yes, I know, the nurse filled me in about the particulars."

The waiting room walls are mostly windows on all four sides, and I feel as if I'm in an ant farm, peering out at the halls. The only other person in the room besides us is an elderly gentleman in the corner, sleeping with his head propped against one of the windows. The nurse's station and the elevators are next to the open door, and the large, terse woman I spoke with when I arrived is still seated at her desk, studying us with a suspicious eye.

Apparently Arthur had his heart attack in the faculty dining room at Carson and was brought here by ambulance. The nurse told me the paramedics had to revive him en route, twice, when his heart stopped.

I feel as if I have a fever. My head is throbbing, my mouth is dry and a thin layer of cold sweat is covering my skin. As much as I've grown to loathe Arthur in the last year, one thing is certain: I do not want him to die in this dreadful place, with his chest opened up under hot bright lights, and tubes sticking from his body, and the smells of rubbing alcohol and disinfectant filling the air.

He's Arthur Donovan, and he deserves better than that.

Oh, Arthur.

Don't you dare die on me yet, old man. If anything kills you, it should be me.

Caitlin glares over my shoulder at Alex and Eric. "You two don't belong here. This is a family matter."

I face her down. "Alex is with me, Caitlin, and he isn't going anywhere. And Eric drove us here, and will likely need to take us home, too."

Martha shifts in her chair. "Good God, Hester, you're *drunk*! I can smell it from here."

I look down at her with as much courtesy as I can muster. "Hello, Martha. How are you holding up?"

The question seems to startle her. She studies my face for a long time, and her lovely pointed chin quivers. "Not well," she mutters at last, reluctantly. She pauses again before forcing her next words out. "And you?"

I have some idea what those two syllables cost her, and for an instant the blistering hatred I feel for her cools the tiniest bit.

I shrug. "About the same."

She nods and drops her eyes. "I know."

She picks up a *New Yorker* magazine from her lap and pretends to read.

Thank God that's over. As long as she stays quiet and continues to ignore me from here on, there's a chance she may live to see the end of this day.

Caitlin was attempting to flay Alex with her gaze as Martha and I were speaking, but now she returns her attention to me.

"I understand Paul's in jail." She snorts. "I assume you had something to do with that?"

I unbutton my coat. "You assume incorrectly. Paul assaulted Evan this afternoon in their shack, and Evan called the police."

She grunts. "I see." A flicker of what might be amusement passes through her eyes. "With any luck they'll execute him."

"Amen," Alex whispers behind me.

Caitlin stiffens, and I intervene before she can begin her attack.

"Hush, Alex," I say over my shoulder. "Why don't you and Eric go get some coffee?"

"Okay." He touches my arm. "But I'll check back in a few minutes and see how you're doing."

I smile at him. "Thank you, dear. Please do."

The boys exit, in a hurry, and I watch them through the glass as they pass out of sight down the hall. Eric clearly has no desire to be here, and is probably regretting his decision to function as our designated driver. In the car on the way here he was quiet; when Alex asked him if he needed to be someplace else anytime soon, he said he was supposed to meet some young lady named Sofia for supper, but he could change those plans if necessary. Alex's jaw tightened at this information, and for the rest of the ride he was silent, too.

Poor Alex. No amount of jealousy on his part will alter Eric's sexual orientation, and wishing for things to be otherwise will only make him miserable. Still, it's good to see that Eric has apparently forgiven him, and is willing to be friends after all.

I wonder what made him change his mind since their conversation this morning.

"Hester?"

Caitlin recaptures my attention. My mind is wandering about like a ferret.

"Yes, sweetheart?"

She makes a face. "Don't call me that, please. I wouldn't want anyone to think we were close."

Martha snickers into her magazine.

It seems the gloves may be coming off, after all.

No. I recall my resolution, and keep a bridle on my temper. I will not make a scene.

"Very well," I sigh. "What shall I call you that will meet with your approval?" I remove my coat and sit in the row facing them.

Caitlin stares down at me for a moment then sits again as well, in the chair next to Martha.

"Caitlin will do," she mutters. There's a long pause, and when she speaks again, she's slightly less antagonistic. "Anyway, I hate to say this, but do you think we should attempt to bail Paul out of jail so he can be here?"

"Why?"

She shrugs. "I don't know. It seems the decent thing to do, don't you think?"

I shake my head. "As intoxicated as he was this morning, I'm fairly certain the police won't be releasing him for many hours yet, even if we were foolish enough to post his bail."

She leans forward. "So you *did* see him earlier today."

"Yes. He stopped by the house before his brawl with Evan, to bully me into evicting Alex. He also insisted I relocate myself to the gulag."

I almost tell her about Paul's confrontation with Alex in the street, then decide not to. The fewer people who know about that, the better.

Caitlin sniffs. "You *should* evict Alex, Mother. You had no business letting him move into the house in the first place."

It's clear she wants a fight, and it's all I can do not to give her one.

I search in my purse for a mint. "Let's not argue, please. This isn't the time or place for it."

The reality of that statement creeps up on me, and I take a shaky breath as another wave of anxiety over Arthur surges through my chest.

Dear God. I really may never see him again.

I recoil from that thought, and nearly retch. Life without Arthur in my house is acceptable, but life without Arthur at all is unthinkable. I couldn't bear to lose him. Not this way.

The night Caitlin was born, Arthur was on tour in Australia. (Caitlin was premature by over a month, and so caught us by surprise.) When I reached him with the news, he immediately cancelled the rest of his performances and flew home to be with us. He came stumbling into town two days later, exhausted from the journey but carrying roses for me and a koala bear and kangaroo mobile for Caitlin's crib, and he cried as he held her for the first time.

When Jeremy got in a fight in second grade with an older, bigger boy who gave him a black eye, I had to pry the phone out of Arthur's hand to keep him from challenging the other boy's father to a duel. And when Paul got a severe case of food poisoning, Arthur sat by his bed in the hospital all night, reading to him and watching old westerns on the television, and pestering the night nurse with anxious questions about Paul's condition.

My Arthur.

Arthur in my bed, Arthur in the shower. Arthur lifting me off my feet and kissing me on the staircase at the conservatory, the day I was given tenure. Arthur attempting to dance, Cossack-style, at a Russian festival in St. Louis, and knocking four other men down, like dominoes, when he fell. Arthur pursuing me around the house with his violin, playing sappy, gypsy love songs by way of an apology for an argument we'd had; Arthur on the front porch with three-year-old Jeremy, trying to teach him solfeggio syllables for an aria by Bizet. Arthur in the kitchen one midnight, wearing nothing but a Batman beach towel and a pair of dress socks, lecturing Paul about upholding the dignity of the Donovan name by respecting the family curfew rule—then bursting into laughter when he realized how absurd he looked.

So many, many good moments, just like these. Thousands of them, maybe tens of thousands. Can this truly be the end of all that?

If it is, I won't be able to stand it.

What good is my life without Arthur?

Unfortunately, Martha chooses this exact moment to drop the magazine in her lap and begin to blubber. "I simply don't know what I'll do if Arthur dies," she sobs. "He's my whole life."

Caitlin and I stare at her for a moment, then we look at each other and she rolls her eyes.

Martha puts her face in her hands and convulses with grief, and there's no power in the universe that can make me hold my tongue any longer.

"There, there," I say dryly. "I daresay you'll soon find another woman's husband to fornicate with."

Her head snaps back on her neck so hard it's a wonder it doesn't fly off her torso and take out the vending machine behind her. She balls her hands into fists, and her chair creaks as she leans forward.

"I will not put up with any more of your ugliness, Hester. I'm warning you right now." Her mascara is a mess from weeping, and when she squints at me she looks like a demented raccoon. "I have more of a right to be here than you, and you know it, and if I have to, I'll have you thrown out."

I laugh. "If that's the case, why was I the one who just filled out all the insurance forms? Could it possibly have anything to do with my last name still being Donovan, while yours isn't?"

She fumes. "That's only because your divorce isn't final, and Arthur hasn't yet had time to make the appropriate changes."

I nod. "No doubt that's true. Nonetheless, I'm still legally married to Arthur Donovan, and you're not. Shall we speak to the nurse and see which of us she chooses to remove?"

She clutches at her sweater and beads of sweat sprout on her upper lip. "You wouldn't dare."

I glance over at the admitting desk and raise my hand. "Oh, yoo-hoo! May we have a moment of your time?"

"Hush, Hester," Caitlin admonishes.

The nurse is on the phone and doesn't notice me. I open my mouth to call out to her again.

"Stop it, Mother," Caitlin insists. "Don't be malicious."

I blink at her in disbelief. "Surely I didn't just hear the word 'malicious' from you. Aren't you the same woman who once told her ailing grandmother her breath smelled like the inside of a diaper pail?"

She blinks back. "For God's sake, Hester. I must have been sixteen at the time. How long have you been waiting to use that against me?"

"Ever since the moment it came out of your mouth, of course." I resume my search for a mint. "I knew I'd eventually get a chance."

Martha isn't through with me yet. "You may be Arthur's wife, Hester, but we both know who he loves."

I study her closely. "You have food caught in your teeth, dear," I lie. "It's very unattractive."

She closes her mouth and runs her tongue over her teeth, checking. I can tell that Caitlin is entertained by this, but she tries to cover it up by patting Martha's arm in a kindly fashion.

"You're fine, Martha. Don't pay any attention to her."

"You are such a child, Hester," Martha huffs. "I have no idea why Arthur put up with you as long as he did."

Alex and Eric are coming back down the hall, walking slowly. Eric is only carrying one styrofoam cup but Alex has two; presumably they found a coffee machine, and he's bringing some for me. Coffee sounds wonderful right now. The elevator doors open behind them, and they make room for a pair of orderlies who exit the elevator, pushing a bearded male patient on a table with wheels. It's not Arthur, but he looks similar enough to spin my mind out, yet again.

Somewhere else in this building are the operating rooms, and in one of these operating rooms is Arthur, being dissected like a frog. He's a supreme violinist and a brilliant man, a teacher and a father, and his damaged heart is literally being held in someone else's hands at this very moment, as the surgeons try to save his life.

And meanwhile, I sit in this godforsaken waiting room, exchanging insults with this frivolous, beastly woman. In my mind's eye I can see him there, under the knife, as surely as if I were standing beside the doctors and nurses as they cut into his big, burly body.

His body. I know every hair on his chest, every wrinkle on his brow, every muscle and pouch of fat on his abdomen. I know every scar, every mole, and every freckle on his back, and I know the soles of his feet and the nails on his fingers, and I know the contour and texture of his penis, and I know where he's ticklish on his aging, ample bottom. There is no part of him I haven't touched and fondled a thousand times, no spot on him I haven't kissed and stroked and tasted.

Every inch of his body belongs to me—up to and including his sick, weak old heart. I hold it in my hands, too, this very instant, just like a surgeon, and feel it beating.

I have no doubt Martha loves him, but there is no way on this earth she can feel his presence right now the way I do. She may have been his mistress for a long time, but I have been his wife for close to half a century, and I will not allow her to pretend that what she has with him can ever compare to what Arthur and I have meant to each other, regardless of how this last year has pulled us apart.

I finally find a mint and pop it into my mouth, framing a reply to Martha as the boys enter the waiting room.

"I don't know how he put up with me, either," I tell her. "But let me tell you what I do know." I gaze into her eyes without pity. "I do know we had thirty good years together before he began his relationship with you, and in those thirty years we raised three children together, and we shared a house and a bed, and a great deal of love. I know that even after he began cheating on me, he was still coming home to me for another fifteen years, night after night, when he could have chosen to leave me at any time and move in with you."

I pause to take a quick breath and go on before she has a chance to offer a rebuttal. "I also know the only reason he finally decided to divorce me was because he's afraid of getting old, and afraid of dying, and being with a younger, prettier woman allows him to pretend he isn't nearing the end of his life."

My voice is gruff as Alex and Eric come to stand by my chair; I summon my last bit of courage to finish my speech. "And most of all, I know that he's with you, Martha, because the guilt he's been carrying all these years for Jeremy's death finally caught up to him last year, and being around me makes it impossible for him to repress or avoid his part in our son's suicide."

I'm referring, of course, to what Arthur finally chose to reveal to me only last year, on the same night he told me was leaving me. And just like that, the memory of that terrible evening comes crashing back all at once, and I'm helpless to block it out.

Arthur was in his office, mourning, when I found him. I was on my way to the attic to get another box of Jeremy's things for Goodwill, because we had finally gotten around to preparing the attic apartment for use as a rental unit. I stopped at the office door and asked what was wrong.

I was struggling to hold back my own tears at the time, too. Getting rid of Jeremy's things was taking a major toll on me, even though by then he'd been dead for more than twelve years. It was especially difficult because Arthur hadn't been able to bring himself to help. The attic had been unused all this while, and though we both knew it was for the best to convert it into a rental space— instead of letting it continue to serve as a tomb for the dead—the actual act of removing our son's belongings was proving to be far more traumatic than we had anticipated. Arthur had gone up with me once to look around at the wreckage, but he had bolted for the stairs after one glance through the window in the kitchen that overlooked the driveway.

Now he had his face in his hands and he glanced up, startled to find me standing there. He had aged so much in the last decade, I could barely fathom the change. His coal-black hair had turned solid gray, and he was stooped in his chair, and his skin was pallid and loose on his face. He looks so old, *I remember thinking. Then again, I reflected, the years had treated me no better.*

It took him a while to register that I'd asked him a question. "I don't really know what's wrong," he answered. "I came up here to do some work, and . . ." he broke down again.

I walked over to him and pulled his head to my breast. He clutched my waist and wept, and I kissed the top of his head and hummed to him until he quieted.

He pulled back finally and raised his face. "There's something I have to tell you, Hester," he rasped. "I should have said something a long time ago, but it was too hard."

His expression was so earnest and sad, it wrenched my heart. I stroked his hair and nodded. "All right. I'll listen."

His jaw tightened as he fought for control. "I knew Jeremy was going to kill himself before he did it."

I flinched. We hadn't spoken about Jeremy or his death since the days following his funeral. It was too painful for both of us.

I shook my head. "Of course you didn't, sweetheart," I whispered. "Jeremy and I kept you in the dark about all the times I found him up there."

Nine times. I found him up there nine times, to be exact. And there was still hardly a day that went by when I didn't recall all nine of them, one after another, and think about the things I should have said, and what I should have done differently.

I called my mind back to the present. "How could you have known what he was going to do?"

He winced. "Because he came to talk to me about it the month before he died."

My hand stopped moving in his hair. "He did?"

He nodded against my stomach. "Up at Carson. In my studio."

I couldn't have been more stunned. Until then I'd believed Jeremy had no other confidant but me, and I had no idea why Arthur had never said anything about this before.

I disengaged myself from him with a weary sigh and seated myself on a leather footstool near his desk. (The chair he was ensconced in was the only one in the room. Arthur liked it that way, to discourage visitors from staying overlong in his private domain.) I was suddenly bone-tired and wanted nothing more than to curl up on the floor to sleep, but I squared my shoulders and tried to prepare myself for whatever it was he had to tell me.

"What did you speak about?" I finally asked.

He smoothed his hair and dropped his eyes. "He was distraught about several things."

"I'd imagine so." I crossed my legs and looked around the room. Arthur's office was a mess; there were piles of paper everywhere, and hundreds of books overflowing the shelves and taking over the floor. Many of them were open and face down, as if he'd begun reading them and been forced to abandon them midsentence. I took a breath and focused on him again. "What was upsetting him the most when he came to see you?"

He bit his lip. "Work situations, mostly. Concerns about his career, and if he'd made the right choices in life, that sort of thing."

I nodded. "The usual, then." I sighed again as the memories started cycling through my head. "So did you get the 'Oh, woe is me, why did I have to be so talented' spiel?"

He raised his eyebrows. "No, not at all." He frowned. "Was that something he complained about?"

"Yes. Several times. Didn't I tell you?"

He shook his head. "No. You never mentioned it."

"I didn't?" I shrugged. "I'm sorry. I should have. He claimed our family's talent was the root of all evil. I'm paraphrasing, but that was the gist of it."

He scowled and grunted. "That's the most ridiculous thing I've ever heard."

I grunted back. "Yes, isn't it?"

There was a long silence as we listened to each other breathe. I sensed he had more to tell me, but for some reason I was reluctant to ask him about it. I told myself I was being foolish, and decided to prod him along. "Was there anything else he said?"

He hesitated, and without quite knowing why, my chest tightened.

He met my gaze, and his face was full of pain. "He accused me of various . . . things, and said that if I didn't stop doing them, he'd find a way to make me regret it."

I blinked. "I see." After a moment I waved a hand, suddenly wanting this conversation to go no further. "Well, he was semi-delusional most of the time for the last couple of years of his life," I said, briskly. "I wouldn't take anything he said too much to heart."

There was another very long pause.

I swallowed in a dry throat, and I hugged myself. An abrupt chill filled the room, and my hands and feet were cold. Arthur seemed in no hurry to divulge any more bombshells, so I gathered my courage to ask the next question.

"Arthur? Precisely what sorts of things did he think you were doing, dear?"

"Oh, Hester," he whispered. "You'll hate me forever."

I recoiled for an instant, but then I reassured myself that everything was going to be okay. I had my suspicions about what he was going to say next, but I was also sure the truth of it would prove to be less awful than my imagination was making it. After all, I knew my husband.

"I could never hate you, darling," I murmured. "It's simply impossible."

And I gave him my sweetest smile.

Dear God, I was a stupid woman.

He took a ragged breath, and then another, and he opened and closed his mouth several times before he finally began to speak.

"I'd been having an affair with Martha Predel for about three years when Jeremy came to talk to me." He didn't give me a chance to react; the words came gushing out of him. "And somehow Jeremy found out about it, and that's why he came to see me, and he threatened to do something drastic if I didn't put an end to it. I told him he was wrong, and that he had no right to speak to me like that, and I basically threw him out of my studio and told him to never say a word to you about any of this."

He stared over my head at the wall, avoiding my eyes. He needn't have been afraid of my reaction; I was too astonished and horrified at the moment to have any access to outrage or anguish. All I could do was gape at him, witless, my mouth ajar.

"When I got home that night after our argument," he continued, "I was expecting him to make a scene, but he never said another thing to me about the situation, or acted as if we'd ever fought in the first place. It was as if he'd forgotten all about it." He paused. "He even wished me good night on his way to bed, and he patted me on the shoulder as he passed by my chair." He tugged at his beard. "I remember being moved by his affection, because I was certain he was still furious with me."

He found the courage to look at me again, and his face crumpled at whatever he saw. He lurched forward, awkward and heavy, and knelt on the floor in front of me with a groan. "Oh, God, Hester. I am so sorry."

I struggled to say something, anything. "Martha?" I stammered at last. "Martha Predel?"

He bit his lip. "Yes."

I could feel the ice in my extremities working its way inward to my heart. I knew he had even more to reveal; something told me there were far worse things coming.

I somehow found my voice again. "I see." The words felt like two small stones in my mouth. "So did Jeremy specify what he meant by 'something drastic?'"

The question spun in the air between us, gathering force with each passing second.

"Yes," Arthur croaked at last. "He said he'd kill himself if I didn't stop deceiving you." He made a helpless gesture. "But I didn't believe him. Given the rest of what he said that day, I thought he was just being melodramatic."

I reeled back on the footstool and almost lost my balance. Arthur reached out to steady me but I shied away from him as if he had leprosy.

"You thought he was being melodramatic?" I repeated, on the verge of hysteria. "Let me get this straight. You were sleeping with another woman behind my back, and our son came to you and told you he intended to kill himself if you didn't stop, and you handled it by throwing him out of your studio?"

He sat back on his heels, stung. "It wasn't like that." He held up his hands in supplication. "Please listen to me. He was being entirely unreasonable, and I talked to him for a long time, but then he became unhinged and started to badger me with what I thought at the time were just childish threats, and so I lost my patience and told him to go home."

Twelve years, I thought. Dear God, twelve entire years.

For twelve years, he had let me carry the entire burden of guilt for Jeremy's death. For twelve years, he let Caitlin and Paul hate me, assigning me the role, through his silence, of chief villain in our tawdry little family drama. For twelve years I had hated myself as much as my children did, never knowing that at least some of that hatred could, and should, be shared.

Twelve entire years.

I nodded. "I see. Well, now it all makes sense. You're completely forgiven. Don't think another thing about it."

I extended my arm and slapped him across the face as hard as I could. He caught my hand before I could do it again.

"Stop it, Hester!" he rumbled. "You must listen to me!"

I tried to pull free of him, but he was too strong. "Let go of me!" I cried. "Was your affair with Martha Predel worth your own son's life, Arthur? Did she comfort you when he died? Did you give her up then, or did you need more time to cry out your grief on her shoulder?"

He shook me until I quieted. Then he closed his eyes for an instant, and when he opened them again, I knew what else he was going to tell me.

"Oh, I see," I said. "I see."

He released me and rose to his feet. "I can't give her up, Hester," he muttered. "I just can't."

They're all staring at me: Martha and Caitlin, Alex and Eric. I have no idea how long I've been silent, but the entire hospital seems to have shut down around us while I was lost in my thoughts. The only sounds I can hear from the hall are a few muted voices and the distant ring of a telephone.

I sigh and cock my head at Martha, and pick up as best as I can the threads of what I had been saying to her.

"So you can believe what you will, Martha, and Arthur can deny this to his grave, but here's the God's honest truth: he will *never* love you the way he loves me. Never. And deep down, I think you know that, don't you?"

Her lips are pinched, and her eyes are brimming, but she says nothing. She looks away, her jaw working.

The silence at last is broken by Caitlin, clapping lazily. "Brava, Hester. Neatly done." She sits upright in her chair, wrathful and frightening. "And far be it from me to defend Dad for his role in Jeremy's death. But Dad wasn't the one on the roof with Jeremy— time after time after time—when he was suicidal. Dad wasn't the one who was with him when he finally jumped. It wasn't Dad who babied him his entire life, nor was it Dad who thought that a good scolding was sound psychiatric therapy."

She's ticking the points off on her fingers, one after another, and the scorn in her voice is more than I can take at the moment. I feel tears coursing down my cheeks.

"Please, Caitlin, you must listen to my side of the story," I plead. "You've never given me a chance to explain what happened."

She cuts me off. "No, Mother, I haven't, and I'm not going to now, either. Listening to you tends to make people hurl themselves off rooftops, remember?" She drops her eyes. "Which I'm feeling an impulse to do in short order, now that I mention it."

Alex is watching me with concern.

"That's enough," he says to Caitlin. "Just leave her alone, okay?"

In an instant, and for no reason I can see, Caitlin is on her feet and screaming incoherent things in his face. He screams back, and the next thing I know Martha is on her feet and screaming at me, as well, and Caitlin slaps Alex, and Eric is holding Alex to keep him from hitting Caitlin. I catch a glimpse of the elderly man in the corner as he wakes to this ruckus, and his face is frightened and baffled. I try to give him a reassuring smile when his eyes flit over my face, but he draws himself into a tight little ball of anxiety in his chair.

The head nurse shows up with a security guard and an orderly in tow, and before I even know how it all happened, I'm standing with Alex and Eric outside the hospital entrance, watching Caitlin and Martha being escorted to their separate cars. The nurse is beside me, as well, telling me to go home, and that she'll call me as soon as Arthur gets out of surgery, which is likely to be several more hours.

Her tone is final, and will brook no argument.

The sun is setting, and it's cold, and between the cars in the parking lot are several large mounds of dirty gray snow resembling burial mounds. I think my husband may be dying somewhere in the building behind me. I watch the nurse re-enter the hospital, and I feel Alex's long arm drape itself around my shoulders as he seeks to give me comfort.

I gaze up into his freckled, earnest face and try to recover some of who I used to be, before this day started.

"Well." I clear my throat. "I daresay that could have gone better?"

He gives me a sad smile. "Nah. It's about what I expected."

"You're probably right." I bite my lower lip, hard enough to draw blood. "Oh, Alex. Please take me home."

CHAPTER 21

W e're on the roof. Alex and Eric and I.
I talked the boys into coming up here with me to admire the view of the stars in the winter sky, and the three of us are nestled together with our backs against the house, sharing a bottle of brandy beneath the kitchen window of the attic apartment. I'm seated in the middle, with Alex on my right and Eric on the left. As cold as it is up here, I'm wonderfully comfortable. We threw a wool blanket over us, and their warm young bodies are like space heaters against my sides. Alex is especially toasty; if you cut into his skin, I'm convinced molten lava would flow from the wound.

It's nearly eleven o'clock, and we have yet to hear from the hospital about Arthur. We returned home mid-afternoon (after the fiasco in the waiting room) and I've called a dozen times since, but all the nurse has told me each time is that his surgery is still proceeding, and there's no news as of yet, aside from that he needed a quadruple coronary artery bypass, and they're having "serious complications" with one of the grafts. I brought my cell phone to the roof with me, but it's resting in my coat pocket, quiet as a cadaver, and I'm beginning to feel as if it's never going to ring again.

Arthur has been in there for more than eight hours.

Eight *hours*.

What in God's name could be taking so long?

Eric was supposed to have had dinner with his friend Sofia, but after downing a few cocktails on an empty stomach, he decided he should remain with us for the evening, instead, which was probably a wise choice. Alex and I had quite a head start on him when he began drinking, but he made a valiant effort to catch up—so much so that now he seems on the verge of passing out. His head is lolling from side to side on his neck, and he grunts and giggles more than he speaks.

Alex is handing me the bottle and asking me something.

I attempt to concentrate. "What did you say, dear?"

He seems nervous as he points at the edge of the roof. "Is this the place?" He clears his throat. "I mean, is this where Jeremy . . ." He looks at me and trails off. "I'm sorry. I shouldn't have asked."

I tilt my head to study him. The whites of his eyes are visible in the light from the moon and the stars, and the corners of his mouth are drawn down in a deep, troubled frown.

"Yes." I take another drink. I have no idea how much alcohol I've had today. I'm surprised at how clearheaded I feel; I'm certain I should be clinically dead by this point. But the brandy must have restorative qualities as well, because my brain seems more or less operational, and when I speak my tongue still does what I ask of it.

"This is where Jeremy jumped." I pause. "Or where he stepped, actually. He simply stepped backward into space, and fell."

There's a long, long silence, broken only by the wind, and a barking dog far in the distance.

"Shit," Eric whispers. "Holy shit."

Alex stirs against me. "Christ, Hester. Why did you bring us up here?" His voice is rough. "Isn't this like the worst place in the world for you?"

I shrug. "Actually, no. You'd think it would be, of course, but for some reason I still find this a beautiful spot." I stare up at the stars and find Orion, hovering over the Mississippi. I've been afraid to come up here for years, but now that I'm here, all I feel is a strange emptiness in my chest, where I thought grief would be lurking.

I tug at the blanket, bringing it closer to my chin. "And the worst place in the world, bar none, is the driveway below. This is a proverbial piece of cake compared to that."

"Jesus Christ," Alex mutters.

Ever since we came home from the hospital, the boys have been talking nonstop. We listened to music and ate dinner, and we sat by the fire as they chattered about this and that, both of them keeping an eye on me and hopping up to refill my glass whenever it was empty. Now they're tongue-tied, though, and I feel guilty for inflicting my bleak mood on them.

The house is full of ghosts tonight. If I close my eyes and listen, I can almost hear my entire family, including me, when we were all younger, quarreling downstairs in the kitchen, or playing music in the front room. I do not fear these phantoms, really, but I would just as soon not listen to them anymore, either.

They are a fractious bunch, and they are wearing me out.

I do my best to lighten my tone. "Anyway, I brought you up here because I thought tonight was as good a time as any to reclaim this part of the house for the living." I nudge both of them with my elbows. "And I knew with the two of you for company, I'd be brave enough to give it a shot."

On cue, Eric slumps against me and begins to snore.

I may be haunted by the past and on the verge of despair about the future, but this still strikes me as somewhat funny. I sigh and reach up to pat his blond head.

Alex looks across me at his friend and snorts. "He seems to do that a lot. He's such a gimp."

The love is plain in his voice, and my heart aches for him. But I'm grateful for the diversion this offers; his problems are so much easier for me to address than my own.

I make sure Eric is indeed asleep, then I lower my voice. "Why did he change his mind about associating with you again?"

He darts a quick glance at Eric, and doesn't answer until we hear another light snore. "He told me he thought about it some more, and decided it was stupid not to hang out with me just because I'd done something dumb while I was wasted." His voice is suffused with relief. "He also said he likes me a lot, and I deserve another chance."

"I see." I ponder this for a moment. "Alex. You're aware Eric isn't homosexual, aren't you?" I study his silhouette. "And you must know he'll never want to be more than just your friend?"

His chin trembles as he nods. "Yeah." He takes the bottle from me and fiddles with the cap. "I know." He leans his head against the house. "But it's okay. It really is." He pauses. "Mostly."

"Mostly?"

"Yeah." He plays with the label on the bottle. "It's just that he used to let me hold him in his sleep, and now I don't think he'll let me do that anymore. And I hate like hell that I fucked up that part of our friendship." Tears appear on his face, glistening like tinsel. "I'm so stupid. No one else has ever let me do anything like that before, and if I just hadn't pushed for more, we could have kept on being close like that forever."

I sometimes forget how young he is. He shared a bed with Eric two or three times, and somehow that translated in his mind into something that might actually be permanent. Foolish child.

I almost tell him he should try being married for forty-five years, if he wants a taste of forever, but before the words come out I fall mute in astonishment at my own blindness.

Dear God.

How am I only now seeing this?

It may be the brandy speaking, but now that I think about it, I'm an idiot.

Arthur is lost to me. Even if he should live through this surgery, there will be no "forever" for us, either, because he is not mine any longer. He belongs with Martha, or (God forbid) with the worms in consecrated ground, but he doesn't belong with me, no matter how much I wish it were otherwise, or how badly I keep behaving in public.

There's only one fool on this roof, and her name is Hester.

Oh, Arthur. What have we been doing? We've wasted so much time.

I want so badly to speak to my husband again, and to tell him goodbye in a civilized fashion. I want so much to be given a chance to repair some of the damage between us, and to part company without killing each other. We have loved each other for decades; surely the two of us can still find a way to let go with dignity and compassion, and a measure of gratitude?

Surely there must still be a way?

I sigh, and return my attention to Alex. "Pushing for more than what you can get is . . . well, it's forgivable, my love. But I wouldn't make it a habit." I rest my head against the shingles, too. "You're actually quite lucky it fell apart so soon, and that you're still friends."

He's staring up at the stars, but I can tell he's listening to me. Fresh tears run down his cheeks and he wipes them away.

"I guess." He finally takes another swig of brandy and coughs, and his voice drops to where I can barely hear it. "But I really, really loved being able to touch him, and I'd give anything to still be able to do that."

"I know." I sigh again and pat his arm under the blanket. "And I'm sorry you're not getting what you want. But trust me. It's better this way."

He searches my face for a long time. "Are you sure about that?"

I snort. "Don't be silly. Of course not."

He manages a grin. "Great. Thanks a lot."

I lean over and give him a peck on the cheek. "My pleasure, dear. Always glad to help."

There's an odd, perfect moment of peace, then, as we watch the sky and listen to Eric snore. I feel the two boys breathing against my sides, and I note, with humility, the conspicuous silence of the ghostly voices in the house behind us, and I fill my lungs with cold, clean air and let it out again into the night, where it hovers before our faces like a cloud of pipe smoke.

And in my pocket, the phone rings.

CHAPTER 22

It's late morning and I'm driving home from the hospital, nursing a five-alarm hangover from yesterday. Arthur was still asleep when I arrived to visit him, and Caitlin was no longer at his side, so I had no choice but to speak with Martha in the hallway outside his room. Our whispered conversation was quick and unfriendly, but I managed to extract a promise from her to tell Arthur I'd stopped by, and would return later today to see him.

The surgery, though difficult, was an apparent success. The nurse who called last night (while the boys and I were stargazing on the roof) assured me Arthur would live to fight another day, at least, and that he might even be around for many more years.

Assuming he takes better care of himself.

But for some reason her cheerful words didn't sink in yesterday evening. I didn't really expect him to pull through, and until I saw him dozing in his bed a few minutes ago, I was convinced I would never see him again. And then there was Martha to deal with, and a hallway full of strangers as I was leaving, so I am only now digesting the fact of his likely recovery.

Only now.

Relief surges through me, and my eyes fill, blurring the road through the windshield. I brush them away but more take their place and I'm forced to pull over to the curb and have a good cry. I park in an illegal space next to a fire hydrant, but I'm on a quiet side street, and in no danger of being harassed by a meter maid. There's a large oak tree next to the hydrant, spreading its leafless branches above my head. It reminds me of a minister giving the benediction at the end of a church service.

I let the tears course down my face, let myself sob in gratitude and grief. Arthur will live, and I will have to live without him.

Thank you, God, for sparing him.

Damn you, God, for sparing him.

It was one thing to sit on my roof last night (when Arthur's demise seemed imminent) and know I needed to get on with my life, but how do I actually *do* that, now, in the clear light of day, when he's still very much alive?

I dig a tissue out of my purse and blow my nose, and I stare out the windshield at the picturesque little neighborhood surrounding my car. It's a Saturday morning, and no one is outside except for a pair of young girls down the street, building a snowman in their yard. Everything is pure white from the heavy snowfall of the last few weeks, except for the gray concrete of the shoveled sidewalks, and the bright yellow fire hydrant beside me, and the matching blue coats and red scarves the girls are wearing.

I remember all three nights Arthur and I made each of our children, or at least I think I do. I remember him resting on top of me as we finished making love. He stayed inside of me, as well, for a long, peaceful time. I remember his handsome, sweaty young face, beardless in those years, pressed against my cheek, and the instinctive feeling that something was different afterwards. I suppose it's ridiculous to say I know, for certain, the three specific times when we created our children. But we quite often used protection of one kind or another to prevent any surprises, and so although there were hundreds of fine, loving moments in our bed, there were only a handful of occasions when it was likely he could have gotten me pregnant.

And three times, only, when I felt as if he and I had somehow changed the world.

The evening I told Arthur I was pregnant with Jeremy, he was performing the Brahms *Violin Concerto* with the Chicago Symphony. He went on stage mere hours after I revealed the information about the new tenant in my womb, and he stood in the spotlight, gazing out into the darkness of the concert hall. He placed his violin between his neck and shoulder, and stood there smiling as the orchestra played the intro. When it came time for his entrance, his bow bit into the strings with such passion that I thought the seams of his instrument would fly apart.

He knew where I was sitting in the audience, and though I'm positive he could barely make out my face through the glare of the spotlight, his eyes never left me for an instant. It was the most public declaration of love I've ever witnessed, and the most thrilling musical performance I've ever heard. He gave away every emotion he was feeling, every ounce of happiness and serenity in his entire body; he emptied himself in front of thousands of people, until he was nothing but a husk on the stage when the piece had ended.

It was the bravest thing I've ever seen. He surrendered himself, utterly, to his art; he stripped himself down to nothing but spirit and fire. And he did that for me. For me, and for the unborn child I was carrying within me.

That's why I loved him. And why I still love him, in spite of everything. Because anybody who can do what he did on the stage that night has a ferocious, open soul, regardless of how he behaves in every other arena of his life. And sometimes that soul of his shines out when I least expect it—when he's washing the dishes, or trimming his beard at the bathroom sink, or dozing in his chair by the fire after supper. I can't exactly tell you how, but I'll glance over at him and he'll be glowing like a firefly.

And I suppose that's why I'm sitting in this freezing car on this fine winter morning, weeping my eyes out.

Because Arthur Donovan is still in the world. And because I can no longer have him.

Paul's red Volvo is parked in my driveway when I arrive home, and as I notice it from the street my heart nearly stops beating .

Oh, Lord. Now what?

A horrid thought races through my mind.

Did I remember to lock the house when I left this morning?

After Arthur moved out, I changed all the locks in the house, and made a point of not giving a new key to either Caitlin or Paul.

But more often than not these days I forget to lock the door on my way out, and I was in a hurry this morning to get to the hospital, and . . .

And Paul is not in his car, or on the porch. He's nowhere to be seen.

Alex and Eric are probably still asleep in the attic. And if Paul is even half as drunk as he was yesterday morning, Alex could be in serious danger.

I fly up the driveway in my Toyota and barely avoid slamming into the Volvo as I stomp on the brakes. My engine stalls and I jump from the car and run toward the house as fast as I'm able. My headache is enormous and each footstep is a gunshot to my temples, but I don't slow for anything until I'm on the porch and at the door.

The wide-open door.

I burst into the house, praying Paul is sitting in the kitchen or living room, waiting for me. And that he's sober.

There's no one downstairs. It's just as I left it this morning, dark and quiet. The bottle of Motrin I set out on the kitchen table (in case Alex awoke and needed pain medication while I was gone) is untouched.

But there are wet footprints on the stairs. The ones on the lower steps still have little globs of melting snow in them, so Paul must not have gotten here too far ahead of me.

When the boys and I came inside from the roof last night, Eric staggered into Alex's living room and passed out on his couch. Alex was still functional enough (barely) to see me safely downstairs to my bedroom, and then he stumbled back up to his bed, where he no doubt has been dead to the world ever since.

So dead he won't hear Paul coming until he's right on top of him.

"Paul?" I call out in panic. *"Alex?"*

There's no answer from the attic. There's no sound at all, anywhere in the house, except for the ticking of the grandfather clock in the study.

I charge up the stairs, which at my age is no easy feat. I'm in fair shape for a seventy-one-year-old woman, but I've never been a fan of aerobic activity, and the three staircases facing me are steep and long. The last time I even attempted such a thing was when Jeremy was out on the roof that final cold winter morning.

Out on the roof, getting ready to kill himself.

I cry out in terror, and my lungs almost rip with the effort. *"Alex! Eric! Wake up!"*

And that's when the yelling begins in the attic.

It's Alex's voice I hear first, as I reach the landing by my bedroom.

"Get the fuck out of here, Paul!" he shouts. He sounds very frightened.

I turn the corner and grab at the handrail for support as I trip up the next flight of stairs.

"What the hell?"

That's Eric's voice, blurry and alarmed. I try to hasten my steps and I lose my balance for an instant, banging my knee into the wall. I bite my lip and regain my footing, and I keep going even though my kneecap hurts like the devil.

I curse myself for leaving my purse in the car. It has my cell phone in it, and if I had a brain in my head I would have already called the police. I also could have used the phone in the kitchen, or the one in my bedroom, but there's no time to go back now.

I finally arrive on the landing by Arthur's studio (where there *was* a phone, too, I remember bitterly, until I removed it to replace the one I wrecked after arguing with Paul), and from here I'm close enough to hear everything clearly. It sounds as if they're all in Alex's kitchen, and their voices echo down the last set of stairs as I stop to catch my breath before resuming my climb. I'm so winded I don't know how I can keep going, but I have to get there before something terrible happens.

"I don't know who you are, dick," Paul rumbles, "but if I were you I'd stay the fuck out of this." He must be talking to Eric, but his tone changes as he apparently turns his attention to Alex. His voice is so hostile it's almost unrecognizable. "We're gonna have a talk now, you little shit."

He's clearly out of his head, again. There's no other explanation.

He would never do something this outlandish if he were sober. Paul is a difficult man, and a bully, but he's not insane.

My heart is beating wildly, and I put my hand on my chest in sudden fear of having a heart attack of my very own.

Maybe they'll put me in the same room with Arthur at the hospital. Martha would have a fit.

I force myself to wait another moment before taking another step. I'll be of no use to the boys if I reach the top of the stairs and die of a stroke.

Alex and Eric are both in far better shape than Paul. I noticed last night that Eric, especially, appears quite strong, and has the build of an athlete. But I hope neither of them makes the mistake of thinking they can handle Paul, in spite of that. He has fifty pounds on either of them, and he's drunk and enraged, and likely to do anything.

Anything at all.

"Be careful, man," I hear Alex say. "This guy is out of his fucking mind."

Thank God. At least Alex knows enough to be cautious.

"We're just gonna have a talk, punk," Paul says. "Tell your little friend to get lost."

I tug myself up another step, frantic, and almost retch from the effort. That mad dash up the first two flights of stairs was almost the death of me. I try to call out again, but I have no air in my lungs and can only gasp.

There's a heavy stomping noise, and one of the boys cries out, "Oh, shit!" Then a tremendous clang reverberates through the house, and what sounds like several chairs and possibly the table being knocked over with a huge clatter.

"Goddammit!" Alex bellows. "What the fuck are you doing?"

I force myself to move. No matter what, I have to get up there. Each step is an agony, but I will not stop until I reach the attic.

There's the sound of glass breaking, and what has to be plates shattering. I'm halfway up the staircase and I almost black out from anxiety and exertion, and then I hear Paul start to laugh.

"Christ," he says. "She's still got this fucking picture up here from when I was in high school. Damn, I was a good-looking kid, don't you think?"

A moment later I hear more glass shattering, and a surge of adrenaline finally gets me moving again. I sail up the last few stairs and come to a grinding halt in the doorway of the kitchen.

Paul is standing with his back to me, facing the boys. He's huge and terrifying, resembling a grizzly bear in his winter coat. The table and chairs are overturned and scattered throughout the room, and the skylight and the other window have both been knocked out. The floor is covered with broken glass and dinnerware, and a cold wind is whipping through the jagged remains of the windows, turning the place into a freezer.

Alex and Eric see me at the same time. They're standing side by side in the corner, as far away from Paul as they can get. Neither must have had time to get dressed before Paul's assault; Eric is only wearing jeans, and Alex is nearly naked in a pair of brown boxer shorts. There's blood on Alex's feet and on the floor around him; he must have stepped in some glass. The house is whirling around me, and the sight of Alex's blood makes my gorge rise.

Paul sees the boys react to my presence, and swings around to face me.

"Oh, hi, Mother," he grunts. "I didn't hear you come in."

He lumbers over to the counter, and while the rest of us stand frozen, watching him, he picks up the toaster, carefully unplugs it, and flings it through the shattered window, knocking out a remaining shard.

"Stop it, Paul!" I scream as more glass flies everywhere.

"Oops," he says in the silence that follows the explosion. "I sure hope that wasn't expensive."

"I called the police before I came up here." I hide my shaking hands in my coat pockets, but my voice gives away my fear. "You had best be on your way."

"You called the police?" He studies me, bleary-eyed. "No, you didn't. You're lying. I can always tell when you're lying. Your forehead does this weird scrunchy thing."

"What in God's name is the matter with you?" I cry.

He jabs a finger at Alex. *"Him,* Mother. He's the matter with me. He's in Jeremy's apartment, and he's got no business being here." He says this as if it's the most obvious thing in the world, then he opens the silverware drawer and begins flinging forks at the wall with all his might. Most of them bounce off and skitter around the room (forcing the boys and me to cower to avoid them), but the last one plunges right into the plaster, tines first, and stays there, quivering.

Temporarily out of ammo, Paul turns to Alex.

"Jeremy lives here," he says quietly. "Not you, you little shit. Jeremy." He faces me again. "He sort of looks like Jeremy, don't you think? Something in the eyes."

I shake my head at him, not knowing what to say. There's madness in his gaze, and a horrible, wrenching sorrow that twists his features and makes him look like a stranger.

He takes a step toward me. "Here's the deal. You don't get to replace my little brother, Mom. Okay? You killed him, so you don't get to replace him. That's only fair, right? I don't get another brother, so you don't get another son. Period."

There are tears on his face and in his beard, and he takes another step toward me.

"Stay away from her," Alex warns. "Run, Hester. He might hurt you."

"Shh, Alex," I whisper, appalled by what I'm seeing in my son's expression. "It will be all right."

"No, it won't," Paul sobs. "It will never be all right." He grabs the top of the refrigerator on both sides, and with a tremendous heave pulls the entire thing over onto the floor. The whole house trembles from the force of it, and the noise is earsplitting.

As Paul stares down at the refrigerator in the moment of stunned silence afterward, Alex and Eric exchange a glance. Eric nods, and without a word spoken, both boys launch themselves at Paul. Alex slips and falls, though, crying out as he lands in more glass, and Paul spins in time to intercept Eric. I step forward to intervene, but before I can reach them Paul catches Eric by the arm and shoves him toward the doorway I just vacated. Eric loses his balance and trips across the hall at full speed, unable to stop himself. His thighs slam into the railing by the stairs and he tumbles over it, and an instant later there's a sickening snap as his legs strike the steps on the other side. He disappears from sight with a scream of agony.

Paul stares after him with a shocked expression, as Alex cries out his friend's name. Paul pivots on his feet to stare down at Alex thrashing around the floor, and takes a heavy step toward him.

"I didn't mean to do that," he says plaintively. "I really didn't."

I look down at my fingers, and find them clutching the old black rotary phone that was on the table beside the doorway.

Eric screams again from behind me, and Paul takes another step toward Alex and then stops. He's only two feet away from the boy, and I don't know what he's intending to do.

"Stop, Paul," I beg. "Please, stop."

He ignores me and leans down toward Alex, reaching out a hand as if to grab him.

Alex flops to the side to get away from him and kicks at Paul's legs, but Paul is undeterred. His hand locks on Alex's forearm, and Alex cries out in panic.

"No, Paul!" I howl.

I run forward. There's a sound of a bell clanging, and the next thing I know Paul is splayed out on the floor in front of me. He's not moving, and there's a small pool of blood forming by his head.

Alex stares up at me in horror.

My chest is heaving, and I can't seem to remember how to breathe as I stand there looking down at my son's prone body. I glance at the old phone in my thin, frail fingers, trying to recall when I picked it up.

This used to be Paul's phone, when he lived up here. Then it was Jeremy's. There's a clump of scalp on one corner of it, now.

Eric cries out again downstairs, demanding to know what's happened. He must be in tremendous pain, but he's asking if we're okay.

I look down at Alex and whisper his name, and I drop the phone on the floor. My eyes fill with tears, and the last thing I see before the room spins out of control and I, too, fall to the floor in a faint, is him reaching up to catch me.

CHAPTER 23

I struck my own son.
The thought keeps repeating itself in my head, over and over, like an ostinato.

The intern finally finishes stitching up Alex and lets him return to me in the waiting room at the hospital. He walks over, limping, and sits beside me.

"Hi, Hester," he says, trying to smile.

I know he has small cuts all over him, but the worst ones are on his feet. He's moving gingerly, but he's dressed again, and he seems all right.

I take his hand and squeeze it. "Hello, dear. How are you feeling?"

He shrugs. "I'm okay. You?"

I give his fingers another squeeze and release him. "I'm fine. The doctor confirmed that I merely fainted at the house. I didn't even injure myself by falling, thanks to you."

I struck my own son.

He nods. "Really? That's awesome." His voice has relief in it. "You really scared the shit out of me when you face-planted on top of me like that. I thought for sure you'd had a stroke or something."

We're alone in the waiting room. A young mother with three toddlers was here when I first arrived, but she left soon after, when her husband was released from an examination. The oldest child was a boy, who clung to his mother's neck, sleeping, as they walked past me on their way out the door.

I struck my own son.

I give an involuntary wince. Alex notices, and studies my face with concern.

"Thinking about Paul?"

I blink, and try a feeble joke. "Psychics used to be burned at the stake, you realize. Just like witches."

He gives me a sad grin but remains silent.

I sigh. "Of course I'm thinking about Paul. It's not every day you almost kill one of your children."

His grin vanishes. "Yeah. But if you hadn't done it, I might be dead, Hester. He was out of his fucking mind." His voice is shaky. "And who knows what he would have done to you and Eric after he was done with me?"

I want to tell him he's wrong. I want to tell him that the man who tore up his apartment an hour ago and hurt his friend was once a sweet young boy, just like him, and would have restrained himself in the end from causing further harm. I want to tell him how much Paul had loved his brother, and that losing Jeremy somehow turned all his demons loose, and it was alcohol that was really the main culprit here. I want to tell him these things, but I can't.

True or not, they make no difference now.

I bite my lip. "I still don't know how Eric came out of that fall with only a broken leg and a few cracked ribs to show for it. He's a very lucky young man, considering."

He makes a face. "Yeah, real lucky." He nods his head in the direction of the forbidding head nurse, who's on duty again today. "I asked that lady how long he was going to be unconscious from the drugs they gave him, and she said at least six hours or so. She said his leg was broken in four places, and he was going to be in a lot of pain when he woke up."

I rub my forehead. "I know. I spoke to her, too, while you were being examined."

Her, and the police.

My son's room is being guarded by an armed officer. Paul's unconscious, also, at the moment, with a fractured skull and a severe concussion. But as soon as he's well enough to travel (which may be several days) he'll be taken to jail, where he's being charged with assault and first-degree burglary. And possibly even attempted murder.

When the ambulance Alex summoned arrived at the house, it came with two police officers in tow, who followed us to the hospital. One of them was waiting for me the instant I was released from the doctor's custody, and wanted to escort me to the police station to get my statement. But he finally agreed to allow me another half hour here at the hospital. I told him that unless he was prepared to grapple with a seventy-one-year-old woman, I wasn't going anywhere until I'd had a chance to speak with Arthur and Caitlin in Arthur's room—and that I would not do *that*, either, until Alex was finished being patched up and given a clean bill of health. (He said he needed to speak to Alex, too, and suggested he take him "downtown" while I was with my family, but I insisted Alex and I would go to the station together, after I had finished my business.)

Luckily he was a young officer, and easily intimidated. But he's keeping an eye on me from down the hall, and he's been glancing at his watch ever since Alex sat next to me. He's no doubt expecting me to spring to my feet now and scurry over to Arthur's room for a quick chat, after which he can cart us off to the police station and have his way with us.

But he can damn well wait another few minutes while I pull myself together for the conversation with my husband and daughter.

I can't bear to speak to them until I've had a while longer to prepare myself, even though they've already been told what happened. I need to be calm before I face them. If they know how undone I am, I imagine they'll move in for the kill.

Out of the corner of my eye, I see the officer check his watch again and take a step in our direction, but I freeze him with a glare and he halts, cowed.

I turn back to Alex with grim determination.

"I have to go speak to Arthur and Caitlin, dear. And then that unhappy-looking policeman over there wants to take both of us to the station for an interview. Can you wait here for me until I return?"

He nods again. "Of course I'll wait for you." He tilts his head and smiles at me. "Just don't let your family give you any shit, Hester. Don't let anybody, okay?"

His blue eyes are surrounded by red—the whites are bloodshot, through and through, and the skin around them is raw and angry looking—and his hair is a dirty red nimbus framing it all. He needs a shower very badly, and a tremendous amount of sleep, and he looks as if a harsh word might be the end of him.

And yet, when he smiles at me with his exhausted face, my fear and anxiety lessen, and even my guilt at striking Paul abates a little.

I want to put my arms around him in gratitude, but I don't, for fear of embarrassing myself if I can't let go of him.

This fragile, damaged boy is so much stronger than he knows.

Arthur is propped up in bed when I walk in the room, with several pillows behind his back, and Martha is seated on the mattress next to him, holding his hand. Caitlin is over by the window, with her back to the door, staring out at the parking lot.

"So you're finally awake." I step to the foot of the bed and disregard the withering glare Martha gives me. Arthur's face remains neutral, however, and Caitlin doesn't even bother to turn around. I straighten my skirt and force a smile. "You were still sound asleep when I came to visit you this morning."

Arthur's voice is weary, but steady. "Yes, Martha told me you stopped by." He's pale as death and plugged into several machines, but his eyes are alert. "I'm flattered you found the time for me. I know you've been terribly busy, what with bludgeoning our son into a coma and all."

I flinch a little, but I keep my eyes on his. "He's not in a coma, as you well know. He was fully conscious for a few minutes when he arrived at the hospital, and he won't even require surgery." I take a deep breath and let it out again. "And you can believe me or not, Arthur, but he left me no choice."

Caitlin snorts and looks over her shoulder at me. "Congratulations, Hester. This is sure to win you yet another Mother of the Year Award."

I'm suddenly so tired I can barely stay on my feet. "What should

I have done instead, Caitlin? Given him a spanking? Sent him to his room without supper?" I sigh. "Trust me when I tell you this, please. He was no longer Paul. He was a monster."

She looks away. "Fine," she mutters. "But all the same, would you mind keeping your distance from the telephone? I neglected to wear my helmet this morning."

I look around for a chair. "May I sit? I'm very tired."

Arthur is studying me, and if I'm not mistaken, there's a great deal of concern in his face. For some reason, though, I'm having more difficulty than usual reading him.

"Of course," he says gruffly. He points to a chair by the bed. "Sit."

"I don't think that's a good idea," Martha butts in. "Arthur needs his rest, Hester, and you being here isn't good for him."

Arthur pats her hand. "It's okay, sweetheart. She'll leave in a moment, but I think the two of us need to discuss a few things first." He hesitates. "Would you mind?"

She stares at him in disbelief. "You're not serious. You can't possibly be asking me to leave you alone with *her.*"

He nods and adjusts his hospital gown. "Only for a minute, darling. I promise." He glances over at Caitlin. "You too, Caitlin. Please? I need to speak with your mother in private."

She turns to face us. "If you're going to discuss Paul, I'd like to be here, if it's all the same to you."

Arthur glances at me. "It's not about Paul, is it?"

I shake my head. "No." I clear my throat. "It's not." I make my way to the chair and collapse into it. "Although the three of us will need to talk about him eventually, of course."

Grief is rising up inside of me, like rainwater in a pothole. I look over at Caitlin and struggle to say what needs to be said before it overwhelms me. "But there's not much we can do for your brother, I'm afraid. I've been told he's facing as much as twenty-five years in jail, even if the boys and I refuse to press charges."

She closes her eyes for a long time, and when she opens them again, they're brimming with tears. "Twenty-five years? Dear God. That's . . ." She makes a queer little gesture with her hands. ". . . that's the rest of his life." Her voice breaks. "*Will* you press charges?"

When I first walked in the room, she was every inch the famous

Dr. Caitlin Donovan, chair of the English Department at Pritchard University. Now she's just Caitlin, my brittle and heartsick child.

My throat closes. The only other time I've ever seen her this vulnerable was after Jeremy's suicide.

"I don't want to," I whisper. "But I don't know what else to do."

I'm certain she's going to argue, but all she does is nod after a moment, and wipe her face. She stares off into space, and a shudder runs through her body. "What happened to him, Mother?" she blurts, crumbling. "What happened to all of us?"

Arthur is crying, as well. He says her name, but then falls silent, and looks at me for help.

And I have none to offer. I look back at him, equally helpless, my own eyes burning with sadness. Our daughter searches both our faces, as if trying to grasp a dialect she's never heard before, but her shoulders eventually sag in failure.

She takes a few deep breaths and composes herself. "I'll be nearby if you need me," she says quietly.

I don't know which of us she's speaking to, but on her way out the door, she touches my shoulder, and I swallow convulsively. I don't even remember the last time she did something like that.

Martha pauses before stepping after her into the hallway. She shakes a finger at me. "I swear to God, Hester, if you upset him, I'll kill you. He's in no condition for another one of your outbursts."

I stare over at her blankly, feeling no need to respond. At the moment, she's only a cipher to me, a nothing, and for all the reaction I give her, I could be a statue—perhaps a distant cousin of St. Booger's, lifeless and weather-beaten.

She begins to squirm under my gaze, but her pride won't let her leave without some kind of acknowledgment. I suppose I can't blame her for that, but I'm at a loss as to what I can do to pacify her.

Arthur speaks up, sparing me the task of breaking the stalemate.

"I'll be fine, Martha." He attempts a reassuring smile, but there's a hint of impatience in it. "Now will you please close the door, and leave us alone for a few minutes?"

"Fine," she huffs. "But I'll be right outside." She pulls the door shut behind her with an angry bang.

Arthur and I study each other for a moment in the stillness.

He's so big. Why do I always forget how big he is? He fills the bed, and his broad shoulders almost extend the entire width of his mattress. It's hard to believe he had major surgery just yesterday, because even now, wan and exhausted, he still seems indestructible.

"You look rather well, dear, considering all the stitches and pigskin you've got floating about in your ribcage." I tug at my lower lip, the way I always used to whenever I teased him. "I understand your heart has been replaced with a football."

That tickles him, in spite of himself. "You may be right," he grunts. He brushes his eyes with the back of his hand. "That's certainly what it feels like."

We smile at each other, awkwardly, and become quiet again. We've gotten out of the habit of being good to each other.

He searches for words. "I . . . don't blame you for what happened with Paul. I know you only did what you had to do."

This startling concession rubs at my conscience.

"Did I?" I lean forward. "Oh, Arthur. I so much wish I were sure of that." My worst fear comes tumbling out. "He was absolutely out of control, and that's the God's honest truth. But he may not have been meaning to hurt Alex anymore when I struck him. He may have been grabbing the boy only to help him up. But I struck him anyway."

I play the nightmare in my mind again, reliving Paul's last conscious moments in the attic kitchen. What would have happened if I'd simply spoken his name again, and asked him to leave? Would he have somehow turned into my son again?

I force out the rest of what I'm thinking, knowing that Arthur will have every right to judge me harshly for what I've done. My voice quivers. "And now I'll never know if some of this could have been prevented."

Arthur considers this gravely, then shakes his head. "You did what you had to do," he repeats. "And from the sound of it, I think you made the right call."

My lips tremble, and something hard and cold in the center of my body begins to dissolve. I didn't expect mercy from him, and it may be my undoing.

I search in my purse for a tissue. "Thank you. You have no idea how much I needed to hear that." I blow my nose and dab at my eyes. "When I first hit him, I thought I'd killed him."

He nods and sighs. "I'm sorry to say it, but it might have been better if you had." He rests his hands on his stomach and turns to look out the window. "Oh, Hester. How did our lives turn out like this?" He lets the question hang in the air for a minute, then swings his head back to me. "Where did we go so wrong?"

There's no bitterness in him at the moment. Just shock, and hurt, and confusion. For the first time in what feels like centuries, I abandon my defenses, and answer him with as much honesty and love as I can dredge up.

"I don't know, darling. Probably a thousand places, a thousand times."

I rise from my chair, on impulse, and step over to the side of his bed. Wordlessly, he shifts to make room for me to sit next to him. I scoot up beside him, ignoring that the mattress is still warm from Martha.

I lift one of his hands and hold it in my lap. "But we also went right once or twice, didn't we?" I gaze into his eyes. "And when we went wrong, at least we did it in public, in as humiliating a fashion as possible."

One side of his mouth quirks up. "That's for damn sure." He takes a deep breath and grimaces in pain. "Ouch. Remind me not to breathe right now. It stings a bit."

"Noted." I study his fingertips, pressing lightly on the calluses he has from his violin. "No more breathing allowed."

This is the first time we've touched since the day he told me about his affair with Martha, and his role in Jeremy's death. We used to be very affectionate, and it seems surreal, and inexpressibly awful, to realize that this is likely the last time we'll have physical contact.

He relaxes again and cocks his head, watching me. "There's something different about you today, Hester." He grins a little. "I mean, something beyond the fact that you're not going out of your way to piss me off."

I glance up and shrug. "It's nothing, really. I merely had a life-changing epiphany on our roof last night, while you were in surgery."

He blinks. "You were on the roof?"

I nod. "The boys and I went up there to stargaze. I needed some distraction." I notice he's no longer wearing his wedding ring, of course, but he hasn't worn it for some time now. Yet the skin where it used to sit is still worn smooth, creating its own semipermanent band. I have one just like it.

"You gave me quite a scare yesterday," I mumble.

He sinks deeper in his pillows. "I scared myself, too." He catches my thumb, playfully. "So tell me. What was this epiphany of yours?"

I so much want to say the right things to him, now. I want to find the words that will set us both free, and end our mutual bloodletting. But there's been so much anger between us, I don't have a clue how to proceed.

With the truth, I suppose.

I disengage myself from him, gently, and place his hand back on his stomach. "As epiphanies go, it wasn't much, really. It just . . . well, it simply occurred to me, all at once, that I've truly, absolutely lost you. And I'm more or less fine with that." I reach up and put my fingers on his lips before he can answer. "Which doesn't mean I won't miss you terribly. And that I won't hate Martha for the rest of my life, just for the fun of it. But when I thought you might die last night, things somehow changed."

There are, surprisingly, fresh tears in his old gray eyes. He removes my hand from his mouth and holds it against his shoulder. "What things?" he whispers.

I study his thick beard, and his small, elfin ears, and his large Adam's apple. I notice the way the late afternoon sun from the window brings out a random orange thread in the collar of his gown, and how a wrinkle in the middle of his forehead is deeper on the right side than on the left. I smell his familiar, pleasant body odor, which underlies the scent of flowers in the room, and the pungent medicinal stink, which must be the dressing on his wound, and I listen to him breathe, shallow and slow.

And I can feel his much-abused heart beating through our linked hands.

I clear my throat. "Everything, my love. Everything. The whole world changed." I turn my head to look out the window. "I saw just how awful I've been since Jeremy died. I saw how much the two of us have hated ourselves for his death, and how we let that ruin us. I saw how I've clung to you like a parasite ever since you wanted to leave me, and I saw how the only hope for either of us to find any happiness from here on in is to just let go of everything, completely."

My voice is even, and almost cheerful, but my face is wet. One tear after another falls from my chin to my lap. I turn back to him, resolved to finish what I came here to say.

"Arthur." I wipe my nose with my free hand. "I have loved you so much. Do you know that?"

He tightens his grip on me and tries to answer, but he can't. He pulls me closer to him, intending to put his arms around me, but the tubes are in the way, and he's still in too much discomfort from the surgery to attempt such things, so I forestall him and lean in for a kiss, instead. His lips are soft and a little chapped, and our breath mingles, warm and moist. We only hold the kiss for a moment, and then I pull away and sit up again, before I get lost and can't find my way back home.

He swallows several times and finally manages to answer me.

"I had a similar experience myself when I woke this morning," he begins, with considerable difficulty. "I was foggy and still feeling the effects of the anesthetic, and when I opened my eyes, I saw Martha. And before she spoke, I found myself wondering why she was here, and not you." He runs his fingers along my forearm and cradles my injured wrist in the palm of his hand. "And then I remembered everything, and it nearly killed me, all over again."

He pauses. "I know you're right. I know we can't go back to what we were, and that we can't be together anymore." He locks eyes with me. "But I wanted you to know that when I woke up today, I was still looking for you. Even after everything that's happened, you were the first one I wanted to see."

He chokes out the next words. "I will always look for you, Hester. I have loved you my whole life, and I will always love you." He fights for control, and I can hardly see him for my tears.

I don't remember anything ever hurting this much in my life. Not the death of my parents, not Paul's descent into madness, not even Jeremy's suicide. Not anything. I thought I could handle this, but I can't.

He does his best to get us both past this moment. He gives my arm a gentle shake, and when he can talk again, his mouth twitches and he sighs. "But that being said, please be aware that when I get out of here, it's likely I'll still want to strangle you, or run over you with a car."

It's a sorry sort of life line, but it's enough. I take hold of it, and let him pull me to safety.

I force my lips to form syllables. "Of course you will, darling. I'd expect nothing less."

And somehow we smile at each other. I don't know how we manage to do that, but we do.

There's a long, aching silence as both of us wrestle with our emotions. He lets go of my wrist, and we sit together, listening to voices in the hall outside the closed door, and the sound of somebody's television in the next room, behind the wall. In that stillness I can feel us withdrawing from each other, bit by bit; without a word spoken, we both understand it's time to end this. In another minute or two, I will walk out the door, and Martha will walk back in.

And that will be that.

He breaks the silence at last. "So, I've been thinking about something." His voice is more removed now—still cordial, but no longer the voice of my husband.

I respond in the same manner, knowing it's the kindest thing I can do for him at this point. "Yes? I'm all ears."

He winces at the subtle change in my tone, but then he nods, as if to himself, and continues. "I'll be needing time to recover from this surgery, and I probably won't be in any shape to deal with all the stairs in our house. Martha's home is more suited to the condition I'm going to be in, so we might as well drop this lawsuit thing for the time being, until I get my strength back."

I straighten in surprise, and nearly begin to cry again.

It's a generous thing he's doing, and unprecedented. There are layers on layers of grief here, for both of us, and he's doing what he can to lessen some of it. And I'm grateful, and moved, by the gesture, especially because I know what the house means to him.

But even so, I can't help goading him, just a little bit.

It's what I do.

I sniff. "That's very kind, dear. But are you sure? Martha could definitely use a few trips up and down the stairs every day, even if it's not the best thing for you."

His eyes narrow and his lips tighten for an instant. But then he searches my face, and something he sees there causes him to laugh, against his will. It's an irritated, rueful chuckle, but at least it's real.

"Good God, woman, you are such a bitch." He yawns, and drops his head on the pillows. "And Martha is really *not* fat, you know."

I nod. "I know. But it's quite entertaining to watch you change colors, like a chameleon."

Whatever energy he had is spent. I rise to my feet to go.

I stop by the door and turn to face him. We gaze at each other one last time, and half a century of memories pass between us. Love and loss, our children, music, hopes and dreams, death and despair, sleep, food and wine, arguments, and sex, and more sex, and winter mornings and autumn afternoons, and days on end, together.

Our life, such as it was.

Going, going, gone.

I tilt my head at him. "Goodbye, Arthur," I say.

"Goodbye, Hester," he murmurs, closing his eyes.

CHAPTER 24

"Alex?" I stand on the third floor landing and call up the stairs. "You have a telephone call."

"Okay!" he hollers back. "I'll be right there!"

He sounds excited. He probably thinks Eric is on the line.

This is Eric's third day in the hospital, in traction. Alex has visited him every day, several times a day, but he's had to share him with a lovely, doe-eyed girl named Sofia that Eric appears to be courting. I know her presence makes Alex jealous, but he won't admit that. He's attempting to pretend his feelings for the other boy are now only "platonic."

He sails down the stairs and gives me a guilty look when he sees I'm a bit winded from the climb up here to get him. I've told him he needs to contact the phone company and have service installed in his apartment, but he hasn't done it yet.

"Sorry, Hester!" He's trying to head off a lecture before I can get my air back. "I'll get a phone line connected next week, I promise." He passes me at a trot, on his way to the ground floor. I've asked him not to use my bedroom phone (I have to maintain *some* boundaries), so he has to go all the way to the kitchen. He calls back up the staircase as he reaches the second floor landing. "Is it Eric?"

"No, it's not." I lean my head over the banister above him as he grinds to a halt in surprise. "And don't run on the stairs. You'll break every bone in your body." I pause. "Alex. It's your mother."

His face falls. "You're shitting me."

"I'm afraid not. She sounds terribly sad."

He stares up at me for a while. "What the hell does *she* want?" There's more anxiety than anger in his voice.

"I don't know. But you'd better find out." I rest my hands on the railing. "And don't be rude to her, dear. I know things are strained between you right now, but she's still your mother."

He makes a face at me, and a few seconds later the corners of his mouth curl up in a familiar way. "Can't I just beat her brains out with an old phone instead?"

I shake a finger at him and growl. "That is not in the least bit amusing, young man. Now go talk to your mother."

I left the receiver in the kitchen resting on the kitchen table, but Alex waits until I return to the ground floor before picking it up. He's been standing down here for some time; it takes me quite a while to negotiate the stairs.

"Hello?" Alex mutters into the phone. His bare toes are clinched into miniature fists on the floor.

I raise my eyebrows at him and begin to leave the room to give him some privacy, but he waves me in before returning his attention to the call. "Yeah, I know who it is. Hi, Mom."

When I spoke with his mother, she was almost pathetic in her need to speak with her son. She made a half-hearted stab at small talk, but it was all she could do to restrain herself from begging me to run and fetch him.

But I doubt she would have had the courage to call if she'd known how cold his voice was going to be at this moment.

His posture is rigid. "I'm fine. I'm doing fine." He pauses. "Why are you calling?"

I sit at the table across from him. "Be nice," I whisper.

He covers the mouthpiece on the receiver. "Why?" he grunts. "She's only calling to piss me off."

I frown. "Just give her a chance."

His mother says something else, and he rolls his eyes. "Yeah, I feel pretty damn bad about it, too, Mom. But now that you've called, everything's all better now. Thanks."

There's a bowl of green grapes on the table, and I snatch one up and fling it at him. "Quit it," I hiss. "Give the poor woman some credit for trying."

The grape bounces off his cheek and he glares at me. He covers the receiver again. "Are you nuts? Whose side are you on?"

I seize another grape and threaten him with it. "Just *talk* to her, Alex."

His mother speaks again, at length, and Alex's face darkens bit by bit until he finally snaps, cutting her off. "Why in God's name would I want to come see you guys? Has Dad changed his mind about me? I notice he's not on the other line. I bet he's out building an electric fence around the house to keep me out in case I should be dumb enough to show up."

Another grape bonks into his forehead, but he ignores me.

He listens to her again, looking more miserable by the second. "Oh, I see." He closes his eyes and breathes. "He's busy." He sounds inexpressibly melancholy. "Well, I've gotta go," he says. "I'm busy, too."

She raises her voice in desperation. I can't make out many words, but I do hear "please come home," and "family."

He swallows hard and opens his eyes. I want to tell him to be kind, and to make peace, but I force myself to stay still this time.

He clears his throat. "I don't think I can do that, Mom," he murmurs. "Besides, I've already got a home, and a family. But really, thanks for calling. And tell Dad I appreciate all his support. He's been swell."

He spins on his heels and hangs up before she can answer him. When he turns around again, I'm waiting for him.

"Oh, child," I sigh. "You're not wrong, but you're not right, either."

Alex isn't the only one to receive an unexpected call today.

I'm alone in the kitchen when the phone rings, and after a brief, awkward conversation, I hang up and wander into the living room, where Alex is sitting by the fire, reading. He should be in class this afternoon, but he's milking his injuries for all they're worth, refusing to return to Pritchard until his cuts and bruises are healed. He says he doesn't want to "feel like a freak," and he's turned a deaf ear to at least three lengthy lectures I've given him regarding the wisdom of this course of action. I fear by the time he does return to the university he may be shown the door (by my daughter, most likely), but there's little else I can do at this point to make him see sense.

He has no health insurance, of course, and no money to pay his emergency room bill, but when I offered to float him a loan, he turned me down flat, saying he'd find a job eventually, and get himself fixed up then. Stubborn child.

He looks up as I sit in the armchair across from him, and I glance at the cover of his book with approval. (It's *The Left Hand of Darkness,* by Ursula LeGuin. Arthur and I both enjoy science fiction novels, and I recommended this one to Alex yesterday when he was hunting for a good book.)

"This is pretty dope," he says, tapping the book jacket. "Weird, but good."

I stare at the fire, too distracted to take him to task for his nonsensical slang. "I'm glad you like it."

There's a long pause, and the sound of a page turning as he continues reading. But after a while I can feel his eyes watching me.

"What's wrong?" he asks.

I stir in my chair. "That was Paul on the phone. He wants to see me in an hour."

His thin, freckled face blanches. "He called from the jail?"

The sun is shining outside, streaming through the windows. I glance out at the driveway and blink at the bright reflection on the snow covering St. Booger's Bible.

I shake my head. "No. He bailed himself out two days ago. He wants to meet me downtown at the diner."

Paul told me his bail was almost thirty thousand dollars, but he was able to access the funds, and the police—at the request of Sam Hastings (the judge who set the bail, and an old family friend)—grudgingly released him. I'm not surprised Paul has that kind of money at his fingertips; he's been drawing a decent salary for many years at Carson, and since he lives in that ghastly faculty bungalow (with a roommate, no less), and never travels or does anything expensive, I'm sure he's managed to squirrel away a princely sum at the bank.

Alex slams his book shut. "Jesus Christ! I can't believe they let the asshole out. What if he gets wasted and comes back here?"

I return my attention to the glowing coals in the fireplace. A log shifts on the grate and is engulfed by blue flames.

"I don't think there's any danger of that. He sounded so . . ." I pause because my chin is trembling. "He sounded sane again. He said he was going to check himself into a detox center tonight, but he needs to see me first."

Paul's voice on the phone was sober and reticent. And disturbingly hollow. There was no life in it, no anger, no energy. He sounded like a robot, except for when he asked to meet me at the diner. When he said "please," his voice broke a little. Which upset me far more than I thought it would.

Alex bites his lip. "I'm going with you. Just in case he does something stupid."

I shake my head once more. "No. You being there is a very bad idea. It's not your fault, but there's something about you that sets him off."

He frowns. "I don't think I'm the only one in this room you can say that about." He leans forward and puts his elbows on his knees to argue. "You really shouldn't go alone, Hester. If you do, you're nuts."

He didn't hear Paul on the phone. He didn't hear my son's voice break.

I pull myself together. "If it's just me, he'll be fine." I give him a reassuring smile. "He won't hurt me."

Willie's Diner in downtown Bolton is hardly the place I would have chosen for a private conversation. It's a small, 1950s-style restaurant, with greasy, salty food, a miniature jukebox at every booth, and two ceiling fans that run all year long. The upholstery on the faux-leather booths and barstools is a black and white checkerboard pattern, and the counters and windows are lined with shiny chrome. It opens at five in the morning and closes at midnight, and it's always busy, day or night.

And everyone who comes here knows Paul and me.

The quick, curious glances I get from the clientele as I enter the diner and walk over to join Paul at his booth are a sure sign that the goings-on at the Donovan househould this last week have been the subject of many a juicy conversation. Janet Green, the wizened waitress behind the counter, gives me a sympathetic smile and says hello as I pass by. I nod at her and come to a stop by Paul's table. He's sitting with his back to the door, so my sudden appearance startles him.

He looks horrible. His complexion is ashen and his big hands are trembling on the table, and his clothes are rumpled and food-stained. He has a full cup of coffee in front of him, and a plate with buttered toast on it, untouched.

"Hello, Hester." He studies me for a minute and then gestures for me to sit. "Are you hungry?"

"Hello, Paul." I slide into the booth, facing him. "No, thank you. I ate a late breakfast today."

We inspect each other in silence, and Janet calls out to me.

"You want coffee, Hester?"

I shake my head. "Tea, if you have it."

"Sure thing, hon. I'll bring it right over."

There's a hum of conversation from the other diners in the background, and no one is sitting close to us, so we have more privacy than I thought we would. But neither of us says a word. He watches me and I watch him, like strangers on a subway train. His beard is tangled and his hair is dirty, and I would wager he hasn't slept or showered in several days.

Janet plunks down a mug of hot water and a bag of Lipton tea on our table, then exits again after checking our supply of sugar and cream. Her stockings have runs in them, and her old ankles are puffy above her scuffed shoes. She may even be older than I am.

Paul fiddles with his coffee mug, but doesn't pick it up. "So how are you?"

I shrug. "Well enough." I become preoccupied with dunking my tea bag in the steaming water. "And you? How's your head?"

His mouth twitches. "Fine, considering."

I expected bitterness in his tone but there isn't any. Just a touch of rueful amusement.

"I'm sorry," I find myself saying. "I didn't know what else to do."

His turn to shrug. "From what I gather, I didn't leave you much choice. I don't remember any of it, but the cops have filled me in." He looks out the window at the parking lot. "How are Alex and the other kid doing? I tried to find out at the hospital when I went to visit Dad, but no one would tell me anything."

I can't tell if he's legitimately concerned, or only being polite, but I decide to give him the benefit of the doubt.

"Both are recovering. Eric is in traction, of course, but he seems to be in good spirits, more or less. And Alex is basically fine. He has about forty stitches in his feet, but he's healing." A thought occurs to me. "You might offer to pay the emergency room bill for him, by the way. He won't take money from me."

His face darkens, but after a moment he nods. "All right. I'll speak to my lawyer about it."

His lack of resistance to this idea is shocking, and I pause. Is it possible he's actually attempting to be agreeable?

I can't help but test him. "Alex was dismayed to hear of your release. He was worried you might do something rash."

He rolls his eyes. "Tell the little dick he can relax," he growls. "I promised Sam when he let me loose that I'd *behave* until my trial." He finally picks up his coffee and sips at it. "It's the only reason he let me go, by the way." He grimaces. "That, and he knows I'm not much of a flight risk."

I'm unable to suppress a tiny smile. Anybody who knows Paul in the least bit is aware of his extreme travel phobia.

He sees the smile and sighs with uncharacteristic grace. "Yeah, I know. It's pretty pathetic." He tugs a cigarette out of his coat pocket on the booth seat and lights it. He must have been here for some time; the ashtray at the end of the table has several butts in it already. "The only good thing about being sent to the state pen is that I'll finally be forced to move out of Bolton."

For some reason, I find myself thinking of Paul's last faculty recital. On the second half he performed the Bach *Cello Suite in G Major*. I snuck into the balcony after intermission so he wouldn't know I was there; we were barely speaking at the time. I found a dark corner and sat alone, and chastised myself for my weakness at being unable to stay away.

But I had to come. No one plays Bach like my son.

He came out on stage in his tux, looking like a scruffy, bipedal orca, acknowledged the applause, and sat down with his cello. I put my head back on my seat and closed my eyes, and I didn't open them again for twenty minutes, after he'd finished the Gigue and was receiving a wildly enthusiastic standing ovation. Unable to help myself, I, too, rose to my feet, and joined the rest of the audience in their praise.

Paul's behavior this past week was monstrous, and for the past few years he's been perfectly detestable. He's boorish, and irresponsible, and unkind, and I will probably never be able to forgive him for his attack on two innocent boys in my house. Or for the way he's treated me ever since Jeremy's death.

But the man can play the cello.

When it comes to music, he's a Donovan, through and through, and an absolute wonder. The richness of his tone, the depth of his emotional control, and the stunning accuracy of his technique are all top-notch; the clarity of his phrasing and the ingenuity of his articulations are masterful. He loves to play; he *lives* to play, and when he picks up a bow he becomes a thing of beauty, an artist on a par with the greatest composers who have ever lived.

And it's just now occurring to me that he will probably not be allowed to have his instrument with him in prison. And if he's to be incarcerated for twenty-five years, he may never have the chance to play again.

Ever.

Without warning, my eyes are filled with tears. Paul flushes and stares down at the table.

"Please don't, Hester," he asks, in a tight, surprised whisper.

For his sake, I force myself to put aside this grief for now. I wipe my eyes and nose with a napkin, and after a lengthy pause I clear my throat.

I do my best to make my voice breezy. "So you're going into detox, you said?"

He relaxes and blows a plume of smoke at the ceiling fan. "Yeah. My lawyer said it was the only chance I had of getting some leniency in my sentencing." He hesitates. "I personally don't believe there's much chance for leniency, but I've decided I should sign myself in, anyway. Recent events have made me think I may actually have a bit of a drinking problem." He manages a grin. "Either that, or I should give up caffeine."

I haven't seen him like this in years. His sense of humor died with Jeremy, but he's almost his old self at this moment. I feel something stir in me in response, but I choose to ignore it, for fear of giving him too much credit.

He chews on his lip for a minute, then leans on the table with an earnest expression. "Look, Hester, I guess we should cut to the chase."

I nod, suspicious again. "Cut away, then."

He stares into my eyes. "I asked you here to tell you I'm sorry." He says this bluntly, almost rudely. "I wasn't sure I'd get another chance to do it, and I wanted to see you before I chickened out."

The grief is back in an instant, rising in my throat. I try a poor joke because I don't know what else to say. "Which transgression are you apologizing for? I've lost track."

My tone isn't lost on him. He snorts. "Take your pick."

He snuffs out his cigarette and his smile fades. "Mostly for Jeremy, I guess. I mean for blaming you for what he did." There are tears in his eyes, now, too, which is unimaginable. "I know it wasn't your fault. I know that, absolutely. But it hurt so much when the stupid shit killed himself that I couldn't stand it. I had to have somebody to blame, and you were the easiest target. I . . . loved him a great deal."

I can't answer. I wasn't prepared for this kind of honesty from him. My throat isn't working, and my vision is blurred.

He sees my distress, and tries to lighten the tone. "Oh, yeah. I'm also sorry for tossing the toaster out the window." He sighs. "I kind of feel bad about that, too."

Somehow I find a way to laugh at this. He knew it would make me laugh; after all these years he still knows me, inside and out.

I blow my nose on the napkin and shake my head. "Yes, well, you were having an off day."

He sobers as he fiddles with his ashtray. "When Alex moved in last month, he reminded me so much of Jeremy, and something inside me just snapped when I saw the two of you together. It was as if . . ." He stops and fumbles for words. "It was like you'd forgotten Jeremy, and moved on. I know you didn't forget him, of course, but I couldn't handle it anyway." He looks into my eyes. "It tore me up inside, Mom. It felt like losing him all over again."

I try to respond, but nothing comes out. His face blurs, and he falls silent.

We take a few moments to compose ourselves. He wipes his eyes on his sleeve and nibbles at his toast, and I stare out the window at a small pine tree sticking out of a snowdrift next to the diner. Some joker has adorned the top of the tree with an upside down Pepsi can, and tied an old mitten to one of its branches. I listen to Paul swallow his food, and he watches the side of my face as he finishes eating and lights another cigarette.

There's so much else to say to each other, but it seems neither of us has the strength left to say it. I want to tell him about that last day on the roof with his brother, and how awful it was. I want to tell him how much I've missed his father, and him, and Caitlin; I want to tell him about the healing conversation I had a few days ago with Arthur. I want to ask him why he decided to be truthful with me and apologize today, and if he's afraid of going to jail.

But I can't. I assume he has things he wants to ask and tell me, as well, but he can't, either.

There may come a day when we can speak to each other again, as mother and child, or at least as friends, but it won't be today. We'll have to let what we've already said suffice for the time being, for fear of going too fast and risking another damaging argument. So we fall back into silence, and we drink our drinks, and after a while he puts money on the table, and stands up to go.

I reach for his hand, then, on impulse, and for an instant he takes it. It's not much of a connection, but it's something, and far more than I ever hoped we'd have again. I watch him leave a moment later, following him with my eyes as he walks out into the cold. I see him through the window as he gets into his Volvo and drives away.

Janet shows up at my elbow and offers me another cup of tea, free of charge. My voice trembles as I thank her, and she pats my hand on the table before leaving me alone. I stare back out at the pine tree, and find myself wondering who owned the mitten before it ended up as a forlorn ornament.

Oh, Paul.

I've lied to Alex twice, it seems.

Once was today, when I said Paul wouldn't hurt me if I came to see him.

And the other time was a few weeks ago, when I said I didn't love my son anymore.

Chapter 25

I step out of the bright, cold sunlight into the relative darkness of Higdon Hall, turning as I do so to wave at Alex, who is watching from the car in the parking lot. He insisted on driving me to Pritchard this afternoon, claiming the roads were too dangerous for me to make the journey by myself. In truth, I think he wanted more time to talk me out of my plan to visit Caitlin.

He saw the shape I was in yesterday after my visit with Paul, and he's afraid I won't survive another conversation along those lines with my daughter.

He may be right.

But I'm sick to death of being at war with my family, and the recent talks with both Arthur and Paul, though terribly painful, have made me believe I can no longer allow things to go on as they have between Caitlin and myself. For better or worse, we're part of each other, and it's long past time for me to make an effort to reconnect.

I check my watch and see I only have five minutes before she finishes with her afternoon class. Alex told me where and when I would be most likely to find her, and I walk up the stairs toward her classroom like a condemned prisoner ascending a scaffold. Higdon Hall is hot and quiet, and my footsteps echo around me as I make my way down the hall to her room.

The door is open, and I can hear her lecturing as I approach. I reach the doorway and find her standing at the front of the room, addressing about twenty students. She's dressed in a striking green skirt and suit coat, and she's leaning her back against the chalkboard.

"You can say whatever you want about Dickens's political views and his scathing critiques of society," she's saying, "but it's his unique narrative voice, just as with Austen and Tolstoy, that makes his work . . ." She sees me in the doorway and falters. ". . . that makes his work timeless."

She frowns at me and seems to lose her train of thought, and after a moment she glances at the clock above her head and abruptly dismisses the class. I step inside the room and her students, studying me with curiosity, file out singly and in pairs. She remains by the chalkboard, silent, until we're alone.

"What is it, Mother?" she asks at last. "Why are you here? Has something happened to Dad?"

"Hello, Caitlin." I force myself to relax my grip on my purse. "No, your father is fine. I just wanted to speak with you for a moment. Is this a bad time?"

She hesitates. "As a matter of fact, it is. I have an appointment in my office in about five minutes." Her voice becomes sardonic. "Are you here to pick up Alex's homework for him?"

I let this pass. Alex seems to upset her almost as much as he does Paul.

"I'm not here about Alex, although we probably should discuss him sometime. You and he have gotten off on the wrong foot, and I believe I'm at least partly responsible for that."

She makes a face. "Don't flatter yourself. Alex Pearl is more than capable of annoying me all on his own."

"How so?"

"As I said to you at the grocery store, he doesn't take his work seriously, and he's disrespectful, and he seems to believe he has the right to intrude himself in our family's business, simply because he rents a room from you."

I sigh. "I can't speak to his behavior in your classes, of course, but that last bit is unfair. He hasn't intruded himself at all. He's just been unfortunate enough to be in the wrong place at the wrong time."

"And whose fault is that?" she snaps.

I remain silent. I didn't come here to fight.

She pauses when I don't answer, and when she finally speaks again it's with visible reluctance. "Anyway, suffice it to say that the only reason I haven't yet revoked his writing scholarship is because he has a great deal of talent, and I would hate to see it go to waste."

I digest this. "Truly? Alex is gifted?"

"I'm afraid so." She grimaces. "He's already a better poet than any of my grad students."

I don't know why this surprises me, but it does. I'm tempted to pursue the subject, but she's looking at her watch again, so I let it go. There's so much more I need to say to her before she leaves.

I step closer. "I came here today because I was hoping we could talk about us."

The afternoon sunlight is coming through the windows on the far side of the room in vertical shafts, lighting the floor in squares and rectangles.

She begins to gather some papers together on her desk. "Yes, I hear you've been making the rounds this week. You must have been visited by the ghost of Christmas past, or something to that effect." She raises an eyebrow. "Did Tiny Tim enjoy his turkey?"

The humor in her voice is tinged with acid.

I bite my lip. "So you've spoken to Paul?"

She shakes her head. "Just to Dad. But he told me Paul called him yesterday after the two of you got together."

I blink. "And?"

She shrugs. "And you somehow managed to have a civil conversation. I was spared most of the details."

I gather my courage. "Caitlin, I'm here to make peace with you, if we can." My voice breaks a little. "I don't know how we're going to do that, but I wanted to tell you I'd like to try."

She looks away. "I see." Her hands come to rest in front of her. "I think it's a little late for that, don't you?"

Her tone is cold, but her chin is trembling.

I take a deep breath. "Your father and I have buried the hatchet, and Paul and I are at least speaking again. Surely you and I can do as much?"

She stares out the window, frowning, for a long time. I begin to think she's not going to answer when she turns to face me again.

"Do you remember that awful fight Jeremy and I had right after he started teaching at Carson?" She's now tentative, for some reason. "The one where he told all of you about discovering me with my friend's husband?"

I nod, wary. "Of course I do. He was being horrible that day."

"Yes, he was," she agrees. "But do you know what he did to apologize the next week, when I was back in school? Did he ever tell you?"

"Not that I recall."

She plays with a pen for a moment. "God, I was angry at him, remember? He was being such a bastard." She takes a deep breath. "Anyway, I was in Chicago again, and I came back to my dorm one morning after class. I stepped into the hall on the way to my room, and I saw a long-stemmed white rose on the floor. A few feet farther on there was a red one, and then a yellow, and as I got closer to my door, there were dozens more, all lined up one after another, all the way to my room."

She sets the pen down and doesn't move to catch it when it rolls across the desk and falls to the floor. "When I opened the door, my entire bed was covered in roses. Just flowers this time, no stems. The whole room smelled like heaven, and there was a note on my pillow." She laughs a little. "The note was unsigned, and all it said was, 'Sorry I'm such an asshole.'"

She looks at me again with an odd half-smile. "I found out later he hired three people, including my roommate, to help with everything. It must have cost a fortune."

Somebody passes by in the hallway behind me, whistling.

I search for words. "That's a lovely story." My heart is aching now. "I can't believe you never told me about this before."

She shrugs. "I didn't want to. It was just between Jeremy and me."

I study her. "So why tell me now?"

"I don't know," she says. Her voice has a tremor in it. "It doesn't really matter, does it?"

I find myself remembering the phone call I made to her last year, after Arthur finally told me about Martha, and about his part in Jeremy's death. I thought, foolishly, that when she heard these things, she might hate me less, but all it did was make her equally furious with Arthur—and me just as furious with her, after she revealed she had been aware of her father's affair for nearly a decade.

I clear my throat. "Caitlin, I don't know what to say to you. What can I do to make things better between us?"

The clock above the chalkboard ticks along in the stillness for what seems an eternity before she answers.

She leans on the desk and frowns. "I don't think I want things to be better between us."

I stare at her. "Please tell me you're joking."

"Every time I'm around you, Hester, I feel so angry I can barely function. I know I should try to forgive you, but I can't seem to do that." Her eyes burn into mine. "When I see you, all I think about is Jeremy, and about how and why he died. I don't think I'll ever be able to stop seeing that. I wish I could, but I can't." She looks away again, swallowing. "I'm sorry, truly."

I think it's her apology that breaks me. I wasn't expecting that. I stare at the floor and feel tears coursing down my face, one after another. I want to say something, but all I can do is cry.

"But it's not just that, either." She's quieter, now, but her bitterness is palpable. "It's you, Hester. It's how you are. I used to dream what it would have been like to have had a mother who looked at me the way you looked at Paul and Jeremy. You worshipped them, and you pitied me, and I had to live with that every day of my childhood. Every single day." Another long silence, followed by an eloquent snort. "In retrospect, perhaps I should be happy about that. The worship thing didn't work out so well for Paul and Jeremy, did it?"

It takes all my strength just to stay on my feet. I want to flee from her, but all I can do is stand here and feel her words cut into me, one after another.

I have no answer for her. I could argue, and tell her how much I always loved her, but there's no point. She wouldn't believe me.

And she shouldn't.

Because some of what she's saying is true. I did pity her, of course. And I treated her differently than her brothers. It was not my intention to do so, but I know I did.

I didn't love her less, but I behaved as if she *were* less.

Her voice becomes a shade gentler. "But then again, I know I haven't been the daughter you wanted, either, so I guess we're even." She pauses. "Maybe we should just leave it at that, and call it quits, okay?"

I wish there were a way to take back all the years. I wish there were a way to undo all our mistakes, and forget all the ways we've harmed each other. I wish I could take her in my arms as she hasn't allowed me to do since she was a very small child, and that we could start over.

But that's not going to happen. Not today. And maybe not ever.

She resumes picking up her things and clears her throat. "I really have to go now, Mother." She waits. "Was there anything else?"

I shake my head. It's all I can do. She lingers a bit longer, but then says good-bye and heads for the door. As she brushes past me, I finally look up again, just in time to see something that hurts far, far worse than all her words combined.

Her face is as wet as mine.

CHAPTER 26

Eric's girlfriend, Sofia, is in his hospital room. She's sitting on his bed when Alex and I enter, and they're holding hands and sharing a quiet laugh about something. A pang of jealousy crosses Alex's face, of course, but I'm afraid he's going to have to get used to that feeling. If I'm any judge of such things, I don't believe Sofia is going anywhere soon.

And even if she does, there will always be another girlfriend, eventually.

Eric smiles when he sees us, and gives us a big wave with his free hand.

"Hey, dudes!" He gestures us over to the opposite side of the bed from Sofia. "What's up? How's it hanging?"

I regret to say he's entirely lost his awe of me in the last few days.

I let his crudity slide, though, because he's truly been wonderful about this entire ordeal. Through no fault of his own, he was assaulted in my home and tossed down a staircase. But in spite of being knocked out of commission for the next several months, he's never blamed Alex, or me, for the fight with Paul, and he somehow stays in a cheerful mood, day after day.

Alex and I step around the weights and wires that are part of his traction apparatus and come to a halt beside his torso. The boys do their odd touching of fists in greeting, and Alex smiles back at him. "I'm good. I just dropped out of Pritchard."

Eric's face falls. "You're shitting me. You're quitting school?"

"He's perfectly serious," I growl. "Perhaps you can talk some sense into him."

"Wow," Sofia murmurs. "Hi, Alex, by the way. Hi, Hester."

She has gorgeous, long black hair, and intelligent, soft brown eyes, and she also seems to be quite sweet. Alex told me he wishes he could hate her, but he hasn't been able to make himself do so.

I return her greeting and find a chair in the corner.

"Hi, Sofia," Alex says, then turns back to Eric. "Yeah. I've been doing a lot of thinking, and I've decided I don't want to do any more school for a while."

Eric frowns. When he's upset about something, his blue eyes darken like a mood ring. "Just like that? You're quitting?"

Alex picks at some lint on the sheets. "Yeah. I'm not leaving town, though. I'm just going to get a job someplace and keep on living with Hester."

"At least until I throw him out on his ear," I mutter.

I've tried to talk him out of this latest plan, but he's being stubborn. He seems to believe he's too far behind in his classes this semester, and feels his time will be better spent in writing on his own.

And given the rancor between him and my daughter, I'm forced to concede he may be right.

Eric shakes his head. "Why are you dropping out of college, man? I don't get it."

Alex shrugs. "It's kind of hard to explain. Basically I just want time to put my life back together. A lot of shit went down this last year with my family, not to mention all the stuff here, and I just want some freedom to figure it all out."

Eric scowls. "And you can do that while you're working, but not while you're in school? Good luck."

Sofia pinches the skin on his arm. "Leave him alone, Eric. It's his life."

"Ow! That hurt, dammit," he says, rubbing his bicep. He leans back against the pillows and studies Alex. His expression becomes gentle, and he sighs. "I'm just pissed because I like having you around." He forces a smile. "Even if you are a total spaz."

Alex looks away. "Yeah, I'll miss you, too. But like I said, I'm not going anywhere. We can still hang out, any time you want."

Eric's eyes bore into the side of Alex's face. "Sit down, dude," he orders.

Alex obeys in silence, settling in next to the other boy's cast. The cast covers Eric's entire left leg, and most of his pelvis, too, circling his waist. About fifteen people have signed the rough white plaster so far. (There's an appalling new contribution by his knee that says *"How do you whack off when you're wearing this thing, dude? Love, Abe."*) I sigh and root through my purse for a mint.

Eric disengages himself from Sofia and leans back in bed with his hands behind his head. "So tell me what's up, man. Why are you really dropping out of school?" He glances at Sofia and me and hesitates. "It's not because of problems with anybody specific, is it?"

I can almost see the troubled thoughts churning around in his handsome head. He's worried Alex may be leaving because of what happened between them, but he can't ask about it directly with Sofia and me in the room.

Alex blushes a bit. He shakes his head, emphatic. "Not at all. It's got nothing to do with anybody else."

I don't know if he's telling the truth or not. I suspect he doesn't either. He's not over Eric, yet, not by a long shot, and one of his reasons for quitting school may indeed be to avoid too much contact between them. Either way, though, he's not about to confess this to Eric.

And I don't blame him. Conversations about unrequited love and balked desire have been scientifically proven to cause hair loss, and many other signs of premature aging.

Eric is skeptical. "Seriously?"

Alex nods. "Yeah. I'm totally cool with everybody at Pritchard." He drops his eyes. "But thanks for asking."

Eric picks up Alex's hand in a curious, tender gesture. His voice is careful as he changes the subject. "So you're going home to see your family?"

Alex has told him about what happened last Thanksgiving in Iowa, and he knows this is a hard topic. Especially because his relationship with his own parents is quite good; I met Eric's mother and father yesterday here at the hospital (they live in St. Louis, and drive here daily to see him), and they seem to be charming people.

"Yeah, I guess." Alex sighs. "Mom called yesterday. I got pissed and hung up on her, but then I started feeling like a complete dick. She was crying and stuff, and I just made fun of her and shit."

Eric shrugs. "She kinda deserves that, don't you think?"

Alex winces. "Yeah, maybe. I don't know." His hand is still holding Eric's, as if it were something fragile and precious. "But either way, I don't want to be mad at them forever, and I'd like to make things better. If I get there and they go postal on me again, then at least I can say I tried."

My eyes drift to Sofia. She's watching them closely, but her face, oddly enough, doesn't have any jealousy in it. Rather, she seems moved, as I am, by the open affection between them. These are two very rare young men. I'm not surprised by Alex, so much; I know him, now, and I know what he's capable of. But Eric is also a treasure.

As a matter of fact, if I were fifty years younger, I'd be pushing Alex and Sofia off the bed to get to him, too.

Eric smiles and finally releases him. "Wow. Listen to you. Mr. All Grown-up."

Alex snorts. "You might want to wait to call me that until after I get back from Iowa. I may need some diapers and a rattle by then."

"When are you going to go see them?"

Alex pauses. "I don't know. Soon. Maybe tonight or tomorrow, even. I don't want it hanging over my head for too long." He looks over at me for a moment and grins. "It's weird. I've avoided conflict my whole life, but now I don't much care if my folks and I have a knockdown-dragout or not. I guess living with Hester has really taught me how to appreciate a good fight."

I make a face. "Wonderful. I've created a monster. But before you make any rash decisions, you might want to remember how well my strategy of engagement has worked for me."

His grin widens. "You've done all right."

The four of us chat for a while longer, but Eric is yawning a great deal. He likely wants to be alone with Sofia again before he has a nap, so after another few minutes I make noises about needing to go home, and Alex takes the hint and rises from the bed when I stand up.

"I guess we better take off," he says.

Eric nods. "Okay." He scratches at the edge of his cast. "But let me know when you get to your folks', dude, and tell me how it's going." He yawns again. "And borrow one of Hester's kitchen knives, just in case things get out of hand." He chortles. "Or better yet, take the phone in the attic. That thing rocks for self-defense."

Sofia pinches him again, and Alex laughs hard.

I sniff. "Another remark like that from you, child, and you'll be in dire need of another cast." I move over to his bed and bend down to kiss his cheek. "Get well soon, dear."

Alex tells him he'll call when he arrives in Morelle. Eric opens his arms, indicating he wants a hug, and when Alex leans in to comply, Eric gives him a quick peck on the cheek as well, and tells him to be careful. Alex pulls back, flustered, and Eric smiles up at him. Sofia giggles at Alex when he just stands there, beaming from ear to ear, unable to think of anything else to say.

We take our leave, and when we're in the hallway, it's all he can do to refrain from jumping around with joy. I nearly tell him not to read too much into Eric's farewell, but then I realize he doesn't need to hear this. I believe he already knows; it's likely he's just happy to find he's loved. It's not the kind of love he wants, of course, but maybe he's wise enough to know that love of any stripe is better than none at all.

And wise or not, as long as he lives, he'll never forget that kiss.

CHAPTER 27

I've decided to loan Alex my car so he can visit his parents and try to patch things up with them. When we arrived home from visiting Eric at the hospital yesterday and he told me of his plan to "hop a bus" as soon as one was available, I insisted he take my car instead, but only after getting a good night's sleep and eating a decent breakfast. He argued about leaving me without a car for a day or two, but I won, of course, telling him I had a pantry full of food, and no reason to venture out until early next week, when I have a meeting with the dean.

It's a bright, cold morning. We finished eating a few minutes ago, and he just backed the car out of the carriage house and tossed his suitcase in the trunk. St. Booger is glaring down at him as he stands there in the driveway, and I'm on the porch, in my robe and slippers, waiting for him to leave.

"Go inside, Hester," he calls out. "It's too cold out here for you to be dressed like that." He walks slowly toward me, kicking at some ice with his sneakers.

"I'm fine," I answer. "What's taking you so long?"

He points over his shoulder with his thumb at the car. "The engine needs to warm up for another few minutes."

I raise my eyebrows. "You already warmed it up in the carriage house, didn't you?"

He frowns. "Yeah, but it needs more time than that. It's not made for this kind of weather."

He's stalling.

I shiver. "My car doesn't need to be babied, boy, and you're wasting gas."

He comes to a halt by the porch steps and looks up at me. The sun is catching him from behind, and I have to put my hand above my eyes to see him. He can no doubt detect every wrinkle and every age spot on my skin in this light, but I don't care; he's gazing at me with affection, and there's something so lovely in his expression that it almost breaks my heart to look at him.

His nose is running from the cold and he wipes it on his sleeve. "Are you going to be okay while I'm gone?"

I sniff. "I'll survive." I smile down at him. "But if there's a snowstorm, send me a St. Bernard, with a large flask of expensive cognac attached to his collar."

He continues staring at me in that odd way.

"What?" I demand.

He shrugs. "Nothing. It's just that you look great, Hester." He laughs. "What happened?"

"Are you certain you can see to drive, child? Ever since your glasses were broken, you squint a great deal, and I fear you're getting blinder by the minute."

He shakes his head. "No, I'm not. I'm serious. You look terrific."

I feel myself flush a little and I stare at the ground. "Thank you, dear." I clear my throat. "I feel rather well."

And I do. I really do.

"Because of your talks with Arthur and Paul?" he asks.

He knows my conversation with Caitlin didn't go well, and is likely afraid to bring it up. But for some reason, even the difficulty with my daughter isn't damping my spirits too much today. She may yet come around, and there's nothing to keep me from trying again. I saw her face when we parted, and I know she still cares for me.

And that has to be worth something. I will *make* it be worth something.

I look up again. "Partly, of course. But it's more than that." I tilt my head. "This may sound a bit self-congratulatory, but it seems I've discovered the secret of life."

I shiver again and he tells me we can go inside and finish our conversation, but I tell him he's wasting daylight, and he needs to be on his way if he's going to have dinner with his parents at their house.

"I've got plenty of time," he protests. "And I really want to hear what you mean, but I don't want you to freeze to death while you're telling me, so we should go inside."

I step down beside him, to usher him toward the car. "I'll tell you in transit, then." I take his arm, and we start walking as I continue. "It's not much of a secret, really."

I stare around at the snow-covered yard, and the carriage house, and the tall wooden fence lining the edge of my property. Where can I begin?

I clear my throat. "It's just that I've begun to enjoy cleaning my teeth at night, for one thing. And I adore the moment of silence that happens when I turn off the bathroom circulation fan after my shower in the morning." I ignore the amused look on his face. "Now that I think of it, I've also grown quite infatuated with the beeping sound the microwave makes after the bacon is done cooking."

He waits for a beat. "Have you been smoking my pot again, Hester? It's okay if you have."

His comic timing is improving.

"Just shut up and listen, will you?" I tighten my grip on him as we step over a slick patch on the sidewalk. "I'm talking about gratitude, son. Simple gratitude. That's the entire secret of life. I know it sounds trite, but there it is. Be grateful for just about everything." I pause. "Good Lord, would you listen to me? I'm in danger of becoming positively *chipper.*"

We come to a stop by the car, and I peer up at St. Booger. The giant statue frowns back at me, as if he's afraid I'm preparing to steal his Bible. Behind him, the blue sky is crystal clear, except for a white puff of smoke rising into it from the neighbor's chimney.

I nudge Alex. "For instance, even poor old Booger here is beautiful, in certain lights, don't you think?" I lean in for a closer examination and snort. "Well, then again, maybe not."

He chuckles a bit, but when I look up at him, he has tears in his eyes.

"What's the matter?" I ask, surprised.

He shakes his head. "Nothing. I'm just remembering the first time I met this strange old woman, not so long ago, and how I thought she was out of her mind. In fact, she was so nuts I almost turned her down when she offered me her apartment." He wipes his eyes. "But that would have been a huge mistake, wouldn't it? If I'd done that, I'd never have gotten to know her. Or myself, either."

His voice is rough. "I guess I'm trying to say that I think I've already got a pretty good handle on gratitude." He swallows. "Thanks, Hester. I mean it. Thanks for everything."

I study his face for a moment, then wrap my arms around him. He's bird-thin, like me, but my head only reaches up to his chest. It's so good to be held by somebody young, and strong, and warm. I'd forgotten.

"Be safe, Alex," I murmur. "And come home when you're through. I'll be here if you need me."

I give him a shove toward the driver's door, then head for the house before he can answer. I take one slow, sure step at a time, being careful not to fall on the ice. He stands by the car and watches me until I'm safely back on the porch.

I open the screen door and call over my shoulder. "By the way, you should have shaved, dear. You look like an overgrown dust bunny."

EPILOGUE

I wave to Alex as he pulls out of the driveway, and I wait until he rolls around the corner at the end of the street before stepping back inside and closing the door. The warmth of the house enfolds me again, and I return to the kitchen to wash the breakfast dishes.

It feels as if it's been a while since I've had the place to myself for any length of time, though in reality Alex has only been living with me for a little over a month. But I've already gotten used to having him home and underfoot in the evenings, and it seems strange to me to know that tonight when I go to bed, he'll be with his family in Morelle, rather than up in the attic.

Only a month. Yet now he belongs here.

I turn on the radio in the kitchen, and the stately, glorious third movement of Mahler's *Fourth Symphony* pours from the over-matched speaker and fills the room. I take my time cleaning the dishes, enjoying the silky feel of the soap suds on my hands in the hot water. The sun is warm enough today to melt some of the snow outside, and I watch as St. Booger's white skullcap slides off his head and breaks apart on top of his pedestal.

An oboe solo in the background reminds me of Oscar Schnei-der, my would-be suitor, who called again last night to ask me out, yet again. Alex listened to my side of the conversation in the kitchen, and whispered juvenile things while I was trying to talk, such as *"Tell him yes, and that you'll wear something slutty."* I made excuses to Oscar for the time being, but I may take him up on his offer at some point.

Just not right now. I'm in no hurry to find romance. There are other things in the world I'd like to explore first.

I dry my hands on a towel and pour myself a cup of hot tea (after giving fleeting consideration to the half-full bottle of red wine left over from last night's supper), and then on a whim I begin to wander through the house, going from room to room.

The fire in the living room is dying down, and as I stop to stoke it up again and stare into the rekindled flames, I'm aware of light footsteps and voices behind me. I drift into the music room and run a finger across my piano, interrupting a heated rehearsal Arthur is having with Paul, then I amble up the west staircase and peek into Caitlin's and Jeremy's old bedrooms. The children ignore my presence; Caitlin has her nose in a book, of course, and Jeremy is sitting on the floor with Paul, playing a semi-violent game of blackjack. Caitlin's face is pensive and withdrawn, and both of the boys are in desperate need of a haircut. I say hello and all three of them instantly become dust motes, floating in the sunlight from the windows.

My bedroom is next, and Arthur and I are in the bed, under about ten afghans. (It must be a Sunday, because Sundays are the only days we ever stay in bed this late in the morning.) It occurs to me that each of those colorful blankets covering us was made by somebody who cared for me; one was crocheted by my mother, another by my grandmother, and all the others were given to me by this or that dear friend throughout the years. I watch with amusement and tenderness as our younger selves make love to each other under this heavy protective shield, but after a moment our bodies transform into nothing but soft pillows and rumpled sheets, and I sigh and continue my journey.

Arthur is in his office beneath a bright chair lamp, reading something historical and boring, and both the guest rooms have hundreds of visitors, arriving and departing, and Alex's apartment is Paul's again, and then Jeremy's. (I toy for a moment with the idea of venturing out on the roof this morning but decide against it. It may be warm enough outside to melt snow, but I'd rather sit by my fire, and listen to music, and sip my tea in peace.) I spend another lazy, sweet minute with Jeremy in the attic kitchen, and I listen to him chatter about this and that as I peer down at the town of Bolton, spread out before me like a medieval village at the base of a castle tower. I take the east staircase on the return trip to the ground floor, and sometimes I'm not alone on the steps, and sometimes I am.

From here on in, either way is fine with me.

I refill my tea in the kitchen, and sit at the table, and hum familiar phrases along with the radio. The Mahler symphony ends, and then the host of the program announces that the next piece will be Franck's *Violin Sonata*, as performed by Arthur Donovan and Hester Parker. It's the recording we made in 1958, at the summer music festival in New York, on the first night we met.

There's a long pause before the music starts, and when it does, it's glorious.

I close my eyes and lower my head, as if in prayer.

There's something else I should have told Alex earlier, but now it will have to wait until he comes home. I told him that gratitude was the secret of life, but that's only part of it, of course.

The rest is forgiveness.